GOLDEN RIFTS

GOLDEN RIFTS

MARION DEEDS

FALSTAFF
BOOKS
WWW.FALSTAFFBOOKS.COM

This book is dedicated the women in the world who fight for freedom and equality.

PART I

THE RIFTS

W hat I say tonight shall not leave this room," Elmaestro Tregannon said. "The parasites of the New Way must never discover what we know."

Erin folded her hands in her lap. The five other people at the small table in the large room represented three countries, all members of the Copper Coalition. She barely belonged here.

Tregannon wore his purple vest tonight, the mark of his office. At the other end of the table, so did Elmaestro Melendres from Pais Lewelyn. Tonight, a band of cinnamon-red fabric shot with gold held her hair back from her face. Melendres nearly always wore a band pulling her hair back, the same way Ruth Stillwater did.

Tregannon nodded in Erin's direction, sprite light glancing off his silver hair. "Tomorrow at dawn, Yorita Dosmanos rides out to meet another guardian, she who holds the compass. One of the Ancient texts tells us the book and the compass, used together, disrupt the messages the New Way send one another, leaving them in disarray."

"Isn't it dangerous, two Ancient artifacts in the same place?" Alder Holay sat across the table, next to Profesor Stillwater. He was a member of the Crescent Council, which was sort of like Congress in Erin's world. Holay was a newcomer to Tregannon's council of war. Tonight, he was here instead of Senior Councilmember Del Rios, the usual group member. Senior Councilmember was like president. At least, Erin thought that was the equivalent position.

Stillwater spoke, calm and authoritative. "Less dangerous than allowing the infection to spread, especially if the parasites find another frontera to their homeworld."

Tregannon followed up. "Risks must be taken. This is a war, Councilmember. In a battle of arms, we could defeat them—"

"Could we, Brel?" Elmaestro Melendres was one of the few people who called Tregannon by his first name. "Taking arms against our own people?"

"My point, Noemi. This is *not* a war of arms. It's one of intelligence and subversion, and they have two years' advantage on us."

"You believe bringing two artifacts together is worth the risk," Melendres said.

Holay cleared his throat. "Why not bring the other guardian here, where both can be protected?"

"We have been infiltrated before," Tregannon said. "I won't risk it happening again."

Tregannon spelled out the plan. Erin would ride in a locked cart. She'd meet Wing Mei, who held the compass, at a small guesthouse near Querida Pass.

The same guesthouse Erin and Trevian had stayed at the night before they'd closed the New Way frontera. The night before she'd— against her will—merged with the hive mind of the New Way and learned more about their plans. Before Tregannon had organized this council of war.

Before Trevian's father had died and Trevian had gone fifteen leagues south for the funeral in White Bluffs.

She wished she'd gone with him. He said he didn't need her, and she was needed here... Mentally she shook her head. No point in worrying about him now.

God, she missed him.

She looked down at her plate. It felt weird to be eating in the long room, usually filled with worktables, piles of scrap metal, sheets of quartz and various mechanical experiments or prototypes. Tonight the tables were clear, except for the one in the center where they sat. The room's size defeated potential eavesdroppers.

"Will the yorita have a security detail?"

Stillwater fielded the question. "We don't want to draw too much attention. She will have a pair of Copper Coalition guards, and one charmcaster in the cart with her."

The woman on Erin's left cleared her throat. "Yorita Dosmanos, could you pass the sugared nuts?"

Seriously? Erin glanced at the councilmember from Madlyn, the northern country. "Sure." She slid the bowl over. The woman—what was her name? Farway?—scooped up a handful.

Her words muffled, Farway said, "I don't understand how these artifacts work."

"Neither do we," Tregannon said. "But they do."

"We are trusting a lot to an out-of-worlder woman who barely speaks our language," Farway said. "No insult meant, Yorita Dosmanos."

Well, *that* was harsh. Erin was starting to dislike the blond woman next to her, in her swishy green skirt and the shiny golden jacket. So far, Farway had skipped at least two meetings, and was always sending her secretary, who had shoulders and cheekbones like a beefcake TV actor, to strut around mailing letters or finding her another bottle of wine.

"Erin has risked her life twice for this world," Tregannon said.

Stillwater chimed in. "And she is one of the Four Families."

Melendres laughed. "If we believe in the Four Families. No insult, Erin. I may not believe in your origins, but I know you hold the Ancient book. And I trust your knowledge."

Oh, right. These people thought mountain ranges grew up overnight, but *her* ancestry was a fairytale?

"Is Querida Pass safe?" Holay again. "What if there is an ambush?"

"The guesthouse is a few hours south of the pass, on the North Road."

"How will we know if it is successful?" Melendres said.

Ruth answered. "Those who are infected will know at once if they've been released."

"And what of those who aid them and are not infected? This Oshane Langtree, for example. What if there are others?"

Melendres was a tough audience, but Erin was starting to like her.

Holay spoke first. "Langtree is a criminal. Anyone who aided these creatures is a criminal and will be dealt with by the Justice Arms of our Councils."

"Our primary goal is to end the New Way's ability to infect us," Ruth said.

"This information cannot go beyond the six of us," Tregannon said. "I must have your word."

"You have it," Melendres said.

"You have mine," said Holay.

The Madlyn woman said, "Of course."

"Good." The legs of Tregannon's chair scraped the floor as he pushed it back.

Ruth turned to Holay. "Councilmember, I have a fine bottle of golden wine from Pais Lewelyn. Will you join me for a glass?"

"Most kind, profesor, but my brain reels. I must rest."

"Another evening, then. I'll use this time to look over the pages Erin gave me from her book."

"Her book? *The* book?" He stared over at Erin, who nodded.

"I made some copies," she said.

"Now that is tempting. I *will* join you."

"They are in the study next door. And I'll bring the wine."

"Wonderful..." Holay followed her to the side door and out of the room.

Noemi Melendres stood up. "I need to speak to the charmcasters and see what progress they have made on those parasites," she said.

"And I need to write a letter," Farway said, scraping the final few nut segments from the bowl.

"Stay a bit," said Tregannon.

"Really? Is there more to discuss?"

Tregannon carried a bottle of wine down the table and added a splash to Melendres's glass. "There may be more to discuss in a few moments," he said.

Farway held out her glass, and he added a bit to hers as well.

Erin laced her fingers together over her head and stretched. Her spine popped in several places. She'd been scared the plan was too obvious, or Ruth and Tregannon would oversell it, but the two of them were good enough to do community theater. Now it was just a waiting game, hopefully a short one.

The three countries, Madlyn, The Crescent, and Pais Lewelyn, ran in north-south line, traded with each other, and spoke the same language. Perlarayna, a country far to the east, was sending a contingent here too. The threat they were up against might be global. They didn't know.

Melendres narrowed her eyes at Tregannon. "There is no locked cart, is there?"

"No."

A few minutes later, they all heard a soft thud from the next room.

"Join me," Tregannon said.

Melendres let Farway follow Tregannon, and said, "Yorita Erin, what's happening?"

"It's part of a plan," Erin said.

Tregannon opened the door and entered, standing to one side. Farway strode in and stopped, gasping, clutching her wine glass. Erin glanced around, trying not to make it obvious, and spotted the Copper Coalition guard in the corner. Two cups and a green glass bottle sat on the work-table beside an uncapped jar.

The study had a second door into the hallway, and near it stood Senior Councilmember Del Rios, wearing a short blue and green jacket, the colors of the Crescent. She stared at the floor in the center of the room.

Holay, on his back, head tipped to one side, lay there. As they watched, he gave a faint snore. Ruth knelt beside him, her hands on her thighs, looking up at Elmaestro Melendres.

Before anyone spoke, Ruth brought her finger to her lips.

Tregannon pointed at Holay. His shirt was unbuttoned and folded aside. On his chest just below his collarbone clung a leathery pinkish bladder, pulsing in a sleepy rhythm.

Farway gave a squeak.

Ruth pointed to Farway and then to the uncapped jar, but the Madlyn councilmember shuddered and backed away. Melendres stepped forward, picked up the vessel and held it out to Ruth, who drew out a flat-bladed knife. Gently, Ruth slid the blade underneath the New Way node, prying it loose.

The node flattened, but it was still pink, still inflating and deflating. Erin's breathing adjusted itself to the node's rhythm, and she looked away, breaking the pattern consciously.

Ruth dropped the node into the jar, sealed it, and handed it to the guard, who carried it out of the room.

Del Rios approached, staring at Tregannon. "Just as you warned us. How did you discover him?"

"We have a technique," Tregannon said.

Del Rios said, "I'll need it."

"I'll need it for Madlyn too," Farway said.

Melendres said, "We all will. What was this, Brel? A proof of a concept?"

"A field test, the Ancient used to say." Tregannon let his gaze sweep them, then nodded. "Senior Councilmember del Rios, Councilmember

Farway, Elmaestro, we will provide you all with the means to identify the infected."

"And what about Alker?" the green and blue woman said. "Will he die from this? What do I tell his family?

"He should be well, Senior Councilmember." Ruth sheathed the blade. "About his family, we should send someone to see his wife. She could not have failed to notice that creature."

"You think she is infected? How?"

Ruth nodded at the supine man.

"Do they know your true plan now, whatever it is?" Melendres said.

Erin said. "I don't think so. They seem to go dormant when the hosts—"

"Hosts?" Melendres raised her eyebrows.

"Infected people, then. When the infected sleep. If they're detached during sleep, they go into a dormant state before they die. Before the New Way shuts them off, I mean."

"How do you *know* it's dormant?"

"I don't. We're not sure. It's why we don't talk much when one's in the room."

Tregannon said, "We have uncovered an infected person on the Crescent Council, and we know the charm Erin used in Madalita is successful."

Melendres nodded. Senior Councilmember del Rios wasn't satisfied yet, though. "Surely those parasites know their...host?....host was drugged."

"The potion in the wine induces a sensation of extreme sleepiness, nothing more alarming," Ruth said. "Holay said he needed rest. It should seem as if sleep overcame him suddenly."

All Tregannon needed was a big *Mission Accomplished* banner behind him. Erin wasn't being fair, though. He wasn't wrong. They'd achieved their goal. One fewer nodes spied on them, or directed things, out in the world. And the Madlyn, Pais Lewelyn, and Crescent politicians had seen a node in real life for the first time.

Farway said, "Any one of us could be these, these hosts. Would you know?"

"With nearly complete certainly," Tregannon said. "Still, we request each of you to submit to a search, with the guards we have chosen."

Del Rios said, "Of course."

"I want Brevik with me," Farway said. Brevik, the secretary with the cheekbones.

Tregannon nodded. The secretary would have been searched anyway.

Farway sighed. "Well. Is there any wine around that isn't dosed with a sleeping potion?"

Tregannon led them away, to the designated guards.

Ruth sat cross-legged on the floor next to Holay. "I'll stay with him until the healers' apprentices come," she said.

Erin leaned back against the door. One infected person freed. Seven hundred ninety-eight to go.

2

(III) Dear Dare—I hope you and Mama are all right. I'm going to write this like it's a letter and pretend you'll see it someday. They took all our devices—what a laugh, we couldn't connect to anything anyway—and all my books and notebooks. It's just lucky they didn't find this one in my weekender bag underneath my towel, which I guess is me admitting I never pulled it out after you were so sweet to give it to me.

I'd have said it wasn't much of a search, just done to flex their power, if they hadn't taken all of my notebooks. And they won't tell me if Richard is alive.

I don't know what's going on but I can guess they're keeping us isolated from one another is so we can't compare notes. It may be my imagination, but things feel wrong here—the corridors feel colder. I say "here," but I'm at the installation... except it all feels wrong.

I think they're going to do to us what they did to Aperture One, whatever that was. Baby, I wish you were here to hold me right now. I'm so scared.

From Telma Lewiston's Journal

Aideen woke before sunrise. She stretched, Ilsanja a line of warmth against her back and thighs. She kept her eyes closed, seeing for a moment the torch, her hand and Trevian's gripping it, as they set Father's bier alight.

The three of them had accompanied the Voice of the Mother to the funeral site. The Voice, a woman from Sheeplands, spoke the final plea, wishing Father a good journey to the Mother's arms. Aideen and Trevian, with Ilsanja as witness, carefully drenched Father's body with lick, and heated up the whiterock chunks with the torch until they glowed and the gray wrappings enveloping Father's body flared up green and orange.

He was gone.

This morning they would review his will. It was customary to attend. She didn't want to. She knew what the document would say. Father had left Trevian as his heir, and Ilsanja was Trevian's wife. For the few sennights of Father's fading, she'd experienced freedom. Now, once again, she lived in someone else's house, dependent on their good will. Ilsanja loved her, but that didn't change the facts.

Sleep came again, and when the smell of sisuree and kokalatal woke her, the room was full of light. Ilsanja sat by her side of the bed, holding out a cup of the hot drink. A plate with warm morning cake sat on the bedside stand. "I've slept long," Aideen said, sitting up suddenly.

Ilsanja drew the cup back quickly. "You have all the time you need."

Aideen glanced over her friend's shoulder at the tall clock Ilsanja had brought with her. The polished, elaborate piece was a wedding gift from Ilsanja's father. Aideen bit her lower lip.

"What?"

"I'm wondering what Don Leo would think if he saw where you've put the clock, and where I sleep."

Ilsanja smiled. "My father rests easier when his mind is not burdened with complexities."

Aideen grinned back and took the cup. Her dark mood lightened for a few moments, at least. The sisuree was stimulating, and Susanah had mastered the art of adding kokalatal, Ilsanja's discovery, to pastries. In this moment, perched on a rock in the rushing stream of the world, she could pretend nothing more was in store today than visiting the cages to review the repairs, or spending the day as she most often did, in the Langtree Company offices.

"Trevian returns to Duloc today," Ilsanja said, knocking her off her safe perch with five words. "After the reading."

Aideen pulled her legs up and swung them over the edge of the bed. "The reading." She broke off a piece of the fragrant bread.

Ilsanja said, "You know what to expect."

"Nothing. I know to expect nothing." Aideen stood up and headed down the hall for the latrine before Ilsanja could answer. When she returned, her friend stood by the mirrored dressing table, straightening a hairbrush resting near the table's edge.

"I doubt he left you with nothing," she said.

"He already gave me my mother's jewels, most of them," Aideen said as she sat down. Her mother's favorite necklace had vanished with her.

Ilsanja picked up the brush.

Ilsanja loved to brush Aideen's hair, and Aideen loved for her to do it, but it provided no comfort this morning.

"I meant coin." Ilsanja drew the brush along Aideen's scalp and then down the length of her hair.

"Yes, a portion to tempt a husband, probably."

"If he didn't leave you something, Trevian and I will arrange an income for you."

Arrange an income, as if she were just come of age, worried parents carefully paving their child's way in the world. She sighed.

Ilsanja set down the brush with a precise click and stepped back. Her voice was calm, a little distant. "What will it take to make you happy?"

Feeling wronged and yet somehow *in* the wrong, Aideen shook her head. I live in this house on sufferance, she thought. Everything I value hangs on the whim of other people, people I love, and who love me, I believe, but still… "Forgive me," she said. "I sound like a small child who stayed up too late at Long Year's."

Ilsanja's shoulders relaxed. She leaned forward and put her arms around Aideen. "You sound like a woman who has lost a beloved parent. A troublesome, beloved parent. Don Oswald's stubbornness, his blindness, in no way lessens your value."

Aideen pressed her hands over Ilsanja's. "I am glad I have you in my life, to say those things to me."

"Settled, then." Ilsanja reached again for the brush. Watching her face in the mirror, Aideen said nothing more about her fears.

Yor Numinov had an office overlooking the central plaza. From the second-floor window, Aideen watched the late morning sun sparkle on the flat surface of the canal. Numinov offered sisuree, its spicy scent filling the air, which both Aideen and Trevian declined. Ilsanja took a cup. Aideen was glad to see Trevian had draped an ash-gray scarf over his rough brown shirt, and his battered boots were clean. Family members lined up in front of the desk in mourning gray must be a common sight for the lawyer.

Aideen drew her fingers down the fabric of the gray mourning smock, remembering Ilsanja drawing her close as she tied the sash, Ilsanja's lips, warm and soft, touching Aideen's nape.

Numinov was a brisk, practical man. With no ceremony, he removed the sealed envelope from his desk drawer. He gave it to Trevian. He and Aideen examined the seal, to ascertain it had not been broken and resealed. Aideen gave it back to the lawyer who opened it, slipped out two sheets of paper, and began to read.

First, Father named Trevian as his heir, with control and responsibility for all assets not otherwise addressed in the document. He left the conventional small bequests to the household staff, with a larger payment to Dolores and to his valet, Dimitri. Dimitri meant to move down mountain. The extra coin would be welcome, no doubt.

Father left a collection of curiosities assembled from his prospecting days to Yor Armando Montez, the minor partner in the company, and two paintings by a renowned Madlyn painter to Jefe Leo Silvestro, the other major partner. The paintings were angular and horrible, depicting battles from the Interval, and Aideen was glad they were going.

She tried to remain attentive, but her thoughts drifted to the tunnel through the mountain, the one she and Ilsanja had taken on their journey to the capital. No one in the company knew, yet, that Yor Lopez had gone there on her suggestion, and was searching ways to excavate the long rifts, home for fire elementals. If they could harvest their radiant energy...

Her name. She brought her attention back into the room.

"...my daughter, who has been capable and loyal in attending to the house and assisting with other matters, I leave all rights to the property and income of my blackrock mine. And I remind my son Trevian his duty to ensure that his sister always has a home."

Ilsanja stirred. "There," she whispered.

Perhaps Numinov had read it wrong. Aideen glanced at her brother. His face was as expressionless as always, but he nodded slightly.

The mine still produced well. The income would keep her comfortably, if not lavishly, if circumstances ever changed and she must be on her own.

"As to my company, Trevian is my heir, as stated above. To him I leave thirty-one shares."

Aideen's stomach lurched. What had her father done with the other twenty? Sold them? Had they lost control of the company already?

"To my daughter Aideen I leave twenty shares to acknowledge the work she has done to learn about the company, our family's legacy, when others would not."

"Pardon, Yor Numinov," Aideen said. "I thought you said...will you read it again, please?"

Numinov studied her over the top of the pages for a moment. "He left you twenty shares. Your brother, with thirty-one, remains the majority partner in the business."

"When did this happen, this change?"

"About four months ago." He raised his eyebrows. "Yorita Langtree, did you truly think your father was blind to the help you gave him?"

"I did." It was an impolite answer, but since she had started, she finished the thought. "Perhaps not blind but taking it as due him."

Numinov lay the will flat on the desk. "He *did* believe it was due him. Jefe Langtree was a difficult man, and I'll be the first to admit that. He was slow to trust and slow to love, but he wasn't a fool. And he wasn't..." the lawyer thought for a moment, "... unjust."

The loans he had held, impoverishing neighbors and colleagues... Aideen saw no reason to argue out loud. Numinov must have seen something in her face though. He cleared his throat. "And you were his family. He valued that above all."

Aideen cleared her throat too. She nodded. Ilsanja reached for her hand.

There was very little else, and Aideen did not even try to concentrate now. Twenty shares. Trevian—Ilsanja actually—still held the majority of shares by one, but no longer automatically controlled any vote. Aideen could, theoretically, vote with Don Leo Silvestro and overturn Ilsanja's wishes. She snorted at the thought, turning it into a cough when everyone glanced up at her.

Father had left her a stream of coin, not a token bride-gift portion but an income, and shares in the company. It upended everything she thought she knew of him.

When Numinov finished, Aideen and Ilsanja rose and left to wait outside while Trevian signed papers and finalized a new proxy statement. It wasn't needed, but after last time, he was taking every care. In the waiting area, Aideen turned to her friend. "I'm not dreaming this?"

14

"You're not dreaming." Ilsanja squeezed her hand. "You have a seat at the partner's table now."

"I wonder what your father will think."

Ilsanja gazed into the distance, smiling. She came back to the moment and said, "Well, Yor Montez will be pleased. He appreciates your intelligence and always looks to you for ideas."

"He is kind."

"It's not kindness."

Aideen glanced at the day's *White Bluffs Report,* the town's daily newssheet, which draped across a chair. Yesterday, front and back on the sheet had been devoted to Father. Today the item in the largest print seemed to be about a missing caballo; a feud between neighbors was suspected.

Moments later, Trevian joined them. Ilsanja held out her hand to him. "Come, husband," she said. "I think the new partner must buy us sisuree and cakes."

Trevian leaned down to hug Aideen one-handed. "I agree."

"I sense a conspiracy," Aideen said. As they reached the outer door at the bottom of the stairs, she said, "I realize I know nothing about blackrock mining."

Ilsanja said, "You'll learn."

They brought back frosted cakes for the household and stable staff. Dolores was partial to a certain style of honeybread, so Aiden had bought a loaf for her.

After lunch, Trevian completed his packing. A hug for Dolores and Aideen, a handshake with Ilsanja, and he mounted his caballo and rode north.

Aideen took refuge in her father's study, hers now, perhaps, and read over the papers on the blackrock mine. The mine manager, a woman Father trusted, had been in place for years, and the vein of rock still produced steadily. Even with the expansion of the company to Sheeplands, thirteen leagues down mountain, there would always be a need for blackrock in the countryside to provide additional light and heat. The mine was a two-hour ride down mountain, easily visited and inspected.

"Working already?" Ilsanja leaned against the door jamb.

Aideen pushed away the papers. "And ready for a distraction," she said.

"I mean to check on the mares. Join me?"

Aideen stood up. "We can take your father's paintings to him in the same visit, if you wish."

"Yes. Dolores practically ran to take them off the wall of his room when I told her. We can wrap them up. We'll need a cart, though."

"Would you mind if we visited the cages after?"

"We'd need saddle-caballos then, wouldn't we? Then we'd be a caravan. Or we could take two of mine, I suppose."

"We take carts up to the cages all the time."

"You do?"

Aideen smiled. "*We* do. How do you think the quartz and copper gets delivered?"

"I didn't think the trail was wide enough. Well, do you want to talk to the stablemaster?"

"You can."

Ilsanja straightened up. "Aideen, it may be years before I remember to say 'we' about anything to do with the Company."

"I'll remind you."

Ilsanja said. "Every time?"

"Every single time."

The paintings went well with the dark wood of Don Leo's house, but he liked them most because he knew of the fame of the painter. When Ilsanja explained, with poorly concealed delight, that Aideen, who now held one more share than Yor Montez, had become a partner, he grunted. "We'll have to find a chair," he said.

"Oh, don't worry, Father. I'll find one."

Ilsanja's knowledge of her caballos, their lineage, the strengths and weaknesses of each line, humbled Aideen. To her, except for the color, the useful animals all looked much the same, but Ilsanja pointed out wider chests, longer legs, stronger flanks, differences in hooves and necks that Aideen could not even see. "How will I keep track of all this?"

"You don't have to. I do," Ilsanja said.

Aideen waited silently as her friend and the stablemaster reviewed the progress of the foals and discussed who was buying and who was selling. Ilsanja had always been beautiful and sharp-witted to Aideen: stylish and socially adept. This was a proficient woman of business. As they climbed back into the cart, Aideen said, "I am in awe of you."

"Even though I didn't know you could drive a cart up to the cages?"

"Yes," Aideen said, and basked in quiet the rest of the way.

M oises Lopez, the senior engineer, gave them a tour. Aideen couldn't tell if Ilsanja was bored or baffled. For herself, she was glad to see the needed repairs being made. Yor Lopez proudly showed off the latest cage, nearly complete, large enough to hold a sibling group of fire elementals.

Finishing the tour and arriving back at the mouth of the caves that held the operation, Ilsanja accepted a cup of the bitter tea the workers drank and struck up a conversation with a team leader who was on a rest break. Aideen grasped the opportunity. She picked her way across a labyrinth of coiled leather-sheathed copper cords to where Lopez stood, jotting a note in his log. "What do you think of the rifts in the tunnel?" she said.

"There must be a vast colony of flames. When he lived, the jefe explored it, but couldn't see a way to draw up the radiance."

Father had explored it? "There must be one, though."

"I remembered a method of slanted drilling Yor Montez used before we opened the installation here. We can dig shafts closer to the colony. But there is no room for cages."

"I wonder if there is a way to harvest the energy without the cages."

"Yorita, you know we need the copper to draw off the energy."

"Can we lower cords to the edges of their colony and absorb the waves above the emberbeds?"

Lopez put his cup on the table. "Jefe Langtree tried that first. The copper melted. That is why he partnered with Jefe Silvestro. Close enough to the emberbeds to draw up enough radiance, I think even Yor Montez's charmed steel drill-bits would melt."

She quelled her disappointment. This project was a distraction, and her attention should be on the Sheeplands expansion, but the tunnel and its deep rifts drew her.

"We could design narrower cages to fit in the tunnel," he said.

"I think there must be a safer way than cages." Someday, she would talk to Yor Lopez about the story Trevian had told her, of Erin's flames, who came not only to Erin's rescue, but to Trevian's aid as well. Not today, though. "I'm merely curious," she said.

"It's used as a shortcut by many people. Who owns it?"

"It's unclaimed, I checked. I'm writing the claim, with the proviso to leave rider space for the public."

"Difficult to run an energy installation that way," Lopez said.

She nodded.

Ilsanja had drifted over and stood within earshot. Seeing her, Lopez said, "Have we answered your questions, Jefa?"

Ilsanja pointed with her chin at the thick leather gloves draped over the end of the table.

"We use charmed leather gloves when we're working with the cords. The aprons and hoods are for when the fire elementals leave the rifts to watch us—"

"They do that?"

"Often. And the leather sheaths protect from the burns and jolts the live copper cords would give otherwise."

"I see. More elaborate than I imagined. You will me see here from time to time, but more often you will see Yorita Langtree. I rely on her knowledge and judgment completely."

Lopez gave her a brief bow. "Then you will do well, Jefa."

Aideen untethered the caballo and Ilsanja took the reins. The cart rattled a bit when they went over a rut. Ilsanja said, "Now it is I who am in awe. This place is a maze, and you know your way to its center and back."

"Just familiarity."

"Familiarity and far more. What does Yor Lopez think of the rifts?"

"He wasn't encouraging. The copper cords melt too quickly."

Ilsanja *hmmed*, and they rode along quietly for a while. Aideen pondered ways to protect a copper cord, while still using its properties to draw up elemental energy. There must be some way.

Ilsanja said, "The rifts are not our first order of business, though."

"No. What is, do you think?"

Her friend glanced sideways at her, grinning. "Finding you a partner's chair."

CONTENTS OF A LETTER

They trust no one here. The out-of-worlder speaks of parasites sharing thoughts across leagues, but they tell us little of value. They speak of Orchard Hill but do not name its location.

There is more I could tell you, but you have not delivered what you promised. I will risk no more for you until you uphold your end of the bargain.

3

————————

Erin cut the last line into Melendres's arm and blotted away the blood. "Done," she said as she spread singeweed ointment over the mark and reached for the cloth bandage.

"Nothing to recite?"

Erin shook her head. "The charm requires concentration while you're marking it but that seems to be all. Be careful when you stand up. You'll feel lightheaded." Everyone got lightheaded as the charm settled on them.

"Are you carving all of them, Yorita Dosmanos?"

Erin tried not to flinch at "carve." "No. Charmcasters and copper-hunters can both apply the charm effectively."

"Good, since we'll need to protect many," the Pais Lewelyn elmaestro said. "Must they wear the mark first?" Clearly, she was taking mental notes.

Her headband this morning was dark green with a black and yellow geometric design along the edge. It wasn't as flattering as the brownish-red one, but she'd worn it several times so Erin thought it was probably a favorite.

"No, it's not needed. But it's just a good idea for people with access to sensitive knowledge to have one."

Melendres moved her arm and winced a little. "Thank you. Now I'll be able to recognize an infected person?"

"Yes. Your skin will feel like you have a mild burn."

"Unpleasant, but necessary." Her eyes widened, and she gripped the edge of the table. "Lightheaded... Yes, I see."

The door opened behind Erin. Melendres said, "Good morning, Brel. Alker, are you well?"

"I am ashamed." Holay sounded subdued. Tregannon sat down across from Melendres and motioned Holay to the chair next to him.

"No more need for shame than if a mestengo hit you on the head and emptied your purse," Tregannon said.

"I betrayed us."

The door opened again and Farway entered, holding her arm away from her side the same way Melendres was.

Over breakfast, Erin told Stillwater she didn't think much of Councilmember Farway. Ruth laughed and shook her head.

"She doesn't waste breath on much beyond asking where the wine is, but Madlyn's charmcasters are the best on the continent, and she brought us three, so I'm happy with her."

"Is she an effective leader?"

Ruth shrugged. "She's one of nine, how effective must she be? Her mother and grandfather were both councilmembers, and her district likes the idea of a family tradition, I guess."

Farway sat down now, fluffing her hair. The long sleeves of her tunic gleamed with intricate embroidery in pink, purple, and yellow.

Holay took his seat, staring at the table's surface. His gray-blond hair was slicked down with water, and he looked hungover. Erin recognized node withdrawal. Holay was pretty coherent. He couldn't have been under their influence for too long. Some of the Madalita villagers, who'd been controlled for nearly two years, were still not fully back to themselves.

"Alker has some things to tell us."

"First, how did you become infected?" Melendres said.

Holay fidgeted. "I invested in an expedition into the far north of Madlyn. There is a great vein of Ancient there, barely tapped by prospectors, or so I was told."

"I know the place." Farway fussed with a sleeve.

"The caravan master came to my house three nights ago, with news, he said, of great importance and secrecy. He had found an Ancient artifact of unknown rarity and uncalculated value. No one must know of it, except me. I took him into my study. He even put a chair in front the door. And I suspected nothing."

Distracted by greed. Erin hoped the thought didn't show on her face.

"He took the parasite out from under his coat. At first, I thought it *was* the artifact, and then…"

"The next morning, you petitioned Senior Councilmember del Rios to add you to this council."

"I didn't petition, Elmaestro Tregannon. I *demanded*. I said the caravan master had identified a strange illness, and as you know, I implied I had some special knowledge."

Melendres leaned forward. "Your wife, children? Are they infected also?"

"I told my wife I would be sleeping at the Coalition, because of an urgent matter needing day and night attention."

"Yora Holay and the children are not infected," Tregannon said.

Erin stepped in. "You know things now, right? It's a two-way street when they take you over."

He frowned. "Don't all streets run two ways?"

"It's an exchange," Tregannon said.

Holay gave a jerky nod. "Whatever the Langtree family is doing in White Bluffs, providing light without sprite lamps or blackrock, they are interested in. They wish, they *need*, to control it. And someone named Oshane Langtree, who they call the unreliable source, is no longer of use to them."

"Why not?"

"The unreliable source had a way of locating frontera for them, but he has it no longer."

"Trevian thought Oshane had a charm," Erin said. Oshane wore a string of stone beads around one wrist, and Aideen had torn it off him while he was trying to strangle her. "Aideen destroyed it."

"He is a liability now. He has reached out, but they do not answer. They fear him because he has an air elemental tethered to him."

His forehead scrunched up. "There is an object they want to build, a pole. They think it will help them subdue us."

Tregannon said, "How?"

"Something to do with ripples in the air."

"Can you draw this object?"

He closed his eyes. "It is…yes, I can. It….It looks very simple, but I don't understand it."

Tregannon rose, going to one of the worktables and opening a drawer.

"They want the artifacts, the lantern and the compass, because with those, at a place called Orchard Hill, they believe they can open a frontera, or, failing that, create a new one."

Tregannon, walking back with paper, froze. *"Create?"*

"You mean reopen," Melendres said.

"Both."

Tregannon's head whipped around. "Erin, can they do this?"

Erin shrugged. *"They* think so. The experiments the Ancients were doing at Aperture One *did* open something. I was always told frontera occurred naturally, but maybe people created the early ones."

Tregannon slapped the paper down on the table, making Holay rear back. "I thought we had stopped the threat, and only had to find and end these nodes. Instead, they'll just choose another place and—"

Holay said, "They only think of Orchard Hill."

Melendres said, "Do you have any idea where this hill is?"

Tregannon didn't hesitate. "The Ancient books Profesor Stillwater collected speak of it. They do not give a location."

It wasn't even a lie. Erin kept her mouth shut.

"How would the New Way find it if we can't?" Farway said. "It seems we are secure on that score at least."

Tregannon scowled. "How many prospectors are there in Madlyn, and in the Crescent? All of them searching every fissure and crevice, every defile and cave, every valley for riches. And we don't know how many of them are infected."

Farway's eyes widened. "You cannot mean to limit prospecting! They are the root of our wealth."

"I mean for you to understand the danger," Tregannon said.

"We need to find the location first and destroy it." Farway said.

"Secure it, at least." Tregannon rolled a pair of pencils toward Holay. "Alker, can you draw for us this device, this object, they wish to build?"

He nodded, chewing on his lower lip. "I will try," he said. "As I said, it seemed simple." His hand moved slowly over the paper, the pencil scratching quietly.

Erin stood up. "I'm going to get sisuree," she said. The others, leaning toward Holay, nodded without looking up at her. She didn't think they noticed when she left.

The hallway was filled with students, technicians, profesors, assayers, and apprentices, going about the daily business of the Copper Coalition. So far, only the profesors and the guards were aware of the infection. She made her way toward the kitchen.

Orchard Hill—clearly Tregannon didn't want the location leaked. He didn't even want to tell the group he supposedly trusted. Erin was sure the complex Aideen had described in her letter to Trevian was the actual place. On the other hand, at least one member of Tregannon's council of war wanted to blow it up, so Erin had to agree with Tregannon on this one.

They knew part of the New Way's plan, at least, and they had one form of protection: the charm. Zachary, Tregannon's apprentice, had been their guinea pig. He'd insisted.

R uth had said, "We could try the charm on me," when Zachary brought in a tray of sisuree and bread.

He set the tray down silently and said, "Profesor, I request the mark be put on me."

"There's no need, Zachary."

"They made me betray the Coalition, Profesor."

"No one thinks you betrayed us," Tregannon said.

Zachary straightened up. He was kind of a wispy kid, but right then he looked almost soldier-like. "I do, Elmaestro. When I was six, my father let me join him when he took a wagon of Ancient to the Coalition office in our town. I watched the assayers and the copper-hunters, and I knew then this was where I wanted to be. My whole life I have worked to come here, and they took it from me."

Ruth said softly, "Zachary, you were controlled by one of those things. It's possible the charm will not work on you."

He raised his chin. "Then we will have learned something," he said.

Ruth smiled in spite of herself. Erin, who had heard those words come out of Ruth's mouth more than once, gave the contest of wills to Zachary right then.

She carved the protection mark on the inside of his left arm. Then Ruth and Profesor Machios spent two days parading him past ten covered quartz cages. Ten times out of ten, Zachary stopped in front of the cage with a node in it. When Machios put two of the dormant nodes out, Zachary stopped at the first one, scratching at his arm, and said, "Something's wrong. I think there's one in here, but I think there's another one."

When there was no node in any of the covered cages, Zachary walked around and around, shaking his head. He was not guessing. He could sense them, just like Erin could.

Ruth got the mark next, then Trevian, then Tregannon. Tregannon tested a pair of Coalition charmcasters, and Erin put the mark on them. She had them practice the mark with pencil and paper, and then they began marking guards.

Half the guards were protected. Tregannon's war council all had the charm now, and today they would start on the Crescent Council and the Council Guards. There was still an element of secrecy, while the politicians worked out how to explain to people what was happening without causing distrust or a panic. That wasn't Tregannon's concern, though. His was strategic.

She came around a corner into a nearly empty stretch of hallway. Farway's secretary Brevik held an apprentice by the arm, waving a packet of papers with his other hand. Erin recognized the gangly apprentice, Tonio, assigned to Profesor Machios. She lengthened her stride.

"—must be delivered to the mail van at once," Brevik said.

"Tonio, is everything all right?" Erin said, easing in so she crowded slightly into the secretary's personal space. She hoped he would pull back, but he didn't.

Tonio's voice shook slightly. "Yorita, Yor Dougal needs a message taken to the morning mail van, but I have a task from Profesor Machios I must complete."

Dougal smiled at Erin. So Brevik was his first name. "Councilmember Farway sends regular reports back to Madlyn. This must go out with the first mail van."

"Why didn't you leave it at the mail station the way everyone does?" The Coalition had a designated box for messages.

"The councilmember was delayed."

"So why not use a private messenger?"

Back home, Erin thought mail delivery was kind of quaint when so much could be done electronically. Here, four groups of riders and wagons, called vans, went out and back twice daily. Each van had a region they delivered to and received mail from. It was an impressive system and made her admire the post office back home more, in retrospect. If you needed something delivered even faster, there was always a fast messenger, or private messengers. Melendres, for instance, brought two messengers in her entourage.

She ignored the smiling secretary and focused on Tonio. "What are you doing for the profesor?" she said.

Tonio tugged until Dougal finally let go of his arm.

"I'm taking this to Profesor Ludo and her charmcasters." He drew a glass bottle from his pocket. Erin could feel the charms on it. At the bottom, odd bits of metal and plastic rattled. "These came from inside a parasite. Profesor Ludo hopes she can craft a charm to stop them, if she has more knowledge."

"How long can it take to run to the mail van and back?" Dougal said, his voice jovial. He set Erin's teeth on edge.

She ran through the options. She didn't know where the mail van stopped. Clearly, Dougal'd just grabbed the first apprentice he'd seen. This wasn't about delivering a letter. Dougal wanted to be important. On the other hand, Tregannon was trying to pull this group of people together so they'd work as a team, and Erin didn't want to mess with that.

"Tonio, can you get the letter delivered if I take the bottle to Profesor Ludo?"

"Yes, yorita. Will you explain why I, why I left my duty?"

"Of course. You didn't leave, you were pulled away by one of the Elmaestro's guests." As Dougal handed over the packet, she gripped his wrist. "Coin," she said.

"What?"

"Tonio needs coin."

The packet was addressed to someone named Farway, but Erin couldn't make out the rest.

Dougal dug out some unos for the postage. "Go on now," he said, smiling. "Run!"

Tonio darted away.

"Pardon me," Erin said, sidestepping the man.

"Of course," Dougal said. "You're an out-of-worlder and ignorant of the ways of society. I know you don't realize you're encouraging an apprentice's disrespect. You have my pardon."

"Oh, *do* I?" Erin walked past him. "Wow, thanks."

On her way to Profesor Ludo's study she decided the Madlyn contingent was not impressing her.

S he put down the pot of sisuree and the tray with cups and sliced fruit, but no one looked up from where they were circled around Holay. "I am baffled," Tregannon said. "It looks like a child's toy."

Melendres moved aside, making room for Erin. "You were gone long."

"Sorry." She leaned over the table and craned her neck to see the drawing. Holay gave it a quarter turn so she could see it better. Like he'd said, it was a pole. At the top, rods branched out in four directions, like a spikey crown, terminating in rectangular vanes. He'd labeled the rods, "Copper" and "loomin'", and drawn wires spiraling down its length in a crisscross pattern. "It looks like an antenna."

"Which is what?" Melendres sounded impatient.

Erin was learning the hard way to simplify her answers to the tech questions, and she tried to do it now. "A device that lets them send messages farther through the air." Maybe that was too simple.

Holay nodded vigorously though. "Yes! Ripples in the air, too tiny and too fast to be seen."

"Like wind? Like an air elemental?" Farway was frowning. "Yorita, will you bring the fruit down here?"

"Not an air elemental. The New Way fear them," Holay said.

Erin moved the plate of fruit. Radio waves. That was how her phone had kept the New Way at their outpost from contacting their homeworld through the frontera. She didn't really understand how an antenna—a transmitter, basically, she guessed—would help them create a new frontera, but she was pretty sure they were dealing with radio waves.

"What are these cords?" Melendres tapped the drawing.

The room was quiet, and Erin figured out they were asking *her* the question.

"In my world, a thing like this would need power. Energy. To generate, um, create the ripples."

"Could they use sprites?"

"They would need a lot of sprites. A *lot*. More than I've ever seen in one place here."

Melendres said, "What would they use, then?"

Before Erin could frame an answer, Holay said. "The Langtree Company's experiment, with the flames."

Melendres frowned. "Energy from flames? I thought the Langtree project merely provided lights to some homes." Plainly, she'd heard of the company, even in Pais Lewelyn.

Tregannon said, "Oswald Langtree is, was, an eccentric. His experiment garnered him much interest, and much coin, but I think it's mostly a curiosity."

Melendres adjusted her headband. "Yet the New Way wants it. Didn't Oshane Langtree try to take control of it? Isn't that what your infected man in Sheeplands conspired with him about?"

"It was."

"The project must shut down," Farway said. "We can't risk the New Way controlling it."

Erin crossed her arms. Close the Company? It didn't matter to Erin, but it was a big deal to Trevian's sister. A *very* big deal. And could the Coalition just step in and close down a private company? That seemed to go against the rampant capitalism they liked so much here.

"We don't need to close it," Tregannon said.

"Why don't we?"

"Councilmember Farway, how do sprite-takers catch sprites?"

"With nets."

"That's one way."

"With a bit of honey in the bottom of a jar," Melendres said. "Is that what you're saying? The Langtree Company is a cube of honeycomb at the base of a trap?"

"We have control, then," Tregannon said.

"A big risk," Melendres said. "I find your attitude strange, Brel. You want to 'secure' this danger spot, Orchard Hill, instead of destroying it. You want to control an experiment that gives the New Way the energy they need to imprison still more people. And open a new frontera. What are you thinking?"

Tregannon leaned forward and put his hands on the flat on the table. "We can dig and sift and pick off eight hundred parasites one at a time, while still more lie in wait to infect people. Or we can draw them to places where we have the advantage."

Farway rubbed her arms as if she were cold. "You risk lives. All our lives."

"They believe they can create a frontera, Debora. If they can, how many more thousands will they bring here? And the yorita has told us about their energy weapons. This is a war."

"You speak of war often, but you've never fought one."

"None of us has."

Farway's voice rose. "You base your knowledge on fireside stories and bits from old books! If this invasion is a disease, then we must eliminate the places that draw infection, the way you boil the sheets from the bed of a person with a fever, and scrub down the floors and walls of the house with singeweed and vinegar. You don't leave bedding in a pile to 'attract' the disease."

Melendres said, "Debora, this is not a war of weapons and armies. It is not a mestengo band who must be brought to justice. Nor is it strictly a disease. This requires new thinking. I'm not saying I think Brel is right about the Langtree Company, but let's think this through. Let's have a deeper discussion."

"I'll *insist* on that discussion," Farway said, "with Senior Councilmember del Rios in attendance, and perhaps others as well. We don't play games of chance with people's lives."

"I'm not playing with lives," Tregannon snapped.

She glared at him. "You already have, with your charm."

Melendres shoved back her chair and stood up, her hands stretched out. "Enough. We will discuss this again, calmly. Alker, do you remember anything else?"

"Did I say they need the compass and the lantern to accomplish this frontera creation?"

Tregannon nodded. "We have little to fear, since the lantern is not in this world."

Erin bit her lower lip. Oshane knew where the frontera to her world was, and he'd been there. Oh, but the New Way wasn't taking his calls right now. Maybe Tregannon was right.

"A small blessing," Farway said.

Erin poured lukewarm sisuree into a cup and sipped, savoring the flavor of pepper and ripe pears. Unlike coffee, sisuree didn't change flavor as it cooled. "I'm going for a walk," she said. No one stopped her.

4

(VII) Dare—I'm a scientist so let me act like one. I'm going to write down what I remember from right before...this. Right before all our data vanished, for one thing, right before everything went sideways.

I think I've been isolated for seven days now. They've pulled me out twice to answer questions. Not interrogating, more like subject-matter-expert questions. Months ago, when I was arguing with Lichtstrom about funding or something, I said, all self-righteously, "The Defense Agency doesn't own us!" What a joke.

Anyway, they're acting like there was some sort of multi-dimensional event. Which, okay, would explain those things, first at Ap-One and then here, and those crazy-wild readings out of the Pit.

I guess I'm hoping, dreaming really, someday someone will find this and know what happened.

From Telma Lewiston's Journal

The Company had recovered more than half of the copper Vallis Majeur and his father had stolen, and the cage fabrickers were on schedule. Over the next few days, Aideen reviewed the reports and invoices. The Sheeplands expansion was progressing, and one of the expanded cages was ready to put into operation.

When she wasn't with Ilsanja, or working on Company business, she reread the passage Trevian had left her. He'd had it copied out of Erin's charmed book. He felt it would answer her skepticism for his story of the flames who followed Erin and fought for her. The passage didn't convince her, but it gave her much to think about. Too much.

"You read that over and over as if it is a love letter," Ilsanja said as she came into the room. "Should I be jealous?"

"No love letter. It's from Erin's book." Aideen pushed the paper across the desk.

Ilsanja sat down across from her. "Is this based on the story he told us, about the elemental rescuing him from the New Way?"

"Partly."

Ilsanja leaned forward. "I believe his account, but I think he overlooks the most obvious explanation; Erin is an out-of-worlder, and she holds a charmed artifact. Simply because she did not *knowingly* tether the flames with a charm doesn't mean there isn't a charm in effect."

"And so he gave me this." Aideen waited while Ilsanja read. She knew the passage by heart now.

The flames can do much useful work within the carapace, whether earth, wood, or metal, although wearing it weakens them to the point of extinguishment. When the control drops away, as it does if the wearer of the object lets attention waver, the carapace vanishes. Often the flames lash out at the person who controlled them, with disastrous results. The vigor with which they turn on that one, even in a group of people, creates the illusion of understanding and intent among the creatures. It is disquieting.

"Trevian said he saw them create these carapaces, at his camp." Ilsanja turned over the paper to be sure she'd read everything.

"The charm created it, not the flames themselves. They were imprisoned."

"The lantern does this?"

"No. The collar. Oshane had it."

"And where is the collar now?" Ilsanja sat back.

"It's a mystery," Aideen said. "The elementals seek out and punish the person who imprisoned them. They attacked Oshane, when Erin released them, with no urging from her."

"Understanding and intent. Do fire elementals think?"

"My very question."

"Do you fear they will attack you, and the workers, because you cage them?"

It *was* her fear, or part of it, but even now she hesitated to speak it out loud. "We do not misuse them. Or we were not, until recently, when we held them too long. Would you lash out at us?"

"I'm a person, not a fire elemental. And they return to the cages. That doesn't seem intelligent, Aideen. Perhaps the things simply don't have memory, as we understand memory."

"Or we are enticing a different elemental each time."

"Then they must not speak to each other," Ilsanja said.

Aideen laughed. "You're right. Anyway, it's a puzzle."

Two days later Dolores carried in a message delivered by fast messenger. "It is addressed to both of you, yorita," she said as she laid in on the desk in front of Aideen. "From Yor Langtree."

There had been nothing so urgent from her brother that he couldn't use the regular mail caravan, not for nearly a month. "What now?" she said. "Is Jefa Langtree still at her father's?"

"Due home in an hour, yorita," Dolores said.

"We'll wait."

Aideen's fingers itched to open the packet, but she swore to herself she would wait. The hour crawled by, lasting as long as a rainy winter day, before the door opened. Ilsanja said something to Dolores. A moment later, she stood framed in the doorway, smelling of caballo, dressed in her work trousers and frock coat. "An urgent message from Trevian? What now?"

"I don't know."

"You could have opened it," she said, striding over to what was now her usual chair.

"It is addressed to both of us, I thought I should wait."

"In the future, don't be so polite."

Aideen slipped her finger under the seal and cracked it, unfolded the letter.

Elmaestro Tregannon had sent a handful of builders, a copper-hunter and guards to Merrylake Landing, where they were acting like prospectors. In reality, they were inspecting Orchard Hill to see where gates could be built. He had done this quietly, Trevian said, but Aideen and Ilsanja might see members of the crew in White Bluffs buying supplies.

Members of the Crescent Council, and people Tregannon invited to his war council, want White Bluffs to close the Langtree Company. It is of interest to the New Way, as we already knew. Nothing has been decided yet but be on your guard. Tregannon does not want it to close, so he may be your ally in this.

Aideen stood up, knocking back her chair. "No! I will not lose this company now!"

Ilsanja said, "Tregannon is no friend of White Bluffs."

Aideen could not stand still. She began to pace. The attacks on the Company never ended. "Why would they want it closed? What has it to do with the New Way? The Council fears our influence, and this is an excuse to take it from us."

"Does the New Way plan to power a device?" Ilsanja said.

"What device? And we *are* prepared! Who warned them about the New Way? Who closed their main door to our world? My brother!"

She reached the door. She longed to kick it, or the wall, anything. Any moment she grasped a particle of happiness, the world conspired to tear it from her. She would not lose her company. She would not let her company fail. She held herself still and drew deep breaths. This anger was good, it powered her, but she needed focus. She needed her wits. She spun back to face Ilsanja. "What pretext can they have?"

"That the New Way wants to seize it. And with the parasites, those nodes, perhaps they can infiltrate."

Aideen unclenched her fists. "Then we make it impossible to infiltrate us. We apply the charm Erin used. You and I will wear the mark, Yor Lopez, the team leaders and all the workers at the cages. And key people in the office."

Ilsanja cleared her throat. "The partners?"

Aideen shifted her weight from one foot to the other. "The partners have seen a node themselves; they know the risk we face, but others... I— We need to think this through. I want many people wearing the charm, but I don't want to start a panic. The sheriff has kept the charm from public knowledge."

"Tregannon calls the New Way a disease," Ilsanja said. "We can say it's a charm against infection."

Aideen had a direction now. "I suggest we call a partner meeting," she said. "Let's share Trevian's letter and put forth our plan. I want us to be ready, already protected, so we can batter down any excuse the Council makes for why we must close."

"I agree," Ilsanja said. She came around the desk, sat down in Aideen's chair, and reached for a pen.

Ilsanja's father bellowed like a wounded ram and stomped around the room. Aideen's throat tightened, but Yor Montez and Ilsanja watched the man without reaction until he came back to the table. Aideen wondered how she had looked, back in her study.

"This is another feint by the Crescent Council," Jefe Silvestro said. "They are pleased to take our taxes, but every day they seek ways to hobble us."

"Those parasites are real," Yor Montez said. "We should protect our workers and ourselves against them. We don't need to wait until the Council speaks."

"Agreed." Ilsanja nodded to Petrie, Silvestro's secretary. "Please put Yor Lopez and the cage workers first on the list for the charm, followed by all the partners."

Petrie, already writing, said, "Yes, Jefa."

"Do we give a disease as our reason?" Ilsanja said. "It might be a good tale to tell, if we need to institute searches later."

Silvestro frowned. "How does calling it a disease serve us?"

Montez said, "Some diseases create marks on the body, rashes or swellings. We can say we search for those."

"Why do we not say a parasite carries the illness, and we are searching for it?" Aideen said.

Silvestro rubbed his forehead. "So much to think about."

"The three of us will manage this, Father," Ilsanja said. "Edmund and Petrie will assist."

"Very well. Is there anything else? I'm meeting friends on the southern green, I don't want to be late."

"Don't let us keep you from them, Father. We will work out the details."

Aideen said, "I will write to the Coalition and ask for a trained charm-caster to come and begin the marks."

"The Coalition?" Ilsanja raised her eyebrows.

"Tregannon is our ally in this, remember? For now, at least."

"Very well."

Montez cleared his throat again. "Yorita Langtree, I have a question on another matter. Why would Yor Lopez be digging in the old tunnel?"

"He and I discussed the rift there," Aideen said.

"Ah." He nodded. "For a further expansion?"

"Is there a problem?"

"None, merely curiosity."

"It's unclaimed land," Aideen said, "but it could be claimed."

Ilsanja made a sideways sweep of her hand. "Shall we focus on the threat to the company first?"

"Of course," Montez said.

Two charmcasters came from the Copper Coalition, arriving three days later. Even though they both wore the mark, the Sheriff searched them. While one went with Sheriff Tanden to speak to the Town Council, Aideen escorted the other up to the cages and introduced her to Yor Lopez, who had assembled his team leaders.

Aideen explained that they would be given a mark to protect against a new parasite-borne illness showing up in various parts of the Crescent. Yor Oakley, from the Copper Coalition, had carried the infection, and the company wanted its workers safe. The charm would alert them if they came close to an infected person.

A team leader raised her hand. Aideen recognized her. When Father had first fallen ill, the woman had given her a prayer bead.

"Yorita Langtree, is it the disease that struck Madalita in the north? My cousin is a caravaneer, and he said the town ran mad."

Aideen tried out the answer she had crafted. "The disease seems to make some people behave strangely, speak strangely. Madalita was the location of one outbreak, and those people are healed now."

Another voice from the group. "Where is it coming from?"

Before she could answer, someone said, "Prospectors are bringing it. They go everywhere, with no safeguards, no limits. Will that be stopped, yorita? Will they be rounded up until this disease is finished?"

"There is no indication that prospectors carry any greater infection than others," Aideen said, hoping she sounded as confident as she meant to.

Someone muttered something, but the first woman spoke up. "What should we expect, yorita, with this charm?"

Aideen explained. She warned them about lightheadedness. Lopez told them the operation would run on half-shifts while the marking took place. People would be paid for a full shift, he was quick to add. Aideen, Ilsanja, and Montez had all agreed with no debate.

The group had drawn numbers to determine their order. Lopez was prepared to go first if others were reluctant, but the leaders lined up with no discussion. Aideen stayed, wrapping the cuts with bandages, and reminding each person to sit quietly until the lightheadedness passed. The charmcaster added that some might dream of the mark—a normal reaction.

Lopez moved his arm experimentally after the charm had been cut. "I planned to go to the tunnel on Weyves," he said, "but perhaps I'll go today."

"Do not injure yourself. You'd do better to rest," she said.

He grinned at her. "I'm not good at rest."

After the leaders were marked, the charmcaster motioned to Aideen. She sat down and rolled back her sleeve, trying not to wince as the loomin blade sliced into her skin.

While the charmcasters were working, they found no parasites among any company staff or cage workers, a relief to them all.

Aideen wrote a letter of thanks to Elmaestro Tregannon. She commented, as if casually, on how many people had been protected by the charm, and said they found no instances of infection in the company. It might read like just a wordy letter, but every sweep of her pen was a brick in a defensive document, and she knew it.

At least they had done what they could to fend off both the New Way parasites and the Crescent Council. Daily operations went forward, and Aideen settled again into a sense of familiarity and comfort until Weyves afternoon a sennight later, when Dolores came up to the study to say, "Yor Lopez is here and says he must speak to you."

"Lopez?" It was the engineer's free day. Why would he come to the house? Her heart thudded as she hurried down the stairs. She hoped there hadn't been an injury.

He stood in the center of the sala, holding his hat in both hands. "Yorita," he said. He was dusty. He'd been up at the tunnel, she was sure.

"Are you well? Is everyone well?"

"Everyone is, yorita, but I was at the tunnel, and…" he stopped.

"Sit down," she said.

He shook his head. "In a moment, yorita. I…discovered something odd, and I thought you needed to know."

"What was it?" She tried to read his expression. He didn't seem frightened, but his demeanor was serious.

"Bones, yorita."

"Bones?" It was rare to find bones, though not unheard of. "The remains of a kiote lair?"

"I don't think so, yorita. Only one set of bones I think and kiotes… there would be many bones, rabbits, ardiyas and even lambs. And they would be…scattered. These are not, not animal bones."

For a moment her voice failed. "Human?"

He nodded.

"An earth elemental… No, of course not." Earth elementals devoured everything. "An oso kill?"

"No oso sightings here in my lifetime, yorita. It's not impossible, but… again, the bones aren't scattered."

A hidden death. A murder, Lopez stopped short of saying. She straightened up. "Any clothing, a purse or a knapsack, anything?"

"One thing, yorita." He reached into his trousers pocket. "This." He held up a fine chain, with a glittering pink stone swinging at the end.

Aideen was in a waking dream where she struggled to move and could not. She could not feel her own heart, her own body. Her hand, unbidden, rose, and Lopez dropped the necklace into her cupped palm. She remembered the stone, flashing pink, and her mother's voice rising and falling as she recited a poem to Aideen.

Her voice spoke from somewhere behind her. "I know this," she said. "It was my mother's."

5

The courtyard hummed with human voices, punctuated with the clang of scavenged metal. From her place on the steps, out of the crowd, Erin watched the combination of caravans and individual prospectors. This was how the courtyard usually looked and she discerned the pattern easily now. A line of prospectors S-curved through the open gates, while closer to the steps, two caravans waited as assayers and scribes reviewed bills of lading, and red-vested guards checked the inventory on the wagons.

Trevian slipped up next to her and took her hand. "It's a good thing Harald and the delegation from Perlarayna does not return today," he said. "There's another caravan waiting beyond the gates."

"Two more days, Mei said in her note."

"Traveling through Pais Lewelyn shortened the journey," he said.

It didn't seem so to Erin; Harald had been gone for nearly four sennights now.

At the edge of the steps, a messenger dismounted. Brevik Dougal darted down the steps and shouldered aside another man, waving a folded square of paper. The messenger took the paper and Dougal hurried away.

"That guy is really something," she said.

"What?"

"Farway's secretary. Really eager to get his letters out."

Trevian shrugged. "Farway is not organized. Perhaps he rushes to get things done because she delays him."

"Yeah. Maybe. The message he was muscling Tonio to deliver was to a family member."

The man Dougal had cut off stepped forward and spoke to the carrier, conducting the business he'd been waiting to do. As he turned away, slipping his hands into his pockets, Erin recognized Lauris Diebell, a charmcaster from the Madlyn contingent. His expression was distant, and he didn't see either of them as he made his way up the stairs.

Maybe the two men had history, or more likely Dougal was just being his usual rude self.

"The Perlaraynans have battery-operated sail-wagons," she said, remembering something Mei told her in a letter.

"Ah, your magical energy storage devices."

"Not magical. Chemical."

"Profesor Machios would love to see one," Trevian said. "Are they bringing a wagon? Or a battery?"

"The wagons need wind, and they don't do well in the hills, so I don't think so. And I don't think they'll take a battery off the vehicle." She smiled at him. He was back to himself.

He'd been quiet when he came back from the funeral. The second night, in their room, she said, "How was it? Are you all right?"

He reached for her hand. "There were many people at the memorial, all speaking of his greatness, saying nothing of how he treated his daughter, or me...or how he drove his wife away. I felt nothing, and I felt nothing at the bier. The reading of the will went better. In the final months of his life, he did the right thing, although now Aideen will have to fight the Crescent Council to keep the company alive."

"If it's a wager between the Council and your sister, my money's on Aideen."

He gave her a small smile. "Mine, too. And you were right, about Aideen and Ilsanja. They share a bed."

"How do you feel about it?"

He glanced around the room as if he thought someone might overhear. "I feel happiness for my sister. But here, between us, alone, I will admit...I mostly feel relieved. I owe Ilsanja nothing now except respect. I am free."

"Except for fighting this war against the New Way."

He stroked her hair and drew her down against him. "Free in the ways that matter," he said.

Now, he scanned the courtyard idly as he spoke. "Machios will be disappointed—" His grip tightened and his whole body tensed.

"What?"

With his free hand he pointed. "There! Do you see—"

He let go of her hand and shot into the crowd like a crossbow bolt. After a second of shock, Erin followed him, or tried to, skirting bored caballos and drowsy caravan guards. "Trevian! Wait!"

It took her less than a minute to lose sight of him completely. A couple minutes later she'd managed to squeeze and sidle her way to the gate. "Did Trevian Langtree come through here?"

The gate keeper looked up from the prospector he was questioning. "He dashed out, headed south, yorita."

She stepped beyond the compound wall. What the hell was Trevian doing? She swiveled her head, checking both ends of the street. A long caravan snaked its way out of sight to the north, caballos pawing the pavement and tossing their heads. Sprite carts, saddle mounts, and people on foot all crowded into the right lane to avoid the wagons.

South, the lanes were less congested, but the sidewalks were jammed with people, mostly prospectors headed off to spend their money.

She sighed and started south, twisting her way between clumps of people. At the next block, she found Trevian pressed up against a wall, his gaze sweeping the street from side to side.

"What happened?"

Without stopping his scan, he flattened his arm against her, pressing her into the wall next to him. "Didn't you see him? Oshane?"

Erin's back prickled, and she pressed herself tightly against the stone, clutching her bag with both hands. "What? Where? Where is he?"

"I lost him in the crowd. He saw me and fled through the gate."

Erin's heart rate dropped back closer to normal. "Did he come with a caravan? What was he wearing?"

"Black, a black hat, with a gray scarf over his nose and mouth."

A scarf over... "Could you see his face?"

His eyes still bouncing from side to side, he shook his head.

"Um, he was wearing a gray scarf, like you were at the funeral? Mourning?"

"He was trying to obscure his face. I know it was him."

A different unease filled Erin. "How do you know?"

"His gait."

Erin let her gaze sweep the busy street too. "Where'd he go?"

"I don't know." Trevian clenched his fists. "I lost him."

She touched his arm. "Okay. Let's go back. And don't do that again, okay?"

"What?"

"Don't bolt off like that. We could have let the guards know, or the gatekeeper."

"There wasn't time." He glanced down at her for the first time. "Erin, there wasn't time. I feared he would flee."

Which he had. "When we get back inside, let's ask the gatekeeper."

She gripped his hand in hers the whole walk back. It wasn't clear at all what Trevian had seen, probably a random prospector. The gatekeeper wasn't any help. A clot of men and women, flush with coin, had left just before Trevian ran past. Several had worn black, some had worn scarves, and the gatekeeper knew nothing more.

"You think this was a fancy, a waking dream," Trevian said.

"Not necessarily. I just don't know what you saw. There are a million people in here."

"A hundred fifty, maybe a few more," he snapped.

She wasn't going to argue. "Let's go tell Tregannon. If—" She was about to say, "If Oshane *was* here, then..." Instead, she substituted, "It might not have been the first time he's been here."

"You saw a man in a hat, in a crowd of people wearing hats, for a matter of seconds. And his face was covered." Tregannon wasn't even trying to hide his skepticism. If Erin recognized it, Trevian must too.

"I know it was him. I know how he moves."

"He was wounded by Justice Arm Stuart. He moves differently now." Tregannon leaned back in his chair. "Why would he come with a caravan?"

"It's a plausible cover, I mean, something no one would question," Erin said.

"Why take such a risk to stand in our courtyard? We are guarded. He could do little damage or gather little information."

"I disagree," Stillwater said. "You can learn a lot from listening to the caravan masters or gossiping with the guards. Not just our guards; the caravaneers, too." Stillwater was taking Trevian's claim more seriously than Tregannon did. Maybe more seriously than Erin did.

Tregannon rolled his eyes. "In one afternoon?"

"He's been missing for sennights," Stillwater pointed out. "It may not have been just *one* afternoon. We should alert the justice arms."

"Because a copper-hunter saw a man in a hat and a scarf?"

Stillwater's voice had the level quality she used a lot with Tregannon. "Because we thought we saw Oshane Langtree, a wanted fugitive. Nothing more. They will decide what action is warranted."

"You think I am some sort of fool, spinning fancies," Trevian said.

Tregannon sat upright, glaring at Trevian. "I think your uncle murdered your father, and you burned your father's bones barely a sennight ago. I think your grief and rage are playing tricks on your mind. You need to rest, Langtree, and you need to hand the reins to your reason, not your passions." He settled back a little. "And, Ruth, you *should* notify the justice arms. We'll let them decide."

"I'm not turvy," Trevian said, but there was a note in his voice that worried Erin, like maybe he thought he was.

"No one thinks you are," she said. "C'mon, let's go get something to eat."

"I have no appetite," he said. His shoulders slumped. "Yes, let us go." He followed her out. "Do you think I imagined him?"

"I don't know what you saw, but I think we should be careful," she said. "He's always taken risks, right? I mean, he had his air elemental carry him right into your father's office. And he's desperate now. He's injured, the New Way have cut him off—he's someone with a lot less to lose."

His gripped her arm and pulled her to a stop in the middle of the hall. "But do you think I saw him?"

His intensity worried her. "I don't *know* what you saw. You were gone before I could look where you were looking."

"It was *him*, Erin. The way he turned his head, the shift of his shoulders..."

"Okay."

She wanted to be convinced, but for all his conviction, Trevian hadn't really spent much time with his uncle. Oshane had already been sickened by exposure to copper magic—stolen copper magic—the last time they'd both seen him. She pressed her fingers over his where they clutched her arm. "Okay," she said again, "I just want you to consider one other possibility. You said he wore a gray scarf. It is possible there was a prospector in the courtyard this morning who was also grieving someone, and wearing one? And it caught your attention?"

He stared at her. His grip dropped away, and he pivoted away from her.

She blurted out, "I'm not saying it's what *did* happen. I'm saying consider it."

"Of course. He wouldn't be wearing mourning, would he? I am a fool."

"You aren't." She put her hand on his shoulder. "I'm not saying you were wrong. I think we should assume he was there and take precautions. Trevian, I think maybe you should get some rest."

He raised his head, his back still turned to her. "I will lie down, at least, if you will join me."

"I...I would, in a heartbeat, but Ruth and I are going through the books looking for Orchard Hill references. I promised her."

Sighing, he reached up and touched her hand. She felt good, until he lifted her hand and ducked out from under her touch. "Of course, you must. You are needed."

"You're needed, too."

"I will do as you suggest. Perhaps visit the bathhouse and then rest."

"I'll come up as soon as I can."

"Good." He walked away without looking back.

Trevian hoped the hot water and the scent of the soap would calm his swirling thoughts, but they did not. Perhaps Erin and Tregannon were right, and he had imagined Oshane's presence. But Erin, at least, could she not believe him? He had taken her word for so many things.

He sat up, his shoulders chilled as they erupted from the water. No. Erin was clear-sighted and smart. He could not wish her to turn away from those things for anyone, not even for him.

Had it been the scarf, worn by a prospector mourning a claim partner or a parent, fooling him? Or had he seen someone who moved a bit like his uncle and imagined the scarf as well?

Or had he seen Oshane?

He clambered out and toweled off. He'd said he had no appetite, but now he was hungry. Erin was busy with Ruth Stillwater and the Pais

Lewelyn elmaestro, searching the books in the archives. As usual, there was nothing he was needed for.

He dressed in the clean trousers and shirt he had brought down from his room. He thought back to the good news they'd had these past sennights. Tregannon's ambush plan, at the guesthouse, had not only uncovered Holay, it had proven successful and they had freed eleven people from the infestation. According to Aideen, The Langtree Company had carved the mark on the workers at the cages, so they would be warned if an infected person approached. This, he hoped, would be enough to stop the Crescent Council's drive to shut down the Company.

Soon Harald Stuart would return with a contingent from Perlarayna, and the second guardian, Wing Mei. With another guardian, there would truly be no need for him. He had no magic artifact, no great skills beyond copper-hunting. He brought nothing useful to the war.

Well. He *did* hold an artifact, the collar. He did not wield it as Erin did the book, but it was in his care.

The kitchen apprentices waved him over to a sideboard where cheese, fruit, and bread waited. Only a few people sat in the dining hall this time of day. Dougal, the self-important Madlyn secretary, sat with a group of copper-hunters newly returned from prospecting. At a bench under the windows, one of the Madlyn charmcasters hunched over paper, his pen flashing as it moved. Trevian reached for his name. Lauris Diebell. He was a slender man with pale skin and short, shiny black hair wisping around his face in what one of the apprentices said was the latest Madlyn style. He glanced up and nodded at Trevian, who nodded back and found a table across the room, not wanting to disturb the man.

His tea had steeped enough, and he closed his eyes at the first swallow, transported back to his prospecting claim on the great field of Ancient, in his camp, before Erin had come into his life. How simple things had been. Close by something rustled and he opened his eyes. Diebell smiled at him. "Are you in meditation? My apologies."

"Just old memories."

"I yearn for company," the charmcaster said.

"You seemed deeply focused, I had no wish to interrupt."

He shrugged. "Yes. Letters. I write to my brother and his family. They've never been outside Coyle's Crossing, their little village on the Serpiente, and my nephew Pipjin longs to know all about the Copper Coalition—and Duloc. And I write to my padrey."

Trevian gestured to a nearby chair. Trevian hadn't known diosos sent letters to their temple keepers. Diebell must be very devout.

Here was a purpose, though. "Have you been to waterfront to watch them load the ships?" He could be like those in the city who took newcomers about for an uno, showing them the sights. "It's an interesting process."

"Ah! Pipjin would love to read of that! He dreams of boats, that boy." Lauris rummaged for paper and made a note, this time with a pencil. Did he carry his writing case with him everywhere?

Trevian rotated his plate. "A council of war is not the best topic for family letters I guess," he said. A moment later he worried. Did he sound like he was making a judgment?

Lauris, busy writing, nodded. "There is little I can say of the daily goings on, and I fear once we begin this expedition the chances to send letters will be few."

Trevian took a bite of bread and cheese. The size of the expedition to the underground complex his sister had discovered was daunting to him, with representatives from all three nations and perhaps even Perlarayna taking part. Historians, charmcasters, copper-hunters, guards, and messengers, it numbered more than twenty. Not an easy thing to keep a secret. "Elmaestro Tregannon plans to bring messengers," he said.

"Yes, but there will be little I can write to a curious nephew. Normally I would share views of our journey, but even the location is being kept a secret. I did hear a rumor there was a dried-up lake nearby."

"Merry Lake," Trevian said. "Where did you hear of it?"

"Just gossip among the guards. No one has betrayed Elmaestro Tregannon's order of secrecy." He laughed softly. "To be honest, there is very little I do know. Councilmember Farway shares nothing with anyone except Yor Dougal. With him, she shares everything. The rest of us, we aren't like you, at the center of this crisis."

"As you can see, I am at the center of nothing. I assist the Yorita Dosmanos, and she is the guardian of an artifact, but nothing more."

Lauris folded up the paper. "Your humility brings you honor, my padrey would say, but I see how important you are. The out-of-worlder looks to you before she makes a single move."

Trevian picked up a slice of fruit. Plainly, Lauris Diebell did not know Erin.

The charmcaster pushed back his chair. "Well, I think I'll arrange a visit to the waterfront. I should fill at least two letters. I hope we speak again, Yor Langtree."

"It would be a pleasure," Trevian said. How weak he must be, to get a glow of importance from Lauris's words.

E rin clung to his hand. The first of the expedition guards dismounted, waiting while a marked guard checked each of them for parasites. Erin's nerves, he knew, were humming like plucked guitarra strings.

"How long since you've seen her?" he said.

"Wow, um, okay. About a year, I guess. We've never actually met in person until now."

"Only through letters? Oh, no, through your devices."

"Yeah. All the Four Families met that way a couple of times a year. And Mei's been here about a month longer than me, I think."

The gatekeepers were thorough, but the process went quickly. From their behaviors, the visitors from Perlarayna understood what was required and why. Soon Genaro was helping Harald off his mount. Harald paused to grin at the two of them and squeeze their hands. "Duty commands," he said. He beckoned to Tregannon, leading him to where a man dismounted a stocky black caballo.

"Capitan Espinosa, please meet Elmaestro Tregannon of the Crescent Copper Coalition."

The newcomer twisted his torso slightly and cocked his right elbow. Tregannon, who'd prepared, did the same, and the two men lightly brushed elbows. Perlarayna had suffered a plague twenty years before, and many lives had been lost. They did not embrace or clasp hands outside of family.

Capitan Espinosa was a short muscular man, with cropped black hair. His knee-length black coat had a sigil of some kind embroidered on the breast, but Trevian could not make it out.

"Capitan," Erin murmured. "A military rank."

"Not his name?"

"I don't think so. Where's Mei?"

As Espinosa and Tregannon strolled toward the steps, two more riders came through. They both wore coats with black hoods. The rider on the left had embroidery on hers as well, a long creature like a snake or a lizard, picked out in glinting red, green, silver, and gold threads. Erin gasped and took a step forward as the other rider flipped back the hood, swung her leg over the pommel of her saddle and jumped down from her mount before it stopped moving. "Erin!"

Espinosa whirled. "Mei, wait! Stop!"

The woman didn't stop. At nearly a run, she held out her arms and threw them around Erin as the two women met. She held tightly as they rocked back and forth.

"Finally!" the newcomer said. "Finally!"

"Thank God you made it. And you're okay," Erin said.

The rider with the lizard sigil dismounted more decorously. When Espinosa halted, his hands on his hips, Mei stepped away from Erin and said, "It's all right. It's Erin!"

Espinosa muttered something under his breath but stayed where he was.

Mei still clung to Erin's hands. "You look different. Tough." There was a lump on her back, but as she moved, Trevian saw it was a knapsack, in a shade somewhere between pink and lavender. Like Erin's messenger bag, did it house an artifact?

"You look exactly the same," Erin said.

Trevian didn't move. Orbited by Espinosa, the lizard-sigil woman, Harald, and Trevian himself, the two women still seemed to be in a world of their own. Maybe for a moment they were, in their homeworld.

"I'm so sorry, Mei, about your parents. Are you all right?"

Mei shook her head. "I'm not, but I will be. And I'm sorry about yours. Now, we need to send these parasites away so we can go home. Oh, Juanita! Come meet my extranjera friend Erin."

The woman stepped forward and extended her bent elbow. "Juanita Gunnarsdottir. Es un placer, Señorita."

After a second, Erin said, "A mi tambien. Um, Gunnarsdottir? Is that...Icelandic?"

Gunnarsdottir started. "You know of Icelanders? Many generations back, yes." She flipped back her hood, revealing reddish hair braided close to her scalp in two tracks. Trevian hoped Erin would explain what Icelanders were later.

The courtyard filled, and they all retreated to the steps. Erin found him and guided Mei up to meet him. He'd been curious to see another person from Erin's world, especially since she was from a different nation, on a different continent. The second guardian was almost as tall as Erin, a slender woman with delicate features, whose black eyes reminded him of Ilsanja's. Her skin was fair but had a glow to it as she if she was lit by sprite lamps wherever she went. Like Erin's, her hair was black but sleek and straight instead of curly, cut short with tendrils like fern fronds brushing her face. Her speech was strange but not *so* strange, and he guessed he'd adjusted to Erin's accent enough to recognize it.

The bright-colored knapsack had faces drawn on it, not human ones. He couldn't make out what they were supposed to be.

The Perlaraynan delegation all spoke English, Mei had said, even though their home language was Spanish. He didn't know what Spanish was, but he knew Erin spoke some.

He touched elbows with Gunnarsdottir. Was she a guard assigned to Mei? Mei answered the unspoken question a moment later. "Juanita is a historian. She knows a lot about the Cataclismo."

Erin said, "In the Crescent they say, 'when the earth turned.'"

"Juanita has access to first-person accounts," Mei said.

Erin gave a little laugh. "So do I. They're not very helpful."

"Hers might be."

Tregannon's voice boomed from the top of the steps. "Let's let our honored guests get settled, and then we can speak. We have important matters to share."

The military man and Gunnarsdottir led the way, and a cluster of Perlaraynan guards followed. Behind them, the Copper Coalition guards and charmcasters hurried up the steps, leaving Harald, Genaro, Erin, Mei, and Trevian standing. From the doorway, Tregannon scowled at them, but hospitality commanded too, sometimes, and he was forced to lead the visitors inside.

Mei took Erin's hand again. "Before we get into anything else, explain. How can the parasites build an antenna when you say they don't even have electricity here? And do you really think they are AI?"

6

(VIII) *But enough about Richard. Enough speculating. Let me recap:*

After they shut down Ap-One, I tried to get hold of Bea Talavera, every way I could think of. No luck. I think she's dead. I'm not giving in to fear or catastrophizing. This is theorizing from data. I think they're all dead.

That didn't stop Lichtstrom from recreating their experiment in The Chapel and opening the exact same *dimensional rift they did, bringing through one of those banana-slug things. It lived six and half hours and then vaporized into dust. And just like with Ap-One, when it appeared, the readings out of the Pit went gonzo.*

I wasn't in The Chapel the next time they opened it. I was monitoring the Pit when my board went crazy. This is what I remember. I'm pretty sure I'm not hallucinating or imagining—this is what I remember. My board went crazy, and the world turned black, only I could see everything. I mean, everything. I saw the quantum level, and I saw all the way out to the end of the universe, all in one, well I'm going to say moment because I have no idea how long it was, and then it felt like the world turned sideways. I fell over, the console cracked and the air all around me was blue. Klaxons and alarms were blaring, and the place went into auto-lockdown. And I swear, it felt like I was in an elevator suddenly rushing upward. Like I left my guts somewhere down around my feet.

I told our friendly jailors from Defense all this. They just wrote it down without saying anything. When they were bringing me back to my room I said, "We've moved, haven't we? The facility moved." One of them said, "You need to stay calm, Dr. Lewiston." I swear if I wasn't so scared, I'd be pissed off at the condescension.

From Telma Lewiston's Journal

Edmund set a pitcher of sisuree and one of water down on the conference room table. Aideen smoothed her skirt and gave him a nod of thanks.

Jefe Silvestro muttered, "When the Council visits, we offer refreshment."

"No." Ilsanja was adamant. "When we *invite* a councilmember, we offer refreshment. We are not supplicants. They came to us. They demand of *us*. They will get what hospitality requires and nothing more."

Edmund had just taken his place in the corner when Petrie tapped on the door. "Yora Quinn has finished her body-search of the Senior Councilmember's assistant, and Councilmember Dunstan is ready as well."

Ilsanja glanced around her. Yor Montez, Silvestro, and Aideen each nodded, and Ilsanja said, "We are ready for them, Petrie."

Keir Dunstan was the elected member for their region. He came from a down mountain town in Sheeplands. No real friend of White Bluffs, he had never worked against it either. Aideen knew very little about Senior Councilmember del Rios, or who she might have sent to represent her in this meeting.

The two representatives entered. Dunstan was a surprise for Aideen. He looked about Yor Montez's age, with a wrinkled, tanned face and dusty blond hair pulled back in a queue the way her brother wore his. He stood behind a chair, his head tilted toward the woman who entered behind him, wearing a short jacket in blue and green over a blue skirt and sturdy boots.

Ilsanja said, "Welcome."

The woman nodded and held out her hand. "Thank you. Jefa Langtree? My name is Naedra Kortas. I speak for Senior Councilmember del Rios."

Ilsanja rose and shook her hand. The representative reached out to each of the partners. She seemed nondescript, with plain brown hair pulled back in a braid, plain brown eyes, ordinary features. With a flicker of amusement, Aideen mused that she was looking into a mirror.

Dunstan followed with handshakes, and once Kortas was seated, he sat down as well.

"It seems we are addressing all the partners." Kortas's gaze swept the line of them.

"You are," Ilsanja said.

Kortas folded her arms on the table. "You have prepared for the risks of the parasites. In her discussion with me, the senior councilmember advised me that you, more than most, were intimately aware of the risks of this infestation."

"My husband, Yorita Langtree's brother, is companion to the out-of-worlder Erin Dosmanos. He has fought these parasites twice. And sadly, his uncle is in league with them, or has been."

Silvestro said, "We've seen one of those vile things personally."

"This will speed this conversation. The Crescent Council got information from a person who was infected, saying the Langtree Company is of interest to these creatures, particularly the energy harvesting apparatus itself."

"The Copper Coalition has made us aware of this," Ilsanja said. It wasn't technically true since the word had come from Trevian, but Aideen did not interrupt.

Dunstan frowned. "It did? Without discussing it with the Council?"

Aideen raised her eyebrows. "I thought the Copper Coalition to be independent of any nation's Council. It works with the Council, not under its orders."

"It's true," Dunstan said. "I wish they had thought to tell us so we could have coordinated the message."

Ilsanja said, as smoothly as spider silk, "And did you discuss *your* visit, and your request, with the Copper Coalition, Councilmember Dunstan, before you came here today?"

Kortas spoke before Dustan could answer. "This is new ground for all of us. We all wish communication was better. I'm gratified to see you have taken steps to protect yourselves here at your offices, but the cages seem to be the focus of these New Way parasites. What have you done there?"

They had agreed Aideen would speak to the steps they'd taken there, and she recounted the addition of the mark on the cage workers. Kortas leaned forward. Her gaze never left Aideen's face.

"What did you tell people? About the reason?"

"I said there had been an infestation of a parasite. It changed people's behavior, and this mark would help them identify anyone infected."

A shallow nod. "What was the response from the group?"

Ilsanja stepped in. "There were no problems. They all cooperated with the charm."

"There was one cord-runner who thought prospectors carried the infestation," Aideen said. "I told them all, we'd traced the original infestation to a settled town. His team leader spoke to him too."

Kortas chewed on her lower lip. "We fear that people will rise up and turn on each other, blaming certain groups for spreading the things."

"The caravans," Dunstan said. "If mobs begin attacking caravans, our nation will unravel. We cannot have that come to pass."

"And some have already suggested prospectors," Kortas said, "because they move about so."

"I read the *Crescent Noticias* every day," Aideen said, "And I've seen no notice, no comment, no editorial from the Council. You say you are concerned, but you are silent on it."

Dunstan sighed and leaned back in his chair. "We've torn apart draft after draft. We pick apart each word and send it back again. And again."

"I've drafted two versions myself," Kortas said.

Yor Montez said, "Why so many, Councilmember?"

"Because we are afraid," Dunstan said. "We don't know what we face. The Crescent Council has faced crises before, but not one like this."

"They fear they will make the situation worse," Kortas said.

Silvestro twitched in his chair. "What has this to do with us?"

"We are concerned that the parasites have in interest in your company, Jefe," Dunstan said. "They have targeted it by name. And because of Oshane Langtree, it seemed they might have better access than we would like."

"Is Oshane Langtree even alive?" Aideen said. "Justice Arm Stuart wounded him with a crossbow. No one has seen him, have they?"

"There is a search throughout the mountains and the capital," Kortas said. "But he is a wily man and a desperate one."

"I do not believe you are concerned for our company," Silvestro said, as if he'd followed none of the conversation. "I believe you wish to close it. The Crescent Council is no friend to White Bluffs. You take our taxes but seek to break us."

"We are concerned for our nation, Jefe, as you should be."

"I didn't vote for you, Dustan, and I know well your stance on the cinco coin."

Dunstan's patience seemed to slip a little. "It matters not whether I got your vote, Jefe. I represent your district, all of it. All of *you*. This isn't about a coin, but about lives. The least you can do is listen."

Silvestro folded his arms.

Aideen leaned over to Ilsanja and whispered, "Refreshment?"

Ilsanja cleared her throat. "Edmund, would you find some bread and fruit for our visitors? They've had an early morning."

Without a flicker of expression Edmund glided out of the room.

"I thought we—"

"Father, the discussion of White Bluff's right to choose its own way is an important one, but as you said, you saw the creature yourself. It could be our workers, and those who subscribe to our services, who become infected."

"Well, I don't see what we can do."

"Jefe Silvestro, you've already helped us," Kortas said, to Aideen's surprise. "You've followed a plan of preparedness others could model."

A silence drifted over the table, and moments later Edmund came back with a tray of sweet bread and fruit, as if it had been ready and waiting somewhere. He passed the tray, the cups, and the sisuree pitcher. After a few bites, Ilsanja said, just as they had discussed, "We believe there was talk of asking us to close."

"There was," Kortas said.

"You see!" Silvestro sat upright and bellowed. "Closed! What did I tell you!"

"There *was*," Kortas said again. "It did not come from the Crescent Council. The Copper Coalition and the Council has drawn together delegates from neighboring nations. Even a contingent from Perlarayna is expected. Many suggestions, from the reasonable to the wild, have been raised. No one on the Council wishes to close down the Langtree Company at this time."

Silvestro stabbed the table his finger. "At this time!"

Kortas set down her cup. "Jefe, we've spoken of isolating whole towns, outlawing prospecting, stopping travel if we have to. Yes, we'd close a company if we believed it would protect us. That is not what we think now."

She lifted the cup and sipped from it, directing her next comment back to Ilsanja. "Jefa, you have taken good steps, rapid ones, to protect your workers from the parasites, but as Oshane Langtree demonstrates, there are people in league with these creatures who are not infected. They could still attempt to overtake your operation."

Aideen said, "That has always been a risk, but we can take greater steps to secure the cages."

"Yor Lopez added watchers after the attack on Don Oswald," Yor Monez said. "We can build on it."

"The Council can offer assistance as well," Dunstan said.

Don Leo snorted. "So they get a better look at our operations, and our charms."

Ilsanja rotated her cup. "We will accept whatever help we need, and we will offer whatever help we can," she said.

Montez said, "The Crescent is our home, and we wish to keep it safe. White Bluffs is our home too, and the people of this town rely on us to provide light and warmth. We wish to keep them safe too. Our guiding star, Councilmember Dunstan, is to keep the balance."

Dunstan ducked his head. "Well stated, Yor Montez."

Silvestro paced, ranting about the hidden motives of the Council, before he left the room, and probably even the offices themselves.

"I expected a clenched fist and a demand," Ilsanja said. "Not a reasonable discussion."

Aideen said, "Is anyone but me frightened?" She smiled, to lighten the words.

Montez did not smile as he answered. "Not frightened perhaps, but... it worries me, those creatures having a plan for our cages."

Ilsanja said, "It worries *me* that the Council seems frozen like an ardiya in front of a kiote. This reluctance to speak because people will rise up. I don't understand this. Have there been uprisings? I remember none."

"Father spoke of one in Three Hills, in Sheeplands," Aideen said.

Montez nodded. "Yes. Some issue with water. People came to the town center and milled around in front of the town council offices, shouting insults. They did this every day for a month. Two council members stepped down, and the council re-voted and undid their decision. I remember no details though."

He stared into the distance. "But when I was a boy, there was an uprising in Duloc, over grain prices. The Council loosed its guards on the people. It didn't go well. The Copper Coalition stepped in to mediate. It's part of the reason people trust the Coalition guards more than those of the Council."

"If the worst thing happened, and we needed to close," Ilsanja said, "it wouldn't be enough to suspend operations. We would have to remove the charms so no one else could use it."

"People count on our power," Montez said. "I know nothing about wars, but how long would one last? What if it lasted until winter?"

"People would need to store blackrock for lamps and stoves," Ilsanja said.

Montez countered, "And blackrock brokers would seize a chance to reach deep into the purses of our neighbors."

"We could defray the costs, if we stockpiled some blackrock," Aideen said.

"At company expense?"

"If it came to it," Aideen admitted.

"An unpleasant thought, but not as unpleasant as those things controlling our town," Ilsanja said. "Here with the three of us, we do all realize some of these decisions will mean banding together and outvoting my father."

"Oh, yes," Montez said. "We're aware."

"Well. Much to think about. Aideen, will I see you at home?"

"In an hour or two."

Ilsanja smiled at her as if the world held only the two of them. "Very well. Yor Montez, pleasant day."

"And to you, Jefa."

Ilsanja swept from the room, her bright yellow skirt rustling.

Aideen gathered up her portfolio. At least for the past few hours, preparing for this meeting, she hadn't thought about the bones.

The bones, wrapped in a leather bundle, lay in a drawer at the office of the sheriff. Lopez had been right, and further excavation revealed all the bones of the skeleton including the skull. They found scraps of fabric so old and grayed by burial they could not tell its original color, and a pair of leather shoes, nothing else.

The skull was smooth, unmarred. There were bones broken in the third and fourth fingers of the right hand. Otherwise, the bones kept their silence on the death of their wearer.

The sheriff, who had captured mestengos and dealt with deaths caused by theft, by anger, by fighting, shook her head when Aideen approached her. "This is beyond my skill, yorita. I've sent a letter to the justice arms in Duloc, but I have no way to determine who this was. We don't know how long the bones lay there. Certainly long enough for the flesh to feed the earth, but otherwise—" She rolled her shoulders in a shrug. "The necklace, which you say belonged to your mother, is a help, but she might have given it to someone, or had it stolen."

"Surely other people have gone missing over the years," Aideen said.

The sheriff turned the inkpot on her desk, lining the pen up with the corner. "Until I know how old the bones are, there is no point is asking about people who have vanished. And there truly aren't many."

Aideen stopped asking questions. She knew what was unspoken. The sheriff was protecting the Langtree reputation. Serafina Langtree was the most famous missing person from White Bluffs. Trevian always said she'd gone west to the nations of Shevastin. She'd vanished two nights after Father had sent Oshane away from the house.

The town believed Serafina had fled with Oshane.

Now they would believe Oswald Langtree had killed his wife. This was the cupboard door the sheriff didn't wish to open.

And now...the company, and the Council.

Workers had dug leagues of narrow trenches, and copper cord now ran close to the town of Circle Springs, in Sheeplands. Nine leagues of cord. She should shift more workers to the project, pushing it closer to finished. Instead, she jotted figures on a sheet, remembering the yield from the blackrock mine she now owned, trying to calculate how much of the town's needs it could meet, and for how long.

Edmund tapped at her door. "Yorita? I bring a message from the sheriff, for you and Jefa Langtree. Shall I have it delivered to the house?"

Aideen held out her hand. "I'll take it."

When he'd left, she snapped the seal and unfolded the sheriff's note.

Jefa Langtree, Yorita Langtree;

The Crescent Council informs me Justice Arm Aquila Lodros will arrive in White Bluffs on Veyernes. Justice Arm Lodros has experience in the study of bones and a record of success in solving deaths many years old. She will need to interview both of you and members of your household as well as others.

Well, progress, at least.

She slipped the note into her trousers pocket and returned to her drafts. It was good news, but she couldn't let the bones distract her from the immediate threats facing the Company.

7

It was a relief for Erin to talk to someone without finding metaphors or simplifying concepts she didn't really understand herself. She led Mei into one of the study rooms, Trevian with them, bypassing the delegation assembling in the dining hall.

Mei sat down. "Artificial intelligence?"

"They evolved from AI." Erin recapped her experience with the consciousness of the New Way. "They're definitely a collective, but there's a hierarchy. I got a sense of their homeworld, but it felt like a, a projection, almost. The nodes are biomechanical, with electronic components."

Mei frowned. "You're sure they were human created?"

"Yes, but they've evolved beyond that."

Erin thought for a moment. She hadn't told anyone this part, not even Trevian, largely because she didn't have the vocabulary for his world. At least she and Mei had a common jargon.

The New Way had started out as an enhanced smart system run through a personal device. People on the New Way's homeworld wanted better, faster access to everything, with more convenient tech. Even carrying around a phone was too much bother. The companies tried various things to meet that desire.

"Like those glasses with a heads-up display and a network connection," Mei said. "It didn't work, though, at least not at home."

"It didn't work for the New Way's world either, but something else did."

Researchers found a way to create a biological terminal for data access.

"They created those creatures?" Trevian sounded shocked.

"And made them pink?" Mei made a face.

Erin chose to answer Mei's question. "They made pink, stripes, glow in the dark, customize your own, everything you can think of. Once the New Way formed and, well, took over, all the bionodes reverted to pink."

"What did they make the nodes out of?" Mei said.

"Human genetic material but I don't know the details."

Mei shuddered.

Even with a perfected bionode, the system didn't catch on at first. People thought it was gross. At the end of five years, only thirty percent of the population wore a node. Those users connected directly with the "instant system," as it was advertised, and that system analyzed the years of data in detail.

A group of tech-billionaires formed a philanthropic foundation and offered the system to low-income areas and countries. Within the next two years, eighty-two percent of the total world's population were integrated. More and more people could communicate, nearly instantly, with each other.

"Was it self-aware by then?" Mei asked.

"Yes. It was operating in stealth mode."

"The billionaires were controlled?"

"Definitely."

Trevian shook his head. "I understand none of those words."

"It was acting harmless, but it was in control."

"What you're describing sounds nothing like elementals," he said.

"I don't think the New Way is directly elemental. Some elemental energy may feed them, but they were created by humans, absorbed human impulses, and grew from those. Remember, all this was three hundred years ago."

Mei gasped. "What? They were that advanced back then?"

Erin nodded and continued.

The New Way discovered a mechanical intruder had entered their world through a dimensional rift, a frontera. They disabled it to study it. When a second one came through, they attached a node and sent it back. Upon the limited data they got from it, they sent through several more nodes. Once they had a foothold in the other world, they prepared to send human hosts through, expanding their control.

"My world," said Trevian.

"Yes. The Ancients stopped them at Aperture One, by firebombing the installation and burning the town."

"Wow," Mei whispered.

"But the New Way knew about other worlds now. They found another way through about six months later, at Orchard Hill, but something went wrong. The Collision. Since then, they've been searching for another frontera, so they can control this world and keep it from creating another Collision."

"Is that when the earth turned?" Trevian said.

"It has to be, by the timing, but I still don't know exactly what happened."

"You should talk to Juanita," Mei said.

"Anyway, they think they can use radio waves or something to open a frontera at Orchard Hill and bring through an actual army."

Mei looked at Trevian. "You said the people in the cave with you had crossbows. Did the New Way keep their weapons primitive?"

"No," Erin said. "The people they sent into this world had to blend in, but at least one of the three who attacked Trevian had an energy weapon. If they don't need to be all stealth-mode, I think they'll bring more of those."

"Oh, God. Colonialism," Mei said.

"These things were created and matured in a competitive, market-driven environment," Erin said. "I don't see how they could be anything other than imperialist."

"We know where Orchard Hill is," said Trevian, "but we don't think they do yet."

"Good," Mei said. "Can they communicate through a closed frontera?"

"Maybe, but they couldn't open the frontera while my cell phone was searching for signal."

"Do we know what frequencies they broadcast on?"

"Seriously, Mei?"

Mei spread her fingers. "It was worth asking. How many cell phones do we have?"

"Yours and mine."

"There are hundreds," Trevian said.

Erin nodded. "Yeah, thousands actually. Dead, and they've been dead for three hundred years. And there is no signal for them to find, is there, even if we could charge them?"

"Perlarayna has electricity," Mei said. "In limited quantities. It's hydro-electric. But it's three weeks at least to get there, and we'll probably need the phones at this Orchard Hill place. To block their signal."

Trevian looked from one to the other. "What are weeks?"

"Sennights."

Mei said, "I don't know what you expect me to do, Erin. I have the compass, but all it seems to do with the books is pass objects."

"Well, you're the hardware genius. Wait, *books*? Plural?"

"Perlarayna has two books like yours."

Erin's stomach dropped. "Like mine?"

"Not exactly like yours, for sure. Theirs don't have any magical spells in them. The one I've seen has a lot of botanical information, mostly medical. But it has a puerta. Each book has a puerta, Marco said, and—"

"Who's Marco?"

"Sorry. Capitan Espinosa. The Presidenta has one book in her office and the other is at the university where Juanita works."

It was weirdly comforting to hear Spanish words with standard endings, but she wondered how the Perlaraynans would feel when they heard some of the Crescent's words, like "elmaestro," or "profesor" for either gender. It was still a hard one for Erin. Not pro-*fess*-or; pro-fes-*sor*, when Ruth didn't even do the conventional things a professor might do at a university. And then the names. Trevian's wife pronounced the J like in juice, instead of the softer nearly-h sound other words had.

A university. Electricity. Mei's frontera was definitely in the upgrade nation.

"The compass doesn't only deliver stuff, can it? I thought it worked with the book."

"My mother thought it worked with the lantern, but we don't really know. Is there anything in your book?"

"Not about the compass." Erin looked, really looked at Mei. The other woman was hunched over, and her eyes were dull. "Okay. Enough talking for now. Let's get you something to eat."

As they reached the door, Erin said, "Seriously, though, I thought you were a hardware nerd. Didn't you used to build radios?"

"I *am* a hardware nerd. I could build something, theoretically. We have to know what to build, and I need the raw materials."

"Well, we've got the materials," Erin said, "and they're raw. Really raw."

H arald was in the corner of the dining hall, talking to a woman in blue and white plaid smock, kitchen staff. Her arms were crossed, her back stiff.

"Do they think we carry disease?" she snapped as Erin eased past her.

Harald did not raise his voice. "They faced a plague. Many of them are old enough to remember it. Three out of every one hundred died. Think for a moment, Elya. Imagine your own family, your neighborhood. No one spared. Fishers, sailors, cooks, fabrickers, builders, singers, and poets, justice arms, council members, scientists. Every town, every city."

Eyla didn't uncross her arms, but her posture softened. "Well, but that didn't happen here."

"They still do not know where the contagion came from. If they wish to wipe down their utensils with white lick before they eat, we do not need to take offense."

Erin stepped out of the doorway so Mei and Trevian could get in. "Is that true?" she whispered to Mei.

"Yes. Um, Marco is waving at me."

Erin got out of her friend's way. She slid over against the wall. Trevian joined her.

"I understood almost nothing the two of you said. Will she help us?"

"She wants to, but we don't know how yet." Mei had gone to a place in this world that had electricity. Erin hadn't quite gotten over that. Of course, at home, Mei's frontera was in a national forest. A hundred years earlier, some Wing ancestor had built a simple rock building around it, and now visitors thought it was some kind of ancient shrine. Mei's frontera was in a shrine. Erin's opened in a culvert. Why shouldn't Mei get electricity and universities?

Kitchen staff began carrying in food and loading it on a side table. Two attendants went directly to the tables where people were seated and put bottles filled with a clear liquid on each one. Some carried in additional napkins. White lick was high-proof liquor, and its alcohol content would probably kill any microbe out there. Knowing about the epidemic, the Perlaraynans looked practical, not eccentric, with their elbow bumps and their disinfecting rituals.

Harald joined them. "I did not think how their desire to wipe everything with lick or very hot water would be received."

"I met two Perlaraynans before today," Trevian said. "They were prospectors. I had forgotten they doused everything in hot water."

Harald jerked his chin at Espinosa, who was talking to Mei. Or maybe lecturing her. Erin couldn't tell. "That one brought birds in a cage. Birds! I'd never seen so many in one place. Apparently, he conducts some spiritual ritual with them."

A qualm of nausea rolled through Erin's stomach. "What do you mean?"

"Every three days, he would remove a bird from the cage. He fed them from his hand, with some grain he carried, so they didn't flutter away from him. He'd attach something to the bird's leg and toss it into the air, freeing it. I confess, watching them fly was a joy and a wonder I had not expected."

Erin's smile-muscles kicked in and she didn't even try to look serious. "He was sending messages."

"So I gathered, instead of a prayer bead or a candle."

"I don't think so. In my world, anyway, there are birds who fly thousands of miles to return to where they were born. They do it every year. I think he was sending a report back to whoever he works for."

"The capitan reports directly to their ruler, someone called a presidenta. He is part of their military, but no longer works with soldiers. I was not clear on exactly what he did. But birds? Truly?"

"Truly." Erin pushed away from the wall. "Maybe later I can get Mei to tell me what he does."

The three of them found seats at the end of the table, and a moment later Mei joined them. Erin looked around for familiar faces before she remembered Stillwater and Melendres were already on their way to Orchard Hill. Farway spooned fruit onto her plate, Dougal grafted to her side.

Gunnarsdottir caught Erin's gaze and pointed with her fork at the broiled vegetables. "These are good."

"I like them too," Erin said. "What do you do at the university?"

"I am a historian. My area of expertise is the Cataclismo and the period immediately following it. The threat we face seems to have come from that time period, so I was chosen to accompany Señorita Wing."

"Mei said you have a first-hand account of what happened during the Cataclismo."

Chewing, Gunnarsdottir nodded. "Do you know what a skald is, Señorita?"

"Um, burning yourself with very hot water?"

Gunnarsdottir frowned. "What?"

From across the table, Mei giggled, covering her mouth. "With a *k*, Erin. They were poets and chroniclers in Iceland. They were in our world too."

"Right, in like, the Middle Ages or something."

Gunnarsdottir laughed. She speared a chunk of lamb from the platter as it was passed down the table. "Yes, long ago. But more recently…"

Tregannon stood. He waited until the two tables quieted. "Welcome to our guests from the gateway to the eastern continent," he said. "Especially to another member of the Four Families, Señorita Wing."

"Oh, God," Mei whispered. She raised her hand, then dropped it and stared down at her plate, blushing.

People joined in a chorus of welcomes. Half-rising from his chair, Espinosa gave a nod.

"Elmaestro Melendres from Pais Lewelyn and our own profesor Stillwater are not present tonight. They have gone ahead to prepare for an expedition to the area we think provides our best defense against these parasites. Within three days, we will be ready to join them."

Espinosa got frowny and looked down at his lap.

"What's up with Espinosa?" she whispered to Mei.

Mei leaned over, her lips close to Erin's ear. "He didn't want to stay. Pais Lewelyn? He doesn't like them. The whole journey he planned to deliver me and return. Something changed."

"Something Tregannon said?"

"Marco used the compass to send a message to the presidenta."

"He doesn't look happy with the answer."

Dougal rose. "Where is this location, Elmaestro?"

"Now, Brevik," Farway said. "The elmaestro will come to it in his own time."

Tregannon inclined his head in the direction of Farway. "That time is now, Councilmember. We believe the location of Orchard Hill is near the empty town of Merrylake Landing. The settlement is close to a thriving hill town, White Bluffs, so food and equipment will be available. Secrecy will be a challenge, but we have put the story about that we are prospecting."

Gunnarsdottir raised a hand. "You said the town is empty. Why? Was it the victim of infection?"

"No. The lake dried up, other towns became more prosperous, and earth shudders blocked a wide pass from Boskey. Sprite carts did not move well on the steep trail running east to the North Road. The world passed the town by."

Erin shot a sideways glance at Trevian, who grimaced. Merry Lake, he'd told her, was not simply drying up. White Bluffs channeled its water, first as a source for drinking and crops, and now to feed the decorative waterfall and canal, the city's centerpiece.

Gunnarsdottir persisted. "But you believe these infectious parasites visited us before, at or near Orchard Hill."

Tregannon smiled at her. "Yorita, you would do better to ask the person sitting across from you. Yorita Dosmanos believes the parasites came to our world twice before but were eradicated by the Ancient."

Faces turned toward Erin, who didn't bother hiding her sigh. "When I was joined with the New Way, I learned they found another way to enter our world, at Orchard Hill. Some catastrophe at Orchard Hill ended their second foray. They didn't come here again until they found the frontera above Madalita."

Capitan Espinosa said, "What happened?"

Erin said, "I don't know."

CONTENTS OF A LETTER

Perlayraynans have arrived and with them the guardian of the compass. We go to Merry Lake.

8

...We were on auxiliary power except one of the backup generators got crushed when the cavern collapsed, so it was three-quarter power and no connections; phones, devices, nothing. The emergency radio worked but Lichtstrom commandeered it. The first couple of hours I just spent finding people and getting the injured ones to the infirmary. They dug Richard out of the rockpile that's The Chapel, now.

Then I tried to call you and Mama—that's when I found out we were cut off.

Defense showed up, and we're all confined to quarters. But a bunch of the people I talked to said the Pit chamber turned blue. It wasn't just me who saw it. It wasn't wind. It was an air event of some specific kind and it seemed to move with intent.

One thing my friendly Defense interrogator said to me was, "This was a non-localized event."

From Telma Lewiston's journal

I would say it is the largest colony of flames I have ever encountered," Yor Lopez said, guiding Aideen around the pile of earth he'd shoveled up. He had drilled at an angle and lowered braided copper wire and a thicker copper cord, but both had melted.

"The copper mesh on top of the cages doesn't melt," Aideen said.

"No, but it does decompose after a time, yorita. When, back at the cages, we use a sibling group as planned, I'll need to calibrate the copper mesh."

She dug the toe of her boot into the rocky soil. She had not asked him if this was the place the bones had come from. "Is it worth claiming?"

"The reason to do so would be to prevent another sharp-eyed person from claiming it with a plan to rent it back to you at great cost."

"Reason enough."

It was nearly time to head back. The justice arm had arrived the previous afternoon and planned to meet with her and Ilsanja today. As they walked back toward the opening where the caballos waited, she said, "Yor Lopez, do you believe the flames can reason?"

"Reason?" He walked a few more paces. "Does a kiote reason? Does an ardiya? I would say ardiyas do not reason, but I watched a female once, determined to steal a knapsack from a traveler. Plainly he had food inside. She hid, she feinted, she crouched immobile until he dozed off, then scampered out and seized the straps of the sack. She would have made off it with it, but I was there and snatched it back. It looked like strategy, but we do not say ardiyas think."

Aideen smiled at him. "And the flames?"

"Ah. Well, they are curious. It's how we trap them. But no, I do not think they reason."

"You have heard of Erin Dosmanos?" They stepped into the light. Aideen stroked her mount's face. "In her book, there is a passage about imprisoned flames, when freed, turning on the one who imprisoned them, even singling that person out from a group of many."

"We are always careful," he said.

"I mean, do they recognize faces?"

"They have no eyes, yorita."

"Earth elementals do not seem to have eyes or ears, but they open the earth directly under their prey."

"They sense vibrations in the earth."

"You have worked with flames every day for years. Do you believe them witless?"

He considered her words, flipping the ends of his reins back and forth. "I think them...strange. Not like us. I understand what you are asking and there is a sense, sometimes...but no. Mostly I find them strange, and dangerous if we are not careful and respectful of their power." He waited while she mounted, then did the same. "I hope I have not disappointed you."

"No. I seek information, and you provided what I asked." She nudged her caballo around to head down the hill. "The capital has sent a justice arm to study those bones. She may wish to speak to you."

"Whatever you and the jefa need."

They parted ways at the cages. Full summer had arrived. It seemed like only yesterday had been early spring, but everything had changed, not just the seasons.

At home, she changed her skirt and waited with Ilsanja in the sala until Dolores entered. "Jefa Langtree, Yorita Langtree, please meet Justice Arm Lodros," she said.

The blocky woman with her held out her hand first to Ilsanja. "Jefa." Her hair, as gray as blackrock ash, was drawn back from her face in one severe braid. Her eyes, Aideen noticed as she stepped forward to shake hands, were the same color. The Justice Arm settled into a chair, set down the bulky satchel she carried, and accepted the cup of sisuree Ilsanja poured for her. After a few sips, she set the cup aside and drew out a notebook and a pencil.

"I have examined the bones your employee discovered," she said. "Yorita, I've been told you believe they might be your mother's? Is this because of the pink stone on a chain that was found with the skeleton?"

"Yes."

"How long has your mother been missing?"

"Since I was six. Sixteen years."

Lodros made a note. "Is there anyone in the house now who knew her?"

"Yes. Our housekeeper, Dolores Noudin."

Lodros made another note and then set down the pencil. "I have examined the bones using my eyes only, and I confirm what you already observed. There was no injury to the head. Many deaths on the road— murders, I mean—are caused by blows to the head. There was none here. The neck was not broken. There were two broken fingers, which might mean a struggle. My next examination will be with a set of magnifying lenses. A blow with a knife or a crossbow bolt will often nick or scratch a bone."

"You're sure it's a woman?" Ilsanja said.

"Oh, yes. Clearly a woman, an adult."

"One thing for certain, then," Ilsanja said.

"It is possible the woman died naturally, of an illness. If she had a fever, she may have wandered into the tunnel. It doesn't explain the broken fingers, or why the bones were covered. The bones tell us little." Lodros reached down and opened the squat satchel. "The shoes, however…may I speak to your housekeeper?"

Aideen rose. "I'll get her."

Ilsanja gestured at the bell cord, but Aideen shook her head. Dolores sat in her alcove outside the kitchen, reviewing the accounts. She rose without speaking and followed Aideen back to the sala, where she reluctantly accepted a seat near the table.

"Do you recognize these?" Lodros thumped the shoes down on the table. Bits of soil spattered onto the surface and Dolores flinched slightly. She leaned forward, squinting.

"May I touch them?"

"Touch, pick them up, whatever helps you," Lodros said.

Dolores picked up the closer shoe and held the heel up to her eyes. "This shoemaker's mark, I know it. Jefa Langtree—Jefa Serafina Langtree, these were made by her favorite shoemakers."

"I suppose many people bought shoes from them. Do you see anything specific about this pair?"

Dolores bent the shoe and twisted it slightly, raining more dirt down on the table. "They're well-worn, so if they belonged to the jefa, they were her everyday shoes." She swapped out the shoes and rubbed soil away from the toe of the second one. "These are aged in dirt," she said. "May I apply some leather soap to this one? It will help me answer your question."

Lodros stared intently at Dolores. Just as Aideen was about to move or speak to break the quiet, the justice arm said, "Yes, if you think it will help."

Ilsanja reached for the bellcord. "We'll get the chica to bring some," she said.

Nila appeared, left, and came back with a tub of leather soap and a soft cloth. Dolores scraped and shook off as much dirt as she could. She scooped a small portion of the soap onto the cloth and brushed it onto the leather upper. Using her finger, she spread it around. After a few seconds of staring at the shoe, Dolores sighed. "Here." She held it out to Lodros. "With the leather moistened, you can see a stain here. It came when the Jefa spilled a glass of wine one night. The shoes became her everyday shoes after that."

"Can you swear these shoes belonged to Jefa Serafina Langtree?"

Aideen's heartbeat pulsed in her throat. It was her turn to stare at

Dolores. She'd already known, and this issue of shoes shouldn't matter, but somehow...

"I can swear it," Dolores said.

She put the shoe on the table, carefully lining up the pair. Staring down at them, she touched the top of the nearest one gently with her finger, then folded her hands in her lap.

"My thanks," the justice arm said. She wrote in her notebook, but Aideen thought her attention was on the women before her, not on her scribbled words.

"He did this," Dolores said.

The words struck Aideen like a blow to the stomach. "No," she said. "I do *not* believe Father did this."

Dolores glanced up, scowling. "What? No, not Jefe Oswald, yorita. Him. Oshane Langtree."

"There's a name I've heard," Lodros said, "from a colleague of mine. Not available now, sadly—he's on an expedition. Was Oshane Langtree in White Bluffs when Serafina Langtree went missing?"

"He came back," Dolores said.

Lodros shifted her position in her chair, like someone getting ready to hear an eagerly awaited fireside tale. "Came *back*?"

"The jefe sent him from the house. I don't know what was said, but Oshane Langtree was angry, and the Jefa stayed in her room with me while he left." Dolores blinked. "I was not the housekeeper then. I came with the Jefa, I was her chica."

"How did she seem, while the argument went on?"

"Relieved. She was weary of staying out of his reach, fending off his compliments, trying not to spark the storm that could roar up between him and the jefe at any moment, for any reason. Then he was gone, and she went to bed. I was preparing to sleep as well when the cook came to get me. Oshane Langtree was at the kitchen door, demanding to see the Jefa."

"Will the cook remember this event?"

"Susannah was not the cook then, she was a kitchen chica, but she might. The cook now lives in Bois with her daughter and son. I can tell you where she lives. We write often."

"It may be useful. But go on."

"I went out to see him. Oshane Langtree was a smiling man, his green eyes twinkled, but the anger *always* crouched right behind those eyes. When I told him the jefa didn't want to see him, he unleashed it like a wildfire, telling me no chica would keep him from her if he wanted her. The cook called the stable workers, and they drove him away. All the doors and windows were locked."

"What did the jefe say when you told him of this?"

"I didn't tell him," Dolores said.

"No?"

Warmth flowed into Aideen's hand. Ilsanja had taken it in her own. Only then did Aideen realize how cold hers were.

Dolores stroked the upper of one of the shoes. "The jefa did not wish it. She did not wish to upset her husband further. Someone in the household may have told him. I did not."

"You say she wished to avoid him, but those green eyes, a smile… perhaps the thought of forbidden kisses drew her, a little?"

"You did not know the jefa. She would do no such thing."

"Her marriage satisfied her, then?"

"Her marriage…" Dolores raised her head and looked at Aideen. "Forgive me, yorita."

"My father was a difficult man, Dolores. This is no surprise."

Dolores bit her lower lip and nodded. "She wasn't as happy in her marriage as I am in mine, but she loved her children, and she was satisfied with her life. She had honor, Justice Arm, and she was no fool. She would not bring scandal on herself or her family…and if she were to risk such a thing it would not be for one like him."

"A person can break," the justice arm said, thoughtfully.

"She did not break. The next morning, she was relaxed and cheerful. She took the children to the midwinter pageant on the green, do you remember, yorita? And two days later she was gone."

"The story in the town, I take it, was that she fled."

"That was what people said, yes."

"Tell me what happened the day she disappeared."

"The day was a usual one. She broke her fast with her family. We made a trip to her dressmaker's. She visited a worker from the cages who was home with a burn."

"Was Oshane Langtree present?"

"He had already been sent away from the house."

"Did you see him in town?"

"I did not."

Lodros made a note. "This was after midwinter."

"Yes. It rained much of the day. Late in the evening, the rain stopped, and the jefa went out for a walk before sleep, as she often did. She said the night air helped her rest more deeply. I went to bed. The next morning when I went into her room, she was not there, and her room had not been slept in."

"Was anything missing from her closet? Her coin, her jewelry?"

"Nothing. I told the housekeeper. She spoke to the jefe. He sent the entire household out to look for her. We feared she'd taken ill, or fallen, or been attacked by kiotes."

"Just to be clear, did the jefa share her room with Jefe Langtree?"

"She did not." Dolores tapped the knuckles of her right hand with the fingers of her left. "We spoke to her friends and others who were in her social circle, but none had seen her. Jefe Langtree thought she had been taken for ransom, but no message came, and he went to the sheriff. They searched for seven days but there was no sign of her."

"Tracks?"

"We found tracks, perhaps they were hers, but they stopped with no warning, and by then the rains had softened the ground so much any traces were gone. The jefe offered a reward for any information, and a few people from Sheeplands came forward but they were shown to be liars, or turvy."

Aideen was surprised to learn Father had offered a reward.

"What did you think happened, Yora Noumin?"

The housekeeper shifted her shoulders as if they ached. "I couldn't say."

"No? You knew her the best of anyone in the house. She took no extra clothing, no jewelry, and no coin. You must have had a theory."

Dolores raised her head. "I simply hoped she would return."

Lodros gave her a small smile. "Do you remember if Oshane Langtree had a flautine then?"

Aideen spoke on impulse. "He did, he played it nearly every night. And he had the amulet of Cheviot the Ram. I remember I loved its red eyes."

Lodros noted that down too. "Harald Stuart believes the amulet traps the air elemental here, tethers it, and the flautine commands it."

"Calls it forth, at least," Aideen said, touching her neck. "Do you think he used the air elemental to attack my mother?"

"It is not the most likely explanation, but it is one." Lodros closed her notebook and stowed it away. "If a closer examination of the bones yields anything," she said, rising to her feet, "shall I notify you?"

"Think before you answer," Ilsanja said.

"Why? Of course I wish to know."

"You may not."

Lodros, picking up her bag, said, "This death happened sixteen years ago. I can offer possibilities, but most likely, Yorita Langtree, you will never have a satisfactory answer."

Aideen collected herself and stood up too, as did Ilsanja, with a graceful swirl of her skirt. "Thank you for your time, Justice Arm."

Dolores, who already stood by the door, said, "Shall I call for a sprite cart, Justice Arm?"

"No need. I wish to walk for a bit."

In the silence following their departure, Aideen said, "I *don't* believe Father harmed her."

"I know you don't."

"You heard her. Oshane set the air elemental on her just as he did with me."

Ilsanja studied her. "I did hear her. She said it was a possibility, not the most likely one."

She reached for Aideen's hand, but Aideen pulled away. "I need—I'm going up to the cages."

"You were just there."

"No, I was in the tunnel with Lopez."

"Aideen, please. Don't flee." Unspoken, Aideen still heard, *"Don't do what your brother does."*

"I'm not *fleeing.*" She stalked to the door. "Dolores! Have them saddle a mount for me." Although she stared into the entryway, the presence of Ilsanja radiated into her back like the summer sun. She said to the air, "I need to think. We'll talk more later. I promise."

Ilsanja's voice was so soft Aideen barely caught her words. "Very well."

9

The northern sky grew lighter, and Trevian could make out the details of the preparation in the courtyard. Guards, Copper Coalition, Perlaraynan, and Crescent Council, all checked girths, bridle straps, and hooves, while apprentices, kitchen workers, and healers loaded packets onto the backs of the placid mulas and pack caballos. Wagons were too wide for the narrow trail through the mountains, and pack animals were the alternative.

Trevian turned to Erin. "So few?"

She shrugged. "Well, Ruth and Elmaestro Melendres took sixteen with them already, right? We've got nearly twenty. And there was this idea that it would be sort of secret."

Trevian snorted.

"No argument from me," Erin said, turning her head this way and the other. "Mei's surrounded by the Perlarayna contingent. I can't talk to her."

Trevian tensed. "They keep her from you?"

After three days, he knew how much Capitan Espinosa despised those from the Crescent. The word for primitive was similar in his language and the capitan said it often enough.

Espinosa was a man of the military, but not battlefield or troop movements or any of the things Trevian had read of. He identified possible threats against his nation, he said. Erin called it "intelligence," but Trevian didn't see what it had to do with soldiers and an army. Like Harald,

Trevian decided the most interesting thing about Espinosa was his caged birds. He had released the last of them the night before, saying his contingent would rely on Yorita Mei's compass for messages.

"They're not keeping us apart," Erin said. "They're just protective. And, well, she knows them." He thought he heard sadness in her voice.

"You know her," he said.

Mei—at first, he thought the differences between her and Erin were few, but he'd changed his opinion. The cadence of her speech like the rhythm of a dance he hadn't learned yet, and her voice was lighter. She spoke fast, and often seemed to wait, quivering, until another finished speaking so she could rush in with words. And sometimes she and Erin would speak, and it was like a spring storm; one sentence taken up by the other and completed, words flashing like lightning, gusts of laughter like rain-laden wind. It was a sharp reminder they shared a world, one he did not.

Harald directed his caballo to them and leaned down. "Machios is sending three of the nodes with us," he said. "If Señorita Wing's theory about the plaques and energy is correct, we will be able to test it." He called her Señorita now, in the Perlaraynan fashion.

"Let's hope the New Way isn't in a big rush to shut those down," Erin said.

"So we all hope," Harald said.

Trevian picked up the set of saddlebags next to him and approached his mount, who was drowsing, one rear leg bent. He settled the bags and turned to help Erin, but she was fastening hers into place with no difficulty. Seeing his glance, she pointed with her chin to the steps.

Tregannon led the Madlyn charmcasters down the stairs. Two were coming, while one stayed here to work with Profesor Ludo. Both charmcasters carried knapsacks and saddle bags.

"At least the rude secretary's not coming," Erin murmured.

Tregannon marched up to Harald's caballo, and the justice arm leaned down to hear him better. Trevian smiled. It must pain Tregannon to put Harald in charge, just as it had pained him to send Harald on the mission to meet Mei. Tregannon was self-important and rigid in many ways, but he didn't let his rivalry influence his decisions. With Harald and Genaro leading this expedition, Trevian was confident about the outcome of this journey.

Erin said, "I don't know exactly where we're going."

"On a road that runs around the lake. Hiring the needed number of boats would invite gossip. By land will add two hours to our journey. It's why we're leaving at dawn."

"Hokay."

They both mounted up.

Harald led the way out of the Coalition courtyard into the street, where sprite-takers releasing the creatures from the streetlamps gawked at them. Trevian, who had traveled much in the past two years, had never been part of a column like this one. Guards rode behind Harald, and brought up the rear, while the Perlaraynans, Mei, and Erin were closer to the center. The shapes of the stone walls of the buildings grew sharper, the sky greener, while the air filled with the scents of baking bread, smoke, and lakewater. He looked down at his hands holding the reins, the veins smooth under his skin, and at the flicking ears of his caballo, furred like certain kinds of caterpillars. This moment felt new to him, like nothing he'd experienced, or even dreamed before, even though he was only riding a caballo down a road he'd traveled many times. He twisted in his saddle and found Erin two riders behind him. She stared past him, serious and sad, until something made her look up and catch his gaze. Then she smiled.

As they rode along the lake's edge, Erin had a new view of Duloc. There were more low buildings, houses probably, spread out along the western edge. It was an area she'd never visited. They passed several groups on foot heading into the city, and soon short piers and small boats decorated the shoreline. Across the road, more small buildings came to life in the growing morning light.

Soon they joined the North Road, and Erin figured out they were south of the ferry landing.

Trevian, two caballos ahead of her, might as well have been on another planet. Mei was somewhere behind her. Harald, who had led the expedition out of the city, had trotted back down the line once, checking in, and smiled at her, but now he was somewhere behind her, where Mei was. Ruth wasn't even here.

She'd never thought of herself as a needy person, but she couldn't remember a time in her life when she'd felt this alone. Talking to Mei only made it worse. Mei was eager to get home to aunts, uncles, grandparents, and a life. She *had* a life.

And, she had weeks in the country with a university and electricity, while Erin got outhouses and sleeping on the ground. She knew it made no sense to be envious. Fronteras opened wherever they opened. It was what it was. It's what her parents, her grandparents, all the ancestors had said, among other things. Although when it came down to it, not a single one of them had ever been through a frontera. Not a single one of them knew jack shit.

Okay, snap out of it, she said to herself. Enough self-pity. She reined her mount off to the side and waited as the riders passed until Mei caught up with her.

Mei smiled and didn't cover it. "Hi!" She nudged her mount to the side. "It's pretty here."

"A lot of countryside," Erin said. "Where we're headed, it's mostly steep mountains."

"What's with the animals? The horses seem regular-sized, but I saw a freshwater eel—Juanita called in an anguila, and it was the length of an eighteen-wheeler."

"Have you seen an ardiya yet?" Erin grinned. "They're squirrels, and they look like just our squirrels, only they're size of a cocker spaniel."

Mei flinched. "Eee!"

"Yeah."

They rode for a bit. Glancing at the shadows ahead of them, Erin said, "You get the direction thing, right? East versus north?"

Mei tipped her head and widened her eyes. "Why, *yes*, I do. My artifact is a compass, were you aware?"

Erin said, "Really?"

Mei giggled. "Although it doesn't do much as a compass except point to magnetic north, which truly is where the sun appears on the horizon."

"And the mountains, and lakes, they just... I don't know. Bloomed."

Mei ran her fingers over the pommel of her saddle. "I feel bad, Erin."

"Bad how, are you sick?" Erin started searching the line for the healer.

"No, no. I feel... You have done so much already, risked your life, and I've done nothing."

"That's not true. Your main goal was to keep the compass out of Oshane's hands, and you did. And you sent me a lot of useful information."

"I hope I can be more useful. I wish the Agustos were here. We could experiment with the lantern."

Erin's stomach churned at the thought. She'd seen the lantern misused by Oshane and the New Way, but Mei was right, clearly it was a powerful tool. If only they knew what to do with it.

"If this were a movie," she said, "we'd build a generator out of, I don't know…"

"Hair clips and quartz crystals," Mei said, "and an old cereal box. Coco Balls, maybe."

"Is that a Taiwanese brand?"

Mei looked surprised. "I don't think so. It's Kellogg's."

"Maybe they market it there under a different name."

Mei rode in silence for a few minutes. "Can I change the subject? Juanita is afraid of deltierras—you call them earth elementals. They all freaked out when one surfaced on the journey here, and it wasn't even attacking us."

"Perlarayna doesn't have them? I thought elementals were everywhere."

"She's really familiar with delaguas, because Perlarayna is a maritime country with lots of ships and boats. And they have manifestations they call velas, which seem to be localized. Delaires and deltierras are rare. Anyway, she's still a bit freaked out, but nobody here seems worried."

Velas, candles, or fire elementals, Erin thought. The other three; from water, from air, from earth. "Trevian got attacked by a baby earth elemental. I sent it away—oh, God! Did I send it to you?"

"I would have mentioned it," Mei said.

"Maybe I sent it to the presidenta's office or something."

"I think *they* would have mentioned it."

"Anyway, yeah, they're common here, but those braided cords with the copper disks on the hooves of your caballos aren't just decorative. They're warding charms."

"Oh, I thought they were some religious medal."

"And air elementals are pretty rare." Erin only knew of one.

"Could you tell her? I think it would mean more, coming from you."

"Well, sure."

Mei guided her horse out of line. Juanita Gunnarsdottir rode up next to Erin, eyebrows raised in a question.

Erin explained about the charms, and the scientist nodded. "The one we saw, the earth liquified and a kiote disappeared into the ground without a yip. Our caballos shied away and nearly bolted. Señor Stuart had put those coins on our mounts, but I didn't understand why. We're safe, then. And velas? They are very common, I understand."

"Where we're going, they are. There's a lot of volcanic activity and they seem to gather there."

"And you have a pair that follow you, or so I've heard."

"They don't always follow me. They seem to show up when I need help."

"I didn't know they could be trained."

"I didn't train them. I didn't charm them or compel them. They just do what they do."

"Forgive me, I didn't mean to give offense."

"It's just…Oshane Langtree, he compelled them. He tortured them. I don't want to be compared to him."

"I simply didn't realize, señorita. I meant no insult."

Great, now she was causing an international incident. "So, was your father from Iceland?"

"I don't know of such a place in our world, but he was from Desturvalur." Juanita looked at Erin's face and laughed. "Don't worry. I won't ask you to say the name."

She straightened the hood of her coat. "My mother was born in the capital. She is a biological scientist who specialized in water and came to the valley when the town dug some new wells, and needed the water's purity tested. My father is a carpenter and a skald. You remember skald?"

Erin dipped her head.

"That's their story. I'm the youngest of three, I studied at the university, intending to study plants and agriculture, but the history of the Cataclismo seized me and wouldn't release me. And here I am."

"You and Ruth Stillwater have a lot in common."

"I look forward to working with her, and seeing this place, which might be nearly intact. A site this much closer to the center of the Cataclismo must yield much knowledge."

"For us, too," Erin said. She really hoped so.

After four hours they stopped to rest and water the mounts. Erin found a patch of grass to sit on. Trevian joined her.

"Are you well?"

Their version of "Are you okay?" But Trevian was always asking. Did he think she wasn't? "Of course," she said.

"You seemed sad earlier."

"Did I?" She laced her fingers through his and set their hands on his knee. "Well, I'm happy now."

He glanced around. Seeing few people watching them, he planted a kiss on her temple. "Good."

Across the road, Mei stood with Juanita and a guard from their group. Was she frowning? Erin took a gulp of water and offered her canteen to Trevian.

Harald had them back on the road quickly, and it seemed like the next leg of journey passed quickly. Soon they left the prospecting town of Lily Bend behind them and turned down the narrow winding trail Erin remembered walking. Even making better time with the horses, Erin didn't think they could make it all the way to the rough little shelter in the grove of trees, the albergue, without stopping for food, and Harald didn't think so either, because he called a halt an hour past noon, to eat. Harald and Genaro joined them. Erin beckoned to Mei and Juanita, but Mei hesitated, looked at Espinosa, shrugged an apology at Erin and sat with the Perlarayna group.

"Already he is writing a letter," Trevian said idly, swirling his canteen.

"Who?" She looked around and saw the charmcaster from Madlyn, hunched over a piece of paper. "How does he think he's going to send that?"

Harald said, "He asked me if it was possible to send personal messages with the regular messengers. My first response was "No," but he writes to his dioso padrey."

"I thought he wrote to his nephew," Trevian said.

Harald nodded as he chewed a slice of dried apple. "He did. His nephew is ill and lives his life through his uncle's letters, but he told me in his recent letter to the boy said he might not be able to write further, to protect the secrecy of the mission. His letter to his padrey is part of a prayer challenge he accepted before he was assigned to the delegation."

"Are you worried he'll give something away about where we are?" Erin said. "I mean, what's he writing to his priest?"

"He is to describe his actions and take responsibility for any harm they may have caused. No details of the journey, he assured me."

"Every day?" Trevian said.

"Every three days."

Confession by mail? *Somebody* was keeping their congregation on a short leash. Or maybe the quiet, studious Lauris was really a very bad boy. The thought made Erin smile.

The group remounted. Harald took advantage of the longer summer day, and pushed the group, with a plan to reach Merrylake Landing before sunset. As the line of riders started back on the trail, Erin ended up behind Mei, with Juanita Gunnarsdottir behind her. The trail wound down into the stand of trees. Soon the gray and red cliffs rose on her right. The chasm on the left was lined with lush green bushes and the burble of running water reached them in snatches. The trail widened a bit as a decline led away to a formation of natural rock pillars. Erin remembered it. They were nearly there, maybe two more hours of riding.

She waved her hand to drive away the whining insect next to her ear. It didn't work. Her caballo's ears flattened and it snorted, tossing its head.

The whine got louder and deeper. It wasn't an insect.

Blue. Everywhere. Singing.

Someone screamed.

Mei, it was Mei, wrapped in blue, rising into the air as her mount reared, squealing, rocks cascading over the ledge, thrown by its hooves.

Erin dug her heels into her mount's sides, urging it forward. The rider ahead of Mei turned, but Erin could hear nothing now over the high-pitched hum of the air elemental clutching Mei.

She stood up in her stirrups and grabbed at Mei, catching her around the hips. She couldn't breathe. Her mount plunged underneath her. Her arms slipped down fabric, her lungs screamed for air, and suddenly there was nothing underneath her. She fell, thudding onto the ground, Mei on top of her, as the caballos squealed and curvetted, hooves coming down on either side around them. Still blue, everything, still airless.

Mei rolled underneath her panicking mount, and Erin followed, trying to shield the other woman from the hooves of the caballo. Her vision dissolved into black dots. Still no air. The elemental still had a grip on them, but it didn't seem able to lift both of them. But she couldn't hold on.

Hot.

Animals screamed over the steady hum of the thing gripping them. So hot.

Air whooshed into her lungs. Mei panted so hard that each inhalation sounded like a scream.

Erin wrapped her arms around Mei's head as the caballo's rear hoof grazed them. The two women rolled up against the cliff face as the mount whirled.

Funnels of flame danced on either side of them. The undulating shape of singing blue narrowed, slipped between them, and aimed at Mei, but the flames intervened. Now the air elemental elongated, trying to wrap around all of them. It suffocated. Could it kill the flames? Could the flames wound it? Erin threw herself across Mei. The flames melded, the wall of heat holding back the other elemental, temporarily at least. A crossbow bolt shot through the air elemental and sank into the cliff face behind her.

A man's voice, shouting. A light flashing. The flames broke apart, spinning, to wait on either side of Erin and Mei, as the charmcaster from Madlyn approached, whirling a flashing silver thing over his head like a riata. The air elemental gave way. Lauris planted himself between Mei and the pulsing blue shape, snapping the silver chain at it.

The elemental fell back, feinted, and tried to come in from the side, but the flames advanced. Mei's coat smoked slightly. Falling back, the air elemental levitated. It swooped down on them. The flames blocked it, a burning arch. The air elemental rose higher, pulsing, and vanished.

"What. The. Hell," Mei said, panting.

Lauris knelt at her side, slapping the arm of her coat, a silvery chain studded with iridescent stones trailing beside him. "Yoritas, are you well?"

"Mei?"

Mei sat up. "I'll never take breathing for granted. Ever again."

The squealing and snorting of caballos still filled the air. Lauris caught Erin's gaze. "Yorita...?"

"Oh." She concentrated on the flames. *Can that thing hurt you?*

The response was affirmative. Air elementals could hurt them. She also felt a vibration of satisfaction—they could hurt *it*.

Don't risk yourself for me, she thought.

She didn't understand the response this time. There was a sensation of heat, of light, and something else, but it flickered away, just as they did.

Stay safe, she thought after them.

Juanita flung herself down next to Lauris. "Mei, are you well?" Capitan Espinosa strode up behind her.

"Erin!" Trevian pushed his way between the mounts, followed by Harald. "Erin!"

"Here. Fine, we're fine." Erin got her feet. Her knees shook, but she was all right. Lauris walked backward on his knees as Espinosa stepped over him, reached down to help Mei to her feet. Erin met Trevian's gaze. "Well. I guess we know who you saw in the courtyard that morning."

"Who?" Mei said. "What do you mean?"

"Oshane fucking Langtree."

Mei gasped. "Erin!"

"He's earned it."

Mei's voice shook. "Is that how my parents...died?"

Erin didn't need to answer.

Trevian curled his fingers around the chain Lauris carried. "Where did you hear of this? I'd never known of a charm to repel an air being."

"Moonstone and plata," Lauris said. "I'd read of it. I wasn't sure it would work, but I tracked one down in Bois before I came south. Cost me half a year's rent."

"Melendres sent to Pais Lewelyn for some, to be delivered to Merrylake Landing," Harald said. His face was red, and he flinched slightly as he shifted his stance. The prosthetic leg must be troubling him.

Mei touched Lauris's wrist. "You saved my life."

"It went straight for you," Erin said. "How did Oshane know who you are?"

"She rides with the Perlarayna contingent," Harald pointed out. "If, as we conjecture, Oshane was listening in taverns and bars, and gossiping with those who went in and out of the Coalition, he would have known when the Perlaraynans reached us."

"You promised Señorita Wing would be protected," Espinosa said.

"I'm safe," Mei said.

Espinosa ignored her and pointed at the moonstone chain. "That needs to be in her possession for the rest of this journey."

"You do not command here," Trevian said.

"But I agree with the capitan," Lauris said. He draped the three-foot chain around Mei's neck.

Harald said, "We have sworn to protect both guardians and we will. Erin, you will ride by Mei's side, with guards around you, the rest of the journey. We know Langtree is an interested in you as he is in her."

Erin didn't argue, but she wasn't sure that was true anymore. The New Way wanted the compass for their tower. Mei was in far greater danger.

"Do we go forward?" Lauris said. "We cannot protect against another attack from the air."

"Let us turn back," Espinosa said. "At the compound, we can provide protection."

"We will not turn back," Harald said, his voice calm. "At Merrylake Landing we can also provide protection. The way back is much farther than the distance to our destination, and we would be in just as much danger."

"You have launched this plan with no intelligence, no grasp of your enemy's whereabouts, and you endanger Señorita Wing."

Trevian's face flushed. Harald still spoke calmly, but Erin thought he was mad. "I assure you, among us there is *plenty* of intelligence."

"He means knowledge. Like from spies." Erin glared at Espinosa. "You may have a great intelligence network, but you don't know where the New Way hosts are either. Maybe you're the one who should leave."

"Since you are fearful," Trevian said.

Espinosa's breath hissed in, and he stiffened like he'd gotten an electrical shock. Trevian's hand hovered over his knife sheath.

Mei stepped between them. "Erin and I are the guardians," she said. "We decide. I say we go to Merrylake Landing. They've got those warding charms and there's probably shelter. We know Langtree's still around and still after the artifacts. Useful news, Marco."

Juanita spoke. "And it is our duty, isn't it?"

Espinosa snorted, turned on his heel and mounted his caballo without another word. Trevian stalked past him, took the reins of Mei's caballo from a guard and brought it back to her. Deliberately, he helped Mei mount her calmer animal, and held the bridle of Erin's caballo as she mounted.

Everyone went back to their caballos and mounted up.

Great, Erin thought. Everything's going great. Just peachy.

PART II

THE PIT

10

(VVI) Dare—I got your letter. Did you get mine? I don't believe you wrote it, composed it, I mean. I think they stood over you, like they did me, and gave you "guidelines." Mine sounds like a kid writing home from summer camp, and yours does too. I pray to the Mother that you and Mama are at least okay.

I write in this under the covers, like a kid, actually, with that gag light-up ink pen you got me on the boardwalk, a hundred years ago.

I think it's been eleven days. They let us out of lockup today and assembled us. Lots of people were missing. They said we were the epicenter of a "global, atmospheric and seismic disturbance which is ongoing." And "The ramifications are still being studied." Oh, and we could be tried for crimes against humanity but we probably wouldn't be if we cooperated.

Lichtstrom's dead.

They didn't want us talking to each other, but a couple of us managed to. Nameah and Linus both think the dimensional rift opened wider than the team could control, and two realities converged, violently. I know how crazy it sounds, and I'd dismiss it if I hadn't seen those banana-slug things...and the Pit. Like me, Nameah thinks Orchard Hill has physically moved. We both agree we've got no objective data for that theory.

They've brought in a couple of extra generators—not the little ones—in armored vehicles. Linus thinks they're trying to reopen the rift and pry the two realities apart. His cognition might be more affected by the situation than he realizes.

A guard in Copper Coalition red met them at the base of the mountain. Whispers ran up and down the line as Harald and the guard talked. Erin loosened her grip on her reins, forcing her muscles to relax. What had gone wrong now? After a few minutes, Harald raised his arm, and the group continued forward. The guard remained.

The town looked different, not just because people from the Copper Coalition had moved in. Even more buildings had been demolished, the wood and stone dragged off, making the streets appear twice as wide as she remembered. The group dismounted, leading their mounts toward a cleared area near the mudflats, where a trough filled with water and some feedbags sat.

Stillwater came out of an intact building, making her way to them. Instead of the blue tunic Erin was used to seeing her in, she wore a thick wheat-colored shirt, sturdy black trousers tucked into boots. Her hair still puffed out behind a blue band. "You made good time," she said, smiling and holding out her hands to Harald.

"We were attacked," Harald said. He gripped her hands and then pulled her to him in a brief embrace. "Is that why you have the camp warded?"

Fear pinched Erin's stomach. Warded? Langtree had warded the entire settlement when Trevian had brought her here the first time. She searched around, and saw Trevian watching her, looking grave.

"What sort of attack? The mestengo band fled, from all accounts."

"Air elemental," Harald said, "Langtree."

Stillwater frowned, her gaze sweeping the group before her. "Erin, Trevian, are you well?"

Erin gestured to Mei, standing in front of Juanita. "We weren't the target, Wing Mei was."

Stillwater left Harald's side and came to Mei, her hand extended. "It's an honor to meet another guardian, Yorita Mei. And are you well?"

"Fine," Mei squeezed her hand and dropped it. She was looking around.

"My name is Ruth Stillwater. I'm a profesor at the Crescent Copper Coalition. I study history and languages." Ruth turned away from the newcomer. "Now, what happened?"

Harald gave her the details. Ruth nodded when he mentioned the moonstone charms. "A packet of those arrived two days ago," she said.

"Not enough for everyone, but we can make it work if people double up. And now we know they're effective."

Looking around herself, Erin saw two people she recognized, David and Miriam LaFish, two of Oshane's captive copper-hunters. She waved, and David bowed, while Miriam held up her hand. It was nice to see people she knew a little bit at least.

"I made a mistake," Harald said. "I misjudged Langtree. I thought he would concentrate his attacks on White Bluffs. And I dismissed it when Trevian thought he saw Langtree in the capital."

Trevian said, "You weren't even there when it happened. How are you responsible?"

"Tregannon told me of the incident, and I, like him, thought grief and fatigue were driving your judgment."

"Thank the Mother, Diebell was present and he had one of those charms," Ruth said. "The guardian is unharmed. I'll show you where people are sleeping."

"Why was the town warded?" Erin said.

Ruth smiled. "Our disturbance was annoyingly human. We've kept the town warded since a double-handful of drunken fools from White Bluffs staggered up here, hurling rocks and threatening us with crossbows, saying we brought a plague. We sent them home to sleep it off, but we've been cautious since then, and it has slowed our work. Come. Settle your animals, and we'll show you where you're to sleep."

"Juanita Gunnarsdottir from Perlarayna is eager to meet you," Harald said.

Ruth's smile vanished. "You brought Perlaraynans into camp?"

"Yes. Guards, and two envoys from their presidenta."

"Soldiers?" Ruth's gaze searched the party, and her fists clenched. "Elmaestro Melendres won't be pleased."

"What's wrong with Perlarayna?" Mei said.

Harald frowned. "Our continent is at risk, Ruth. If they are willing to help…"

"Brel should have sent a messenger to let her know," Ruth said. She wheeled away before Harald could say anything more.

When the animals were unburdened and the tack stored away, Erin touched Trevian's arm. "I know he bothers you, but please don't go off on that Espinosa guy again, okay? It's more important than ever."

"I don't understand what you just said."

Mei said, "The capitan makes you angry. Don't let him."

89

"How can I not, Yorita Mei? I am primitive and ignorant, am I not?"

Erin sighed. Mei wasn't bothered though. "He's protective and he bosses people around, but he's a good person. He promised to keep me safe, and that's what he's trying to do."

"He does not command here."

Erin said, "Maybe he doesn't know any other way to act. You're pretty protective of me, you know. It's the same thing for him."

Trevian looked at Mei, shocked. "Is it? The same thing?"

"Uh, well," Erin said. "Maybe not *exactly* the same. But he's guarding her. He's trying to do the right thing."

"I'll try not to fail you again," Trevian said. "I think Harald and Genaro can use my help." He strode away, leaving her staring after him. Fail her?

She shook her head. Mei was giving her a judging stare.

"What?"

"Nothing, just...are you being fair to him?"

"What's are you trying to say?"

"I'm not judging, Erin."

"Aren't you? Feels like you are." She crossed her arms. Even *Mei?* "I think we should get you to the infirmary building so they can check you out."

"Erin."

"You coming?"

———

There was good news. She and Trevian had a house to themselves in an intact cottage Ruth was also using for storage. At least, Erin hoped it was good news. Trevian barely spoke over dinner. Of course, with all the introductions and data flying around, he'd hardly needed to. Melendres met the newcomers with cold courtesy and her two guards dropped their hands to their knife hilts whenever anyone from Perlarayna approached.

Erin didn't want to deal with politics. She needed to get to the cave site, with Mei, and see what they could find. Ruth looked smug about it, so there had to be some goodies in there, something they could use.

Right now, though, she had to figure out what was going on with Trevian.

As they spread out their bedrolls, she said, "You've never failed me."

"No?" He didn't look at her. "The first thing I did when you arrived was lead you into danger."

She tugged on his hand until he looked up. "Come sit down. Your uncle tricked you. And frankly, if he hadn't, no one would know about the New Way and what they were trying. They'd have the lantern and the collar."

"He was using the lantern for his own ends."

She sat cross-legged on the floor. After a moment, he did too.

"There's this expression in my world for people who steal money from the place they work. We say "skimming." Scooping a layer off the top before anyone notices."

Trevian nodded. "We do as well."

"Oshane was skimming energy to feed the charms he'd stolen, but the whole set-up was an experiment by the New Way. Anyway, my point is, we stopped it. Not a failure. Closing the frontera, not a failure, and *you* closed it."

"When you and Mei speak, I don't understand your speech. It's obvious you wish your frontera opened in Perlarayna instead of the Crescent. Daily I am aware of how simple and primitive we are compared to your world."

"No, I—" Erin sighed. She reached for his hand. "Okay, yes. I *do* wish I'd ended up in the place with electricity and a center dedicated to learning. But I didn't, and I don't regret it. I do understand that I'm the outsider here."

He met her gaze. "With you and Mei, I am the outsider."

"Well, Mei and I aren't getting along that well either."

"You finish each other's sentences."

It was her turn to look away. "I thought we'd connect with her and put the book next to the compass and something magical would happen, and it would give us a road map, a clue at least. Instead, nothing. And it turns out the book isn't even important. She said there are others."

"Other books made using the same technique. Not the same as yours."

"Yeah, well…the lantern, the collar, even the compass, all have power themselves. The book is clearly the weakest artifact." She didn't know where the next words came from, but they bubbled out of her. "I guess I thought I was the hero, but I'm just a sidekick."

"A sidekick sounds like a part on a wagon."

"In our stories, there is a hero who has a helper. An assistant. They run errands, they get information, they tag along."

He nodded. "An apprentice."

"Sort of."

"You are an apprentice hero."

It made her snort with laughter. "Please! I'm trying to be self-pitying here."

He shifted his body and took both her hands in his. "You uncovered the New Way's presence here. We closed their frontera, and you gave us the charm that identifies them. I think you are a journey-level hero, Erin."

"Well, then, you are too. No more talk of failing me, okay?"

"Hokay," he said, blowing out the first syllable. Did he really think that was how she said it?

"And...I know Capitan Espinosa is really irritating, but try to keep your temper?"

"I will try."

———

At half an hour past dawn, they headed up to the cave, festooned with moonstone chains, carrying sprite lamps, quartzlights, and a set of unlit blackrock torches. Instead of starting up the trail Erin was used to, Ruth led the group down and to the right, along the steep edge of a trickling stream for below. The planks set over the stream shivered under their steps. Here the way broadened and led up.

Erin looked around. The creek ran parallel to the trail they'd come in on, until the trail curved northeast, and the creek ran straight. They stood on a plateau overlooking the dwindling lake.

Capitan Espinosa followed her, with a Perlaraynan guard, then two copper-hunters, Lauris Diebell, then Melendres, flanked by two Pais Lewelyn guards, and finally a Pais Lewelyn charmcaster. Melendres had limited how many Perlaraynans could attend. Juanita, who might have been useful, had been excluded.

When they reached the ledge, Ruth stopped and waited while they gathered around. "We believe there were originally three entrances to this complex," she said. "The south entrance is thoroughly blocked by a rock-slide, most likely caused by an earth shudder. The rocks flow down into a narrow, twisted ravine. Many of you have ridden past it. Yor Langtree,"— Ruth was being formal this morning—"the east entrance your sister and your wife discovered was difficult to reach from any trail, but clearly not impossible. We have blocked it for safety. This entrance is stable and clear, but we will navigate rockslides as we go deeper. There are frequent earth tremors in the cave complex."

Mei whispered, "'No beverages and no flash photography inside.'"

Erin snickered.

Once inside the cave, the air took a golden hue from the radiance of the sprites. Quartzlights flicked on as people whispered to the charms to awaken them. Ruth led them into the passage Aideen and Ilsanja had discovered. Ruth talked as they moved, the walls amplifying her voice.

The corridor they walked ran the length of the complex. From it, three passages branched. Erin imagined a capital letter E. One passage ended at the abyss Aideen had discovered, while the other two held numerous rooms—including living quarters and a couple of rec-room- looking spaces.

The complex extended down a level several in places, Ruth said, like a laboratory and a supply area. So far, they had managed to open every door they found.

Ruth halted the group at the first right-angle corridor. "This one leads to the abyss. We call it the Pit."

Erin raised her hand. Oh, wait, she probably didn't need to. "Is it related to the 'pit' Lewiston and Talavera referred to in their text conversation?"

"Certainly, it was my first thought."

Trevian stirred. "Aideen spoke of sounds emerging from it."

"…Yes. Those sounds. Most of us hear a sound like wind moaning, or laughter, at times. But others… Well, as we get closer, perhaps you will find out for yourselves."

Capitan Espinosa cleared his throat. "And what purpose does this tour, and this pit, serve?"

"It may be a frontera," Ruth said.

Ruth led the way down the corridor. Erin thought she heard rushing wind, but maybe that was only her imagination. And maybe it was her imagination too, but it seemed lighter. She raised her voice. "Is it lighter in here, Ruth?"

"Definitely."

Erin craned her neck searching for holes in the rock above them, and from the rustling around her, she wasn't the only one.

Without turning, Ruth said, "The light does not emanate from above. It seems to come from the Pit itself."

"Aideen described blackness," Trevian said.

"I know. It's a puzzle."

Erin thought back to the words in Ruth's old book. When the New Way had first breached this world, entering through Aperture One, the Pit had given off crazy readings, Lewiston had said. Was the Pit awake in some way? And was that good or bad?

At the moment, Erin didn't see any way it could be good.

The walk gave her time to look at the paintings on the wall. She wanted to see the huge portrait of Lewiston, but it was behind them, on the spine of the capital E. These were whimsical, cartoonish but well painted.

"...a baseball game?" Mei said, pointing.

Trevian said, "A sport? We have one like it."

They walked on. Erin moved her jaw from side to side to stop the ringing in her ears. It didn't help. The whine grew louder, and with a rush of cold up her spine she recognized the sound. Trevian whirled, his arms out, and flung Mei and Erin against the wall, standing over them.

"What!" Espinosa shouted, leaping forward.

Diebell cried out, "What is that?"

"What's going on?" Mei said.

"Peace!" Ruth said, her voice echoing.

Trevian pivoted, his moonstone chain in his hands, his head sweeping from side to side. "Air elemental!"

Espinosa bounded toward him; his knife drawn.

The guard from Perlarayna drew his knife, whirling to protect the Capitan's back.

"Knives down! Peace!" Ruth shouted now. Echoes bounced around them. "There is no danger! No danger! Well. No immediate danger. Sheath your weapons."

Erin stared at Mei. "Can't you hear it?

Mei frowned back at her. "Something like running water?"

Erin edged away and stood up. "No."

"Whining, or singing," Diebell said. The copper-hunters and the other charmcaster nodded.

The Pais Lewelyn charmcaster said, "Like a hive of angry bees, only higher-pitched. Small insects that gather over water in our wetlands make a similar sound but not as strong."

Espinosa sheathed his knife but stepped back. "Señorita Mei, esta bien?"

"I'm fine."

Trevian lowered the chain. "Profesor Stillwater, I wish you had warned us."

"I wanted to see what, if anything, people experienced without a story already in their minds," Ruth said. "I didn't expect hostility."

The capitan leveled a stare at Ruth. "The señorita is my responsibility to protect."

Melendres gave a sharp laugh.

"It makes the same sound an attacking air elemental makes." Erin looked at Mei again. "You sure you didn't hear it?"

"I heard it yesterday when the elemental tried to pull me off my caballo," Mei said. "Not here."

"Only copper-hunters and charmcasters hear it," Ruth said.

"You're a copper-hunter?"

Erin said, "It seems so." She brushed off her sleeves, not that she needed to. "Should we get going?"

"Is everyone well?" Ruth said. Hearing affirmatives, she started on.

Mei said, "So you're magical?"

"I guess."

After a few seconds, Mei said, "Well. That's nice."

It grew steadily lighter in the passageway. Ruth stopped them again. "Yorita Wing, Yorita Dosmanos, can you decipher these letters?" Back to formality.

No fanciful paint and whimsical figures here; large red letters had been stenciled on the wall.

W RNIN OBSERV LL NON INC SION PROTOCOLS

"Even I can figure out 'Warning,'" Mei said, "and 'protocols.'"

"I believe we use the word 'procedures,'" said Ruth.

"Protocolos," said Espinosa. "Orders to be followed."

"I'm going to guess 'observe.' 'Warning, observe…all non-something protocols.'" Erin looked at the mystery word.

"Inclusion?" Mei said.

"Incursion?"

They said in unison, "Non-incursion!"

"This is not heartening," Ruth said.

"A warning to observe all non-incursion protocols," Harald said. "They expected invaders from this Pit."

Espinosa stepped forward. "Incursion is not an invasion," he said. He glanced at Melendres. "It precedes an invasion. You should destroy this place."

"It's just on the wall," Erin said. "And they were studying it. It was a precaution. Wasn't it?"

Mei said, "Marco, do you still have warnings on walls in public places, about your epidemic?"

After a moment he nodded. "Yes. Especially in temples and iglesias and medical facilities."

"And we are nearly to the Pit," Ruth said. The group moved forward.

A moment later Trevian stiffened and reached out to touch Erin's arm. "Look." He pointed with his chin.

"Are those...musical notes? Like the ones in the book?"

"Yes."

Erin didn't want to dig out the book in front of everyone, and she was sure Trevian was right. "They closed the New Way frontera."

"It appears between the warning and the Pit itself," Ruth said. "Do you suppose that *is* the non-incursion protocol?"

"It's not stenciled or printed like the other message."

It looked like it had been painted quickly, with whatever brush was at hand.

"You think it is not official," Espinosa said.

"And yet we know it works," Trevian said.

Erin put up her hand. Damn! She had to stop doing that. "Copper-hunters, charmcasters, is the sound getting worse?"

Headshakes, immediately. Diebell said, "Louder, most definitely, but not rising or falling in pitch, at least for me, and I've adjusted to it."

"The same," said the Pais Lewelyn charmcaster, and Trevian nodded.

"Okay." Seeing Ruth's quizzical look, Erin said, "Just interesting."

"We learn more each visit," Ruth said, and led them forward to an area that opened suddenly, the spots of lamps and quartzlights reflecting back at them from the barrier. Beyond it yawned the Pit.

11

I know what you are doing," Ilsanja said from where she sat behind Aideen's desk, papers spread out across it.

Aideen stopped in the doorway. "And what am I doing?"

Four days had passed since Justice Arm Lodros's visit. Aideen meant to talk to Ilsanja, to explain how she felt, but the moment had never occurred.

"You are calculating how much blackrock the town will need for six months if we shut down the cages, and preparing to shift the yield from your mine."

"You've been thorough." Aideen changed her direction, walking to the window. She stared out, watching Susannah picking herbs from the garden for the evening meal. "In fact, you are wrong. I've already done the calculations. I sent a letter to the mine manager yesterday to stockpile until I notify her otherwise."

"Without discussing it with your other partners."

She spoke without turning. "You'll recall I own the mine outright. I have no partners."

Ilsanja sighed. "You do not need to impoverish yourself. This is a Company issue. If we are preparing for a war, the Company should assume some of the responsibility and the cost."

"I thought of that." She relented, striding back to the desk and sitting down across from it. "Here is what I thought. If the Company suddenly begins buying up blackrock, blackrock miners will know there is some risk, and they will drive up our prices. And word will get out, and there will be a panic."

Ilsanja, lounging back in the chair, nodded thoughtfully. "Yes, a concern, the same one I raised when I discussed this with Yor Montez, who asks us to call him Armando, by the way."

"You discussed this with Yor Montez?"

Ilsanja raised one eyebrow, a gesture Aideen recognized as a danger sign. "Did you think you were the only one who could foresee a problem and seek a solution?"

"No." As Ilsanja stared, she said, "Yes."

"Yes."

Aideen twisted her hands together. "I did not reason through to that conclusion. I…I don't have the habit of remembering I have others who will help. That's all it is."

"Not all." Ilsanja said. She flicked at the papers on the desk. "Yes, you move forward alone, and I do understand why. But you try to impoverish yourself at the first chance. You have some wealth now, Aideen, and power. Stop tossing it away."

"Did Yor Montez have a solution?"

"A suggestion, at least. He has written to two blackrock dealers. They know of the expansion into Sheeplands. With any project there may be setbacks, and clever companies plan for setbacks. Yor Montez offers a flat sum of money now for first rights on blackrock at a fixed price anytime within the next twelve months. We will renew the agreement then, if we need to."

"Won't they bleed us, with the flat sum?"

"They'll try. Everyone knows our expansion into Sheeplands won't be as complete as our White Bluffs operation. The distance between towns and villages prohibits it. Regional blackrock dealers will still find a market there. They will still reach as deep into our purse as they can. But you and I have a cache of money, from your father's loans."

"Oh. I'd hoped to use some of that for the exploration of the tunnel."

"Ah! At last!" Ilsanja threw back her head. "Finally, a sacrifice you admit it would pain you to make! Progress."

Aideen wished she didn't feel so diminished by her friend's mockery. "Since you have solved this problem without me, perhaps I'll go for a walk."

"Or perhaps you'll stay and talk to me."

"And be reminded of how unnecessary I am? No, thank you."

"Come now, Aideen…"

She didn't look back. Ilsanja would not follow her. Her friend was proud. Well, she could be proud too.

Why, then, as she walked north to the edge of the neighborhood, into the golden green meadows beyond it, did she feel small and miserable?

Her conversation with Dolores had been as disappointing. She'd called the housekeeper into her study and asked her to shut the door. Instead of sitting behind the desk, Aideen sat on one of the chairs and motioned to Dolores to sit across from her. The woman's face was calm, and her hands rested easily in her lap as she settled herself.

"You said Oshane Langtree killed my mother," Aideen said. "Do you believe that now?"

"I do not doubt it, yorita."

"But you must have decided so after he attacked Father."

Dolores lowered her head.

"Before then, did you think Father killed her?"

"I did not think, yorita. I wished. I wished she had fled west and was safe and—"

"Dolores, I am not a justice arm from the capital. I am not the sheriff. From the time I was six, you might as well have raised me. Tell me the truth."

Finally, Dolores lowered her eyes. "In the small hours of the morning, in the dark of winter, yes. As time passed, I would go for months, years even, forgetting, imagining her somewhere in the west, laughing. And then the Jefe would do something, even some little thing, and I would doubt. And at first I was sure he had."

"But you stayed. Why?"

"For you and Yor Trevian. I couldn't leave two children alone here if he had indeed killed her."

Aideen's throat ached. "I don't believe he did, Dolores."

"Nor do I, yorita. Plainly it was his vicious brother and that elemental monster."

"I don't believe Father killed her, but I think he *could* have," she said.

Dolores stared, as fierce and alert as she had when she found Aideen crying as a child, and then gave a short nod. "I think you judge him rightly, yorita. The Jefe was a difficult man, a harsh man. But you think you have the right of the situation too. He did not kill Jefa Serafina."

I think he could have. Those were the words she should say to Ilsanja, but they clung to the inside of her throat with claws.

She walked until her feet ached. Not so long ago, with Ilsanja at her side, she'd sworn she would never walk again. They'd grown closer than she had ever dared dream. Now there was a rift between them, a chasm, and Aideen was driving it wider with every word and action.

***

Susannah tried a new recipe for river fish. Three tiny crescents graced Aideen's plate. The first bite was sweet and insubstantial on her tongue, but she could barely swallow, and now she stared down at them, her hands in her lap.

The only sound in the room was the clink of Ilsanja's utensils.

Aideen carefully aligned her wine glass with her plate. "Yor Montez's solution is a good one," she said. "I certainly should have spoken to both of you about my idea."

"Yes, you should." Ilsanja drove the side of her fork through a fish, neatly severing the flesh from its network of fine bones.

"My plan...I think I will still set aside this month's yield and next month's. Then we'll sell half and stockpile half, to be safe."

"That seems well thought out," Ilsanja said. "If unnecessary." She picked up her wine glass and took a swallow.

The lamps cast a shaft of light through the golden liquid in Aideen's glass. She reached for it, furled her fingers, and drew her hand back. "I've been quiet these past several days," she said.

"Quiet? You've been *silent*." Ilsanja looked up, directing one of her distant, measuring stares at Aideen, who felt herself shrink and grow cold. "I know my feelings for you, Aideen. If yours for me were just an early-morning glamor, fading as the sun rises higher, you must let me know. I assume you will wish to continue living here, and if so, I must make a plan for how we will behave with each other."

"What? Are you saying I must leave this house?" Aideen couldn't swallow; her heart thrashed at the base of her throat like a fish in a bowl.

"I'm saying, tell *me* where I stand with you."

"You must know where you stand."

"I do not. You shut me out at every turn. I reach out. Always, I reach out. Always, it is my hand extended and I never know from one moment to the next if you will take it or turn your face away."

"I've never turned away from you!"

"Most recently, this afternoon."

"I…" This wasn't what she had expected. "My feelings for you could never fade."

"Am I an ornament then? The one thing I required of you was that you not discount me, not shut me out."

"I've never shut you out." Aideen closed her eyes, trying to think over her pounding heart. "I don't *mean* to shut you out. Ilsanja, for sixteen years if I've been hurt, fearful, or doubtful, I buried it inside and tried to make things right as best I could. I don't *know* how to speak of…of things."

Before Ilsanja could answer, before Aideen could stop herself yet again, she blurted, "I don't think Father killed my mother, but I know he *could* have. Father drove his rage down inside and compacted it. It would flare like a bolt of lightning, and then it was gone, and all was cold again."

"Like the trader with the bird that did not return," Ilsanja said.

"Yes. These past sennights, no, since early spring, everything I knew—well, everything I thought I knew about my father, good and bad, has gone turvy. Those terrible loans, leaving me the mine, and now…"

Ilsanja said, "I cannot climb this hill for you." She sounded cautious, as if she were talking to a turvy stranger on the street.

"And I do not wish you to."

Aideen opened her eyes. Ilsanja sat across from her. This time, she knew, Ilsanja would not rise and come to her side. If either of them was to move, it would have to be her.

She pushed back her chair. Ilsanja swallowed. She feared Aideen would turn toward the door and not toward her, and Aideen knew it in a flash, like she knew how to breathe. Ilsanja's coldness was not all judgment. It was protection against hurt.

She walked around the table and crouched next to Ilsanja's chair. "It's my hill to climb, and I am never discounting you, or shutting you out, when I grow quiet."

Still staring at the table, Ilsanja moved her hand across its surface. Aideen reached up and covered it.

"What am I to do, then? Your silence, Aideen, is like an impending storm. The air in the room all rushes toward it."

"Surely not."

"Surely, yes."

"Well." Aideen thought she would never get warm again. As if Ilsanja's words were charmed, they conjured up the way she had felt around Father, so often. It could not be true, but then, how did Ilsanja know to use those very words? "This, then. I will…" she discarded the word "try." "I will *work* toward sharing more with you, in the moments of doubt and fear. And when it comes to Company matters, any of them, I will speak to you right away, even if I seek a solution within my own power. Will you be patient with me?"

Ilsanja sighed deeply. She did not look at Aideen, but turned her hand and entwined their fingers. "I believe you know patience is not my strongest feature."

"I do know."

"But I, too, will work toward patience."

"Then." Aideen stood up. "I *do* know we may never uncover the truth about what happened to my mother."

Ilsanja squeezed her hand. "I cannot walk this hill for you, but I will walk by your side." She reached for her glass. "Now, please try to eat some of Susannah's delicious fish."

Things seemed settled, but they had bad news from the cages two days later. Yor Lopez sent them each a message, advising them a morning shift worker had died on his way to the cages. They rode up to the site together, where Lopez waited with the night manager.

"It seems to be an accident, but it's a strange one," Lopez said. He was not due at the cages for another hour, but he was the first one called for any irregularity. "Stayben Sykes. He lives in the hills south of here and walked to work every day. This morning he did not appear."

Threedeer Potter, the night manager, spoke. "He is the shift leader, and I was due to go off shift. His team was here, so I sent a runner to his house, and they told us he had left at the usual time, so we began a search along the trail." He paused, his mouth working. "We found him halfway down the cliff."

Aideen reached out without thinking and squeezed the night manager's hand. "Good journey to him," she said.

The man gulped and nodded.

She continued. "Was there a disturbance on the trail? A rockslide? It's still dark when he arrives, usually?"

"Yes, gloaming at best, but he'd walked that trail four days a week for six years, in all weather, and he carried a lamp. The trail was clear. Narrow, but safe."

Ilsanja said, "What age was Yor Sykes?"

"Thirty."

She nodded and said nothing else.

"Where have you taken him?"

Lopez answered Aideen. "To the sheriff's."

This was the procedure for an unexplained death, even if it was plainly an accident, as this one was. "We sent word to the family, and they have gone there as well."

One small relief, Aideen thought—she and Ilsanja were spared, for an hour at least, the pain of meeting with the family. She felt selfish thinking it. A husband and a father gone was far worse than the awkwardness of trying to offer comfort. "And the workers?"

The night manager shook his head.

Lopez said, "Dazed, whispering to each other, quiet."

"Shall we speak to them?"

Ilsanja gripped her hand, but both men brightened.

"If you would, yorita," Lopez said. "I know your words will offer comfort. I will have them gathered."

"What do we say? What do *I* say?" Ilsanja whispered.

"Say that you share their sadness, you wish Yor Sykes a good journey, and offer prayers for his family. It's all they expect."

"They wish to hear from you."

"You are the majority partner. Your words, however simple, will mean much."

Ilsanja said what Aideen had suggested. In her faith, she said, people lit candles to help guide the departed along the path, and she would do so today. Aideen followed. Lopez dispersed the workers.

"Should we close and bring in the afternoon crew to keep the operation alive?"

Lopez shrugged. "We've lost workers before, usually to illness. The team leaders will keep an eye on things."

"We trust you to know what to do," Aideen said. Neither she nor Ilsanja spoke until they were mounted and headed back to town.

"Are we cursed?" Ilsanja said.

"Like in a fireside tale or a stage play? Surely there are no real curses."

"Just an accident."

"Just an accident," Aideen said.

12

(VVVI) Nameah and Linus are gone.

They have me reviewing formula and reports from everything we worked on. If I approve it, they print it out, stamp it and put it in a binder. Some of this is from Ap-One.

There are hundreds of binders already, it seems like.

I'm never going to see you again. I'm never going to see anybody again. This notebook is stupid, a dream. Even if they don't find it, no one else ever will. They'll bomb this place or implode it.

Don't care. Writing it down anyway.

I think they were right, Linus and Nameah. I think we violently interacted with another reality and merged with it, in some really bad way I think the Pit had something to do with it, but mostly it was the Aperture One experiment that we recreated in The Chapel. Something flew out of The Pit though and the Pit's still acti

Final page of Telma Lewiston's journal

"Okay. Wow." Erin said.

The cavern they were in was almost perfectly circular, with a domed ceiling. The air was gray, as dark as a winter morning back home, without any lights on. Light enough to see furniture and steps, not light enough to read by. She glanced over her shoulder and confirmed the corridor they'd just left was substantially darker.

And the grayness came from the roughly circular hole, surrounded by a transparent barrier.

She still heard the whine, but it hadn't gotten any louder or deeper, and now other sounds were mixed in with it. She said, "What are people hearing?"

Ruth said, "Wind, or rushing water."

"I hear moaning," said the Capitan.

A few others murmured agreement, including the guards.

"It sounds like voices singing to me, but it fades and swells," Mei said.

"I hear the whine, and the ripple of water," Trevian said, and this time the other copper-hunter nodded. Erin heard the same.

She advanced a few steps. "The top isn't covered," she said. "So they weren't trying to keep anything in."

"There is a ramp and a platform extending over it," Ruth said. "We believe the barrier was simply to keep people from falling."

Mei followed Erin and tipped her head back, staring up. "Are there holes in the roof, letting in the light?"

"There are," Ruth said. "Like you, we thought they were the source of the light. Two guards went up and covered them with wood and cloth, but the lightness in here did not dim."

Erin shot Mei a glance. "You ready?"

Mei shrugged. "Sure."

"Wait!" The Capitan strode forward. "Señorita Wing, I know what you're planning, and it isn't safe."

"It's why we came here," Mei said reasonably, settling her fuchsia-colored backpack more firmly over one shoulder.

"I will accompany you," Trevian said, stepping forward.

"Wait." Erin had misgivings. No one in the group knew it, but Trevian carried an artifact too. Having three of four of them on a platform over an abyss didn't sound like a good idea. "Let's think this through. Aideen got really disoriented when she went out there."

"My sister fears heights."

Right, but it read like more than that, in the letter. Erin glanced from the group to the barrier, paralyzed with indecision. After a moment, she slipped her messenger bag over her head. "Trevian, will you hold this? And stay at the end of the platform? I don't want to lose both artifacts if something goes wrong."

"Maybe I should leave mine, too?"

Espinosa came up to stand next to Trevian. Erin tried not to roll her eyes. There would be another international incident if she asked Mei to hand the compass to Trevian.

Trevian reached out, took the strap of Mei's pack, and handed to it Espinosa, who blinked, but gripped it in both hands.

Mei looked at Trevian. "If we freak out, will you come get us?"

"Freak out?" Espinosa said.

"Yes yorita," Trevian said. "I will come get you."

"*We* will come," Espinosa said.

"Or we can tether you," Ruth said. "That's what the first of us did. It *is* an unsettling experience."

Erin glanced at Ruth. Beyond her, Melendres was still watching Espinosa with a look just short of a glare.

"Let's try untethered," she said. "We'll be careful."

Mei nodded. "Here we go."

The barrier split around a ramp about six feet wide, with a waist-high wall along the sides. Erin drew her fingers along it. Acrylic? No, glass, probably tempered. The ramp was steady under their footsteps, even if the view below it was a seething blackness, devoid of any distinguishing feature. Erin didn't understand how the thing could make it lighter in here when there was no light source.

Mei whispered, "Is it moving?"

"I think so, but I don't know *why* I think so." Erin was baffled. Her brain was telling her there were currents and eddies in the blackness, but she wasn't *seeing* them, exactly.

"It's like hot oil in a pan," Mei said.

They walked all the way out. The whining settled into a steady tone, and now, like Mei, Erin distinguished other sounds, some low-pitched and resonant, some trilling, and under it all the steady rushing.

Erin leaned against the waist-high safety barrier and peered straight down.

Blackness, and a sense…of something.

Silvery dots sparkled in her vision. Dizziness swept over her, and she stepped back, staggering. Mei caught her arm. "All right?"

"Yeah, a little lightheaded."

Mei had not been looking over the side. She'd been studying the barrier, and now she pointed. "There was something bolted here," she said. Erin squinted, spotting the four holes down the corner of the material. "I'm guessing some kind of console."

Erin knelt and looked at the other side. She found four more holes.

Mei said, "But what *is* it?"

"No idea."

Trevian said, "What are you finding?"

"Come back to the ground," Espinosa said.

"Just a minute."

Trevian, surprisingly, backed the capitan. "Come back *now*. I saw you stagger."

"Okay, fine." Erin did roll her eyes now, and Mei grinned. They returned to where the group stood.

Mei reached for her bag. "Thank you, Marco." She opened it and lifted out the compass.

"What are you doing?" Erin had only seen the compass in videos. It was flashier than her book, but nothing too impressive: a thick disk with a curved glass cover over the compass face, blue opals studding the sides.

"Seeing it if reacts." Mei stood up and pivoted back to the ramp.

"Mei, maybe you shouldn't—"

Holding the artifact in both hands, Mei advanced along the ramp in measured steps, her head tilted down. Erin, who'd reached out for her, let her arm drop with a little sigh.

"This is how you are with me," Trevian said.

"What? No." She shifted her weight. "I should go after her."

Trevian put his hand on her shoulder, holding her in place.

At the edge of the platform, Mei looked back, shaking her head. "I thought I got a flicker, but now, nothing."

"Come back, then."

"Are you going to try with the book?"

"Not yet." Erin glanced at Ruth for help. "I think we should take a systematic approach, maybe have a plan."

"'Kay." Mei came back and tucked the compass safely into her backpack. "What about the rest of the group?"

Lauris said, "We would be interested in seeing what else Profesor Stillwater's team has discovered, and discussing what it might mean, against the New Way."

"Yes," Espinosa said.

"Good. This way, then," Ruth said.

B ack the way they'd come, and up a long line of shallow steps, they encountered the murals Aideen had described. Along the way the floor beneath them quivered—a mild tremor.

"'She brings us the future,' implies this Lewiston was a deity of some sort, or perhaps half-deity," Ruth said. "Some people call them Walkers."

Melendres added, "And we wonder what a beaver is."

Erin went straight to the context of THE EAGER BEAVERS OF ORCHARD HILL. "An eager beaver is a figure of speech. It means a go-getter."

"Like a hunting dog?"

Okay, she should have seen that one coming. "A person who always shows up early, works hard, takes initiative."

"But Telma Lewiston was going to bring them the future. How is that possible?" Melendres said.

Mei spoke first. "Do you have slogans here?"

An exchange of glances, several nods. Mei went on. "It's a slogan. A goal that is...not specific but unites everyone in a vision. They thought they were creating a different future."

"How arrogant." Melendres sounded personally offended.

"Well, you have to be, don't you? To question everything around you? To dare do things differently? Isn't it all possibly changing the future?"

"They certainly changed our world, if our theories are right," Melendres said, crossing her arms.

No, Erin thought. They changed *their* world. For good or bad, they *created* yours. No wonder Melendres was huffy.

"The painting is interesting, but not the puzzle I wish us to explore," Ruth said.

Ruth led them past the middle corridor and turned them down the dark eastern passage, forcing them to rely on lamps and sprite lights. Erin peered into the small rooms—probably offices—they passed. Many were empty, some piled with metal and scrap wood forming makeshift seats and work surfaces, as if they'd been in use after the facility shut down. Or whatever happened to it.

While there was a fine grit under her shoes, she couldn't help noticing the lack of dust. The place was almost hermetically sealed.

Ruth stopped in front of a pair of double doors set with wide rein-forced glass windows. Ruth pushed them open. Erin and Trevian stepped through first, and Erin was overwhelmed with familiarity, déjà vu. They stood on a gallery stretching the length of the long room in both directions, a metal railing in front of them. Directly before them ran a set of shallow steps down in a long decline to the open space below. Erin looked both ways. To her right was another staircase, and to her left a stairless ramp shared the same trajectory. She looked down through a bank of hanging fluorescent lights at desks, tables, electrical equipment. Consoles and flatscreens still lined the workspaces. Behind her, Mei said, "Whoa."

Automatically, Erin touched the wall beside her. Her fingers found a toggle switch and flipped it without thinking, but of course nothing happened.

"I feel like we're in a science fiction movie," Mei said.

"If we were, we'd find a door labeled Utilities, you'd go in and fiddle around and we'd have lights," Erin pointed out.

"The techie Asian? Racial profile much?"

"At least I didn't ask you about your martial arts moves."

Mei giggled, which made Trevian shoot her a startled glance.

Ruth eeled her way to the front. "Shall we go down? More lights to the front, please. I would like the yoritas to be first behind me, because they might recognize what we're seeing."

Sprite lamps and charmed quartzlights shifted forward, and Ruth started down the stairs. "We've moved some of the texts already, so Noemi and I could read them," she said. Noemi? Melendres's first name, Erin remembered.

"Texts?" Mei said.

"Yes, we found many. But several we left because we want Erin to see them in place."

They all stepped down onto the lower floor. "No prospectors made it this far," Trevian said. "They would have taken the metal fence above first thing."

"I don't think anyone have been here for centuries," Ruth said. "This apparatus, these…machines. Do they have meaning for you?"

Erin stroked the cool surface of the flatscreen on her left. The keyboard in front of it was like nothing she'd seen before. Instead of a plate of letters and characters, the board had three rectangular blocks of keys in two different shapes, and the keys were circular. Still, the purpose was the same. "This machine allowed people to calculate quickly, study images, and get messages from great distances."

Melendres spoke from behind her. "Many of your devices did that, it seems."

"These may not be exactly the same as the devices in our world," Erin said, "but they're close."

Mei pointed past Erin's shoulder. "The pale square against the far wall? It looks like a screen used for projection."

It looked like a huge flatscreen, where data might have been posted, or images. Images from various places. Erin stepped back and looked at the workstations and the chairs. The seemed to be arranged in shallow arcs, all facing the screen.

"Where did you find books?" she said.

"Come down this row," Ruth said, guiding them on the long walk to the far wall, where empty metal shelves clung.

"I don't get it," Erin said.

Ruth pointed. Along the bottom row a bunch of black binders lay dumped on their sides, as if the shelf had been half-emptied and they'd fallen over. Erin picked one up. The flimsy plastic covers bent in her hands.

"These are only shells of texts," Ruth said. She stepped back, revealing a three-drawer file cabinet. She drew one of the doors open. Erin peered inside. More binders. These were full.

Erin opened one. Light from Ruth's quartzlight threw a circle on page after page of printouts, some lines of text, some rows of figures and formulas, some graphs and images. Each page had a red stamp in the lower right corner. *Official Copy.* "I think these are some kind of a backup," she said. "Maybe a backup *to* the backup."

Mei looked over her shoulder. "Did they think they would lose access to the data? Were the servers failing or...?"

Before Erin could answer, Melendres said, "Who were the servers?"

"*What* were they," Mei said. "More machines. All these things are machines, and they all ran on electromagnetic waves."

"What Holay spoke of," Melendres said.

"I'm sure these were important to whatever they were studying here, but I can't figure them out," Erin said. "Mei?"

"I'm not a physicist or a mathematician," she said.

"Some are all words," Ruth said. "And this one..." She opened the top drawer and lifted out a black binder, just like the others. One page was marked with a strip of cloth. "This one was hidden behind this cabinet."

She knelt and put it on the floor, opening it to the marked page. "I thought this looked familiar."

Erin knelt too. Behind her, Mei was checking each of the empty binders and looking behind them in case any more were hidden. She turned her attention back to the page.

A node, flayed open, notations in fine print all around it. Auditory. Visual. A column of numerical figures, captured in a text box, sat at the bottom of the page. There were some tiny letters next to the numbers and Erin could barely make them out.

"This image of the node, it's in my book," she said. "The page Harald had."

Melendres joined the group. "Ruth commented on it once. How did it get into your book?"

"Someone copied it," Erin said. Copied it and then stamped it onto aluminum, thinking that would be more durable. "Someone knew it was important. They didn't copy those numbers though. I think they were guessing a lot of the time." She looked up at Melendres. "More importantly, they'd seen a node. They dissected one."

"There is still more," Ruth said. She flipped the pages back to the front cover. For a minute, even with the quartzlight, Erin couldn't see what she was pointing at. Inside the pocket on the front cover stuck a small black book.

Erin slipped it out. "Mei, look."

The cover was slick, and the volume was flexible; a journal, the kind Erin could find in specialty stores and bookstores in her world.

"It's the only one we've found," Ruth said. "And we can't read it. And this…this binder was hidden."

Erin flipped the journal open. Ruth aimed her quartzlight at the pages. Black ink, or dark blue, the small, crunched script was impossible to read. Erin riffled to the front. Printed words graced the first page:

This is the journal of:
If found, please Contact:
Reward:

Next to **Journal of,** someone long ago had printed, "Telma Lewiston."

"She hid it," Erin said.

"Not very well," Mei said. "Maybe she was rushed and slipped it into the first place she could."

"Why didn't they take the binders in the cabinet though?"

Ruth said, "We believe they got interrupted. Earth shudders perhaps. I think perhaps this whole row of shelves was once filled with shells filled like this one. Someone took them away, but they were rushed."

Erin reached for the journal. "Anyway, may I bring this back to camp?"

"I hope between the two of you, you can read it. We still have rooms to visit, though, and Erin, there is something else you must see."

Erin tucked the journal into her bag. "Lead the way."

Espinosa stood in the aisle Ruth chose, blocking it. "I thought we searched for a weapon," he said.

"Or the materials to make one," Erin said. "We need to see what's here. Everything that's here."

"Should we not bring one of these parasites into this space to see how it reacts?"

"Perhaps," said Ruth. "Later."

She led the group up the ramp. Erin let Lauris, whose head swiveled from side to side, pass her. "This is a wonder," he said.

Melendres stopped next to Mei. "I asked who the servers were because there is a door marked Server Room One."

"There is? Can I see it? I need to see it!"

"Of course, Yorita Wing," Ruth said, after the smallest hesitation. "We'll take you there next. What do you hope to find?"

"Equipment I can use."

When Mei reached her, Erin said, "What good will equipment do without power?"

"There might be something I can do. We can take a look, at least."

Ruth and Melendres help open the doors while everyone else trouped through. "We will go south now, only a few paces."

"I'll direct the yoritas," Melendres said, "while you take the others as we planned. We'll meet you."

Ruth sought out Mei. "Does that satisfy?"

Mei shrugged. "Sure."

Espinosa stepped forward. "I accompany Señorita Wing."

"Not without guards," Melendres said.

Mei hissed out a sigh. "What's he going to do in front of the whole group?"

"You do not know what Perlaraynans are capable of," Melendres said.

"While you try to invade—"

Trevian took two strides, to stand next to Melendres. "Capitan Espinosa and I will both accompany you."

Mei closed her eyes. "Fine."

113

Melendres marched off. "As Ruth said, it is only a few paces," she said, as Ruth's voice faded slightly down the corridor behind them. Melendres's light carved a yellow beam through the gloom, while Espinosa held up a sprite lamp. Melendres was right, and it was only a moment of two before she stopped in front of a door on the right.

NOC SERVER ROOM 1

The doorlatch looked like the kind in offices or schools, a long lever. Erin pushed it down, sure it was locked, but the handle gave, and the tongue of the latch clicked as it retracted. She pulled open the door and stared into a wide black tunnel lined with tall metal shelves on either side. On each shelf rested a shadowed rectangle.

"Oh, yes!" Mei said. "Señora Melendres, are you coming in with us? Marco, can you stay and keep watch?"

Espinosa peered around her. "These metal walls are high. They create hiding places."

"I'm more worried about the door locking behind us, leaving us trapped inside," she said.

"We will wait," Trevian said.

Erin pulled open her messenger bag and dug past her book until she touched the cylindrical surface of her flashlight and pulled it out. She flicked it on. It was a bit brighter than Melendres's, with a wider cone of light. She hadn't needed to use it much here, and the batteries were still strong.

The three of them advanced. Mei *hmmed* and nodded to herself.

Erin had thought the room was a closet, but it was deeper and wider than she'd supposed. Three rows of shelving ran back from each side of the door, rising up until shadow swallowed them.

"This is Room 1, meaning there are others?"

"Oh, yes, there'd be others," Mei said.

Melendres said, "This is the one we have found. Who is Noc?"

"Network Operation Center," Mei said.

Melendres's light wobbled. "Network. Like the parasites use?"

"Purely mechanical, not like them," Mei said. "But there are similarities."

Erin played her light along the ceiling, and, on impulse, switched it off. Dots of light still gleamed. "Is that phosphorescence, or are there openings in the roof?"

Mei stared up. "Openings, I think—skylights. Mini ones. They don't let in much light, though."

She stopped in front of one of the units. In a matter of a few seconds, she disconnected the component and slid it out. Melendres gasped. "Yorita!"

Mei knelt, turning the piece of equipment every which way. "Well," she said. "This one's a doorstop."

She stood and shoved it back into place. Lengthening her stride, she headed down the aisle, leaving Erin hurrying to catch up.

For a second, she lost track of Mei. Panic fizzed up inside her. Then, "Now, *this* is what I'm talking about," drifted back to her. She rounded a corner to find Mei squatting, studying two machines placed side by side, and nodding to herself. Once again, Erin directed the beam of her light over the machines.

Dos Torros Inverter 15 kWatts

"Generators?"

Mei's voice sounded like velvet, "Yes, and if I'm right there are two more on the other side." She got brisk again. "Señora, did you find any large metal barrels? It's a very long shot, but—"

"You think there's still fuel after three hundred years?"

"Maybe, if the barrel was airtight."

Melendres said, "There is a ruined room filled with machines and other things. It's unsafe."

"We need to see it."

"Why? What do you plan to do?"

"See if we can activate some of the equipment, of course," Mei said. "If we can create the killing frequency, killing the parasites' communication, I mean, we—"

"It's unsafe."

"It's what we're here for."

Erin tried to figure out Melendres's sudden hostility.

"We need energy to do *anything*," Mei said.

"That room is not safe."

Erin could see this was going nowhere. "Let's discuss this and make a plan."

"You may discuss it. We will join the others now." Melendres wheeled and started back up the walkway, her boots clicking.

Mei said, "What is happening?"

"I don't know," Erin said. Melendres was afraid, somehow, of what Mei was saying. She hadn't struck Erin as fearful. "Did they run this whole place on those four generators?"

"Those are portables, backups. Backups to the backups, like you said."

When they reached the door, she said, "Good news, Marco. This equipment might be something we can use."

Espinosa nodded and let the door shut. Trevian stood a few feet away. It didn't look like they'd been fighting. Small blessings.

Melendres led them in the direction Ruth and the others had gone. "There's something for Yorita Dosmanos to see," she said, but it was all she would say.

13

———

Trevian felt like Oldest Son in the Shevastin fireside tale, who fell into a cavern between worlds, trapped until he was rescued by Youngest Daughter and her dog. There was little in Orchard Hill he understood, even when Erin tried to explain it. Beyond the generalities of doors, rooms, tables, and chairs, all was strangeness.

Elmaestro Melendres led them past a closed door. "That's room's nothing but rubble," she said. She opened the next door, one closest to the intersection of the east-west corridor. Profesor Stillwater and the others waited for them just inside. A pile of rubble and scavenged furniture lay in the center of the room, and the walls were bare. This one had been ransacked, most likely by prospectors.

"We think this room was used after the earth turned," Stillwater said. "During the time of the warlords. The materials we've found show us that the Ancients had already learned about the frontera, and even danced across one. They had already brought back the collar."

The collar, made of gold and the same blue stones as were in Erin's book, lay at the bottom of his knapsack. He said nothing.

"It is of interest, but it is not the reason I brought us to this room." Stillwater took another step back and spun, heading for the alcove at the back of the cavern. A moment later she rolled out a small cart made of a material he did not recognize. The wheels rumbled on the stone floor.

"These carts have been very useful, but we left this one until Yorita Dosmanos could see its contents. Erin?"

When Erin didn't move, he touched her shoulder. She threw him a look of confusion—fear—and stepped forward.

Stillwater reached into the cart and drew out a book, its cover copper, bound at the spine with steel rings.

From where he stood, Trevian saw the tremor in Erin's hands as she gripped the volume.

The world seemed to hush, but a moment later Trevian glanced around and realized others were watching with mild interest or, in the case of Espinosa, impatience. Few of them had seen Erin's book. To them, this was just another Ancient volume.

Erin lay the book on a worksurface and opened it. One ring shrilled. "There's..." Erin swallowed. "There is writing, like mine, but no decorated borders. Is this...?"

"We believe it might be a companion to yours."

As they turned another page, Erin fell still, then touched the top corner. "There's a socket, but no puerta stone."

"There are five holes drilled, as if they planned to add some," Stillwater said. "The text of all this is foreign to me, like the early pages of the book you carry, but some of the diagrams are, well, I think they have value for us."

Erin's face was in shadow, and Trevian could only see her hand gripping the edges of the book.

"This one," Stillwater lifted out a third volume, "is completely blank."

"They mass-produced them, then," Erin said. "To have them ready. Perlarayna has two, right?"

"Yes," Espinosa said.

"So maybe there were meant to be five. There were always pages missing from mine, but maybe not all the pages we've added came from my book originally." She lifted her head. "One of the pages we added had a blank border."

"This book, like yours, seems to deal mostly with charms and elementals."

"Were they meant to be together? Did something go wrong?"

Stillwater shrugged.

Mei said, "Are the other artifacts mentioned? Is mine?"

"Yes," Stillwater said. "The lantern may be depicted, but I have never seen it, so I don't know."

"Maybe it has a way for us to defeat the New Way," Mei said, sounding as eager as a young girl going to her first fair.

"Maybe," Erin said. "They were fighting warlords. They sent the artifacts away because of them, not the New Way." She hefted the volume again. "May I bring this with me?"

"That was my thought," Stillwater said. She could have brought the book herself and had it waiting in Merrylake Landing. This had been a stage play, and he thought Stillwater had planned it so, even without thinking about it.

"What value does it serve, if it does not provide help against these parasites?" Espinosa said.

Erin paused before answering. "We won't know until we look at it, obviously, Capitan."

Obviously was a word Erin used when she was getting angry. Trevian tried not to grin.

They looked around this space, but there was little of interest after what they had already seen. Following Stillwater, they started back for the camp. A small second group waited at the mouth of the cavern, including two guards to replace the ones whose shift was ending.

Seeing the fresh guards, Mei said, "Señora Stillwater, can they accompany us to the storage space you found?"

"What space?"

Melendres shifted closer to Stillwater. "The yorita wants to see the large cavern with the rockslides. She believes there could be fuel for a device to bring energy to the machines."

Stillwater frowned. "The space isn't safe, yorita. We just had an earth shudder which may have damaged it even more."

"Can we figure out a way to do it safely?" said Erin.

"Is it so important?" Stillwater said.

"Yes." Mei did not hesitate. In that sense, she was very like Erin. "It's vital to—" She straightened up and said, "I am so stupid!"

Erin said, "What?"

"Screw the cell phones," Mei said, or something like those words. She whirled around again. "Where's the radio room?"

"What?" Melendres frowned at her.

"Radio Room. Communications Room, maybe." She spun again. "Erin, they had radios somewhere."

Profesor Stillwater took a step away from Mei, watching her carefully.

"There is a room labeled with such a word. It's in the middle passage, with the infirmary and the dining hall."

"We need to go there, now."

"Why?" Melendres said.

"We need radio waves to defeat them. That's what radios produce. Get me fuel for the generators and a working radio and I can get started."

"You mean to awaken a machine that speaks to the New Way?"

"It can *block* the New Way."

Erin started to speak. Melendres spoke over her. "But it also speaks the same way they do between each other." Melendres turned her head to stare at Erin. "You have said the parasites are animal and machine."

"Yes."

"How do we know the machines here are not infected? And she wants to awaken them."

"It's really unlikely," Erin said.

"Why is it unlikely? You believe the New Way's frontera is here. Plainly they have been here. If these machines are dead, we should leave them dead."

Mei spoke slowly, shaping her words in an exaggerated way. "We. Need. Equipment."

"This equipment is not safe," Melendres said. "And it cannot be our only choice. You yourself said NOC meant 'network.' That's what you call the parasites."

"It is." Mei held out her hands. "Hokay. It's barely, *barely* possible that the machines we saw in there became corrupted in some way. It isn't like getting a disease, but…let's say it's a risk."

"It is," said Melendres.

"The radios are something different."

"How can they be different when they all run on these waves in the air?"

"Hokay, so caballos need water and dogs needs water, but they aren't the same animal."

"Do you mock me, Yorita Mei?"

Erin said, "A network is like a net, Elmaestro. It's…they're bound together. The radios are not part of the same net. Right, Mei?"

Mei said nothing, but the muscles in the corner of her jaw bunched.

"Our devices run on the same kind of waves as radios," Erin said, "and my device blocked the New Way's communication. If there's a radio room, it might have what we need to stop them."

"Or aid them," Melendres said. Her gaze shifted from Mei to Espinosa. "We know of at least one person, Oshane Langtree, who helped the parasites without being infected. It stands to reason a nation might also be willing."

Mei said, "What does *that* mean?"

Espinosa said, "Pais Lewelyn knows better than anyone here how *we* respond to those who would invade us."

"I know nothing of how you respond to an invasion, Capitan. I know you steal ships and abduct innocent fishers."

Ruth raised her voice. "This does not help us decide about these radios. It's not a discussion for this time and place."

Melendres said, "I disagree. The out-of-worlder was in the company of the Perlaraynans for many sennights. I do not know what thoughts they put in her head."

Erin said, "Stop! Everyone stop. Mei and I are in agreement, and we're here to do the same thing, stop the parasites. You can't doubt *that*."

Mei's eyes widened. Her cheeks were very pink. "If we don't stop them here, they'll invade my world next. All I want to *do* is stop them."

Erin stood behind her, and he couldn't remember ever seeing such a shuttered expression on her face.

When Melendres spoke again, she was not as stern. "I believe both of you, yoritas. I simply worry about what you've been told. If you believe this radio room is indeed tied to a different net somehow, we will take you to it. And, before you ask, Yorita Dosmanos, Yor Langtree, Profesor Stillwater, and Capitan Espinosa will accompany us, along with his guard and one of mine."

Trevian exhaled. He felt as if he could breathe safely again.

Yor Diebell raised his hand. "Shall Madlyn be included, Elmaestro?"

"Lauris, of course. Yes, join us."

Espinosa's voice was cold "Maestra, you and I will speak of this later."

Melendres said, "Address me properly and use my title, Capitan."

His voice was cold. "That *is* your ti—"

"I am *Elmaestro* Melendres. And we will speak when I make time for you." Hers was just as cold. Trevian hunched his shoulders. They prepared for a war with the parasites when they had one in this very cavern.

14

W hy are we buying blackrock? And why are we having so many meetings?" Once again, Silvestro paced the meeting room. "For years, we ran with one meeting a month. Now it's every sennight, it seems."

"Father. Things are changing."

From where he stood at the window, Don Leo glared at the three of them. "Not for the better. We provide light and warmth *without* blackrock! We meet monthly! We do not justify ourselves to the Crescent Council! You, Aideen, see your help with the ledgers as an understanding of this company. Ilsanja, raising trail caballos is not the same as running a business."

Aideen felt her face heat up but held herself still. She would not react to Jefe Silvestro's insults. He understood the company far less than she did, and it was obvious to everyone in the room. Everyone, she thought, staring at him.

Yor Montez said, "We face risks we've never seen before. It's wiser to prepare and have preparation go unneeded than be caught unawares and desperate."

"You've drunk from the well of their panic, Armando." Now his glare bounced from Ilsanja to Aideen and back. "You two make decisions behind my back, and Armando bows his head because he does not want to offend."

"We do not make decisions behind your back, Father. We make them in meetings which you choose to leave."

"You have used a morsel of power, which you *married*, to feed your insolence," Silvestro said. "I have done nothing so bad in this world to earn such a faithless daughter as you."

"Jesu Cristos!" Ilsanja threw up her hands, a gesture Aideen had seen before only on a stage. "Father, you saw that parasite! You know Oshane Langtree killed Don Oswald! Can't you see we are trying to protect our company and our town?"

"I see how badly you go about it!" He strode away and banged the door behind him.

"He didn't mean what he said, Jefa," Montez said.

"Oh, he did, Armando, but thank you." Absently, Ilsanja added, "Please call me Ilsanja."

Aideen reached for her hand. "It is usually easier without him, honestly."

Ilsanja took two deep breaths and straightened up. "Certainly, at times at least. So, Skaggs Mine has accepted our letter, Don Armando, correct? We can begin to prepare for the possible worst."

A t least Silvestro had stayed for the vote to pay the Sykes family six months' salary for Stayben.

That action fit the picture he had of himself; fair, generous to the families of his workers. Preparing for a crisis comprised largely of unknowns was plainly no skill of his.

Ilsanja carried on through the meeting as if nothing cruel had been hurled at her and said nothing for most of the ride home. She clutched Aideen's hand, though. Close to the house, she murmured, "Which you *married*," and gave a little laugh, but it sounded like a sob.

"Sometimes your father is a fool," Aideen said, when they sat finally in the sala. "He loves you, though, in spite of his words."

"I do not doubt it," Ilsanja said. "And it should help that I do not doubt it. But I am *not* faithless."

"You are not, and the world knows it," said Aideen. "You do not respect him, and he senses it."

Ilsanja's eyes opened wide. "Well." She fidgeted for a moment, a thing she rarely did. "It's true. I love Father, but I cannot respect him. I hoped it didn't show."

"I think..." Aideen hesitated. Until the conversation started, she didn't realize she had formed a theory. "I think respect, for Don Leo, is like coin was for Father. No matter how wealthy Father was, he never had enough coin. Hence the loans, payments he did not even need, stacked up in a strongbox and ignored. But he needed a pool of coin. Your father needs a pool of adulation. Even if you behaved in a more... ingratiating manner, it would not be enough. And now, he is no longer a majority partner."

"'Ingratiating,'" Ilsanja gave a soft snort. "Well, I suppose I should be relieved there is little damage he can do."

"Jefa, yorita? A message from the sheriff," Dolores said from the doorway.

Aideen held out her hand. "I'll take it, Dolores. Thank you."

Aideen moved to sit next to Ilsanja on the couch and unfolded the letter, tilting it so they both could read.

The sheriff had released Yor Sykes's body to his widow and children. Yor Ofalson had examined the body. A fall down the cliff from the trail could have left Yor Sykes with a battered skull, or a broken neck, or a broken back and ribs, but not all those injuries, normally, Yor Olafson said. Such damage came from a much higher fall.

"Perhaps he was not on the trail," Ilsanja said. "Perhaps he climbed above, in search of something, and fell from there."

"Missing the trail completely?"

"Perhaps someone beat him? That would be murder."

"It is murder, I think," Aideen said. "But I don't think he was beaten. I think he was carried up and dropped."

The next day, a messenger delivered a message from Trevian. Not a fast messenger or the letter van, Dolores said, a messenger in the red of a Copper Coalition guard. The rider awaited a reply.

Inside the folded paper was another note for Aideen, but Ilsanja shared the contents of hers. "He explores the caves we discovered and hopes he and Yorita Dosmanos—he does not call her 'Erin' here—can visit us during the next sennight. They had an uneventful journey except for a bad moment near the end, but no one was harmed. He ends with, 'the journey has been a disappointment, but the Copper Coalition still hopes for riches.'"

"Is it some sort of code?"

"What does yours say?"

The letter was short. "They faced a lone mestengo and a sudden unseasonable storm but weathered both. Oh, definitely a code. He thinks I would find the cave complex interesting. There is one among the party, who has traveled a great distance, who longs to meet us. I wonder who it is. And the 'lone mestengo,' with a storm. My uncle."

"The letter was delivered by the Copper Coalition, yet he fears it might be intercepted?"

Aideen shrugged. "Shall we say we welcome them? Do we?"

"Of course we do." Ilsanja reached for pen and paper. "What if the visitor from a great distance is the other guardian?"

"That would be a great curiosity," Aideen said. "If my uncle attacked them on the road, then he is not far from here."

Ilsanja did not look up from her writing. "You believe he set the elemental on Yor Skyes, but why?"

"Simply to harass us? The Company, I mean? Out of anger?"

"I suspect a deeper plan than anger," Ilsanja said. "We must remind the guards our enemy has an air elemental."

"And order some more moonstone chains," Aideen said. "I will ride up there now." She held out her hand for the letter and carried it to Dolores. The stable worker brought her caballo a few minutes later, and she rode up to the cages.

She advised Yor Lopez of the sheriff's conclusion. Lopez listened intently. "We'll develop a plan for the night shift and early shift workers, especially those who live in the hills as Skyes did. Although I do not know how we guard against an attack from the air."

"The moonstone charms have proven effective," she said. "Yor Lopez, do you know of any place in the hills, or even up mountain, where a mestengo could be hiding?"

The manager shrugged. "There are several hunting cabins, yorita. Jefe Silvestro has one. And, as everywhere, the caves could provide shelter. I've never looked closely."

"We can organize a search," Aideen said. They needed to take the fight to Oshane, not cower in the shadow of his tethered creature. "I will have Yora Qinn order more charmed chains for us."

The lobby was quiet this time of day, although the offices themselves were filled. Coming down the stairs, a young woman at his side, Yor Montez hailed her, waving. "Yorita! Stay a moment."

"Please, Armando. Aideen," she said.

The woman next to him had inherited his eyes and the shape of his forehead. Her black hair was drawn back in a simple style, and she wore a plain jacket, a calf-length skirt over sturdy trousers. Aideen had met Lucia Montez years ago when they had both been small. Now, as Armando introduced them again, she shook Lucia's hand with pleasure. "Are you with us long? I had heard you were in Shevastin."

"Yes. I went to study their music. Now I'm heading to Pais Lewelyn, with my pledged man. We are staying with Papa for a day or two."

"Pledged! Much joy to you! And is there a style of music in Pais Lewelyn you wish to study?"

Lucia's gaze darted sideways. "Not music, now. Um, some business."

No doubt the pledged man's. "Will you have the wedding here? May we help with the event?"

Armando Montez blushed. "You are generous, yor...Aideen. We'll speak of it later. Lucia's plans are in the middle distance, not immediate. There might be another matter I wish to discuss to with you, also."

"Of course. Yor Montez, speaking of matters, there is a small one I would like your help with. But this is a time for family. Will the three of you come for dinner, tomorrow night?"

He exchanged a glance with his daughter, who nodded. "It would be a great pleasure."

Perhaps it would be the first time Yor Montez had been invited to the Langtree house. Aideen pushed the thought away. "Was your journey uneventful?"

"A bit longer than we hoped," Lucia said. "I planned to cut through one of the old passes near Merry Lake, and come through the tunnel, but we were warned away. There's a group of prospectors up there, infected with some parasite. No one's done anything about it. We rode clear over to the North Road. It added a day."

"Infected? Where did you hear this?"

"Valentin, my pledged. He heard it from a traveler on the road. It's well known, they said. I'm surprised, and a bit worried, if you haven't heard here. Something should be done."

"The rumor is not true," Armando said. "There is a group prospecting in Merrylake Landing, but they are from the Copper Coalition. There *is* a parasite, but they are not the ones who carry it."

Lucia's forehead wrinkled slightly. "Papa, I hope you don't plan to go up there. I wouldn't trust the Copper Coalition's judgment, especially when weighed against profit."

"In this case, I think we can." Armando gave Aideen a glance she read clearly. This rumor was growing too quickly. There seemed little they could do, when even Lucia Montez did not believe the facts.

"Well, tomorrow night," Aideen said. "We look forward to it."

"And so do we," Armando said.

Aideen took her leave, seeking out Paloma Quinn.

When she returned home, she told Ilsanja and Susannah about her dinner invitation. From the sparkle in Susannah's eyes and the wide smile on her face, she was delighted at the thought of guests. Ilsanja seemed pleased too.

Over dinner, Aideen asked about the Silvestro hunting cabin. Ilsanja thought for a moment. "I remember it. I would say 'hut' rather than 'cabin." My father has not used it in ten years or more, I think, but as far as I know he still owns it."

"Do you remember where it is?"

"I was very young the last time I was there. Father will be able to tell us."

"If he deigns to."

A smile flickered over Ilsanja's lips. She sipped her wine. "Perhaps the sheriff could ask him."

This night they chose not to end the meal with a sweet. They both settled into the sala. Ilsanja was reading a new novel from Pais Lewelyn, a story of hidden heirs, stolen babies, and a secret treasure hidden in the mountains of Shevastin "I do not believe this storyteller has ever visited Shevastin," Ilsanja said, "but the tale is gripping."

Aideen took refuge in old poetry, some of the poems she remembered her mother reading to her. After a while, she said, "Did Yor Montez ever come to your house?"

"Every nameday," Ilsanja said without looking up.

"Three-quarters of White Bluffs attends your nameday celebrations. Any other times?"

"Yes. A few."

"For a meal? Did he bring his children?"

She shook her head, still not looking up from the page. "Usually something related to the Company, something my father had forgotten, or Yor Montez wished him to know, and he hadn't been present for the meeting."

"He hasn't been treated well."

Now Ilsanja looked up. "What do you mean? He's a partner. He lives in a lovely house in the canal district, has educated both his children well."

"He's not a jefe."

"Well, not everyone can be a jefe. His drill bits were no longer as valuable once they stopped drilling the shafts into the colonies. The Silvestro charms are still needed every day. Your father's land... our land, needed every day. A drill bit, rarely."

"I suppose."

Ilsanja closed her book. "He could always have sold his shares and used the money to start a business of his own. Bettered himself."

"I think the Company has not treated him well. I think the reduction in the partners draw hurt him."

"It was the same percentage as we took. It was fair." Now she half-turned to face Aideen. "One uno out of ten is *always* one uno out of ten. It struck them all the same...except for your father."

"When a majority partner has three piles of unos, and the minority partner only one, one uno out of ten doesn't seem right," Aideen said. "I understand the arithmetic."

"It's just how life works," Ilsanja said. "Perhaps this Valentin is a wealthy one in Shevastin, and Lucia will bring more coin to her father's strongbox. Would that satisfy you?"

"It's a nice thought." Aideen turned back to her poems. Somehow, she wasn't saying what she thought. Perhaps a night's sleep would clear her brain.

The next morning, she spent a few hours in the office, and when she came home, Susannah's raised voice rang into the entryway. The cook never shouted. Aideen ran for the kitchen.

"Turvy, I tell you, this entire town!" Susannah waved a wooden spoon as she shouted, while the kitchen chica dodged, reaching for the bags on the long table.

"Susannah! Are you hurt? What has happened?"

Susannah lowered her spoon, a dark flush heating her cheeks. "Yorita, my apologies! I am well, I...I'm angry. I went to the market, for tonight's dinner. I want to do something different. I hope you and the Jefa like it, I—"

Aideen said, "And did something happen at the market?"

"They—yes! A prospector and her husband were shopping for supplies, and the daughter of Markow the weaver...you know the one, she married a Fenster, she began to whisper and point, accusing them. Not a single merchant would serve them! And a whole group of people gathered. Those poor prospectors!"

"Why? What did the crowd do?" Cold gathered in the pit of Aideen's stomach.

"People accused them of bringing disease!"

"Where were they from, do you know? Had they come down from Merrylake Landing?"

"It looked like they came up mountain from Sheeplands, as prospectors always have. The woman swore she knew nothing about disease. I tried to speak for them. I said I worked for the Langtree family, and I knew prospectors were not the source of the parasite, but no one listened!" Susannah glanced down at the floor. "I gave them a bag of our goods, at the end, yorita, and they left."

"You did a good thing, Susannah. This is out of hand. I'll speak to the sheriff about it." She remembered she wished to speak to the sheriff about the Silvestro hunting cabin as well.

The rumor was flying, and it was so specific. Why? What purpose did it serve except to frighten people?

She sent a message to the sheriff, and reviewed reports from the cages and from the mine. Lopez reported bad news. Two cord-stringers had quit work this sennight. People left work all the time, seeking fortune elsewhere, but with the death of Sykes, it left Lopez short-staffed, and once again slowed the expansion. It made her pause. Was the Sheeplands expansion the true target? She made a note to tell Lopez more moonstone charms had been ordered.

Ilsanja came home. They bathed together, which took a long, pleasant time, and dressed for dinner. Tonight was not a night for mourning gray; after all, they were not going out. Aideen wore her dark red skirt and jacket, while Ilsanja chose a new dress, a shade between gold and green, with crimson trim on the neckline and the narrow cuffs of the belled sleeves.

Armando, Lucia, and Valentin, her pledged man, arrived on time, and he carried a bottle of Shevastin lick as a dinner-gift.

Valentin and Lucia made a fine picture. He was a few inches taller than her, with hair a bright shade of yellow Aideen rarely saw, suntanned skin, high cheekbones, and pale blue eyes. He spoke quietly but carried himself with confidence. He wore black trousers and a knee-length black jacket. His shirtfront was a mass of tiny tucks. Ilsanja eyed the tailoring detail with approval. Lucia's skirt and jacket were the same cut as Aideen's, in the dark green of pine needles.

Valentin came from a part of Shevastin called Kuono, which Ilsanja thought she had heard of. Aideen never had. His father ran a weaving team and sold cloth throughout the various Shevastin nations, and his mother was a fabricker, working mostly with quartz and glass. Shevastin made and used much glass, and the business was very successful. Perhaps Lucia was marrying into a deep stream of coin after all.

Lucia spoke with passion about Shevastin music but said far less about her plans to move to Pais Lewelyn, while Armando sipped sisuree, smiled and said little. After a few moments they seated themselves in the dining room. Ilsanja picked up the small tongs lying across her plate. "What are these?" she said.

"I don't know," Aideen said. Each plate had a pair. "Susannah said she was trying something different."

The kitchen chica brought out a narrow tray of tiny dumplings. The steam off them raised saliva in Aideen's mouth, and Lucia gave a soft murmur. They passed the tray around and finally figured out what the tongs were for. The dumplings were soft and chewy, with a filling of pork and rice and some new spices. The tray made the rounds again.

The chica brought tiny bowls of thin broth, which was peppery and salty with a sweet tang at the end.

"This soup, Ilsanja," Armando said. "It is delicious."

Ilsanja gave Aideen the closest thing to a panicked glance she'd ever seen from her friend. Aideen was fearful too. A few dumplings and a swallow of soup, was this all?

The chica delivered another tray holding small cakes topped with smoked fish, a tray of roasted vegetables, and some stuffed buns. The pressure in Aideen's chest eased.

"This is an unusual way to enjoy a meal," Armando said.

"For us too." Ilsanja used the tongs to grip a bun. "Susannah has surprised us."

Lucia shifted some vegetables onto her plate. "It has the pleasure and discovery of eating from the booths at a festival, without the inconvenience. No struggle to find a seat and balance a plate."

"And avoid spilling, always my challenge," Aideen said.

Lucia laughed. "How many times did I come home to soak my blouse in cold water, to remove the sauce stains?"

"Juggling a plate and two glasses of wine, while trying to find where my partner sat," Valentin said. "That was my ordeal."

"And mine," Armando added.

"Are you a musician, too, Valentin?" Ilsanja said.

"I play the mandolin a little, but my occupation is charmcaster."

"Lucia, I've heard you play the guitarra and the mandolin, and we've heard you sing. Do you play other instruments as well?"

"In Kuono, I was introduced to an instrument I never saw in White Bluffs. It is a stringed instrument shaped like a table, with keys you press instead of strings you pluck. It's called a piano."

"I heard one in Duloc once," Aideen said. "It sounded like a difficult instrument."

Lucia smiled. "We were speaking of challenges, and it was one for me. And I play the flautine, of course..."

"Ugh," Ilsanja said, shivering. "No disrespect to you or your craft, but I never wish to hear a flautine again."

"I don't either," Aideen said. "The villain who murdered my father controls an air elemental, and it seems the flautine is part of it."

"Father spoke of it. This man, your uncle? He's tethered an elemental with a flautine?" Lucia looked from the two of them to Valentin. "He would have to play the instrument constantly."

"He has a golden amulet we believe holds the tether. But the flautine controls the creature, directs it," Aideen said.

Valentin nodded. "It seems possible," he said. "Sound is a large part of a successful charm. Even the substances we work with, metals and quartz, or glass, respond to sounds."

"How can that be? Copper doesn't respond to singing."

Valentin grinned. "Have you even seen a sheepdog cock its head and stare into space, yorita Aideen, when you saw or heard nothing? There are sounds we can't hear. We believe earth elementals contact each other through sounds so low we can't hear them."

"Is that how they loosen the earth around them, when they surface to attack?"

"Quite possibly. And probably, directed sound could dissolve one, the way enough water will. It's a hard thing to test, though. Shevasti studies show that metals do respond to sounds we cannot hear."

"We know someone who speaks of vibrations through the air, tiny ripples traveling for leagues and leagues."

"We know it's true with music," Lucia said. "Some notes cause people pain. Charms and music may be more closely related than we know."

Two more plates came out. Aideen said, "Is Ricardo still designing roads and bridges in Pais Lewelyn?"

Chewing, Armando nodded. "Yes."

"Although I think my brother is bored," Lucia said. "He engineered a tunnel through a long hill, and everything grows pale in comparison to it."

"Not bored," Armando said. Was there a warning in his glance? Aideen didn't even know why she thought that.

"Will you be near him, in Pais Lewelyn?" Ilsanja said.

Lucia nodded. "Part of the time, at least, we hope. His current work takes him many places."

The chica brought sisuree and Susannah herself carried out the dinner sweet, small kokalatal cakes frosted with even more of the new spice, in a creamy, honeyed base.

"We speak of charms, but your cook is a master of them," Lucia said. "Susannah, this was a delight!"

Susannah blushed again. "Thank you, Yorita Montez. Jefa Langtree has brought kokalatal to us, and I have wasted many hours baking with it."

"Not a moment was wasted," Aideen said.

They lingered longer than usual at the table, sipping sisuree and the after-dinner lick Valentin brought, which tasted of berries and cinnamon. Eventually they moved back into the sala and spoke until all were yawning. Ilsanja insisted on calling a sprite cart for them because of the late hour.

Armando touched Aideen's arm. "There was a matter you wished to discuss?"

"Yes, but not tonight. Perhaps on Veyernes, at the office?"

He gave a quick nod.

"Valentin, what metal do you work with?" Aideen asked, a final idle question as they waited for the cart.

"Like my mother, my affinity is with quartz," he said.

Behind him, Ilsanja's bright eyes suddenly narrowed a bit, but she said nothing, embracing Lucia and shaking Valentin's hand. Her shoulder bumping Aideen's, they watched until the cart was on its way.

"New friends, soon leaving though," Aideen said.

"Yes. Perhaps we can visit them in Pais Lewelyn someday."

"Why do you care that Valentin works with quartz?"

"It's nothing...exactly. It paired, in my mind, with our conversation about Yor Montez."

"I see no connection," Aideen said.

"No... Your mind is not as devious as mine."

Aideen slipped an arm around her waist and pulled her close. "Let's go to bed," she said.

15

As she reached Mei's side, Erin whispered, "So, two nations here are having a Cold War? Great."

Mei shivered. "It's just like home. At least now I understand why we camped out when we were in Pais Lewelyn. They must hate Perlaraynans."

Erin said, "Someone could have mentioned it."

Ruth had come up behind them. She said quietly, "We did not think anyone from Perlarayna was joining this mission."

"Tregannon didn't mention it?"

"Not in any message to me, and if he said so to Elmaestro Melendres, she didn't speak of it." Ruth walked a few more paces. "I knew there were disputes. I didn't know both sides felt so strongly."

The Radio Room was at the end of the middle corridor and Ruth led them in. It was smaller than Erin expected, but Mei *hmmed* and nodded as she inspected the machines neatly lined up around the walls.

"There would have been an antenna array somewhere, probably on the top of the mountain," she said. "I'm sure it's long gone, scavenged. But if we had power, I could make something work."

"Something that calls the New Way right to us?" said Melendres.

Mei was quiet for a moment or two. "We'll make sure that doesn't happen, Elmaestro," she said finally.

The walk back down to the camp was silent, and Trevian feared the day's wounds among the group would not be easily healed. As they reached the shore, Mei said, "Once we find some fuel, we'll be set."

"Seriously?" Erin said. "After three hundred years?"

"You don't have to be negative too."

"I'm not. I'm being realistic. You're not going to find gasoline after three hundred years."

"You don't know that."

"Pretty much do."

They both looked around and stopped speaking. Stillwater neatly guided Erin and Mei out of the pack and said, "Yoritas, I'd like us to review the books we found today."

"Sounds good to me," Erin said, and the three of them went off to the house Stillwater had designated a library.

Trevian found Miriam LaFish refreshing some ward charms and helped her. Harald moved through the camp, on the way to the town hall, and Trevian guessed a meeting was happening.

Between them, they refreshed fifteen wards, and the weight of the day settled on him all at once. He walked over to the library, where raised voices reached him. In the doorway he paused. Erin stood in the center of the room with her arms folded, and once again Mei's cheeks were bright pink. There was a sheen to her eyes. "—and now you won't even help me find gasoline."

Trevian said, "What is gasoline?"

"It's a liquid fuel. There might be some in the supply depot."

Both the metal-paged books were open on the table behind them, but Trevian would wager they hadn't looked at them in a while.

"Next to the laboratory room?" Trevian remembered the door Stillwater had waved at as they passed, dismissing it with the words, *It's rubble.*

"What? No, I don't think so. Sounded like it was...further south in the east wing."

Trevian looked around. The house's main room was filled with tables now, the tables stacked with books from the cavern. The glow of sprite lamps filled the room, making it brighter than the early afternoon sky outside.

He stepped inside and half-sat on the edge of a table. "I will go with you if you wish," he said. "If I go, though, so will the Capitan. Will we hamper your search?"

"Not if you do what we ask," Mei said. "Marco won't like it, though. He's more used to giving orders."

"Melendres's the one kicking up a fuss," Erin said, "so she'll probably want to tag along too."

He knew what "tag along" meant.

"No way," said Mei. "She's not coming."

"She's the head of the expedition," Trevian said. "You cannot stop her. What does she fear?"

"A cave-in or a rockslide."

"I don't like the sound of that," he said.

"We don't either," Mei said, "but we *have* to look."

Erin ran her finger along the edge of the metal pages. "We *do* have to look. But we don't want anyone getting killed either."

Trevian said, "Do you remember Dorotea?"

"Who? Oh, the prospector at your camp, yes."

"She and her partner loved to prospect in caves. They wore rope harnesses and took turns. One would go down, with a line tied off above and the other feeding out the rope. In this way, if the ground gave way the one above could pull the other back up, and if the ceiling caved in, there was a way to follow the line and dig out the other. At least, so was the hope."

Erin exchanged a glance with Mei. "It could work."

"Why are you even agreeing to come, if you think there's nothing we can use?" Mei said.

"I never said I think there's *nothing* we can use. I just don't want to get your hopes up about fuel." Erin faced Trevian. "Is there enough rope?"

"If not, David LaFish and I know where we can find some."

"Where?"

He hesitated. "Oshane's mestengo lair, the old sheriff's house."

Erin shuddered. "Oh."

"We will go. I'll see if Genaro will join us. You do not have to come."

"Good."

"Have you found anything of interest? In your books?"

"We kind of got sidetracked," Erin said.

Mei said, "Plenty of interesting things, but nothing really useful."

"Yet."

Mei echoed, "Yet."

E rin hadn't expected Mei to be a problem. But the other guardian's high-intensity focus seemed like a bad combination with Melendres's attitude. How bad would it be when Mei finally remembered how fast gasoline evaporated?

Maybe Erin was totally wrong and there would six fifty-gallon drums of perfectly usable fuel. And they'd have no trouble persuading Melendres to let them have the equipment.

Right.

"Do you want to look at the new book some more, or the notebook Ruth found?"

"Whichever." Mei looked away from her. "This house, where Trevian's going, what is it?"

"It's where Oshane held everyone captive." Another shudder shook Erin as she remembered. "He sicced his air elemental on Trevian, and his fire elementals on me. And he had the Agustos and a bunch of local copper-hunters from here trapped by the lantern. David LaFish, he was one, and his girlfriend. They all had those parasite things."

Mei rested both hands on the tabletop. Her short hair fell across her cheek, obscuring her profile. "The air elemental killed Mama and Ba. They were...hanging in the air. Now I know what they—what they went through."

"Me, too. Only it was the flames. He used them to accelerate the wild-fire, and then they came to the house."

Mei said, "I didn't look back. I didn't try to help them. I just ran."

After a few seconds, Erin said, "They trained us to run, Mei. It what they've always told us to do. Us, and all the ones before us."

"I know," Mei swiped her knuckles over her check. "But did you ever think you'd *have* to?"

"God, no." She'd grown up with the book as just a thing in her family. When the Carews had disappeared, Mom and Dad immediately started looking for a house less than a mile from their frontera, instead of their home four miles away. The house they bought they could barely afford. When Chip was killed, Erin knew she'd be a checker at Pierson's Grocery for the rest of her life. Even then, while she never seriously considered rebelling, she hadn't thought any of it was...well, concrete. "Magic, yes. My grandmother showed me some of the spells in the book, and they worked. But...other worlds? I never thought I'd see one."

"I didn't either. At least you can do things here. I'm useless."

"Not useless. We need you if we're going to defeat the New Way once and for all."

Mei ran one hand through her hair. "You need the compass, not me. I could go home. I could leave the compass with you, and Marco could take me back to my frontera right now. Whatshername would be happy."

"None of us knows how to use the compass."

"And you think I do?"

"Better than I do," Erin said. She struggled to turn the conversation to a lighter note. "Besides, you're my hardware nerd, remember?"

Mei's smile let Erin know the other woman knew exactly what she was trying to do. "I'm going to go for a walk. Then we can look at the notebook together, yes?"

"Okay." A moment later Erin remembered to say, "Be careful."

The sheriff's house had collapsed even further since Trevian had last seen it. While the large room Oshane had stored his cache of copper in was intact, the kitchen roof had fallen in completely. All the copper was gone, and Trevian was glad about it.

Treading with care, Genaro, David, and Trevian made their way to the back of the house, where they found three large coils of rope, probably from the days when Merrylake Landing had a set of thriving piers. Digging slowly and carefully, David unearthed three stiff leather slings, their sides pocked with grommets. They creaked as he rolled them up.

Back in the center of the camp they deposited their findings in the supply building. Trevian went in search of Elmaestro Melendres, finding instead Yorita Mei sitting on a block of dressed stone, watching the workings of the camp. Not many people were out and about right now. Most of the scientists and scholars, he judged, were in the complex, making notes and plans. He spied Capitan Espinosa several feet away, standing, his gaze never wavering from Mei.

Trevian sat cross-legged at her side, leaving her plenty of room. "Yorita, are you well?"

"Yes," she said. "This is all strange to me."

"As strange as it was to Erin, no doubt."

"She fits in here."

He changed the subject. "I have a question, but often questions I think are simple can be seen as rude, so I don't know how to ask."

A smile flitted across her mouth. "Rude to Erin and me, or rude in general?"

"Sadly, I am seen as being rude in general."

"I can relate." She was silent for a moment. "Just ask."

"I thought your family name was Mei, and your personal name was Wing. Did I have that backwards?"

"Yes. Where I come from, the family name comes first. Mama named me Mei because it sounded more western...more like the names where Erin is from."

"You are not from the same continent, and there are oceans separating you, but you seem similar to me."

Mei tilted her head, watching as a Pais Lewelyn charmcaster refreshed a set of charms. "We're similar technically, scientifically, medically. And because of our technology we can see and talk to each other. But in everyday ways, I would say deeper ways, we are very different."

"Yet you speak the same language."

Mei's smile was a bright light now. "Where I live, many people learn to speak Erin's language. But her people don't often learn the languages of others."

"Why not?"

Mei laughed. "No one knows, they just don't. But my alphabet, food, songs, all are different from hers. How you address people is different, even things like, I don't know, how you receive a gift, or give one, is different."

"Is it more like Perlarayna, then?"

"No. Perlarayna is more like your country than mine."

"I have trouble imagining it," he said.

She nodded. They shared a moment of silence. "I was sitting here wondering what my family is doing. My aunts and uncles, my cousins. If they're gathered at the house, waiting for me to come back through the frontera."

"They must miss you greatly," he said.

"I miss them. And I worry. About the parasites."

Trevian could think of nothing to say, so he nodded.

She stood. "I told Erin I'd look at the notebook with her."

"Have you spoken to Capitan Espinosa about tomorrow's task, in the supply depot?"

She sighed. "No. I guess I should."

"I would talk to him with you, but I fear I'd be no help."

Another smile. "I think you're right. I'll handle it."

Based on the loudness of Mei's sigh, she was as exasperated as Erin was. "This handwriting!" she said. "This is impossible!"

"It's terrible." The letters, tiny, cramped loops, reminded Erin of scrambled eggs on a plate. In places, the words ran off the page. "You know, I'm going to see if Harald brought a magnifier." She straightened up and blinked her dry eyes a couple of times. "Do you want some sisuree?"

"Would they have hot water? Just hot water? I have tea."

"You thought to bring tea. Smarter than me, I only had water and some energy bars."

"I brought a little, not enough, but they grow it in Perlarayna."

"Oh. Why don't you come with me? You could use a break."

"I just had one."

"Come on, Mei. We're not cubicle rats. Come with me."

Mei curled her shoulders in, but after a few seconds, she said, "Okay."

Ruth, Harald, and Melendres were gathered in a large room in the town hall building. Melendres said, "—no more wisdom than we, and by their ages, far less experience." When Erin and Mei appeared, she stopped talking and turned away.

At Erin's request, Harald pulled a magnifier stone from his vest pocket and handed it to her. She thanked him and said, "Is there a problem Mei and I need to know about?"

"We are working it out. There's much here you don't know, Erin." He glanced beyond her to Mei but didn't seem to include her in the comment.

Harald pointed to a nearby open door. "Perhaps you could stop there and take Señorita Gunnarsdottir with you? She hasn't eaten since dawn, poring through the books we carried over here."

"Melendres let her have books?"

"Ruth did," Harald said.

When Mei was out of hearing, Erin said, "Harald, Pais Lewelyn and Perlarayna may have some kind of undeclared war going on, but they don't need to fight it out *here*."

"I had that discussion with Elmaestro Melendres," he said, "But the history between them is long, and neither of us guides their nations."

"Fine." She walked away.

Juanita grunted something when they entered but didn't look up from the leatherbound tome she was studying. Mei stood behind her and said, "We're going to talk *right here* until you join us."

"I am working, I hope to help, I can't just…"

Mei held up a hand. "No. *This* is work. You must tell Erin about Vesturdahlur. And if you do it over some food and a cup of tea, so much the better."

Juanita surrendered. "Very well." She stepped away from the book and followed them over to the dining hall.

They settled at a table in the corner, Erin with her hands curled around her cup of sisuree. Mei poured hot water over the dried leaves in her cup. The smell of green tea filled the air, reminding Erin momentarily of her own world.

For a minute or two, Juanita spooned soup into her mouth so quickly she left no time to speak. She took a bite of bread and dried pork and wiped her mouth with her napkin. "You were right," she said. "I needed to eat."

"Did you know joining the expedition was going to be a problem?" Mei said.

Juanita shrugged. "I'm a scholar, I don't pay much attention to politics, but I knew it might. I assumed people from Pais Lewelyn would be here. I just didn't think one was in charge."

"What's the big deal?"

"Pais Lewelyn encroaches on our ocean border all the time. They hide their spies on their fishing boats. We've warned them off again and again, but they keep trying it."

"Or maybe they're just fishing boats," Erin said.

Juanita said, "You are naïve, Señorita."

Mei said, "You could have headed home. You didn't have to come."

She nodded. "The Capitan wanted to. He was angry when the Presidenta told him to stay and assist. I thought the scholars at least would be fair, and Profesora—"

"Profesor," Mei said. "Trust me."

"…Profesor Stillwater is. The Pais Lewelyn Maestra—Elmaestro tolerates me."

Mei nodded and didn't speak, letting Juanita finish the bowl of soup.

Erin felt despair seeping into her. This was the group they had to fight off the New Way, and they couldn't even get along with each other.

"Now might be a good time to tell your story to Erin," Mei said.

The Perlaraynan pushed away the bowl. "Very well," she said. Her gaze met Erin's. "Here is the story of Vesturdahlur, the west valley town, as it was told to me."

16

The sheriff sent three deputies, armed with crossbows and clubs, to the Silvestro hunting cabin. It was vacant, but a quartz and loomin charm disclosed the presence of recent blood. Oshane might have been there and fled. The steep mountains to the east of the cage complex were riddled with gaps, caves, and chasms. A person could find many places to shelter.

Aideen read Justice Arm Lodros's final report on the bones. Aside from the broken fingers, there were no marks on the bones, no scratches where a knife or an arrow might have pierced flesh. The tongue-bone, a bone at the back of the throat, was not broken, as it might have been if Serafina had been strangled. Lodros was left with the possibility of natural causes, which the jefa's disappearance and burial argued against, and suffocation or poison. And no idea of who might have done those things.

Aideen had hesitated to write to Trevian of this thing but there was no reason to wait any longer. They had whatever answers they could glean, and they both knew who had killed their mother.

She reached for paper and pen.

On Veyernes, she rode up to the cages. With the short staffing, she wanted to make sure they weren't falling behind or taking dangerous shortcuts. Lopez looked greeted her politely, but his jaw was clenched.

They were keeping current, he said. "The new worker Jefe Silvestro hired is eager to learn, although he has no interest in being a cord-stringer."

"The *Jefe* hired someone? Who?"

"A man he interviewed, to replace Yor Sykes. I assumed the partners agreed."

Aideen said slowly, "He is a partner. He has the right to hire, although we all prefer it be left to you."

His jaw relaxed. "Well, thank you for that, yorita."

"What experience does he have?" No one else did what they did, but Lopez had good luck hiring mine workers and people who had prospected where they might have encountered elementals.

"He says he's worked in mines in Sheeplands and Pais Lewelyn, although I hear none of that country in his speech, and on a road crew." Lopez's skepticism rode his words.

"Is he good?"

"Eager to learn, especially the flames and the cages, not so much cord-stringing, which is what we hired him for. He's rough but shows up on time and gives a day's work. We'll help him fit in."

Where had Jefe Silvestro found him? Silvestro was angry and feeling pushed out by the changes. This was only his way of showing he could still take charge. Still, to hire a man without even asking what Yor Lopez needed... She sighed before she could stop herself.

"No other vacancies," said Lopez. Unspoken, *no other deaths.*

"Good."

She took her leave, riding to the office to meet with Armando, who had a pitcher of sisuree waiting in his office. He poured her a cup, and one for himself. "What is it you wish to discuss?"

"Your charm kept steel drills from melting when they draw close to a flame colony. Can a similar charm be made for copper?"

"I suppose it's possible there could be a hardening charm for copper," Armando said, "but I don't know of one."

"Could you design one?"

He smiled. "Like Jefe Silvestro, I am no charmcaster. I purchased the charm, a year or two before I met your father, when I had thoughts of becoming an engineer."

"Could we commission one?"

"This is an odd question, Aideen. Are you concerned about the copper on the cages?"

"No. There are rifts in the tunnel through to Merry Lake. Not the canal tunnel, the one farther east. It holds a large colony."

"Is there no room for cages?"

"I would like to…" She sipped sisuree to give herself time to think. "I wonder if there is a way to draw the radiance without trapping the creatures in cages. It would be less dangerous."

He looked at her without speaking, his brow corrugated.

She said, "It would be safer for our workers, and less distressful for the flames, if they were not drawn away from their colony. Don't you think?"

"They don't experience distress, unless we hold them too long."

"How do we know that?"

"Well." He set down his cup and folded his hands in his lap. "They don't behave as if they are distressed."

"When the delay happened earlier this year, we held a mature flame until it nearly expired. They are communal creatures, yet we draw them apart. Even Father sought a solution, by bringing in a joven sibling group." She needed to bring his attention back to the workers. "And less dangerous work, no transfers to and from cages."

"But our most skilled workers are those who work with the flames. What do you see them doing, if not enticing flames into the cages?"

Here was territory she had hardly mapped, even in her own mind. She spoke slowly, waiting for her thoughts to transmute into words. "I think there is much more we could do with the energy of the flames, and there would be important jobs without daily elemental contact. I believe this energy source is a whole room, or even a house, and we have scraped at the glass of one window only."

The room seemed much too quiet when she finished. Armando looked at her, and she could not read his expression.

He reached for his cup and sipped. "You sound the way Don Oswald used to, after a few shots of lick," he said. He stared past her, and a smile flitted across his face. "I wish you expressed this idea to him. I would have loved to see what the two of you would have done with it." He blinked, put the cup down, and straightened up in his chair. "So, you are thinking we could find ways to harvest the energy differently."

She nodded. "I picture…" For a moment she floundered, not sure exactly what it was she pictured. "A waterwheel instead of a canal," she said finally. "Skimming, or siphoning energy from the rushing surface, without redirecting the flow."

He nodded. "You imagine copper cords lowered close to the colony, drawing up the excess radiance."

"Yes."

"What if you encased the cord in charmed quartz?"

"I don't...I don't understand. They're in charmed leather now, but the leather just burns."

He made two circles with his thumbs and forefingers, and set one behind the other, looking through them at her. "What if you charmed a quartz conduit to keep the copper from melting?"

"But then, would it draw the radiance? Wouldn't it still melt?"

"Perhaps we could enhance the existing charm with the protective quartz, enough so the lengths closest to the colony would stay intact." He chewed on his lower lip. "Or perhaps the final length could be steel."

"Steel? It doesn't draw radiance."

"It does, though a far smaller percentage than copper does. But Aideen —" he leaned forward now, and his eyes were wide. "Even if it is a smaller percentage, we're drawing from a vaster quantity. Do you see where I lead?"

One uno for every ten, Aideen thought. "I do."

"So, if this colony is vast, even though steel draws less per length, if we had more conduits..."

"If steel draws a fifth as much as copper, then we would need five conduits," she said.

"Well, no. There is a loss of energy along any line, even the copper mesh. It would be closer to eight for every one..." The light died out of his eyes, and he slumped back into his chair. "It's a fascinating exercise," he said. "I am not the one to help you, though."

"Why won't you? This helps the company, and you are a partner."

He shook his head. His expression was one of regret. "I am sorry."

She wished Ilsanja, the master bargainer, were here. Was this a tactic? The regret seemed real, but she could not forget how many times she had seen Yor Montez play a role, the simple man, the affable, curious questioner.

"Would you be the one to help me for a greater share of the Company?" she said. "Four shares would bring yours to twenty-three and you would no longer be the minority partner."

To her surprise, he laughed. "Oh, Yorita Aideen, no." He stood, walking to the window. After a moment or two he said, "And why do you not bring it before all the partners?"

146

"I've talked to Ilsanja, and now to you. We are on the edges of a crisis, and I don't want our attention deflected. From this crisis, though, we may find a better way to do things."

He swung around, resting his back against the glass. "Give me a day or two to think about this."

It was the best she would get, she thought. She rose. Another rock in her path. "Of course, Yor Montez. Thank you for your time."

"Please call me Armando. I hope I am still your friend."

She smiled. "Of course." Was he? She hoped it was true.

17

J uanita told the story like a storyteller, a skald.

The town of Vesturdahlur, on the ancient island nation of Iceland, was small. Many of its people rode to jobs in the capital each day, in their vehicles that moved by themselves, but others took up the old skills of the nation: carding, spinning, and weaving wool; carving rostungur tusks; and writing down the sagas of the ancestors. There were no true rostungur tusks to be carved, but they found a nut from a distant land having the same color, smoothness, and weight, and sent for them by the hundreds. They carved the sinuous winged serpents of their ancestors, the dreki, seals, whales, and human figures from the Age of Viking. They shared word of this and soon visitors from all over the world flew to Iceland and rode in caravans to Vesturdahlur, to see the crafts and hear the sagas of the ancestors.

It was a morning in midsummer. The short night before, Northurlios had rippled across the sky in shades of green, purple, and gold. The gray fog of morning melted, and a blue sky greeted them. Many worked in the capital, and others set out about their daily chores.

All agreed, later, they felt and saw the same things.

The world turned to black, and every person, for a space of time—none knew how long—saw down to the tiniest speck of creation and out to the end of the stars. And then it seemed all was as it had been, except their devices for speaking to one another no longer worked. Lights no longer responded to their voices or their touch. People gathered between their houses and in their gardens, raising their voices, shouting, or whispering, questions. They looked at the sky and saw it had changed color.

People fled to their churches. Others met at the town center. And then, because they had begun to look, they saw their mountains were gone.

The mountains could not be gone, but they were, and the sky could not turn green, but it had. The dwellers in Vesturdahlur were used to a gray sky, one cloaked with ash from the eldfiall, the fire-mountains, but not a sky the green of a new leaf, not a valley with its ring of mountains gone.

Their devices and their radios brought them nothing.

And later they commented on how the air felt warmer, moister than they were used to.

In a store for hunting goods, they found horns to amplify speech, and they divided the town into sections, calling out to people to join them in the town center, to discuss what should happen next. They made a plan for dealing with the sick who stayed in a healing center in the town. A mile of so outside of the town, in a land nothing like theirs, they found fresh water, and arranged for it to be carried back to central locations. And after several days, they sent a group southwest, to reach the main road and seek out answers to what catastrophe had overtaken them.

The group took two vehicles. They drove along the valley road, which ended with no warning in a tangle of lush green growth that never had existed in their valley. The wheels of their carts sank in the soft earth. After a discussion, they returned to the village to gather cutting tools, and six set out again.

While the six were gone, the village found ways to forage and hunt for food. They moved the sheep from two ranches closer to town. They would not starve, and they would not die of thirst, but they did not know where they were, or their loved ones were.

After a month and a day, the six returned with six others, with brown skin, brown hair, who spoke a language only a few of the townspeople recognized.

They were not in a place called Iceland. They were in a valley, but it was a jungle valley five thousand miles to the south of their home, on a continent called the Americas. And they were a world away from everyone they knew and loved.

"Okay. Wow." Erin's sisuree was cold.

"The story was written down in two languages, but not the one spoken in the country where they...landed," Juanita said. "One is close to what you speak here, which we learned for trade reasons. The other is the tongue of Vesturdahlur.

The tale been passed down through generations. My father was a skald, the son and grandson of skalds, so he learned it along with many, many others, which speak of things I do not understand."

"This one, though," Mei said.

"Yes. This one. I believe this story describes the Cataclismo, even though I do not know what it means."

"That's a huge chunk of real estate to relocate..." Erin thought about the sky. "... to another reality completely."

"How could that happen?" Mei said.

"I don't know. The stone, the puertas, they move medium-sized objects. I mean, I sent a baby earth elemental...somewhere. Presumably, once you opened a frontera, you could bring other things through, freight, vehicles."

"Land? Buildings?"

"No, I mean, not practically." She thought for a minute. "The New Way call this world Collision."

"I don't understand what that means." Juanita pushed the final scrap of bread around her plate.

"I think I'm starting to. There are mountain ranges are the wrong kind of stone. Or they're...younger they should be. And the accounts I read, they talked about mountains growing out of the ground in days, or weeks." Erin shoved back her chair. "Mei, I want to get back to Lewiston's notebook."

Telma Lewiston's writing only took about eleven pages of the book. After a few minutes of discussion, Mei backed away, literally, with her hands raised. "Even with the magnifying thing I can't figure it out," she said. "I'm going to look at the metal book instead."

"Okay." Erin thought she was doing better with the horrible hand-writing.

Lewiston had started journaling after whatever had gone bad, and she'd hidden the journal from somebody, the military or something like it. She called them the Defense Agency, which was another change from what Erin was used to. And they weren't the good guys.

It was hard to tell who *were* the good guys, though.

(III) Dear Dare—I hope you and Mama are all right. I'm going to write this like it's a letter and pretend you'll see it someday.

The III marking the start of the passage, that must be the third day. Erin didn't know who Dare was, a partner? A sibling? The ending made it seem like they were a spouse or partner. She skimmed the next few pages. Lewiston's tick-marks changed to a mashup of Roman numerals and hash marks.

There were two passages marked VII. The first was directed to Dare like the others were, and she slowed down, hoping for information. There wasn't much. The second had been written later, maybe.

(VII) I thought Richard was probably dead, but they let me see him finally. And they left us alone, which isn't a good sign. It means they know we can't do anything. (It ran off the page) said he had a head injury, but he said no, he'd been trapped in a space when the ceiling came down in the Chapel. Broken ribs, he said, no head injury.

R was in the Chapel for all three experiments. Three, there were three, not two. The first time, he said, one of those things came through, just like at Ap-One. All the Non-Incursion Protocols were observed, and the thing pulverized six hours later. But Lichtstrom ordered the rift penetrated again, a couple days later. I was off-shift so I didn't know this. R says three of those banana-slug things came through this time, and they were different colors and designs. They were almost pretty, he said. Lichtstrom observed the no-touch protocol but put them in a specimen case and kept them in the Chapel. I'm pretty sure if I could go back through the Pit data I could pinpoint exactly when that second penetration took place. R swears when he was called back in the third time, he looked over at the shelf and there were only two of those banana slugs. He could be wrong, or confused, but I don't think so. Maybe one pulverized. Or maybe not.

When Lichtstrom started the protocols, he got upset and started yelling at one of the techs the settings were wrong. The tech just said, "This is the way, this is the way," and nothing else. Two other techs pulled them away from their station and

Lichtstrom was frantically typing in coordinates. The rift opened. R felt like he was a hundred places at once and then the roof fell in.

R didn't feel like I did, stretched to the length of the universe (by the Mother that sounds cheesy). He was in a hundred/thousand places all at once, offices, houses, cars, lakes, ocean bottoms, mountains, desert, forests, hospitals. It was like a thousand transparencies overlaying each other. And then he was in the dark, boulders all around him.

I think maybe the jumbled coordinates created a larger rift, and there was an incursion of another dimension. A big one. And I just read back through this and there's a lot of stuff I haven't explained yet.

The story Juanita's ancestors told, their valley vanishing from one world in a blink, and appearing in another. Mountains and lakes... Oh yeah. The Eager Beavers of Orchard Hill had done something catastrophic.

Mei cleared her throat. "I've found something," she said.

"So have I." Erin joined Mei at the other table. "What do you have?"

Mei pointed to a series of figures on the left-hand page. "That's the compass, and I think this is the lantern."

"It is. And those are...people?...standing around it." Erin remembered people wearing Oshane's metal helmets, but these stick figures didn't wear helmets or any kind of tether to the lantern. Each one had an O for a mouth, as if they were speaking.

"The compass." Mei pointed to the left of the circle and the lantern, where another figure held aloft a disk.

"Those are...lightning bolts?"

"Electromagnetic waves, I think."

Erin looked at the page on the right. An ellipse, in three stages, growing smaller. "A frontera? Closing?"

"I guess. We need the lantern."

"Maybe not, though. Trevian closed one by himself. Maybe we can do it with just the compass. Maybe they didn't know that back then."

"I still think the Agustos should be here, and the lantern. You know what that means."

"I'll have to go home."

Mei said, "It could be good. You could pick up a bunch of supplies." She stared at the image a bit longer. "What did you find?"

"They did open a frontera to the New Way homeworld here, three hundred years ago. And they precipitated some kind of violent merge with another reality. I think that might be when the elementals awoke here."

"Huh." Mei still looked at the metal book. It was like she hadn't fully taken in what Erin said. "I'll start you a shopping list," she said.

ideen sent off her note to Trevian with a private messenger. Perhaps he would at least come, and they could burn their mother's bones together.

The next two days she spent with Paloma Quinn, reviewing payroll and the accounts. As they sat down to dinner on Sabado, she and Ilsanja were interrupted with a message from the night manager at the cages. Another worker was missing.

Because of the death of Sykes, Threedeer Potter had also notified the sheriff. When she and Ilsanja arrived at the cages, sprite lamps bumping against their caballos' withers, a deputy appeared behind them.

Potter met them at the entrance to the cave. Lopez was with him. "Melya Ousten didn't arrive for her shift, and she is never late," Potter said. "I sent someone to her house. They live in town. She left at the usual hour."

"Is she a cord-stringer, like the man who fell?" The deputy spoke before Aideen could ask.

"No, Melya transfers the flames. She's one of our best."

"Is there trouble in her house? Too much lick? A heart yearning for someone else? A sick child needing a healer?"

Potter had started shaking his head at the start of the list and never stopped. "Her husband is out now, with our people, searching the trail. Their children are healthy. Melya will receive a bonus this quarter, and she knew it. There were no problems except for a day worker who waited behind and bothered her earlier this week, and it was easily taken care of."

"What was this?" Lopez said.

"I had it on my list to talk to you about. On Weyves, the new cord-stringer approached her before her shift started. He'd waited for her. He had many questions about the flames. We give trainers a stipend, but he acted as if her knowledge should be his for free. She told him so and walked away. He followed her until her shift-mates set him straight."

"I wasn't told," Lopez said.

Potter shrugged. "She said she'd taken care of it, and then he didn't come back on Veyernes, you said, so I thought the matter finished."

Aideen said, "What is this?"

Lopez turned with a hint of exasperation. "That one I told you of, the one Jefe Silvestro brought on. He has not returned to work for two days. I thought nothing of it since he had no interest in cord-stringing. People do move on."

"Have you looked for him?" the deputy said.

"I sent his final few coins to the address he gave us, a guesthouse on the edge of the southern green."

"And his name?"

"Garth. Garth something."

Ilsanja inhaled a gasp, as Aideen felt her gut contract.

She spoke, hoping her voice didn't shake. "Garth? And his family name?"

"It flees me—ah. Green. Garth Green."

"Father brought him on?" Like Aideen, Ilsanja didn't quite have control of her voice.

"You said he was rough," Aideen said, thinking back now, hating the conclusion she was driving towards.

"Yes, rough mannered, with scars on his neck and hands, but workers do collect scars and...Jefe Silvestro hired him."

"Garth...not *so* rare a name," Ilsanja murmured. She was shivering.

"Not so common. And 'Green,' for a man renting a room on the southern green."

The deputy said, "You two know of this man."

Ilsanja drew in her shoulders and said nothing. Aideen addressed the deputy. "One of the mestengos who abducted us in early spring was called Garth."

"Can you describe him?"

Ilsanja regained some control of herself. "We never saw his face."

"We might recognize his voice."

"You are reacting to the name, then." The deputy's words were skeptical, but her expression was not. "As you said, it is not *so* common. I think we will go to this guesthouse, for a start. And I will send others up to aid in the search. Perhaps Yora Ousten has fallen, or been struck by a fever, and will be quickly found and brought to safety."

"Let us hope," Potter said.

"Is there anything you need of us, Yor Potter?" Ilsanja said.

"No. I thank you both for coming up here so late. I only wanted to be sure the partners knew."

"Our thanks," Aideen said. She and Ilsanja returned to their mounts.

"Did my father hire the mestengo who held us captive?" Ilsanja said.

"Not knowingly," Aideen soothed. Or tried to. Ilsanja was not the only one who was shaking.

The deputy's mount trotted up next to them. "If you do not mind, I will accompany you to your house."

"Do you think we are in danger?" Ilsanja said.

"I doubt it, truly, Jefa," the deputy said, "but I wouldn't want to wager on that doubt."

Aideen said, "We are grateful."

They rode home in silence. Aideen led Ilsanja into the kitchen. She saw no need to rouse Dolores or Susannah, but while she was heating the water for sisuree, Dolores joined them. "I was reading, yorita, not sleeping," she said. "How can I help?"

"We've had bad news, and a fright," Aideen said, taking down a third cup. She poured a generous slug of the sweet lick Valentin had brought into each cup, and dumped in the dried berries, while Ilsanja filled in Dolores on the night's events.

"Would a mestengo be so bold?"

"Garth was the bold one," Aideen said, "and the true leader. Vallis had no strength. He led them only with his false promise of wealth. But if this Garth is the mestengo, I don't think he is acting alone." She handed a steaming cup to Ilsanja and one to Dolores.

The three of them sat down at the table. "Sykes is killed in a fall," Aideen said, sipping the comforting, aromatic drink. "And almost as if by charm, Don Leo meets a man to fill in the position, after we've been warned the parasites want access to our operation."

"It is like a Madlyn ardiya trap," Dolores said.

"A what?" Ilsanja cocked her head.

Dolores carved at the air with her hands as she described the trap. In Madlyn, people wove nets of a vine so tough and resinous even a thieving ardiya's sharp teeth could not gnaw through one easily. "The nets, are long, wide at the mouth, growing narrower. The hunters hook the mouth over the branches of a shrub or bush, and put fruit, grain, or nuts at the narrowest part of the net. Then they wait. An ardiya scents the bait and enters the mouth of the net, sniffing, sniffing. The net grows narrower and tighter but the greedy animal pushes forward until it reaches a point where it cannot move backward and cannot turn around. It is caught, and then it is supper."

"There is a net of events, drawing tighter around us, and we can't see the trap. Is that what you are saying?" Ilsanja gulped the doctored sisuree.

"Well, you are not ardiyas. You have seen the net."

"And we know the weaver. We simply cannot find him," Aideen said.

"You believe Oshane is directing Garth," Ilsanja said. "And eliminating workers from the cages."

The three women were silent.

Ilsanja drank a long draft from the cup, swallowed, and said, "If we were ardiya, we would still have the space to turn around. But the cages cannot reverse themselves. If we moved the apparatus, where would we move it to? We must be near the rifts. There is nothing we can do."

"We can increase security. We could redirect our workers to search for Oshane, although I don't how we would keep them safe doing it. Surely the moonstone charms would help?"

Her empty cup forgotten, Ilsanja began counting on her fingers. "Oshane has an air elemental. We can repel it by moonstone and plata. He has a ruthless mestengo, at least one, in partnership with him. He is in hiding and we cannot find him, and probably he has helpers spreading rumors about prospectors, which might mean he plans to launch an attack on the delegation at Merrylake Landing. And he is an agent of the parasites."

"On the other hand, he is wounded." It didn't sound like much when Aideen said it out loud. "And he is being hunted."

"Sought, but not found."

"Surely the Crescent Justice Arms still pursue him," Dolores said.

"Yes. We could write to the Council and ask for more justice arms to aid in the search."

"Tomorrow," Ilsanja said, reaching across the table for Aideen's hand.

"Tomorrow after breakfast we go to the sheriff, ask her to write the Justice Arm. And we schedule another meeting." Her eyes narrowed; a look Aideen hoped was never directed at her. "And if my father decides not to attend, it will be fine with me."

T he sheriff agreed to write to the Council Justice Arm. "We have been to the guesthouse," she said. "A man calling himself Green stayed there one night and returned yesterday to pick up a pouch of coin from his work, they said. He gave no idea where he was going, but at least we have a description."

Frustrated, Aideen paced her study, trying to think. No blinding lights of inspiration filled her mind, though.

Dolores tapped on the doorframe. "A visitor, yorita. Valentin Agafonov."

"Valentin? Why?"

"He didn't say."

She had him shown into the sala and hurried to join him there. "Ilsanja is checking on her trail caballos," she said. "If you wish to wait, we will have refreshments..."

He shook his head. "No, yorita, it is you I wish to speak with, at Don Armando's suggestion."

"Oh?" Something just below Aideen's ribcage tingled. Valentin, a charmcaster who worked with quartz, had been sent here by Armando. "Please, tell me what it is you wish to share."

"The charm you use to reinforce your quartz cages, so they don't fracture under the heat of a fire elemental, came from Shevastin." He drew a folded piece of paper from his jacket pocket. "Don Armando spoke to me about a project you are considering, where the heat resistance would have to be even greater. This is, I will admit, an experimental charm, but have one of your charmcasters try it. It is from the same blood-clan your charm came from, I believe."

"Really? Thank you. Is there something we can do for you?"

Valentin smiled. "Let me know the results. We will be doing each other a favor, yorita. It would benefit me greatly if I knew the charm worked."

There was only one reason Aideen knew of to have quartz reinforced against heat. She was aiding a competitor. Ilsanja would have plenty to say about it, she was sure. But weren't Valentin and Lucia going to Pais

Lewelyn? And they'd need charmed copper as well. She certainly wasn't going to release *that* spell into Valentin's hands.

"I will be happy to give you an update," she said. "I'm most grateful. Is there a place I can write to you?"

"Let Don Armando know."

"Very well. I don't know how much use the quartz will be, if we can't get the copper close enough."

"He recommended steel?"

She nodded, and Valentin mirrored the gesture.

"I'm not an expert with metals, but most metals will hold a charm to some degree. Gold, copper, and loomin are the strongest. I believe both the white metal with the odd name…"

"Zinc?"

"Yes. Zinc and lead are truly inert. But even plata, which we thought had little use with charms," he cast a pointed look at the moonstone charm across the window, "when combined with certain other elements, seems to hold charmed energy. A few inches of steel, closest to the source of radiance, would direct energy up into the copper, I think." He frowned. "Copper fights with most metals."

She nodded. "We'd be replacing steel tips," she said. They would have to budget for it. She smiled at him, a little more secure now. "And in this, also, you would like to know the results?"

Valentin looked solemn. "It would be most generous of you," he said.

J efe Silvestro came to the partners meeting, but his flushed face and thinned lips made his feelings about it clear. Ilsanja waited for him to sit down and addressed them without greeting him, explaining the loss of Yora Ousten so soon after the death of Yor Sykes, and the disappearance of a newly hired man Garth Green. Jefe Silvestro stiffened.

"This man may have been a mestengo," Ilsanja said, her voice as clear and sharp as the edge of freshly honed blade. "And it is possible he was probing for weaknesses in our syst—"

"What nonsense are you speaking?"

"It is conjecture," Ilsanja said. The words might sound conciliatory, but nothing in her voice or posture gave an inch. "He was untrained, leaving his work to ask many questions about the flames, even waiting past his shift to waylay Yora Ousten."

"He was ambitious! Do you fault that?"

"Then where is he?" Aideen asked, keeping her voice as neutral as he could.

"He waylaid Melya, and now they are both gone," Ilsanja said. "This is disturbing. He was hired without consultation with Yor Lopez, which, I understand, is how it has always been done—"

Silvestro slapped the flat of his hand on the table, a gesture Aideen remembered. "You *understand*!" he shouted. "You are excitable girls, flushed with power, and you understand *nothing*."

"How did you know of him, Don Leo?" Armando asked. His "simple man" mask was firmly in place, but Silvestro glared at him. "Who recommended him to you?"

"I don't need recommendations, Montez. My judgment is excellent! He had experience in road building, and he was not hired to work with flames but to string copper cord. And now a run of bad luck and a few accidents has sent you all into a panic."

"Father. The raiding of our copper caravans was not bad luck. The destruction of your fabrickers' quartz last year, not bad luck. Not an accident. The attack on Don Oswald, the appearance of Oshane Langtree, the poisoned words Yor Oakley offered you, these things are not 'a run of bad luck.' The Company is being attacked."

He glared around the room, his face growing so red Aideen feared for his health, until his gaze stopped with her. He pointed. "Then why is *she* here? She is a Langtree! How do we know she is not in league with her uncle? I know she resented her father."

Armando said, "Oshane set his air elemental upon her and she nearly died."

"So *she* says."

"So I saw," Ilsanja said, and now her voice trembled slightly. "And so Justice Arm Harald Stuart saw. Do you doubt both of us?"

"I acted as a partner would," Silvestro said. "I filled a vacant position. I saw a problem and took steps to fix it, instead of gathering together for endless talking."

"And how did he come to you, again?" Armando said, as if the question had been answered and he had merely forgotten.

"He approached me on the south green when I was leaving a friend's gaming hall." For the first time, Silvestro seemed uncertain. "It was not so unusual. The whole town knew Sykes had died in a fall."

Armando nodded. "True."

Aideen said, "The loss of Yora Ousten is serious. We have more moon-stone charms to ward against the elemental, but I think we should make some arrangements to protect the workers as they come and go off shift."

"An unneeded expense," Silvestro said.

She kept her face expressionless as she said, "We do need it. We must keep our workers as safe as we can."

"Shall we pay for guards at their homes, then? Night and day?"

Armando said, "I pray it won't come to that, but perhaps we should have Yora Quinn draw up a budget for such an expense."

Silvestro gasped as if he'd been punched. "Are you joking?"

"I am not," Armando said. "Things are serious, Jefe. We are trying to prepare."

Ilsanja said quietly, "Will you not help us? One of our workers is dead and another might well be."

In the momentary silence, Aideen saw her future. Every meeting would be like this, every topic, every decision, a fight, while Jefe Silvestro clung to his pride, even if it left his company in tatters. Long ago, or so it seemed now, when her father had plunged from his window, Paloma Quinn had told her she often heard shouting between Don Oswald and Jefe Silvestro, and this was why.

There would be no peace in her life.

"Perhaps I can rein to a stop the worst of your fancies," he said finally, crossing his arms.

Ilsanja had said nothing about Garth being one of the men who had held them captive. There was no reason to, and no proof. But if the time to say so ever, came, then what would Silvestro do?

She cleared her throat and turned to Armando. "Perhaps a covered van for the workers? With moonstones charms on the roof?"

19

Erin felt like she faced a tribunal. She'd brought Lewiston's journal, clutched to her chest like a talisman. Harald, Ruth, and Melendres all stared back at her. She wasn't sure even Harald was on her side at this point.

Mei refused to join her. "They don't listen to me," she said. "You do better with them."

"The notebook confirms this is the place where a frontera opened for the New Way?" Melendres said.

"Yes."

Melendres raised her eyebrows. "How would the New Way know of it, if the place collapsed?"

"Because they were here. One of the nodes was active when whatever happened...happened. Two realities collided."

"Why didn't they come straight here from Madalita, when that frontera opened?"

Erin tried not to sigh too obviously. "Because they didn't know where Orchard Hill was."

"You said they were here, and what one knows they all know," Melendres said. "The hive mind would have known of this place, then."

"It moved."

"*This* place moved? Unlikely."

"Look at Ruth's books. Read the accounts. The earth turning, mountains springing up, lakes disappearing. This place moved. Lewiston writes about it."

"If this happened, and lands shifted, what caused it?"

"Something went wrong when the scientists opened the frontera. The coordinates changed, and I think...two realities merged. Violently."

"This...clash of worlds, wouldn't it have been over in an instant? It didn't take you days to dance across your frontera and come here," Melendres said.

"The scientists called it an ongoing global event. It was a lot longer than an instant."

Melendres relaxed into her chair. "If this is true, and I know *you* believe it, yorita, it is even more reason to destroy the machines here. The New Way had time to poison them, by your own account."

"We're not asking to awaken any of the compu—the machines in the laboratory or the Server Room, or anywhere the New Way might have infected. But the radios are different. I don't think they can even be infected."

"You surmise."

"Based on my experience with similar devices." It was a stretch, but she didn't blink. "If the radios work, Mei can find the frequency that blocks the New Way. We shut down the frontera and we block all their communications at once. We can stop them."

Harald said, "With no allies and no frontera, they would not have a foothold."

Melendres steepled her fingers. "I do not like your friend's alliance with those from Perlarayna," she said. She tipped a sideways glance at Harald. "The Perlaraynans should not be part of this mission. You do not know them as we do. There are those who have helped the New Way without being infected, and Perlarayna may be a nation doing just that. I say this again and again, but my words are not heard."

Erin understood *that* feeling. "I understand they aren't good neighbors," she said.

Ruth spoke for the first time. She didn't look at Erin. "Yorita Gunnarsdottir has been of great value. She has provided much information."

"They boast of how far beyond us they are with their inventions and their culture," Melendres said. "Perhaps they see themselves closer to the New Way than to the primitives around them."

Harald said, "I see one compelling reason why they would not join the New Way. The nodes."

"Why not?"

"They fear infection. Elmaestro, do you believe they would allow an object to attach itself to their flesh?"

"Perhaps New Way has lied to them, promised them an amnesty," Melendres said, shifting in her chair. A moment later she said, "Not likely either, is it?"

"Not likely," Ruth said.

Melendres sat, thinking. "If it were my choice, I would destroy this place," she said.

"No," said Ruth.

Erin said, "We don't know if destroying a cavern or a building closes the frontera."

"Does it matter if it lies beneath a mile of rock and rubble?"

Harald cleared his throat. "Noemi, the New Way expends humans like unos at a carnival. If they found a frontera beneath a mile of rock, would they not force their hosts to excavate it?"

"This is conjecture. All conjecture."

"Sure," said Erin. "But we have a workable plan your artifacts support. We have experience with this technology. Mei's frontera opened in Perlarayna instead of Pais Lewelyn. Is that really enough reason to distrust her?"

Melendres scrubbed her forehead with both hands. "What do you wish, yorita? Just tell me."

"We need to get into the supply depot. Trevian thinks we can do it safely with lines and tethers."

"We've used the technique successfully before," Ruth said.

"And we need to get into the room called the Chapel. I think it's next to the cage room."

"Absolutely not."

Ruth said, "The room is unsafe, it's nothing but rubble."

"It's where the frontera probably is."

Melendres shook her head. "We cannot keep you safe there."

"At least let us in as far as you've gone in. Elmaestro, you're going to have to."

"And you want boxes from the radio room," she said.

Erin nodded.

"I agree to the supply depot, with precautions. And *one* box from the Radio Room. We will discuss the rubble room, and how it may be done safely." Melendres stared at Erin, not quite a glare, but almost. "Let

Capitan Espinosa know his demeanor will be a factor in every decision I make."

———

"Can you talk to Espinosa about being less arrogant?" Erin said.
Mei bit her lower lip. "I don't know if that's possible. It's just how he is."

"You're getting what we need," Erin said.

"Everything is a struggle. Nothing works here. The only things I know how to do, they won't let me do," Mei said.

"They're letting you—"

"*Letting!*" Mei whirled around and shoved open the door, disappearing out into the darkness. Erin rubbed her forehead and realized she was making almost the same gesture Melendres had.

She drifted around the room, knowing concentration was impossible, and after fifteen minutes she went outside. The camp was quiet, and Mei's silhouette blocked the glow of a whiterock fire. Erin walked over and sat down nearby.

After a minute, Mei said, "You know what I really miss? Tacos."

"Really?"

"There was this hole-in-the-wall place in Tainan specializing in tacos. They made these fried tomato and pickled onion ones. Any time we went into Tainan, we'd go there, Mama and me."

Erin felt the tang of pickled onions against her tastebuds, and saliva filled her mouth. "Those sound amazing." Erin shifted a bit, got more comfortable. "I miss coffee, I think, the idea of coffee, anyway."

"Lattes," Mei said. "They were a treat. A latte with a shortbread cookie."

"I wake up dreaming I can taste things I didn't even like much, like barbeque-flavored potato chips."

"I never had those." Mei scuffed the dirt with the toe of her shoe.

"Bacon, I guess. I miss bacon."

Mei wrinkled her nose. "I'm sorry, Erin, but American bacon is weird. Why char a piece of meat until it's like a stick? Pork belly, now..."

"I concede. Pork belly."

After a moment, Mei said, "Chthonic."

"What?"

"A metal band. My grandfather listened to them."

"Your grandfather listened to metal?"

"They sang in Taiwanese. I'd listen with him."

"You'd listen to metal music with your grandfather? While you were building radios?"

"Yes, with Grandfather and Uncle Chen-Jui. And computers, later."

Erin said, "Your life is way more interesting than mine."

They were both quiet for few minutes.

Mei said, "If the New Way takes over this world, ours will be next."

"I think that's the New Way's plan," Erin said. "Wouldn't it be harder, though? I mean, I know they're wireless, basically, but don't we have security and encryption?"

"For this? I don't want to risk finding out." Mei drew lines in the dirt. "All I want to go home and have it be safe. I hate having to fight for every simple little thing. What if...what if things aren't all right back home?"

"Why don't you go back instead of me? You know what you need."

"With a Taiwanese passport and Taiwanese money? Not a good idea. It's your frontera."

"I don't think that matters anymore," Erin said.

Mei shook her head. "It's got to be you."

They sat. Erin tried to think of another neutral topic and settled for an old question. "Who's the figure on your backpack?"

"Detective K," Mei said, "From *Death Note*. The manga, not the anime."

"Uh, okay?"

"The comic book."

Books. Stories she'd maybe never know the ending of. Movies. Concerts she'd never hear. She hadn't thought so much about it, focused on the losses. Mei had things to go back for, but so did she.

"From the hair clip, I expected Hello Kitty," she said.

Mei smiled. "I'm complicated."

Melendres held the meeting in the first room of the town hall. Chairs were arranged in a neat row, and a podium, not a chair, faced them from the front. Okay, Erin thought, as she sat down at one end, message received.

People filtered in. It wasn't a large group; Harald and Ruth representing the Crescent, Espinosa for Perlarayna, and Lauris Diebell for Madlyn. Two empty chairs. Mei had decided not to attend, and Erin had no idea where Trevian was. A moment later Juanita entered, looked at the row, and came to sit next to Erin.

Melendres walked out a moment later, wearing the purple vest of the Elmaestro position and a matching purple headband. Her gaze swept the chairs, noting the vacancies. "This will be brief. Many of you know the guardians wish to enter two rooms in Orchard Hill. We do not believe these rooms are safe but perhaps we can make them so. I have approved Yorita Erin and Yorita Mei to enter the space they call the supply depot. They will use harnesses and lines, and we will bring many assistants to hold those ropes."

Nods around the room.

"Yorita Mei wishes to enter the rubble room with the broken ceiling."

Ruth raised a hand. "That room is unsafe."

Erin said, "It's no bigger risk than most prospectors take every day." Where the hell was Trevian?

Melendres looked at her. "We are not prospectors. It's likely the frontera we seek to close is in the rubble room, though, so we will approach it, but with great caution."

She stood for a few seconds, staring out at them. "Our goal is to close the frontera. It may be best to leave the tracking of the parasites to Elmaestro Tregannon, once we are finished here."

Chairs creaked.

"That won't work," Erin said.

"With the frontera closed, they have no way to bring reinforcements."

"Until they open another frontera," Erin said.

Harald spoke, "You heard Holay yourself, Noemi. They fully plan to open another one somewhere."

Melendres shook her head. "The parasites may believe they can do that, Harald, but it rarely happens."

"Not so rarely," Juanita said. "We monitor frontera. New ones open regularly."

Melendres rolled her shoulders. "So we find them and close them. We have the charm now."

"A constant race, against eight hundred infected people?" said Harald. "A chancey plan."

"We have prevailed so far."

"Once," Erin said.

Harald said, "Eight hundred of them, and a hundred or so parasites waiting for hosts. If they fail once, twice, twenty times, they try again. If we fail once, they invade us. Did they not spend hundreds of years on their world searching for the frontera that opened in Madalita?"

Melendres's sigh was a gust. "Assuming I agree with this argument, once the frontera is closed, what do you suggest?"

Harald said, "We let Erin and Señorita Mei continue their experiment with this radio device."

"And if it brings the New Way right to us?"

"I do not think it will, Elmaestro, but if it does, we will fight."

"Profesor Stillwater?"

"I agree with the Justice Arm, Elmaestro."

Melendres said, "The Crescent has spoken. Capitan, what says Perlarayna?"

"We trust Señorita Mei, and Señorita Dosmanos."

"Lauris, what does Madlyn think?"

The charmcaster shook his head. "These are like the fever dreams my nephew has. Machines, rifts, worlds colliding. I agree the opening into the world of the New Way must be closed. It must be closed." He twisted his hands together. "They must be stopped."

Espinosa didn't keep the contempt from his voice. "Madlyn brings nothing of value to the discussion, then?"

Lauris didn't even look at Espinosa. He stared straight ahead, his folded hands clenched. He, more than anyone, seemed really upset—not angry, freaked out. Erin said, "Lauris may not know a lot about politics, but he was the guy with the moonstone chain when we needed one. Thanks again, by the way."

Espinosa flushed. Lauris said nothing.

"Very well. Tomorrow morning we will visit the supply depot and the rubble room," Melendres said. She strode out of the room like a politician dodging a final question at a press conference.

Ruth waited and approached Lauris as the others wandered out. "Does your nephew have river fever? I didn't know," she said.

"Yes, since he was four. A brave boy."

"There is medicine, you know."

"Not easy to come by where my brother lives," he said.

Ruth said, "I will include him in my prayers."

"Thank you, Profesor."

"I will speak to the capitan about how he treated you."

"He is not wrong, Profesor. I'm not wise politically, I'm a charmcaster."

Ruth sounded disapproving. "Farway should not have put these choices on you. It is no fault of yours."

Erin took two steps closer. "You saved my life, and Mei's, so I'm really glad you're here."

"Are you?" He looked strangely pathetic. "Thank you, yorita, but there is no need to defend me." He left the room.

Ruth stared after him. "No common medicine should be 'hard to come by,'" she said.

"I thought you were all about buying and selling. And trade, and stuff," Erin said.

"Of course we are, but who makes your goods, and who buys your goods, if everyone is sickly? The treatment for river fever cannot cure, but it reduces the pain and the fever. And it is not rare."

"Is he just confused, then?"

"What?" Ruth pulled her attention back to Erin. "Oh, no. He's not confused. Madlyn is different. Well, where do you go next?"

"To find Trevian and figure out why he wasn't at the meeting."

20

At noon, incoming messengers arrived, and the outgoing ones gathered. Trevian and Harald met them, along with two or three members of the group who had letters to send. Lauris Diebell had three; one to Councilmember Farway, one to an address in a town called Coyle Crossing and a third Trevian didn't see. "Your padrey?" Harald asked, with a slight smile. Lauris nodded. Trevian had a note to send to Aideen. Juanita Gunnarsdottir sent a large packet back to her Universidad, and Harald himself was sending an equally large packet to Elmaestro Tregannon.

He handed Trevian a packet from Aideen. "Where is Erin?"

"She and Yorita Mei are planning," Trevian said.

"Tempers seem to be fraying," Harald said. "And we had another handful of trouble-makers up from White Bluffs. The guards sent them on their way."

"Why?" Trevian said. "Why do they come here?"

"To drive us off. A rumor we spread the infestation," Harald said.

Aideen's letter wasn't only folded as usual but sealed. He picked at the wax. Harald was frowning at the papers in his hand.

"That man still writes to his padrey every three days," Harald said. He shrugged and turned to the two messengers who were ready to ride north. After he handed off the packets, he said, "Since you write to your sister, I told Lauris he could write to his nephew, as long as he was careful with what he shared."

"Do you still read our messages?"

Harald shook his head. "No, not after the first few days, although I choose one at random each day. I grew uncomfortable reading Yor Diebell's confessions to his padrey. He wastes a great deal of paper."

"He wears his writing case," Trevian said. "Letters are his lifeblood."

"Wears it?" Harald looked pensive for a moment. He squinted at the sun. "I have a meeting with Ruth. What are your plans, Trevian?"

"I meant to go up to the Pit again. There is nothing the guardians need me for."

"Take care around the Pit," Harald said.

Trevian made his way down to the mudflats. The lake was one-third the size it had been when he was a boy, but right now light sparkled on the water and brought back pleasant memories of Merrylake Landing. Walking slowly toward the trail up to the cave, he read Aideen's first few sentences.

The rumors, and anger against prospectors, increased in White Bluffs. Aideen relayed a story shared by Yor Montez's daughter Lucia, and an incident Susannah had in the market. Once again, Merrylake Landing was targeted as the source of the infestation.

The next paragraph made him stumble. The words jumped around on the page and he was sure he misunderstood them. He stood still and read slowly.

We found human bones in the tunnel east of the town, through the mountain, and a necklace with the bones, one belonging to our mother. It has a gold chain and the pink stone. The bones were intact, a complete skeleton, and the cause of death is unknown. I waited until all the evidence had been examined before I wrote to you. There are no marks on the bones; no crushing, no breaks except for two fingers. She did not fall; she was not struck.

Dolores and I are both sure Oshane did this. I do not know how or when justice will find our uncle, but I pray to the Mother that it is soon.

I wish to burn her bones, and I wish you to be with me when I do. Is this possible? Since you spoke of a visit, I hope it is.

Your loving sister,
Aideen

The world spun around him. He let his hand drop and stared away, across the dwindling lake. He knew the necklace she described. The last time he had seen his mother, she had worn it. As she leaned over to kiss him goodnight, the stone swung out, sparkling in the light of his sprite lamp. The next morning, she was gone.

All this time he imagined her happy, living the life she could not live while married to his father, when she had been moldering in a tunnel less than a league from her home. He had ridden past her, more than once, and so had Aideen.

The paper crackled in his hand; he'd crushed it.

Oshane? Was it not more likely to have been his father? But no. A broken neck, a battered skull, would have been his father's work. But Oshane... *In the darkness, a man screamed. Cosigan was dead. His chest was open and empty, the ribs cracked and blackened.* It wasn't so long ago Cosigan had been killed in the prospector's camp, his claim right next to Trevian's.

Oshane used elementals to kill, fire elementals he trapped and tormented into obedience, or the air elemental he kept tethered to him.

I do not know when or how justice will find our uncle...

Again and again, Oshane escaped.

I will bring justice to him, Trevian thought. He thrust the crumpled paper into his trousers pocket and stroke toward the trail, nearly at a run.

B eneath the steady rush of winds from the Pit, the not-quite-sound of an air elemental tugged at him.

He had planned to come here only to see what he could sense at this place, but now rage filled him, and within the rage lurked a kernel of emptiness, a hollowness.

She had not left them. She had been taken, just as his father, for good or bad, had been taken from Aideen. Just as Oshane had ripped the will from the copper-hunters he had imprisoned with the lantern and the parasites.

He slumped down against the transparent barrier. The letter rustled a protest in his pocket.

What was he to do now, with this knowledge?

He closed his eyes. He thought to push down the rage, but to his surprise, it was like smoke. Instead, emptiness grew, chilling his organs, dimming his senses. She hadn't left him. She'd been taken. He would go to

White Bluffs, he and Aideen would burn her bones, and she would forever be as far from him as if she had fallen into the Pit behind him.

Not living another life, perhaps with other children. His imaginings had filled him with anger and grief, but they were not true. Oshane had taken any choices from her.

Something touched his mind, something distant. The pink stone of her necklace sparkled again in his vision. Her voice filled his ears, singing, laughing. He listened as she read poetry to his little sister, as she planned with Dolores what to wear for a party.

It was Midwinter. He walked along the edge of the canal, his collar turned up against the stinging cold, Aideen's gloved hand in his, his mother on Aideen's other side, on the way to a play in the square, the water beside him viscous with the beginning of ice. Mother sang, softly, and Aideen joined in. Their song swirled out in streamers of breath, and he had never felt happier.

Mother, in a dress of blue and copper, smiling as she handed him an elaborate windup toy with copper cogs to turn the wheels and make the apparatus roll. He didn't remember which nameday, but he remembered the toy.

The memories flowed around him like water from a canal, and he didn't fight against them, didn't try to rouse himself. The sense of another within in, or around him, didn't fade. His mother's spirit? Not what he believed about the spirit beyond death…but his mother's bones hadn't burned. Was she still present? Did she touch him still, one final time?

"Trevian?"

He opened his eyes. Erin stood a few paces away.

"Are you all right?"

He nodded. "I received news. I came in here to think."

"A while ago."

"What do you mean?" He straightened up from where he'd slumped against the barrier. Surely it had only been a few moments.

"It's nearly four. I came to see why you weren't at the meeting."

"Meeting? And it cannot be four. I came up here moments ago."

She sat down cross-legged beside him. "Did something bad happen to Aideen? Or Ilsanja?"

"They are fine. Something bad happened years ago." He pulled the paper out of his pocket and handed it to her.

She smoothed it out and read slowly. He watched her face but saw only confusion. "What happened to her? You said she left."

"Who do we know who has the means to kill without leaving a mark?"

"Your uncle did this?" She looked down at the letter again. "Broken fingers might mean she fought him." She folded the paper into precise quarters and handed it back to him. "Do you think she planned to run away with him, and changed her mind?"

"I do not think my mother liked Oshane."

Her face kept a neutral expression he recognized. She meant to poke at his beliefs. He tried to prepare himself.

She said, with great care, "Sometimes women who are…in love with someone other than their husbands try to keep distance from the person they love, at least in public, to keep it a secret."

He waited for the rage, but it didn't come. He said, "She never approached him. Always, he came toward her. At midwinter, he would seek her out for a dance, and always she would point him to a guest, or one of the chicas, or even Aideen." He recalled his mother even stepping behind him once when his uncle approached.

Erin nodded. "Sounds like a woman avoiding unwanted attention. I thought your father kicked Oshane out."

"He did, but we don't know whether Oshane truly left."

"How did he abduct her from the house?"

"Many nights Mother walked, before sleep, in the countryside beyond the house. Everyone knew this. For this reason, we suspected mestengos at first."

She rested her head on his shoulder. "I'm so sorry."

"I've been remembering her. The memories…" They had been so sharp. He pressed his hand over hers. "What was this meeting?"

"Melendres laying out what she'll let us do. She's hostile, and Espinosa is a pain to deal with."

"I knew that," he said.

She huffed a little laugh. "Yeah, I know."

"You have a plan for defeating the New Way, don't you?"

She sighed heavily and straightened back up. As he watched she scooted around so she faced him. "Well, that's just it. We have *ideas*. We don't have a plan." She bit her lower lip. "We're acting a lot more confident than *I* feel, at least. Whatever we decide to do, we have to close the frontera."

He tipped his head, letting it nudge the barrier. "This is not the frontera."

"I know. We think we know where it is. I'll need your help. You're the only person who's actually closed one."

That was true.

He started to tell her about the sense of something reaching out to him from the Pit. It hadn't been anything, though. His mother, brought to image and voice by his memory and grief, nothing more. He said, "And after, I need to go to White Bluffs, to burn my mother's bones."

She nodded. "I'll go with you, if you want me to."

"It would give me great comfort."

"I wonder..." She bit her lip again. "Could Mei come too, and see the cages?"

"The cages? Why?" The vague sense of shame he always felt at the thought of the cages returned.

"Mei needs energy to use the machines. Anyway, I think she should see how you guys are doing it. She's a lot like Aideen, I think. She understands how things work, how they function."

"She is already invited to the house."

She got to her feet and held down her hand to him. "Will you come get something to eat?"

He was silent on the walk up the passage, and so was Erin. They nodded to the guards and stepped out of the cave. The sun had dropped behind the southern hills, but the sky was still bright enough to walk by easily.

Trevian froze and turned, unsure of what he'd just heard. He ran back a few paces, beyond the mouth of the complex, scanning the ledge and the cliffside.

"What?"

"Did you hear that?"

"Apparently not. What was it?"

"A—" The plateau, shadowed, was empty of life, and the only sound now drifted up from the camp. "Nothing." There was no sign of an air elemental around them. A fancy, he thought, inspired by the Pit, nothing more. "Nothing. I hear echoes in the breeze." He reached for her hand, and they made their way down to the dining hall.

They sat next to Harald. Genaro sat near the charmcasters from Madlyn, engaged in conversation. A moment after Trevian sat down, Mei and Juanita Gunnarsdottir joined them.

Trevian told them he needed to go into the town for a family matter.

Erin said, "Mei, you need to see the operation they have there, with the fire elementals."

"Why?"

"They use them to provide light."

Mei raised one eyebrow. "This would be after we close the frontera, right?"

"Yes."

Harald pushed a scrap of meat around his plate, staring down at it. Trevian said, "Harald? Are you well? What are you thinking?"

Harald's head jerked and he blinked. "Ah, forgive me. Just wondering where Yor Diebell learned of the plata and moonstone chain."

"He told us he'd read of it."

"Yes, he did." Harald set down his knife. "I hadn't, but I encountered few air elementals on my various expeditions. Earth elementals were the more serious threat. Elmaestro Melendres said one province in Pais Lewelyn uses the charm. They face air elementals frequently, although they are rarely dangerous, more of a nuisance because they blow things over with their passage."

"Are there more of them in Madlyn?" Erin said.

Trevian chewed, enjoying the play of light on Erin's face as she spoke.

"Then why did Councilmember Farway not mention it?" Harald said.

"I don't mean to be rude, but Councilmember Farway didn't seem like a very competent councilmember to me."

Harald smiled in spite of himself. "More interested in the next glass of wine and the next handsome young man than in governing, Ruth said, so she would agree with you."

Erin said, "Her secretary was awful. He pushed Lauris out of the way to mail a letter, and he hijacked an apprentice—"

"Hijacked?"

"Sorry. Grabbed him in the middle of a task and insisted he mail a letter. And it wasn't to any 'Madlyn Council,' either. It was to someone named Farway." Her eyes opened wide. "Harald, what if he's a spy?"

Harald grinned. Then he guffawed, slapping his hand over his mouth quickly.

"What?" Erin said.

"Forgive me, Erin. Debora Farway is, as I said, susceptible to handsome young men. Her wealthy husband is aware of it, and quite jealous. I'm sure there was an agreement she would write home each day. Naturally, Brevik would be in a rush to see *those* letters got posted, without fail."

Mei wrinkled her nose.

"They're just having an affair? Eeuww," Erin said.

Trevian snorted with laughter at her tone.

He only ate a couple more bites before Profesor Stillwater approached their table. "Trevian, will you be visiting your sister at any time?"

"Yes." Startled, he wiped his mouth. "Within the next day or two. I have a family matter to attend to. Why?"

"If I give you a list, can you purchase some things?" Ruth met Harald's gaze. She was frowning.

"Ruth, what's happened?"

"The grocer we had an arrangement with sent a note. They will no longer sell to us. They cannot deliver to us, and they do not want us to come into town because they've heard we carry a dread disease."

The plates and silverware clattered, and Ruth put her hand down on the table to steady herself. "Another shudder. There goes my theory about the Pit. No one's been near it today. Anyway, we've no easy way to replenish supplies. Lily Bend takes far longer."

"This—"

"Won't cripple us," Ruth said. "We are not without supplies, but all along we expected to add fresh vegetables and perishables from White Bluffs."

"It's vicious," Erin said.

"Aideen's—Ilsanja's cook can purchase what you need, and they will have it sent up," Trevian said. It seemed like a trivial thing, the rumor, but this was worse than hurling rocks or curses. What if they needed medicine?

Harald set his napkin on the table and rose to his feet. "Excuse me," he said. "I mean to send an urgent message to Tregannon. More guards are indicated, I think."

Ruth hurried around the table to join him.

Erin watched them leave. "Is this Oshane's doing? He isn't working with the New Way anymore."

"He may have won his way back into their favor," Trevian said.

"Great," Erin said.

E rin held her arms out from her sides, staring down at the expanse below her while Ruth and Trevian ran loops of rope under each arm and around her waist. Rubble claimed one whole wall of the domed cavern, a few rock piles dotted the floor, and cracks yawned here and there. As with the lab, they stood on a wide gallery running the length of the wall, and a ramp led down to the floor. It seemed intact.

Ruth snugged up the rope. At Erin's nod, they both moved on to Mei.

Free-standing metal shelving lay like downed trees, and quartz- and-sprite-light struck the sides of metal can and edges of metal. At the far end of the space, shadows hulked like horror movie creatures. Erin thought they were vehicles, but she couldn't tell from here.

Dizziness caught her, and she grabbed the railing. She wasn't the only one—Ruth also seized the rail, and dust sifted down, turning golden in the beams of their lights.

"They continue," Ruth muttered. There had been small tremors throughout the night, according to the guards.

"I came up to the Pit yesterday afternoon," Trevian said. He adjusted a knot of Mei's harness. Marco pushed in close to inspect, and Trevian, after a pause, stepped back. Espinosa checked the rope and the knots.

"Do you think the Pit is causing the tremors?" Mei said.

Ruth ran each line around a vertical post in the railing, to give some torque to Trevian and Espinosa who would be holding the ends. "This land has always been unstable. The town's decline came about in part because a rockslide closed a pass. We've recorded increased shudders within an hour of each time we have approached the Pit. The degree changes. Some, like the last one, we barely feel even in here, and others, like last night, we feel down at the camp."

"And we've had shudders where there had been no one near the Pit," Melendres said.

Mei slid one finger under the rope, adjusting it. "Hard to form a theory."

"Do we have enough rope?" The question sounded more ominous than Erin meant it to.

"If you run short, you will stop where you are until we tie on another length." Like Tregannon, Melendres had no trouble giving orders.

Erin said. "Ready?"

"Ready."

She walked down the ramp ahead of Mei, the drag of the rope a strange sensation behind her. The broken wall to their right was a lost cause. Her nose itched with the smell of burnt hair and licorice, and she wondered if Trevian was getting a copper hit too.

Mei pointed, and Erin aimed her flashlight beam into the distant dark. "What are those? Golf carts?"

"EVs—electric vehicles," Mei said.

Would batteries still work? Erin didn't think "long-life" meant three hundred years. She followed Mei, stopped to roll over a couple of cans with her foot. Peaches, canned corn, various beans. "Food," she said. "The cans, they're not even dented." The next can she toed over had a deep fold running its length. "Well, some aren't."

"I'm not that hungry," Mei said.

"Are you well?" Ruth called, and *ell, ell* echoed.

"Yes!" Erin shouted back.

"Over there, see? Drums."

A double row of metal barrels bounced light back at them. They hurried over. Mei flattened her hands against the closest one. "Do we pry the lid off?"

"I think it's got an opening for a hose," Erin said. "But does it feel full?" She rapped it and the metal boomed.

"That doesn't mean anything. Gasoline isn't that viscous."

"Okay, let's try to walk it out a bit." Erin aimed her light at the base of the barrel, which sat flat on the stone floor.

Erin moved around to the free side and hugged the barrel. Making a wide circle to avoid fouling their lines, Mei stepped close and squeezed her hands between their barrel and the one behind it. On the count of three, they pushed.

The drum rotated, pirouetting away from them in an arc, where it stopped, vibrating faintly.

Mei slumped—not just her shoulders, her whole torso.

They had to be sure. Erin approached the drum, stood on tiptoe and located the round cap on the top. She gripped it and turned. The web of skin between her thumb and first finger stung. Handing Mei her flashlight, she tried again, with both hands, turning until her fingers ached. Just as she was about to give up, the cap gave, turning, spinning free.

Leaning over, they rocked the drum.

"Empty." Mei said. She stepped away. Her rope pulled tight against Erin's ankle. She disappeared.

"Señorita!" Espinosa shouted.

Erin followed, remembered the damn ropes, and went around the drum the other way, to where Mei slumped against it, head bowed, her hands dangling over her knees.

"You okay?"

"Señorita! Answer me!" Marcos sent up a flock of angry echoes.

Mei didn't look up. "Go ahead and say it."

"I'm not going to say it," Erin said. "Well, at least, not yet."

"I wanted there to be fuel. So badly."

"Answer me!"

"We can check the—Excuse me." Erin stood up. "We're *fine!*" *Ine, ine, ine.* She crouched back down. "We can check some others. Maybe some helpers can do it."

"Why bother?"

"Just in case. And is it too stupid to check the batteries in those carts? And there must be other supplies down here, something useful."

"Useful, like Spam maybe?"

After a second Erin got it. "Well, I was hoping for coffee."

Mei lifted her head. "It can't hurt to look." She got to her feet.

Of course the batteries were dead, but Mei roused herself enough to start a cache of materials in the middle of the room. They found three sets of tools, and with those, Mei removed one battery and added it to her hoard. Erin rolled out two waist-high spools of wire, both copper and steel. They found first aid kits and medical supplies, of which the sealed sterile bandages seemed the most useful. One shelf held computer components, the one below it boxes of batteries. Mei shrugged, and Erin grabbed some. She could at least try them in her flashlight.

Behind the reach of their ropes the flashlight beams picked out three long apparatus Mei identified as generators.

Once they'd gathered up what they wanted, it was Trevian's turn. An experienced prospector, he roped himself up and brought down the leather tarps, threading another pair of ropes through the grommets at the corners, he drew them up like handkerchief bundles, steadying them as the others pulled them up over the railing. At Ruth's order they hauled everything out into the corridor.

"The metal cord is a treasure," Ruth said.

"And proof no prospector ventured this far," Trevian said.

"No fuel," Mei said. "Okay. Let's see this rubble room."

Melendres said, "Do you not wish to rest first?"

"Rest? No."

"Are you sure?"

"No risk, no reward," Mei said.

Melendres snapped, "What does *that* mean?"

Ruth said. "We know we have to take risks, yorita, but we will reduce those risks where we can. Elmaestro Melendres asked it you needed to rest because we saw you collapse in the supply chamber."

"I didn't collapse. I just sat down."

"Well, then," Espinosa said as if it settled things.

Erin clenched her fists, furious at her helplessness. Mei was frustrated, and no one seemed to understand, or care.

"I didn't find what I expected," Mei said. "That's all."

Erin moved a little closer to Melendres. "Elmaestro, haven't you ever had a setback? Ever been disappointed? Anyway, I'm ready if everyone else is. Let's go."

Melendres took a few seconds to think about it and stepped to one side. They started up the corridor toward the cage room and Lewiston's chapel, where all of this had started. How appropriate they were going to the rubble room since everything else around them was clearly falling apart.

21

The Chapel was a disaster. After the supply depot, Erin had been hoping they'd exaggerated about this room, but no one had. The gallery ended in jagged thrusts about eight feet from the door, and the floor below them was nothing but rocks. She shone her light up at the ceiling. Instead of the smooth domes of the other large room, this ceiling was pocked with deep craters. Long cracks ran down the walls.

And yet. "Trevian?" she whispered.

He followed lead though. "I feel it."

Mei spoke at normal volume, making them jump. "What?"

"Trevian can sense frontera."

Mei snorted softly.

Melendres didn't whisper, but her voice was soft. "And?"

"There's one here."

Moved mostly by whim, Erin dug into her bag for her phone. Much as she hated to, she powered it up. Immediately the little graphic of four bars began to flicker. "It's searching for a signal," she said. She powered it down quickly. "Something in this room makes the phone think there is a connection nearby. It did the same thing in Via—in Madalita."

"Our frontera." Trevian murmured.

Mei gripped the metal railing, which gave a creaking whine. Espinosa grabbed at her shoulder.

Mei didn't notice. "So, let's go close it. Can Trevian do that?"

Trevian stayed where he was, staring down at the mounds of broken cement, rock and probably some other building materials. "I need to get closer. And I'll need the book, because the puerta stone reacted. It flashed."

"You'll have to lower us down," Erin said. Her stomach gave a sharp twist. She wasn't afraid of heights, normally, but this room...

"Erin, you don't have to accompany me. I closed the Madalita frontera by myself," he said.

"No way you're going down there alone."

Trevian shrugged. "Very well." He still spoke quietly. Everyone except Mei seemed influenced by the room in some way. Maybe that was why they'd called it the chapel in the first place.

He stepped back. "I suggest we put on our harnesses in the hallway where we have more room."

In the hall, they roped up. Erin gave Trevian the book, who slipped it under his shirt. Ruth, thinking ahead, had ordered more helpers, and there were four guards who were going to hold the ropes. Espinosa was silent the whole time. Erin had no idea what to expect, but she hoped she was projecting calm as she clambered over the railing after Trevian.

Even over the shirt and jacket, the rope cut into her flesh. For a minute, she couldn't catch her breath. She landed, and immediately lost her footing as the rock she stood on tipped. She caught herself.

Trevian balanced with ease on a slab of rock. Above them, Ruth and Melendres stared down, trying not to look worried. Erin raised a hand. Remembering the echoes, she hesitated to call up to them in case it triggered anything.

Holding his rope in one hand, Trevian picked his way across the rocks. He seemed to know where he was going, so Erin followed.

"It's here," he said, using both hands to climb up the peak of rubble near the center of the room. He slipped out the book and opened it to the page with the charm on it.

"Do you know what key to start in?"

He shook his head. "At Madalita, it didn't seem to matter, but I'm going to have to sing. At normal voice."

"I know," she said.

He cleared his throat and closed his eyes. He wasn't comfortable singing in front of strangers.

He opened his mouth. The first note flattened and faded in the room, and the following ones sounded thready and weak. As he climbed the octave, his voice grew stronger. She leaned over to look at the book, watching the puerta stone, but it remained a clear blue. Trevian sang the passage five times, climbing each time. He stopped, his swallow loud in the room.

"Nothing is changing."

"Maybe if I joined in? Maybe it's a bigger frontera, it needs more voices?"

He nodded. He started again, and Erin came in on the second note, following his head. The sound spun around them. For a second, the puerta stone flickered, but faded instantly. They sang for five minutes, until Erin's throat began to hurt.

"It's me," she said. "We're never perfectly synced. I'm coming in behind you. Maybe we need to practice."

"I sang these notes through smoke, by myself, in the cave in Madalita, and the frontera closed," he said. "There's some other reason it doesn't work here."

"Is it open, now?"

He shook his head. "No. As with Madalita, I can feel its presence, but it is not open. Which does not mean it cannot be opened."

"Is it the rocks?"

"I think we need more copper-hunters," he said. "More voices might wake the charm."

"Do they need to be copper-hunters?"

He gave an awkward shrug. "I believe so, although I can't say why."

"I trust your intuition," she said. She turned, looked up at the others, and shook her head.

The others pulled them back up to the gallery. Mei said, "Why didn't it work?"

"Trevian thinks he needs more copper-hunters, maybe charmcasters."

"He doesn't *know* that," Mei said.

"Only copper-hunters and charmcasters can do charms, and we know Trevian can find frontera. And he's actually closed one. If he says he needs copper-hunters, I'm going with copper-hunters."

There were six now, and Trevian explained the charm. His voice sounding like a sheep's bleat in his ears, he led them through the notes and the shifts.

The hall was crowded with people; the singers, including Erin, David and Miriam LaFish, Yor Diebell and the other Madlyn charmcaster, guards and more helpers for the ropes, Stillwater and Melendres, Espinosa and Gunnarsdottir, and Yorita Mei.

Melendres was worried the shattered gallery they would launch from could not hold all the weight, so they were lowered three at a time. Each guard who held the rope backed into the hallway, and by the time the third group was lowered, Trevian feared the ropes were so tangled as to be useless. Still, finally there were six singers around the mound. Trevian, holding the book, began.

They sang the notes and shifted, sang, and shifted, shifted again, steadily upward five notes. They began again.

As he sang, the sound emerging no longer felt like it came from his lungs, his throat. He felt like an instrument, the sound coming from somewhere else and flowing through him, mingling with the sounds from the others. The notes wove and twined, and his sense of the copper-hunters around him grew stronger. He felt Erin's grief, and a strange mix of worry and shame from Lauris as he thought of his nephew. Miriam and David's notes wrapped around each other. The Madlyn copper-hunter's song sparkled with curiosity. They wove around him like thread.

The puerta stone did not waken.

Notes faltered and one of the other coughed. The song grew ragged. He stopped them. When he tried to speak, no words came out. Erin nudged him and held out her water bottle. He swallowed and tried again, the words a croak. "I see no change," he said.

David LaFish coughed. "Have we sung for hours?"

Trevian shook his head helplessly. He had no idea how long they had tried the charm. Despondent, he wended his way back to the ledge where Ruth and Mei waited.

"That was half an hour," Ruth said. "Was there any change?"

He shook his head.

Mei leaned over the edge. "Let's try it with the compass."

It took another fifteen minutes to pull everyone up. Trevian was shocked at how weakened and dizzy he felt, and from the way many of them collapsed against the walls in the corridor, so did the others. Melendres passed around water bottles and handed out slices of dried fruit.

When Trevian could speak without sounding like a rusty gate, he said, "Yorita Mei, what are your thoughts?"

"You need the compass," she said. She rummaged in her bag and drew

185

it out. "I had this out part of the time, and the stones were reacting. I think you were merging...energy or something."

The others nodded, and Trevian thought about the flow of the sounds.

Erin's voice was husky. "Should we try it again?"

"Again?" Trevian didn't think he could, but as he looked around, a few of the others were nodding.

"I can sing a few more notes," Lauris Diebell said.

David and Miriam exchanged glances. "And we."

The Madlyn copper-hunter shook her head reluctantly. Well, they had five.

Mei glanced around at the group. "If it needs puerta stones to activate, the compass has more than the book, and they were flashing in a row. This might work."

"Worth a try," Erin said.

"If Señorita Mei descends with you, so do I," Espinosa said.

"Very well." Stillwater rolled her eyes but reached for the coils of rope. "But this must be today's last venture."

Again, they descended. Trevian felt nearly sure-footed across the mounds of broken rock this time. The others were fatigued, and Lauris stumbled twice. Erin caught him and helped him balance both times. Espinosa moved as easily as a dancer, pausing to hold out his hand for Mei.

They gathered, with Mei next to Erin, the compass cupped in her hands.

Trevian's dry throat scratched each time he swallowed. Still, he had sung through smoke before. A little fatigue was worth the risk if it closed the frontera. And by now they were practiced, though they were one fewer.

The five of them came in at once, sang the notes and shifted up one key, singing again. As they cycled through five keys, the stones on Mei's artifact flickered. The flicker grew stronger, settling into a pulse.

The air pressure changed, and Trevian blinked at a barely visible sheet of purple light rippling up from the rocks. He faltered. The light rippled again, in time with the pulse of the puerta stones.

He stopped. "No. Yorita Mei, step back."

The others broke off, discordant.

"Put your artifact away!" He stepped back, throwing David off-balance.

"Oh, no." Erin said.

"What? I—" Mei yanked around her bag and opened it. She pushed the compass inside, backing away too as she did so.

Shouts and screams echoed from the hallway above them.

The world turned blue.

The rocks they stood on shuddered, slipping, and Trevian fell. Erin tumbled down beside him. The blue light was gone but rocks rained down on them. Miriam cursed. "Yorita Mei!" she shrieked, and Trevian looked up as a chunk of rock the size of a saddle cracked loose from the ceiling.

"Mei!" Espinosa bellowed and scrambled toward her, but Lauris was closer. He took two strides and pushed Mei backward into Espinosa's path as the rock crashed down, sending up a spray of dust and stinging rock chips. Smaller pieces pelted down.

The ropes had gone slack but now someone tugged on Trevian's and he slid across the rocks, jagged edges gouging him. "No!" he shouted. "Stop! Erin! Mei!"

Mei screamed as she slid away from a pile of rubble. "Marco!"

Trevian could see nothing. "Erin! Erin!" Dust swirled into his mouth. He spat. "Stop pulling!"

The rocks stopped, except for soft rustling, cursing, and sobbing, the chamber was quiet.

"I'm here, I'm all right," Erin said, clearly, although her voice was shaking. "Answer when I call you! Trevian?"

"Here."

"David?"

"Here."

"Miriam?"

"Here."

"Mei?"

"I'm fine but Marco's down."

"Marco?"

A groan sounded close to Trevian's left elbow.

"Lauris?"

Somewhere, a rock skittered down.

"Lauris?"

"Oh, God," Mei said.

Trevian rolled onto his stomach and carefully pressed down with his hands, levering himself up to his knees. He crawled toward the spot where he'd heard the groan. "Capitan," he said, afraid to yell. "Capitan."

"Uhnnn."

Erin said, "Lauris? Where's Lauris? Who's got his rope?"

A voice from above, "I have, yorita. I am…" The voice shook, too. "I am holding it tight so you can follow it to him."

"Everyone hokay up there?"

Trevian quickly translated. "Are you well?"

"There was a wind, like we've never… Yes. We are well. We are…hokay."

"We need light on us down here. We have injured," Erin said.

Trevian's groping hand touched cloth. Espinosa was down, covered with fist-sized chunks of rock. Moving with great care, Trevian crouched and moved the rocks aside, one after another after another. "Espinosa is breathing," he said.

"I've found the rope." Erin was silent. Then she said, "I've found Lauris."

She didn't speak again. Trevian knew from her voice what she had found.

Rubble clattered next to him. Miriam knelt by his side and helped uncover the Perlaraynan capitan. David said, "Yorita Mei, let them pull you up where you'll be safe."

"No! I need to stay with him." Mei raised her voice and Trevian flinched without meaning to. "Get Juanita down here!"

Melendres's response was swift. "Another person on the cavern floor is not recommended."

"He won't want any of you near him! She's the only one," Mei said.

Miriam said, "Why, because we're inferior? He may be bleeding from an artery, yorita. His superstitions will have to be put aside."

"It's not superstition! He's afraid of disease."

Trevian touched Miriam's arm. He said, loudly, just short of yelling. "If it can be done safely, Yorita Gunnarsdottir would be helpful. We don't know how badly hurt he is."

"Very well," Melendres said. "We are lowering her. Stillwater's sent for help."

Miriam whispered. "What caused this? Why did you stop us?"

"The frontera was opening."

"Did it…cause all this?"

He shook his head. "I don't think so. We stopped before it opened. This…"

He touched the side of Espinosa's neck and was reassured to find a strong pulse there. "It felt like an air elemental swooped through here."

He said nothing else while he concentrated on uncovering Espinosa.

I got somebody killed, Erin thought. She could not stop shivering.

They drew Lauris's—Lauris...up first, because they didn't need to be as careful. Espinosa came out of his stupor as Juanita helped dig him out, and promptly began to move before Mei, Juanita, or Erin could persuade him to lie still. He didn't have a spinal injury, apparently, or he would have paralyzed himself. They lifted him up in one of the tarps, just like they had Lauris, even though he wouldn't let any of the helpers near him.

Melendres stood over him, speaking clearly to the helpers. "You will cover your mouths with scarves, and you will bathe your hands with singeweed and water before you touch the capitan. Is all clear?" Espinosa seemed to relax at those words. Juanita stayed at his side as they carried him away.

Erin sat in the corridor, rubbing her arms.

Mei sat down next to her. "I'm glad you're okay." She caught her breath and started to sob. "Lauris died because of me," she said.

Because of me. Erin put her arm around the other woman's shoulders. "He pushed you out of the way. His choice. He was heroic."

"He suh-saved my life twice. I didn't, I didn't ask for that."

Erin pulled her close. They rocked back and forth, not speaking.

Trevian limped over. "Are you both well?" he said, crouching down in front of them.

"We've been better," Erin said. "But we're not hurt."

"I was a fool."

"Why were you a fool?" Her voice cracked. "I pushed for this. We could have waited."

"What difference would that have brought?"

Mei pulled away, shaking her head. She rubbed the back of her hand across her face. "No one has ever, *ever* said the compass opens frontera," she said.

Ruth came up behind Trevian. She looked exhausted, and stern. "I will hear no more self-blame," she said, "from any of you. Times are desperate, and we took a risk."

"Someone's dead because of it, and it was my idea," Erin said.

"People die in wars, Erin."

She gripped Mei's hand. *I got somebody killed.* Ruth could pep-talk all she wanted, but it didn't change the facts.

"I ordered everyone away from the Pit today because I knew we would be in unstable areas. The guards at the opening swear the rush of blue and the torrential wind that knocked us about and filled the cavern came from the Pit chamber."

Trevian wavered and sat down suddenly. "Do you think my uncle is in here, with us? Now?"

"There is more than one air elemental in the world, Trevian."

"It just appeared now," Trevian said. "A coincidence? Air elementals are rare here."

"I doubt it's a coincidence. I think it sensed the frontera was about to open and became agitated."

Trying to logic that out made Erin's head hurt. She eased away from Mei, braced herself against the wall and pushed herself upright. Lauris lay, wrapped in leather, his face covered. Dizziness washed over her again as she knelt by his side and uncovered him.

Face-up, the damage to the back of his head wasn't so noticeable, but his face looked too full, like a balloon. She looked away. A black stain glistened near his waist. "Is that...fresh blood?" Her voice trembled.

Ruth rushed to her side, but she shook her head when she saw the spreading stain. "Ink," she said.

Erin unbuttoned Lauris's shirt, peeled it back, and untied the straps holding his writing case against his skin. The leather was gooey with ink. She pulled the roll free carefully and lay it on the floor.

A piece of paper, folded several times, fluttered like a bird when she opened the roll. An unfinished letter, she guessed. She knew she had to put it back. The case would be buried with him, or burned with him, or sent back to his family. She started to roll it back up, when another vial caught her eye. This one was unbroken. She slipped it out of its holder and opened it. The liquid inside was clear, with a sharp bitter smell. It wasn't ink. "Ruth, what is this?" She remembered the conversation she'd overheard. "Is this medicine?"

Ruth sniffed the vial as well. "No."

"Some kind of fixative?"

Ruth dipped her little finger into the vial and touched it to her tongue. Her face screwed up. "Ugh, bitter! No, not any kind of..." Her face went blank. She capped the vial and put it in her pocket. "And this letter was here?"

"Yes."

Ruth picked it up. Before Erin could protest, she strode away, calling for two guards to help carry Lauris down to the camp. Erin rolled up the writing case and put it back. "I'm sorry," she whispered.

The Madlyn charmcaster knelt across from her. "He said he could sing a few more notes. And I…I should have gone."

"It wouldn't have made a difference," Erin said. Maybe this was what people did; blame themselves. She made herself hold out her hand to the woman. "He pushed Mei to safety," she said. "He was a hero."

The woman squeezed her fingers and nodded. "I didn't know him well, we only met on the way to the Crescent. He was quiet."

"Pretty devout, I guess. I…dioso, they said he was?"

"Was he?" She looked down at Lauris's face, then away. "I don't think we ever spoke of it. I will walk at his side when they carry him down, with you, yorita, if you wish."

"Thank you." Erin looked around for Ruth, to ask when they would be moving the body, but the profesor was nowhere to be seen.

<hr>

There was some good news. Espinosa had cracked ribs, and a small bone in his wrist was broken, but he was alert, and mobile. He was composing a report for Tregannon with Harald when Erin and Mei found him. Harald looked…angry. Upset. Stern. Erin couldn't quite read it.

"I would have reached you in time," Espinosa said to Mei.

"I know, Marco."

"We found the frontera, and we know it reacts in some way to the compass," Harald said. "Ruth insists the air elemental and the earth shudder originated from the Pit, but I don't know if we have evidence for that."

Erin said, "We've ruled out using the compass to close the frontera, at least, without the lantern too," just to have something to say. Would they take Lauris's body back to Duloc? To Madlyn? And then she remembered Trevian's mother, and her skeleton. "What will happen to Lauris?" she said.

Harald got to his feet. "I'm taking this packet to a messenger now. In it, I advised Brel and Councilmember Farway we will be bringing Lauris to

White Bluffs tomorrow for burning and will send his ashes back to the Copper Coalition. It will be up to Councilmember Farway to see them delivered to his brother." His face was lined, and for the first time since she'd met him, his blue eyes seemed dull. "Erin, Trevian, I wish you to join me and Ruth. There is something we need to discuss with you. And Trevian, I believe you'd planned to go into town anyway."

"Yes. Another funeral."

Harald's face went pale. "Not Aideen? Or Ilsanja, or—"

"No, no. Someone from, from long ago," Trevian said.

Erin looked over at Mei. "Are you okay?"

"I'll stay with Marco," she said, "until Juanita comes back."

"Mei? You all right?"

She looked up, echoing the words she'd said when they first met. "I'm not, but I will be."

Harald led them both outside. Work continued around the camp, but to Erin, it all felt subdued. Voices were hushed, people seemed drawn into themselves. "Where is his body?"

"Ruth had it wrapped and placed in the city hall," Harald said. "We have gathered his effects and will send them on with his ashes."

They walked halfway through the camp before he glanced over at them. "What Ruth and I will share with you will add to your burdens, but you both need to know."

Erin's heartrate kicked up and her hands started shaking. "Someone's infected."

"No infections, but I fear our situation here is more precarious than we knew." They skirted a group rolling the spools of wire to the house where supplies were kept.

The town hall was empty. Erin tried not to look at the table at the back on the main room, where a shrouded bundle lay, but she couldn't pull her eyes away. "Good journey to him," Trevian murmured. Erin wondered what the right thing to say for a dioso was.

To her surprise, Harald led her through the main room and the meeting room into the hall's kitchen. She hadn't seen this room before. Ruth and Melendres waited. Both looked grim. Ruth held Lauris's last letter in her hand.

The room was stuffy and warm, heat radiating off the stove. Ruth nodded to each of them. "It is due to Erin we made this discovery," she said. "I pray it's not too late to help us."

Erin's stomach dropped like she was in an elevator. This wasn't good.

"The vial of clear liquid, its scent suggested something to me," Ruth said. She crossed glances with Harald. "A story Harald told me years ago."

Trevian said, "What?"

Ruth opened the unfinished letter. "Lauris was writing to his padrey. The letter seems, well, personal, but of no import. He speaks of resentments and sleeping late when he should be helping. Look closely at the letter and see if anything strikes you."

Erin peered at it. "Not really, except he leaves a lot of space between each line." She remembered Mei's crowded letters through the book, and Lewiston's journal where the words ran off the page. "Waste of paper."

"My thought as well," said Harald.

Ruth pivoted and held the page out over the stove top, about an inch from the surface. "There," she said, displaying it to them again.

Rust-colored words had grown in the space between the black lines.

I will help you no longer.

"I," Erin swallowed. "Invisible ink, really?"

"As the paper cools, the words fade until heated again. A simple and effective technique for hiding information."

Erin thought she was going to throw up. "He was a spy? Lauris?"

No one nodded. No one had to.

"But he wasn't infected. And he saved Mei's life!"

"Not infected, suborned." Ruth dropped the letter on the table.

Harald said, "I suspect the Madlyn Council will find his padrey is infected."

"But he stopped. He's stopping, right?" Erin waved at the letter. Silvery spots danced in front of her eyes. Lauris was dead now, because of her. He didn't stop on his own. She'd gotten him killed.

"*This* letter was never sent," Ruth said. "We cannot know how much information he shared."

"We must assume the New Way knows of Mei's radio," Harald said.

"Oh, by the Mother!" Trevian said, slapping both hands over his face. "I told him Merry Lake!"

"When?"

"Before the Perlarayna contingent arrived. He said he had heard the search led to a drying lake, and I gave him the name."

"So, they have known since we left," Harald said.

Melendres spoke for the first time. "The blame is Lauris's. None of us saw this side of him. The question is, what do we do?"

Harald said, "I have sent for more guards, and we must expand the wards. I think we should prepare for a show of force from the New Way. If possible, speed up our work here."

"Speeding it up helped get Lauris killed." Erin felt dizzy.

Melendres seemed to understand some of what Erin was feeling. "We must close the frontera. Your experiment was the next logical step. I am in charge of this project, and I knew well the risks, just as I knew the risks when I let you into the room, and into the cavern with the supplies. Yor Diebel's actions have forced our hand. We will have to explore this radio after all."

"We can't do it without power. Energy," Erin said. "And I really think we need the lantern."

"I thought the lantern was not in this world."

"It's not. It's in mine. I'll have to go back to my world."

"How quickly can you manage that?"

"I need to go to White Bluffs first. I want Mei to see the Langtree Company because it produces energy."

"And the Langtree Company needs to know the risks." Harald looked at each of them. "Oshane Langtree is still an unknown. If Yorita Mei can somehow use the energy from the flames, we must know. And do not doubt a New Way army would have little difficulty coming up the Sheeplands Road and invading White Bluffs. They must be ready."

Erin hadn't even thought about an invasion.

Melendres said, "Lauris Diebell sacrificed his life to save one of the guardians. This is how we remember him."

"Even Mei? Doesn't Mei need to..."

Harald shook his head. "I warned you this would be a burden, Erin. I think Yorita Mei should remember him as a man who saved her life."

"Okay."

Harald stepped further into the room and took Ruth's hands. Melendres took no notice as she said, "Why don't you speak to Mei and determine what you need for your journey?"

"Working on it," she said.

On her way out, Erin veered off and to stand at the end of the table. The dioso religion looked largely Christian, maybe even Catholic, with its cross and its candles for the dead. She hadn't been back to church since she turned thirteen, but now she made the sign of the cross, and whispered, "Hail Mary, full of grace..."

22

Aideen held her breath as the vanes of the small carousel shifted and began to rotate. She was afraid to exhale, for fear her breath would drive the sails and ruin the test. The disk spun and behind her, Yor Lopez crowed.

The clicking disk, as wide across as her palm, slowed, and stopped.

"Check the cords," Lopez said, and the workers behind him drew the square tube of quartz out of the slanted shaft. A hose of blackened leather dangled in the middle of the tube, the braid of steel wire poking out the end. The steel looked softened, like uncooked bread dough. At the other end of the charmed tube, where the leather attached to the socket in the carousel, she thought the copper cord there would still be hot.

"Not enough," she said.

"You look at this wrong, yorita," Lopez said cheerfully. "This was the proof. It worked. We drew up energy from the rift. We need to calibrate, but your idea works."

"With some help from Yor Montez, and Valentin Agafonov."

Lopez, studying the quartz tube carefully for cracks, gave a vague nod. "Yes. His charm needs modification, but it functions. Do you think Agafonov seeks partnership?"

"I don't know what he seeks. Do I waste our time here, Yor Lopez? Tell me the truth."

"I always tell you the truth, yorita. It may not replace the cages." Now he looked up at her. "I know it's what you wish. It may not provide sufficient energy to eliminate them completely, but it produces radiance."

"How much more work?"

"I must find a way to keep the conduits from falling down the shafts into the rift. We've lost three."

"Clamps of some sort?"

He nodded. "And a track, so we can draw up the tube and stop the flow of radiance before we unhook the cord."

And claiming the land. The claim must be the next step.

Her next step was to return home and greet visitors. More than they had expected were coming: Trevian, Erin, another guardian from Erin's world, and Harald. It would be good to see them all, but it created a flurry in the household, and the long list of items for purchase Trevian had sent ahead was baffling.

She mounted up. At least there was good news on this front. Now they knew the rifts alone would produce energy, the direction forward was clearer.

Part of her focus on the experiment, she knew, was a way to turn her face from the grief of burning her mother's bones. She avoided thinking of Melya Ousten, and Garth Green, still missing. She had never heard of a family named Green, but perhaps it was a common family name in other places, and she simply hadn't encountered it before. It was easy to put all the blame on Ilsanja's father now, too easy.

Dolores looked calm and unruffled as the chicas glided about the house, preparing. Ilsanja, wisely, had chosen not the sala but Aideen's study as a refuge. She looked up from the squares of fabric she had spread over the arms of a chair As Aideen entered. "Any progress?"

"Until the steel cord melted. Still, we drew up energy. The concept works."

"And now you wish to claim the tunnel, I suppose."

"I do."

"We cannot start on it today," Ilsanja said. "Or tomorrow."

Aideen sat down behind the desk. "Still no sign of Melya. I fear she's dead and I don't know what means for us."

"Too much is happening for me right now," Ilsanja said. "I didn't need yesterday's earth tremor along with it."

"They say the canal sloshed over its banks."

"Don't they always say that, though?" Ilsanja held a square of misty green up to her throat. "Is this flattering, or does it make me look sickly?"

"Not…sickly. It does not flatter, though."

Ilsanja dropped it and reached for a piece the green of a spring leaf. "This?"

"Flatters."

"Good. That's done."

"A new dress?"

"Eventually."

Aideen, who had been opening letters, said, "Why eventually? We have funds."

"I will be frugal until we know what is happening with the cages, and with the New Way." She ran her fingertips over the squares of cloth. "Your brother and his friends will think we have guests every night. He'll never imagine the council of strategy we had to figure out the proper rooms. Dolores has been a wonder. This other out-of-worlder threw everything into the air. At first, I thought Harald would share Trevian's room, and Erin and the out-of-worlder the first guest room. Dolores, however…"

"Said Trevian and Erin no doubt share a bed."

"Which leaves the second guardian by herself. Perhaps we will let them choose."

"A good solution." Aideen wondered if the fabric selection was theater on Ilsanja's part, a way to hide her nervousness. This was the first test of her position as a jefa, a leader of a boss household, and of society, the thing she said she wanted. Aideen decided not to say she doubted Erin or Trevian would notice a moment of it.

Ilsanja returned to the rejected swatch of cloth. "Come closer," she said, holding it up. "This is not right for me, but perhaps for you…"

———

I lsanja said, "You've brought another corpse?"

"He died at Orchard Hill," Trevian said, "while we tried to close the frontera."

Yorita Wing Mei sipped a concoction made of hot water and crumbled leaves like the kind Trevian drank. Her eyes reminded Aideen of Ilsanja's, and her way of speaking was even stranger than Erin's.

Aideen overheard them in the entryway after everyone had been introduced. "Why isn't it Il-san-ha?" Wing Mei had whispered, and Erin whispered back, "It just isn't."

"But you know how to close frontera," Ilsanja said.

Erin said, "We *thought* we did. This one didn't close. We need to get a few more things. And we need to do it soon."

"We fear the New Way are sending fighters even now," Trevian said.

Aideen put down her cup. "How do they know where you are? I thought it was kept secret."

"We no longer believe so," Harald said.

Wing Mei nibbled on a bit of cake. "I wasn't expecting chocolate," she said. "It's different. Good, though."

"You know it too?" Ilsanja said.

Mei, still chewing, nodded.

"Aideen, I regret this visit cannot be leisurely," Trevian said. "Shall we have the funerals tomorrow? Is there need for a memorial?"

She shook her head. "No need, and no need for a Voice of the Mother if you do not wish it."

"Do *you* wish a memorial?"

She had thought about it. "I do not. I think, perhaps at Midwinter if all has gone well, I will have one. But not now, not in such an unsettled way."

"The man who died was a dioso," Erin said.

"I will see if our padrey can say a prayer over him and light the bier. Unless you wish to."

Erin looked at Wing Mei, who shook her head. "I just, I want to be there, if it's allowed."

"Of course," Aideen said. The man who was killed had meant something to this other guardian, clearly.

Erin said, "There's something else. Mei is a technician—"

"Not that educated," the other guardian said.

"And I'd like her to see how you use the fire elementals to generate energy. We need power at Orchard Hill, and there's no easy way to get it."

"A tour of the cages," Ilsanja said. "Easily accomplished. Aideen would love to show it to you."

"I would. Unless you want to rest, is this afternoon too early?"

The woman glanced from Aideen to Erin, startled. "Today? That would be awesome. I mean, fine." She appealed to Erin. "It would, wouldn't it?"

"Sure."

Aideen watched her brother's face. After a moment, she said quietly, "The bones are with the sheriff. If you wished to spend some time in contemplation..."

"I can accompany you," Ilsanja said.

Trevian was silent for a moment. Erin touched his hand, and he said, "I would be glad of your company."

Ilsanja rose. "Harald, do you join Erin and Wing Mei?

"Just Mei," the other guardian said.

"Or will you come with us?"

Harald nodded. "I will join you and Trevian. I need to speak to the sheriff about several matters, and only one is the keeping of Lauris Diebell until tomorrow."

"Good. I will send for a cart."

Aideen went up to change into more practical clothes. A seed of an idea had sprouted in her head, but she looked away from it, determined to let it root fully before she explored it.

When she came out to put on her boots, Wing Mei and Erin stood in front of one of the lights. "It's like the 1890s," Mei said "It's definitely electricity, but I don't know if I can convert it to one-twenty."

"Do we know this world ran on one-twenty?"

Aideen moved nearer. She had no idea what they were talking about.

"Well...I was able to build a converter and charge my phone in Perlarayna," Mei said. "That seems...promising. But I don't think they have gauges."

"I think the Langtree Company is the only group doing this," Erin said.

Aideen said, "As far as we know," and watched them both start. "I don't understand what one-twenty is."

"It's a measurement of strength of the energy," Mei said. She seemed to be struggling to find words. "They're called volts. Where Erin comes from, most places use voltage of one twenty."

"I've never heard that word. We measure by the speed of a carousel or the amount of light the filament generates."

"Carousel?"

Aideen described their test carousel. Erin looked baffled, but Mei nodded. "I'd like to see it," she said. "I'd like to see a sprite cart, too, if it's possible. Physical energy is converted to electricity mechanically, or a chemical reaction is harnessed, but the sprites seem to do neither."

Erin said, "I thought Perlarayna had batteries?"

Mei nodded, but her gaze was fixed on Aideen.

"Our wagon is here. Sadly, it only uses caballos," she said.

Mei actually smiled.

It was a fine day for a ride. Mei tilted her face up to the sun and said, "I'll never get used to this sky. I don't know why it's green."

"I don't know why ours is blue, either, though," Erin said. "I mean, atmospheric condition and light waves and stuff, but still."

Aideen laughed. "You two sound like actors in a stage play." She raised the pitch of her voice half an octave. "'Oh, why do you love me, Melinor?'"

She tried to approximate Trevian's register, which set Erin off laughing. "'As soon ask why the sky is green, my love—only know that it is!'"

"Juanita's ancestors came from a world with a blue sky, too" Mei said.

"I don't understand."

Mei spent the rest of their journey describing events stranger than any fireside tale, stage play or book.

"Is that what you think happened when the earth turned?" Aideen drew rein as one of the newly appointed guards stepped out, crossbow ready. Recognizing her, the guard waved them through. Aideen couldn't help looking up at the surrounding hills. Like Erin and Mei, was she weighed down with a plata and moonstone chain, but she still felt exposed.

"I know it sounds unbelievable," Mei said.

Aideen jumped down from the seat, leading the caballo to a hitching post. "Not so unbelievable. In Pais Lewelyn there is a lake fed by three rivers."

After a moment, Mei said, "A proverb?"

"What? No, a fact." Aideen checked the knot in the reins, and the level of water in the trough. "Things converge."

Erin climbed down. "Okay, but worlds converging seems pretty drastic."

Aideen took the meaning of the word "drastic" from the rest of the sentence. "It is, but we've always known frontera led us between worlds. The thought one could swallow an actual *world*, that's the strangeness."

"It seems to have been a once-in-a-lifetime event," Mei said.

"Well, I hope so, for us." Aideen beckoned them forward. "The rifts and the cages are in this cave. Come this way."

Lopez was still up at the tunnel, but Madalena Cortez, his assistant, advanced to greet them. First, Aideen set up one of the carousels to demonstrate the transfer of energy, then lit up several filaments glowing in their glass bulbs.

"Do you power anything besides lights?" Mei said as she contorted herself to stare at the connection between the copper cord and the plate on the bulb.

"Some people use the energy to generate heat for cooking."

Aideen said, "It can power small machines. One of our newssheets has a flame-powered printing press."

Mei nodded. "How you avoid getting shocked by the electricity? The energy."

Cortez said. "Long thick gloves provide most of the protection, and charmed leather covers for the cords when they are attached to the cages."

Mei followed Madalena deeper into the cave, pausing before the new, large cage which now held a trio of joven flames. "These look like yours," she said to Erin.

"They aren't 'mine.'"

"You know what I mean. Aideen, what does joven mean? Is it a subspecies or a variety? Do you harvest more energy from them or something?"

"It refers to youth. Mature flames are a deeper orange, with purple at their core."

"How long does one last?"

"Live, you mean? Truly, we don't know. We think it takes ten years for the color to deepen and the purple core develop, but we have no way to identify individuals. They may live forever."

"Why the groups, then?"

"The energy flows more regularly. We used individuals before. The energy peaks and then begins to ebb and flutter."

"Interesting."

Erin said, "Can you use this power source?"

Mei gave the same jerky, up-and-down shrug Erin used. "Maybe. At least we could use the illumination. But how many miles of wire would they have to run, and how long would it take?"

"I have some thoughts," Aideen said, "but I would need the Copper Coalition's help."

Mei pointed deeper into the cave. "Can we see the rifts?"

Cortez immediately looked up at Aideen. "Yorita Langtree, it isn't recommended."

"I know. Yorita Mei, I have another site where you can see rifts, and perhaps discuss some other topics of interest. If you wish."

Mei nodded. "I'd like to."

"Then let us go back to the cart."

O ne of Lopez's crew met them in front of the tunnel. She had a crossbow ready and wore a moonstone chain. "Yorita Langtree," she said, lowering the weapon. "I didn't know you were coming back."

"I didn't intend to, but I have some visitors I would like Yor Lopez to meet." Aideen hopped down. There were no hitching posts here, but she found a bush growing out between two rocks and tied off the reins.

Lopez met her at the mouth of the tunnel.

"These are the guardians," Aideen said, "Out-of-worlders who are fighting the parasites."

He shook hands with each of them polite but narrow-eyed. As he gestured for them to walk ahead of them, he murmured, "Is this wise, yorita?"

"I think they can help us."

He started to answer, and instead shouted, "Yorita! Use care." He hurried to Mei's side. "You will burn yourself."

Mei had followed one of the quartz conduits to the edge of the rift. "Are the cages subterranean?"

Lopez said, "No cages here. From what we know of elementals, there are hundreds of flames in this colony, far below us. Yorita Langtree believes we can skim a steady flow of radiance from the edges of their colony without caging them. The concept is a success, but we have setbacks."

"Setbacks?" Mei squatted to stare at the leather hose inside the conduit.

"The heat melts our cords, and we've lost a few conduits down the shafts."

"Steel melts at a higher temperature than copper."

"Yes, and steel works better but it still melts. We have drawn off energy, though."

Aideen's vision suddenly shifted as she saw the place as Erin and Yorita Mei must see it. The tunnel was normally dark, but quartzlight and fluctuating light from the rifts gave it a golden cast. They stood inside the low wall Lopez's workers had built to mark the riding way for the public. Beyond the northern opening of the tunnel, the Merry Lake sky was grayish. The rifts glowed orange.

"Are we right across the lake from our camp?" Mei said.

"Yes, yorita. This tunnel carves an hour of riding off the journey. On the rare occasions some people still use this route. Most prefer the waterfall road, through another tunnel about a league to the south. The canal flows through it."

Mei nodded, staring out the north opening. She was standing close to the U-shaped cutting and fabricking station Lopez had set up near the north end of the tunnel. Sheets of charmed quartz lay next to it. Aideen pointed out the cutting tools and explained the process. Beyond the black and orange lines of the rifts three radiance boards rested on their stands. Only one was live now, five rows of five sockets each, with a small carousel at the top of each column. Above each socket, the glass bulbs poked out, and she was gratified to see two or three glowing dark orange. They needed to be brighter, but it was radiance.

Erin made a half turn, looking behind them, no doubt at the coils of wire and leather and the orderly cubicles of tools.

"This is volcanic, isn't it?" Mei said.

Lopez nodded. "We find fire elementals close to volcanic areas."

"Isn't it a risk?"

"Life is a risk."

Mei gave a little huff of laughter.

Erin pointed to one of the stands. "The light, it's coming out of the rifts?" When Lopez nodded again, she said, "And those are the carousels?"

"It's our way of checking whether the flow of radiance is smooth."

"What reinforces the quartz?" Mei said.

"A charm. We've...adjusted the original charm we use for the cages."

"But you're losing energy because steel doesn't conduct as well."

Aideen watched as Lopez tried out the word "conduct." His eyes brightened. "Yes. We will need many more conduits, and many, many more cords, and feeding them all to boards. The space is cramped as you see."

"Do you bundle your cords into cables?"

Lopez frowned.

"Mr. Lopez—Yor, do you have some drawing paper?"

He brought her paper and a pencil, and in moments they were sitting on a mound of dirt, talking while Mei drew. Aideen and Erin leaned on the dividing wall.

"I thought the cages were amazing, but this..." Erin said.

"Trevian's tale of the flames that follow you got me thinking," she said. "You believe they have feelings, don't you?"

"I do. Don't you? That's why you're experimenting with this, isn't it?"

"I don't believe the cages harm them," she said, feeling as if she needed to defend herself. "But this, it seems like a more elegant solution."

Erin stared at her. She tipped her head. "They're communal...collective beings. They thrive when they're together. And you know it since the energy level dips when you cage one by itself."

"Well, we don't really *know*," Aideen said.

"It's why Trevian hated the cages."

"He never said so in those words, but I always sensed shame from him. It makes me question my own soul, talking to you. It fills me with wonder, not shame, what we're doing. It makes the world better."

"And you're trying to make it *better* at being better," Erin said.

Aideen was forced to laugh. "I barely understand you," she said.

"You're doing a good thing here." Erin glanced around the tunnel. "We're close to Orchard Hill, aren't we? If we needed to use your energy, it would mean a lot less wire to string."

"Far less, and we could do it far faster. But there is an obstacle I need the Copper Coalition's help with, and the Council's."

Lopez stood up so suddenly he stumbled down the mound. "Lucas! Come take a look at this!" Another man joined him at the equipment, and Lopez flattened out Mei's drawing, pointing and nodding.

Mei ambled over to where Erin and Aideen stood. "This could help us, Erin, but I don't want to oversell it."

"What's 'oversell?'"

Mei smiled at Aideen. "Make something sound better or more important than it is. We can definitely use a more reliable light source, and Erin, those rolls of wire you found in the supply depot will help here. I can't just plug in one of those radios and expect it to work, though."

"Can't you try it?"

Mei shrugged.

"There's a problem," Erin said. "Aideen was just about to tell us."

"We will discuss it over dinner, with Ilsanja and Harald," Aideen said. It would save her making the argument more than once.

Her brother returned home subdued. Erin embraced him immediately, and he rested his head against hers. They disappeared down the hall. Ilsanja called for sisuree, and Mei joined the two of them with Harald in the sala. When Harald related the story of the man who had been killed, Mei blinked rapidly. The charmcaster had sacrificed himself for her and it was clear she felt it deeply.

As Harald finished, Trevian and Erin entered the room, holding hands. Mei's glance darted from the handclasp to Ilsanja's face. Then the guardian sipped from her cup of the tea she brought with her, giving it far more attention than it needed.

"I am sure Oshane killed her. He stifled her, either himself or with his elemental." Trevian waved his hand, declining a cup of sisuree.

"There will never be proof," Aideen said. "And though there will be no proof of this either, I believe he has killed two workers, a cord-stringer and a cage worker."

"When? How?"

She filled them in on the loss of Sykes and the disappearance of Yora Ousten.

Ilsanja said, "The sheriff and the justice arms have expanded their searches, but they find nothing."

"Well, he can fly," said Erin.

As she had with the Montez family, Susannah served various trays of pastries and small bites. Trevian looked confused. Mei said, "It's like dim sum."

"Or tapas," Erin said, and while Aideen understood neither of those words, it was plain the out-of-worlders were familiar with a meal of many small courses.

Aideen waited until cakes and fruit were served before she said, "Drawing energy from the tunnel rift eliminates an obstacle for you, Erin and Mei, in your war with the New Way."

"It is *our* war," Harald said.

Aideen kept her expression serious. "Yes, our war. It puts needed energy in your grasp sooner—however, we need your help to achieve it."

Harald said, "Explain how this puts energy in the hands of those at Orchard Hill. The Langtree Company has committed to running copper cord to Sheeplands. You cannot also string miles of cord in the opposite direction, can you?"

Ilsanja raised her eyebrows. Aideen set down her fork.

She barely started to speak when the out-of-worlder Mei leaped in. To hear her, even as she stumbled over foreign words just as Erin did, and tried to substitute common ones, Aideen saw how clearly the guardian understood the cages, and the experiment with the rifts. At least as well as Aideen herself did. She gave Ilsanja a sideways glance.

Her friend was biting her lower lip and the corners of her eyes crinkled.

Harald held up his hand. "Please, yorita Mei, have mercy! Aideen, do you mean you can draw energy from the flames without the cages?"

"Yes. We're perfecting the process."

"Why wasn't this done from the start? Wouldn't it have been safer?"

Aideen said, "I believe Father tried it, but even with the charm, the cords melted. Then Jefe Silvestro provided a charmed cage, and they lured in a curious elemental. Once it worked—"

"It was fixed in their minds, and they never looked away from it." Trevian set down his cup with a clink.

"No one ever said 'instead of caging the flames, let's cage the cords,'" Aideen said.

Harald sighed. "This is good news. I will notify Brel Tregannon—"

"We haven't claimed the land," Aideen said.

"Ah?" Harald glanced from Aideen to Ilsanja. "*Ah.* Land claims must be approved by the Council."

Erin said, "So this is all politics?"

"Yes, Yorita Erin," Ilsanja said.

"Doesn't the Council want the New Way taken care of?"

Harald pushed away his bare plate. "They do. I think if the Copper Coalition approaches Senior Councilmember del Rios, and explains how this a weapon in our war, the Crescent Council will move quickly to approve the claim. If the claim request has been…"

"It's written," Aideen said, and got a glance from Ilsanja.

Ilsanja said smoothly, "We may need more than approval, we may need help. There is work involved, and we cannot ignore our commitment to Sheeplands. If the Council needs things at Orchard Hill to move quickly—"

"They do," Mei said. "*We* do."

"Then they will need to help us. Workers and material."

"We've got some materials we can spare," Erin said.

"But not workers, if what you and Mei have told us is true," Harald said. "I should also say, I am not designated to negotiate for the Council."

"We are confident what you recommend, they will accept," Ilsanja said.

"We need laborers. And charmcasters," Aideen said.

Harald settled himself into his chair. "I must ask; what does the Council gain from this?"

"An end to the invasion is not enough?" Ilsanja said.

"It may not be, for all you are asking."

"We can offer them more," Aideen said.

This time Ilsanja's look was a glare. "*Not* shares in the company."

"No, but an arrangement similar to ours with Sheeplands. Energy."

"You would string cord through the mountains, all the way to Duloc?" Harald stared at her.

"Not all at once," Aideen said. "Perhaps they would have to string the copper half the way themselves. Or, Harald, if Elmaestro Tregannon agrees, perhaps this agreement is with the Coalition."

Ilsanja gave a soft gasp.

If Harald heard it, he gave no direct sign. "Aideen, I am glad Tregannon has won your trust and even that of your brother, but I do not think the Coalition is a favored partner of your company."

"Things can change," Aideen said.

He raised his eyebrows. "So much? Jefe Silvestro raged at the two Council representatives, I heard, when they visited."

"It would be a question of a vote," Ilsanja said.

"You would stand against your father?"

Trevian spoke for the first time. "I believe Ilsanja would have no difficulty doing so."

"The New Way means to take our will, our *selves*," Ilsanja said. "If my father can't be persuaded, he will be out-voted."

Harald's voice was mild, as if he had only a passing interest in the topic. "So we prevail, and this ends, and now you have a company with an angry partner."

"That's our net to mend, Harald."

"Very well. Shall we move to a room where it is easier to take notes? I wish to write down your proposal. If you have the claim written…"

Ilsanja gave Aideen a longer look this time. "It seems we do."

Aideen rose. "If it is well with all of you, Harald and I will discuss this in the study."

As they prepared for sleep, Ilsanja said, "You had the claim ready."

"I had some time." Aideen hung up her skirt. "Your plan to offer them a…well, a subscription to our energy was well-received."

Ilsanja pulled her hair into two loose braids. "I feared you would try to give away your shares."

Aideen tried to quell the spurt of anger. "Well, I did not. I don't know what it matters to you so, but I did not."

"Do you not? Truly? Aideen, between us we have fifty-one percent of the Company."

"Yes, I can do sums."

From her seat in front the mirror, Ilsanja twisted around. "I say so because it seems you do not value the significance of it. We control the Company."

"Of course."

"If you lose even one share, we no longer do."

"Does it matter so much?"

Ilsanja stood up. "Yes. You nearly lost it to Oshane; why do you keep attempting to give it away?"

"Because we were talking first about Yor Montez, who is a smart and reasonable man, for instance, or possibly a handful of shares to the Copper Coalition. They would not have enough to control the company themselves."

"Not alone. You speak as if the minority partner will always be Yor Montez, but what if he sells? And what if he sells to someone who thinks like my father? Or to the Copper Coalition?"

"And you think your father would vote with them, or they with him?"

Ilsanja put her hands over her eyes. "The point is, we cannot know, and you do not give away control. Not if you wish to be...respected."

Aideen couldn't look at her for a moment. She walked over to the clock, staring up at its elaborate face of copper, loomin and red gold. "If I am respected because I own twenty shares, then no one respects me. *Me*, Ilsanja. My thoughts, my spirit, my intelligence."

The room grew very quiet.

Ilsanja said. "I do."

Aideen made herself look back at her friend.

"I do. I am in awe of your amazing mind. But sometimes I see you standing on the precipice, unaware of air beneath your feet. The yors and yoras of this town, they recognize a capable person, an honest one, a smart one, and they admire you, but the ones who control the coin, who gain or grant seats on the town council, they watch you to see if you know you are powerful."

"Those things don't matter to me."

"I know. Just as I know you would rather spend your days in discussion with Yor Lopez at the cages, instead of balancing the payroll. But why did you learn the payroll?"

"Yora Quinn was only one person."

"And?"

"And it needed to be done."

"Right now, we need to control the company, so you can move it forward. I am trying to help you."

She stared at Ilsanja's face and believed her. Ilsanja thought she was helping, but there was still a chasm between them, and understanding had not crossed it. "I agree," she said finally, to have peace. "Now. May we sleep?"

23

Morning mist shrouded the bluff. For a confused moment, Trevian thought he was back with Aideen, setting his father's body alight. This was another day, and Erin was at his side, her fingers cold against his. These were his mother's bones.

"May you have a good journey and find rest in the Mother's arms," he said, along with Aideen and Ilsanja. Once again, he lifted the torch with his sister. The draperies caught and flamed.

Erin's grip tightened. She had lost her parents in a wildfire, but she had insisted on coming anyway, for him.

Next to them, the padrey finished up a prayer Trevian did not recognize, and Mei and Harald gave Lauris's body to the flames. Lauris, who had betrayed them, and who had saved Mei's life. The guardian wiped tears away with her free hand.

Smoke rose. Erin's breathing checked and her body stiffened as the wind shifted and brought the smell of Lauris's body to her. He leaned toward her.

"I'm fine," she said, but he didn't believe her.

"Do you wish to wait at the cart? Everyone will understand."

"No. I'll stay."

They waited until the fires burned down into ashes. The attendants came forward. One questioned Harald about where Lauris's ashes would be delivered. Aideen had already made arrangements for their mother's, and so the four of them wandered in the direction of the cart. Ilsanja kept Trevian and even Erin between her and Aideen. He wondered what had happened between them.

"Does the fire bring back memories?" he said, as they leaned against the cart's slats.

Erin shook her head. "Just a bad moment. I'm starting to wonder what it will be like when I go home."

"You're returning to your homeworld? Why?" Aideen leaned around Trevian.

"To get the guardians who have the lantern."

"You'll return?" Aideen said.

"Yeah."

"I always admired your bravery, leaping into another world," Aideen said.

"I didn't have any time to think about it. I just knew I had to keep the book away from Vianovelle. Oshane." After a breath of silence, Erin said, "I thought you two were pretty brave yourselves."

"Perhaps we've all confused desperation with bravery," Ilsanja said.

"Maybe that's it."

Yorita Mei came down the path. "Harald will be right down," she said. She stood next to Erin, who reached out her free hand.

"Are you doing okay?"

Mei nodded once. She sniffled. "Are we heading back now?"

"Harald wants to have a longer talk with the sheriff, and he said something about meeting with town council members."

Trevian added what he knew. "He asked Elmaestro Tregannon to send two squads of guards to the town. There are rumors, only rumors, of a group of travelers on the North Road, but we fear they might be infected. They were approaching Sheeplands."

"How many guards in a squad?" Erin said.

"Eight, so sixteen guards."

"For the whole town?"

"Armed, and well-trained."

Erin shifted position.

"What?" he said.

"At least one of the New Way hosts has an energy weapon."

"It's one weapon," he said. He remembered the searing burn of the rod intimately.

"That we *know* of."

"What is an energy weapon?" Trust his curious sister to ask.

He thought for a moment or two. "Captured lightning," he said.

Harald came down the path, limping slightly. The justice arm was vital and strong of will and Trevian went for hours, days even, forgetting he had one charmed, artificial leg, but moments like this he was reminded. "They will deliver Lauris's ashes to our camp," Harald said. "They have no fears of infection, but they have heard the rumors."

They climbed up into the cart. Aideen clucked to the caballo, and the conveyance rolled forward.

T his was Erin's first visit to Trevian's hometown. White Bluffs stretched out beneath them, sunlight sparkling on the artificial waterway that split the town basically in half, at least in terms of the short gray and white buildings. Beyond the buildings, a carpet of green rolled out. The southern green, they called it. They weren't big on fancy names here in the Crescent. Beyond the town's edge, orchards and fields stretched across the valley to the southern hills and Sheeplands Road. They called that down mountain, just like Merry Lake was up mountain.

It looked make-believe pretty. Hard to believe a hive mind was threatening it, and the entire continent.

Mei said, "About us getting back."

"I know you're in a hurry, but Harald's issues are important."

"No. I mean, I know. I'd like to spend a little more time up at the tunnel with Mr. Lopez. I think it's a real option for us. I can help jump-start it."

"Oh. Well." It wasn't such a bad idea. "Let's talk to Harald when we get back to the house."

"Did I hear my name?" the justice arm said.

"Twice," Erin said. "We've got something to discuss with you."

Back at the house, food and drink were waiting in the dining room. Erin had struggled to organize a birthday cake for a coworker at the grocery store last year, but Dolores always seemed calm and mellow, and food appeared like magic.

Almost as soon as they sat down, Mei said, "If it's all right with everyone, I'd like to work with Yor...Lopez up at the tunnel while Harald is talking to the political leaders."

Aideen blinked. "Yor Lopez isn't at the tunnel today, he's at work at the cages."

"Well, who's overseeing the tunnel?"

"No one. We work on it when we can."

Mei stared.

Aideen gave Ilsanja a tentative look. Erin didn't know what was going on between the two of them, but something definitely was, and it wasn't good.

Aideen said, "I suppose we could call Madalena in and have Yor Lopez work with you."

"These are extraordinary times," Ilsanja murmured.

"I'll send a note."

"I'm sorry it's going to be disruptive," Mei said.

Aideen grinned. "Yor Lopez would much rather work at the tunnel. It has captured his imagination."

Erin said, "Is it legal?"

Aideen shrugged and snagged a piece of fruit from a plate. "We have not claimed the land yet, but neither has anyone else. We are as precarious as any prospector finding a vein of Ancient in the few days before they file their claim. It is not illegal for us to be there." Aideen got to her feet. "I'll send those notes now."

Ilsanja sipped her sisuree and said nothing as Aideen left the table. She didn't smile at her friend or do anything of the things she'd been doing yesterday. Trouble in paradise, Erin thought. She turned to Mei. "Are you still working on the list of things you want me to bring back?"

"Uh-huh."

Trevian left the table and came back moments later with paper and pencils for Mei. Almost as soon as he sat down, Dolores appeared in the doorway. "There is a messenger for the justice arm, from the Copper Coalition," she said.

"Bring them in," Ilsanja said.

The rider was not from the camp, but all the way from Duloc. While she sipped sisuree, Harald skimmed the note from Tregannon. "He has sent more guards to our site," he said, "and has two squads waiting for White Bluffs to approve them. They will camp by Sheeplands Road until they hear from the town council." His eyes flicked back and forth over the page. "Elmaestro Melendres needs to know the rest of this." He met the messenger's gaze. "Can you return a packet for me?"

"Of course, Justice Arm."

Harald left the room too, returning with a thick packet, probably the claim for the tunnel land.

This was all important, Erin knew, but it seemed like tinkering. She pushed down her impatience.

Trevian hoped his slouch against the doorframe of his father's study, now Aideen's, looked casual. She glanced up, eagerly. The light died in her eyes an instant before she smiled at him. "Come in. I've sent off the notes."

"Mei is busy creating a list of supplies for Erin." He sat in the chair in front of the desk. "I didn't think Erin would come to the funeral with me today."

"Because she has bad memories of fire?"

He nodded.

Aideen set her pen into its holder. "But she has good memories, too, with the flames coming to help her."

"Those are not all good memories. They killed her parents."

Both were silent for a moment.

He said, "I never thought there would be somebody who could love me. I wasn't sure *I* could love."

"Not even Ilsanja?"

"I admired Ilsanja, in the way I admire you."

Aideen laughed. "Admire *me?*"

"Always. You were so smart, so capable, so calm. I was useless at everything our father valued—"

"You weren't, you just hated it."

"My point is, you were a contrast, running the household, managing our father, with almost no effort."

"Constant effort. You simply didn't see it."

"Well." He crossed his ankles. "Mother was the parent who loved me. She loved you too, I don't mean otherwise, but she was my source of love, and when she left—"

"As we thought she did."

"Yes, as we thought...for me, love went with her. I doubted myself capable of it, and I doubted there was much in me to be loved. But with Erin..."

"Ah." Aideen folded her hands. "You are leading this around to speak of Ilsanja and me."

"Yes. Do you love her? Does she love you? I thought as much, when I was here for Father's funeral, yet today you are distant."

He thought she wouldn't answer, but she drew a breath and began to speak.

"It freezes me in place sometimes, how much I love her. And I think she loves me, but she cannot respect me."

"What?"

"Oh, she would never say so. But everything I think or say is wrong. Last night she told me others in White Bluffs couldn't respect me because I didn't wield power. Or words to that effect, anyway."

For a moment or two Trevian was baffled. "Oh! She wishes you to behave like a jefa, and you behave...like you."

Aideen didn't laugh this time; she snorted. "Like me? And how is that?"

"You treat Yor Lopez, Yor Montez and Jefe Silvestro the same. You are as respectful to Yora Quinn as you are to the members of the Town Council. The jefes and jefas of our circle watch every move to determine to whom they should bow, and who to shoulder aside."

"Ilsanja wants me to be like them? I'm not a jefa. I'm just me."

"But you are a jefa. With my marriage, you and Ilsanja are the faces, and the will, of the wealthiest boss family in White Bluffs. I do not wish you to change, but Ilsanja's thoughts on how to deal with jefes and bosses can be helpful."

"She thinks I'm wrong about most things."

He thought of Erin and it made him smile. "Erin thinks me wrong about much. Or she is simply baffled by my thoughts, my judgments. And I by hers."

"She's an out-of-worlder."

He nodded.

Aideen started to smile. "Perhaps I will treat Ilsanja as an out-of-worlder."

"Or pretend you are the visitor to *her* world."

The smile broadened. "Perhaps I will."

E rin wandered out to sit on the narrow bench in the kitchen garden. The smell of familiar herbs was a comfort. Across the space of vibrant vegetation sat the bathhouse, connected to the house by a breeze-way, and now and then a plume of steam drifted past her.

From the swish of fabric as well as the crunch of gravel, the person who walked up behind her was probably a woman, but Erin didn't glance up, just waited.

Ilsanja sat down beside her. "I have a question for you, if you have a moment."

"Sure."

Ilsanja's profile was perfect, unwrinkled, but her hands were tightly clenched. "What is an energy weapon? Trevian said 'tamed lightning.' I don't like the sound of that."

"It concentrates energy into a beam. It burns, and it probably stuns, if it hits you hard enough." She didn't say, *or worse*.

"Do you think the New Way has many of these things?"

She shifted sideways. "Three people from the New Way homeworld came through the frontera before Trevian could close it. One of them carried one of these weapons. We don't know how many New Way hosts brought those other weapons through originally."

"Perhaps they're rare."

"Maybe." Erin was afraid her skepticism sounded in her voice. "They seemed to think they could take over parts of this world by stealth. They *may* not have as many weapons in their world as we do in mine."

Ilsanja cocked her head. "You have energy weapons? Could you bring some back?"

"I don't think..." Tasers suddenly seemed like a possibility. "Not like that one, exactly, but there might be other things." Was there a waiting period for Tasers? Pepper spray?

Ilsanja stood and stepped into the garden, bending slightly to inspect a leafy bush. "I do not want our people wounded with tame lightning."

Erin watched the elegant woman as she rubbed a leaf gently between thumb and forefinger. She pitied any leaf-eating insect foolhardy enough to come into Ilsanja's garden. "If it were up to me, I'd plan for more energy weapons, not fewer."

Ilsanja nodded, brushing her hands over the plant. "Thank you for this guidance."

"Not much guidance."

"It was helpful, Erin." Ilsanja straightened, her slim hands smoothing the fabric of her gray skirt. "Before this spring, I thought the most difficult decision I would ever make would be where to seat someone at the dinner table. And now I face threats against our people, sabotage from those I would trust, and struggles for influence."

"Well, if it's any help, you seem pretty well prepared."

"Hah! I'm not prepared at all, yorita."

Erin thought for a minute. "You're smart, and you understand how people think. You're strategic. You've got strong allies."

"Allies?"

"People who are on your side? Whose interests match yours? Sometimes, groups you don't even think you have anything in common with will help you, because you face a common threat."

Ilsanja looked down at her. "Allies. If the others can see that they face the same danger."

Erin said, "Not being taken over by parasites? It should be obvious, but..." She considered Melendres and Espinosa and shook her head. "Yeah, that's the trick."

Ilsanja's grin was sharp. "You'd *think* it would be enough, but...there are other areas, though." Her mood shifted, becoming brisk. "Aideen and I will not leave our workers in danger. We'll make a plan. Again, I thank you."

"Happy to help," Ilsanja rustled away, and Erin settled her back against the bench, inhaling the scent of rosemary and a sweet, small-leafed herb she didn't recognize.

M ei spent the day at the tunnel, while Harald and Aideen talked to the town council. Harald seemed pleased but did not give a lot of details over dinner. Mei was distracted, sunk deeply in thought, and Erin added "Tasers" to her list, with a question mark. Aideen and Ilsanja were quiet too, but there was less tension between them.

That night, she curled up against Trevian. He stroked her hair until they both fell asleep.

The next morning Dolores gave them packets of food, even though they were less than three hours from the site. Mei didn't want to leave until Erin pointed out how close the rift tunnel was to Orchard Hill.

The longer route, through the town, led them up a winding road next to the waterfall, just past the walking stairs called the Endless Stairs, and through a broader tunnel where the canal ran. Mei zoned back in as if this reminded her of something. "Our tunnel, where Lopez is working, do you think they understand it's artificial?" she said.

Trevian overheard and reined in his mount. "Made by human hands, you mean? We do. At least we assumed it was. It's very regular. The rifts are not human made, though."

Mei looked back at Erin. "Lewiston's journal talked about Orchard Hill moving. Did that open the rifts?"

"It fits with what we've read," Erin said.

They rode around the west shore of the lake for about another hour until they reached the wards, which a guard put to sleep for them. Melendres came out of the town hall building as they approached, Genaro at her side. "We have more guards from Brel," she said after greeting them. "And three more copper-hunters. What news do *you* have?"

Genaro helped Harald dismount. The justice arm pulled Tregannon's letter out of his pocket. "Much in here I need to share. The White Bluffs town council will hold an emergency meeting in two days to discuss accepting the help of Copper Coalition guards. I've asked for someone from the Crescent Council to be present as well."

Melendres nodded. She scanned everyone. The glance looked casual, but Erin had the feeling she was looking for injuries, or dejection. "The guards who rode here faced an attack on the road, just after the turn past Lily Bend. They looked like mestengos, but all the guards felt the burning of their marks. At least two of the six attackers were infected. We have brought one back and questioned him, but I could use your expert knowledge."

Stillwater came up behind her. "Thanks to your housekeeper's son, who delivered a cartful of supplies yesterday," she said to Trevian.

"Good."

Erin caught Stillwater's gaze. "I should probably start packing to head home," she said.

"Yes, and you will take two guards with you to the frontera."

"Guards?" Of course, she should have guards; she nodded her acceptance of the necessity. Not only the New Way, but Oshane would love to get his hands on her, or follow her through her frontera into her world, again.

They unpacked and briefed Melendres and Ruth. From the New Way host, they learned the parasites had drawn large groups of fighters, some targeting White Bluffs. Some headed from the north, through Lily Bend, intending to invade Merry Lake valley. Melendres had deployed guards along the rock-choked western pass too.

Genaro had expanded the wards and put two guards on the south side of the Orchard Hill entrance, because a charmcaster thought she heard a flautine echoing through the narrow ravine at the edge of the plateau. There had been no sign of Oshane Langtree or any air elementals, but Genaro wanted to be prepared.

At dinner, Mei sat with Capitan Espinosa, who seemed to be in less pain. As the meal finished, she came over to their table and perched on the end of the bench. Genaro leaned forward. "Yorita Erin, Yorita Mei, I brought out one of the boxes from the Radio Room. There were, cords, I guess, attached to it, and I brought those as well, although I had to cut one of them because I could not free it from the metal plate it was attached to."

"You're a wizard, Genaro," Mei said.

"Is a wizard good?"

"Very good."

"I carried it down to the house I share with the Justice Arm."

"Cool," Mei said. "Which also means good." She stood up. "Erin, do you have a few minutes to go over the list?"

"Sure." Erin swung one leg over the bench. "I'm leaving tomorrow, and it'll take a day to get to the frontera and a day to get back." Standing, she put her hand on Trevian's shoulder. "I'll see you back at our house. Soon."

Looking up at her, her drew her hand to his lips and kissed it. "Good."

As they left the town hall building, Mei said, "Why are you giving me a time frame?"

"Well, we're on a clock, I guess, if we're worried about getting attacked. It's basically a day there and back, at least one day before the Agustos can fly in from Florida. Expect me to be gone at least four or five days, and I don't know if I can send messages back across a closed frontera."

Mei walked, thinking. "So long? I mean, it's one of the things we don't control, but I don't like being without power, and I'm really hoping you can bring back gasoline." She walked a bit further. Erin looked up at the greenish stars overhead.

Mei said, "I know you don't want to leave him."

"I don't. It's not just me being selfish. He buried both his parents, less than a month apart."

"That's a brutal loss," Mei said. She took the steps up into the house they used as the library two at a time, Erin following. It was. They both knew it.

For the first time since they'd joined the camp, Erin looked at the place as a house, not an archive. The layout was simple, but the place was well-built. The wooden floors were silent underfoot. The windows had thick panes of glass, and the curtains, while frayed at the hems, were clean. The bedrooms, like even the ones she'd slept in at Trevian's house, were not huge, but looked comfortable, and the largest room was the kitchen. Families had grown up here, when Merrylake Landing had been a bustling town, not a ghost town held captive by a crazy man, or an outpost for an army.

Morbid much? she thought.

They unfolded the list. Mei squinted at "Tasers." "Why?"

"Defensive weapons. They may disrupt the connection between the node and the host."

Mei nodded. "No guns?"

"Um, I wouldn't feel comfortable bringing back guns, Mei. The society here, they're not there yet. Wait, don't tell me, Perlarayna has guns."

"I don't know. I don't understand your objection, though."

"Isn't it like a, well, a Prime Directive thing? Shouldn't they develop guns on their own?"

Mei rolled eyes. "We aren't on *Star Trek*. By your logic, should we wait until they develop Tasers on their own?"

"They have charms that basically work like Tasers. Anyway, there's a waiting period to buy a gun, and it's, like, two weeks or something."

"Really?"

Erin put her hands on her hips. "You think we just run around buying guns?"

Mei shrugged. "Yes, actually."

It *did* seem like Americans bought guns the way other people bought groceries. "I'm not thrilled about the Tasers," she said. "There may be a waiting period for them, too, for all I know. But I figure we're desperate."

"Okay..." Mei scribbled down a few more things. "I'm adding some connections and some switches. If we can use power from the tunnel rifts, we might need them. I think that's everything. You'll have security, right?"

"Two guards and a letter from Trevian."

"You need a permission slip from Trevian?"

Erin laughed. "No. Well, yes. My frontera is on his claim."

"Oh. Wow."

"Yeah, weird, I know." Erin folded up the note and tucked it into the messenger bag. Her stomach was clenching. She knew why. As it got closer, her anxiety about going back built up like a killer wave.

Trevian had lit the two whiterock lamps in their house. It was a house, too, a place people had raised families, celebrated events, not just a shelter to camp in. She put her arms around him. "Are you all right?" she said.

"I am well. What about you?"

She rested her forehead against his chest. "I've got Mei's list, Harald picked out the guards, I've got the charm against air elementals. My phone still has a charge. I have my passport."

His hands slid down to her waist and pulled her closer.

"I don't want to go," she whispered.

Trevian rocked her slightly and didn't speak.

"I know I have to, but I'm scared of what it will be like."

"You are brave, Erin."

Tears flooded her eyes. Once before he had called her the bravest person he knew. This simple sentence carried even more comfort.

"I think it is my duty to distract you." Trevian pressed his warm lips against the hinge of her neck and shoulder, making her shiver.

"I should distract *you*," she said, a little breathless.

He held her away, staring into her eyes. "You will never be the distraction," he said. "All the other things, family, betrayal, these are the distractions."

"War?"

"And war." He stroked her hair. "No war tonight." He bent and kissed her. She opened her mouth, letting his tongue touch hers. He guided her back toward the narrow bed. His touch was confident as he drew off her shirt, trailing kisses along her shoulders, down her chest, his fingers untying the drawstring on her trousers as she wrestled with the string on his. His breath came in short gasps. Hers too. She ran her fingers down his warm, bare chest. By now she knew how to touch him, and he her. The room vanished in a tunnel of warmth, sensation, the soft murmurings of their voices. She never remembered what they said, only the blending of their cries.

The next morning at sunrise, flanked by two Copper Coalition guards, weighed down with a moonstone and plata chain, she rode back to her frontera.

PART III

THE TOWER

24

B y a vote of four to one, the White Bluffs town council invited two squads of Copper Coalition guards into town, with a stipulation; the Coalition would pay rent to the homes where they billeted.

Aideen did not think this meeting of the Langtree Company partners would go as smoothly. The back of her neck was a clenched fist as they waited for Jefe Silvestro.

Over breakfast, Ilsanja had said, "This when the fifty-one percent becomes important."

Aideen forced herself to keep her sigh quiet. "I know."

She made herself smile at Yor Lopez, who sat in the extra chair Edmund brought in for him. The manager wore work clothing, but it was fresh. He didn't seem nervous at all, and moments before he'd been chatting with Armando about the Montez children and their plans.

The door swung open. Silvestro froze on the threshold, blinking. "Moises, I didn't expect you."

"He is here to give us a presentation," Ilsanja said. They had agreed; as Trevian's proxy and the majority partner, she would take the lead.

Silvestro stamped over to his chair. "Before he begins, what is this nonsense from the Crescent Council? Some land claim they've approved? They're wrong again. We've claimed no land."

"We did," Ilsanja said.

"What? This tunnel? Are we roadbuilders now, Ilsanja? Do you understand what this company *does*?"

"It's why we've invited Yor Lopez."

Aideen noted the word "we." She had wagered with herself that Ilsanja would say "I," erasing her from the conversation completely.

Ilsanja's voice was low and calm. "We are drawing energy from those rifts. There is a large flame colony there."

Silvestro's head started wagging before she finished the second sentence. "There is no room for cages and the copper cords, unless we excavate, and we have no plan for excavating."

Yor Lopez cleared his throat softly. "We are harvesting energy without the use of cages, jefe," he said.

"Impossible, Moises. We've tried it."

"I know, jefe. I remember. We have added to the quartz charm—"

"The quartz charm is *mine*," Silvestro said. "You have no right to change it."

"Your charm, the foundation, is unchanged, jefe. After some experimentation, we've built another one onto it, one Yor Montez helped us find. It reinforces the quartz at even higher temperatures. By tipping the copper lines with steel, we can harvest radiance directly from the rifts, without caging."

Silvestro swiveled his head to glare at Montez. "You're part of this?"

"Oh, yes. I was curious," Armando said. "And we've had success."

"We've claimed useless land, and we're wasting our workers' time on this project." He stabbed at Aideen with his glance. "This is a fool's fancy."

Aideen's cheeks grew hot, but Yor Lopez threw back his head and laughed.

Everyone in the room turned to stare, and Silvestro's face turned dark red.

"Oh, jefe! I see you remember those words!"

"I..." Silvestro frowned.

Lopez slapped the table. "The very words they spoke to you and Jefe Langtree at the Banco de Duloc! 'A fool's fancy,' when they refused you a loan. You showed them then, too, didn't you, who was a fool?"

"Well..."

"The whole town alight, and them still depending on blackrock and sprite-catchers!" Yor Lopez wiped his eyes. "So many times, Jefe Langtree told that story. I never tire of it."

"Did they say it was a fool's fancy?" Armando said.

Silvestro looked confused. "Perhaps, I…it was long ago."

Armando shrugged. "They were the fools, then."

"Well," Silvestro said. "This is an interesting idea, but it's irresponsible to split our workforce now, especially as we go forward with the Sheeplands expansion."

Armando said, "We will have helpers. Laborers and charmcasters, borrowed from the Copper Coalition."

"What?" Silvestro's calm evaporated. "Surely we are not trusting them! What have we given away to them, for their assistance?"

Ilsanja glided in. "Given away no share of the company or share of the claim. We will discount their price for the energy for the fully operational first year in return for their help."

"Why should they care?"

Now Ilsanja was silent, tipping her head toward Aideen. Ignoring her thumping heart, Aideen said, "The Copper Coalition faces a war with the New Way parasites, and they seek to create a weapon near Merrylake Landing. To charm it and make it effective, they need energy, and they have none. Sprites won't do. They are…eager to help us with our project, in return for the energy. The Copper Coalition takes the risk."

"Well. I don't like their involvement. We can't trust them."

"We can trust them to act in their own interests," Ilsanja said.

Yor Lopez said, "The man I spoke to yesterday promised six laborers and two charmcasters to our project."

"Is that anywhere near enough?"

Lopez gave a brisk nod.

"Well." Silvestro drummed his fingers on the table. "I don't like it."

Aideen folded her hands in her lap. His liking or disliking meant little. They had the votes to move forward. It only meant his ill-will forever when they did.

"But I won't vote against it," he said. "I will hold my vote."

From the silence, Aideen wasn't the only one baffled by this meaningless gesture.

Ilsanja said, "Very well. Yor Lopez, is there anything else about the project you wish to add?"

"Yes, thank you, jefa. Jefe Silvestro, no one was more questioning of this project than I was. But that flame colony is huge. With this technique, we would have a second site in case of an accident or problem at the cages. And most importantly, jefe, it works. We can draw energy directly from the colony! No more burns for our cage workers, no more shattered cages, no more starving flames."

Armando said, "Without your quartz charm, this would be impossible. As with the cages, the quartz conduits protect the cords from the heat."

Silvestro ignored this, staring at Lopez. "Well, you've always been like a boy seeing the stars for the first time, Moises. I'll trust your judgment, but it won't change my decision."

Aideen said, "Yor Lopez, will you wait outside while we vote? There is another matter Jefa Langtree and I wish to speak to you about."

"Of course, yorita." Lopez rose and nodded to her.

Edmund spoke from his corner. "Petrie will have sisuree and some cake if you wish it, yor."

Lopez smiled and left the room.

The vote went quickly. All but Silvestro, with this thirty percent share, voting Yes, and he holding his vote, which allowed him to record his vote later. Now Aideen saw the maneuver for what it was; a way to save face.

"Is that all for today?"

"No. There is talk of a gang of people controlled by the parasite who may be targeting White Bluffs."

"Another rumor? You mustn't believe everything, Ilsanja."

"Of course, but we want to be prudent, and prepared."

Aideen risked a comment. "We had planned for a lone attacker with an air elemental, but a gang of people poses a different risk."

Silvestro gave a half-shrug. "More guards? More cost?" He didn't sound indignant, though.

"An escape plan for our workers. They aren't trained guards or fighters."

Ilsanja said, "And a few more guards, yes."

"An alarm beacon," Aideen said.

Armando said, "I'd like to designate one charmcaster per shift, one who can remove the charm from the copper and the quartz."

"*Remove* my charm?"

"So the invaders cannot use our system or learn our secrets," Ilsanja said.

Aideen stayed quiet.

"When you see one mouse in the grain stores, you don't hire an army," Silvestro said. "You get a cat."

Armando said, "Shall we designate a cat then?"

Now they got the full roll of a shrug. "If it protects the Company, I say yes. Do we need a vote?"

"No, Edmund's notes just need to show agreement," Ilsanja said.

Silvestro rose. "*Now* are we done?"

"Yes. Thank you, Father. We're done."

When he was gone, Aideen sighed and rolled her head. Her neck cracked. "Can we bring Yor Lopez back now? We have another matter to address."

***

L ater, Ilsanja went to check on her caballos, and Aideen sent messages to Trevian and Harald. She was relieved Elmaestro Tregannon had agreed to provide the laborers. Of course, he was doing far more than "helping." His workers and charmcasters would pay close attention to the running of the cords, the mixing of the metals and the charms themselves, with a plan to replicate them. It was an unavoidable risk, and they would not see everything.

While the second part of their plan, the one they'd discussed in more depth with Yor Lopez, was not legally questionable—they had, after all, the majority of partners present—the consequences if it failed could be bad for the Company, and she pushed it resolutely out of her thoughts.

When Ilsanja came home, Aideen tracked her down in their bedroom.

"Play a game with me." She had rehearsed this mentally since her discussion with Trevian.

Ilsanja stood with one boot in her hand. "A game?" She looked around the room.

"A game of words."

Her friend sat down and pulled off her other boot. "All right."

"Pretend I am an out-of-worlder."

"What is this?"

Aideen held out her hand. "Indulge me. Hello, I am Aideen, an out-of-worlder. Explain to me how, in your world, one wields power in a partners' meeting of a company."

Ilsanja dropped her boot and laughed. "Very well. Just as we did this morning, although, Yorita Out-of-worlder, it is an extreme example. One partner lacks vision and is very stubborn, so we take care to arrange things around him."

"Is this how it always is in your world?"

"Yes." Ilsanja unpinned her hair and began to stroke it, looking up at Aideen from under half-closed lids. "There are *other* aspects of our society I could share with you, Yorita Out-of-Worlder."

Aideen tried to stay serious, but a laugh burst out of her before she would stop. "I would enjoy that. But I need to understand things, and remember, I am from another world."

Ilsanja rolled her eyes.

"In my world, a younger child was expected to be quiet and run things smoothly when her mother was gone, and not to speak, not to share what she thought, or knew. I am surprised this approach is the same in your world."

Ilsanja was silent, blinking, her hand stilled against her hair.

"Ah," she said. "I see how it appears so. At times, silence is prudence. At others, firmness is, and at others, boldness is. There is, perhaps I would call it an art? An art to knowing which is required when. And it can be learned."

She dropped her hand, and the flirtatious tone she had been using fell away. "In fact, I learned something this morning with Yor Lopez. Even though he is not a partner or a jefe, he persuaded Father when we could not. He was like a copper cord, running back to a triumphant time in my father's life and illuminating it. No one else could have done it."

"Isn't that why we invited him?"

"I thought he would explain the new process and tease my father's appetite for profit. But he reminded my father of the early days of the company, when he and your father took risks."

"Your father will always hate *me*, though. He will never listen to my words. There is my future in the partnership."

"He fears you, and he should, Aideen. Look what you've already accomplished. But it is not your future forever."

"How is it not?"

Ilsanja stood, reached out, and drew Aideen closer. "We will weather the crisis with the New Way. We will make many of the changes you envision, and he will barely be there. That is the future. He's angry now because he's being forced to pay attention when he wishes to take his partner's draw and pursue his entertainments."

"Will we? Weather this crisis?"

Her friend nodded.

Aideen thought she would go no further with the discussion today. She reached up, curling her fingers into her friend's warm, silken hair.

"Can you show a curious out-of-worlder, then, some of those *other* aspects of your society?"

Ilsanja laughed softly, sliding her hands around Aideen's waist. "I'm sure I can."

S usannah and Dolores both reported the markets were nearly empty of people. Prospectors were skirting the town. Merchants complained to the town council they were losing custom The addition of Coalition guards and laborers helped only a little.

Jefe Silvestro was now interested in security improvement at the cages, which meant he paid no attention to Aideen's meetings with the local doctors and apothecaries, and Yor Genrey, the editor of the *White Bluffs Report.*

Work, and setbacks, continued at the tunnel. Lopez copied a track, and a toothed wheel fastened to the conduit, which, with a set of clamps, raised and lowered them without letting them fall into the rifts. It was a success, but the cords simply did not last, even with the charmed quartz. With each added inch of steel, a cup of energy was lost, as Aideen explained to Ilsanja. ("I am but a poor out-of-worlder," Ilsanja said. "Explain how these charms and cords work and why steel does work not just as well.") Lopez would have despaired, he said, except for Yorita Mei's eagerness. She pushed for making the quartz conduits narrower, something easily done by a company fabrickers, using parts set aside for spare cages.

"When the guardian is not assisting us," Yor Lopez said, "she climbs up to the top of the mountain with the cave complex, and searches for metal. I feared we would lose her, the first time."

"Why did she climb up there?" Aideen said.

Yor Lopez shrugged. "I don't know, yorita. Who knows how out-of-worlders think?"

Ilsanja made no attempt to smother her laughter.

B etween one day and the next, Yor Lopez improved a charm, and radiance flowed in a steady, measurable stream. The out-of-world guardian brought down scraps of Ancient from Orchard Hill, and Lopez incorporated them into the equipment. Even a strange coil of rope that slid through Aideen's fingers like tree silk served a purpose. Trevian brought it down, and she had a chance to talk briefly with her brother before she headed back home. She felt like she was floating on a pillow of air. They would, as Ilsanja said, weather this. They would make improvements, make things well.

The next morning Harald showed up in the middle of a light summer rainstorm. She did not even gesture him into the sala, just stood before him as he dripped water onto the entryway floor. "What has happened?"

He reached for her hands. "It's Trevian," he said. "He's lost."

25

Each footfall puffed up a cloud of ash, and the sky was blinding. Erin squinted, blocking the bright sun with her free hand. The sky arched blue and unbroken overhead.

It smelled like a dead campfire.

She spun around. Behind her, although the sides were blackened, the concrete two-lane bridge and the curve of the culvert were still there. Gala Drive looked untouched by fire, although charred grass led up to it, on this side of the bridge anyway.

A distant rushing filled her ears, one she couldn't place.

The sides of the dry creek, which was a glorified drainage ditch, held the blackened, gnarled skeletons of live oaks. *Those branch tips, snagging her hair as she ran...*

The irregular rushing. She knew the sound. What was it?

Her feet slipping in the ash, she walked until the sides of ditch grew shallow and she was able to climb up easily.

A few blocks away a cluster of houses stood, cars in the driveways, landscaping rusty, pale gray or shrubbery green. In front of her stretched black and gray ground all the way to East Woods Road at the far end of her housing tract. Or where her housing tract had been. The charred plain was broken with twisted squares or tortured loops of metal here and there. The dead campfire smell got more acrid. Jagged stakes loomed over the wasteland. Once they'd been trees.

She couldn't figure out where her house had been.

Over in the standing houses, a woman running a sprinkler hose back and forth over a flowered border stared in her direction.

Erin started to walk, heading vaguely toward East Woods Road.

Had this been the turn onto Apple Press Court? Or was it the next one? She hesitated. This one. And if she walked around the blackened crescent, here was her house, or where her house would have been, right here.

The rushing. It was cars. Just cars, driving by on East Woods Road, lane-changing into the right lane to get on the freeway and head north, toward Guernesburg for wine tasting, maybe. Or staying straight to head out to the coast. Or heading southbound into Fountain Grove, the county seat, to shop at Costco, see a movie, grab a meal, meet a friend for coffee...

Underneath the smell of fire, burnt hair and licorice. Her sinuses started to ache.

She trudged away from the house, following the streets to East Woods Road.

A car slowed behind her, and she moved over. It drifted alongside. "Miss?" Two men, about her age, were in the front. The man in the passenger seat was speaking.

"Yes?" she said, shading her eyes.

"Did you live here?"

She pointed. "2736 Apple Press Court." The car door held a rectangular sign. Preston Security.

He said, "Do you have ID?"

"Yes." She pulled out her passport.

He signaled the driver, and the car pulled in front of her and stopped. He got out of the passenger side. "Do you have a driver's license, something that verifies residence?"

"My license burned up, along with everything."

"So, you don't have proof of residence."

"Um...?" She flapped her hand behind her.

He nodded. He was sympathetic. "Access is limited to people who lived here, for safety reasons. And to control looting."

"Looting?" Her voice went out of control and for a second she was nearly crying.

"I know it seems crazy, but—" he shrugged.

"I don't have proof of residence. I don't know how I'd get it."

"Get a replacement driver's license," he said.

I don't have time. She didn't say that out loud.

"Or mail addressed to you," he said. "You can pick it up at the main post office downtown."

She just stared at him. Mail? Could she get her mail without proof of residence? "I just...I need to get to a hotel," she said finally. "I, um, I need to call my aunt and uncle in Florida. They'll help me."

"We'll give you a ride back to the road," he said, opening the back door for her. She half expected a cage-car, but it was just some regular sedan, and she climbed into the back. Something on the dash started chiming, and they sat looking at her until she figured out it was the seat belt alarm. It took her twenty seconds to fasten the buckle.

And it took them a little longer to reach East Woods and let her out.

A car whooshed by and she flinched. Across the street, a vineyard was intact. She started walking west up to the intersection of North Fountain Grove Drive, staring across the four-lane road at the little strip mall there. Three businesses, including White Doe Coffee, were gone, their store-fronts carbonized shells.

A crosswalk. She started across and a car horn shrieked at her, the car shooting by as she leaped out of the way. She pressed the button and waiting for the sign to show her a walking figure. The back of her throat itched, and her eyes began to sting. She'd been taken in by the blue sky overhead, but near the horizon, above the blackened hills, the sky was a sickly orange-gray.

A metallic voice: *East Woods. Walk sign is on across, East Woods. Walk sign is on across...*

She crossed, then crossed again so she was on the west side of the street. It was about three miles to the city limits. There were big box stores, groceries, and two national hotel chains. She hoped they would take cash for a room.

Beyond the strip mall, nothing on this side of the road had burned. It didn't seem fair. Her entire neighborhood was gone. Here, a couple of old orchards, a nursery, and the exit for the performing arts center looked like they always had. How could this happen? How could White Doe Coffee burn, and all this survive?

The itch in her throat grew worse. Walking, she fished out her water bottle and took a couple of swallows. After about fifteen minutes, she stopped flinching at every car. She'd never realized just how noisy her world was.

The wide space on either side of the road narrowed, and she held onto the chainlink fence with one hand. Cars raced by on the freeway paralleling her. The building for Docker's Four-Alarm Chili was still there, with its plastic banner sign, but there were no cars in the tiny parking lot, and no lights on. Pausing at the entrance, Erin looked past it, across the traffic, and got dizzy.

On the other side of the freeway, the buildings were gone.

She was someplace else. She didn't know where. Then it clicked; footage of a city in Syria, bombed into rubble, on *The Rachel Maddow Show* one night. That was what it looked like. Erin didn't even remember exactly what had been there. A garden center? A big box store? A string of fast-food places? At the northern edge, like the rim of a burned plate, several buildings remained, untouched, beige, fake stucco, embracing black and gray; folds of burnt metal, hulks of...cars? The occasional dumpster, brought in where they'd started cleanup, looked almost shiny. Had there been a medical center over there?

She gripped the chainlink until her fingers hurt, to keep from falling over.

The dizziness abated. She drank some more water and walked for forty minutes, her feet crunching on the decorative lava rock lining the space between the fence and the street.

Except for the orange tint along the horizon, the reek of copper and the persistent impulse to cough, it was a pretty fall day. Fall here; it was early summer in Trevian's world. Just another disorienting difference. She'd assumed the timeframes were the same.

The road curved as it made its way into Fountain Grove, the right turn lane leading cars across the overpass to the west side of the freeway, where the hotels were. She could see one sign from here, and the U-shaped compound behind it wasn't burned. Some good news, at least. Traffic got heavier. Eventually, she stopped at the crosswalk.

She'd been staring west, but the smell of charred wreckage was stronger than ever at the intersection. She turned her head. There had been two high-end hotels right there, one with a golf-course further up the hill.

Both were gone. The once-green hill was a carpet of black. At its crown, an old two-story historic round barn had stood, one of the town's landmarks. She and Chip used to try naming every movie it had been in.

The barn was a tumbled of charred timbers and twin heaps of ash.

She looked away.

The crosswalk stopped chiming, and instead of a figure, the LED sign across the street held numbers, 8,7,6,5...

She didn't even try, just pressed the button again, blinking hard, and waited, and waited, until the light was hers again.

The overpass was longer than she remembered, and hotter. From up here she could see how far the burn had spread. There had been houses back there, west of the freeway, a couple hundred. Gone now.

She wanted to run, run back to the culvert, open the frontera, leave this warzone behind. Mei could figure something out. She couldn't stay here.

More water.

She drank some.

She willed her feet to move, first one, then the other. First one, then the other, across the overpass, to another crosswalk, across the street, past Burger King, Joanne's Fabrics, and a consignment shop toward the driveway into the first chain hotel. In the parking lot, she stopped. Nearly every space was taken. She stepped back and looked at the sign. *No Vacancy.*

The one a block away was also full. She wasn't sure what she was going to do.

The desk clerk inside gave her directions to a motel she had driven by once or twice, the Nationway, about six blocks away. "Motel Six Lite," he said, "but they might have something."

"Thank you." Her voice sounded remote to her, like she was hearing it from under water.

It didn't matter. They just had to have electricity and accept cash. It didn't have to be fancy.

She walked west on Pine Road, past the wholesale flower market, two auto body places, a karate studio, an aquarium store, and a pickup truck bed liner shop. Nationway sat on the corner across the street from the railroad tracks. The two-story L-shaped building was pale gray and the large sign out front said FREE WIFI HBO. She wondered how many years it had been up. Two bare ginkgo trees waded in overlapping circles of yellow leaves.

The desk clerk, a red-haired boy sporting an earbud in one ear, took her cash and swiped a keycard. She paid for three days in advance, $135. "Did you see our warzone out there?" he said. "What d'ya think?"

"That it's a warzone," she said.

"I know, right?"

MARION DEEDS

"My house was off of East Woods Road."

"Oh, shit? Is it—"

"Gone," she said.

"Oh, shit. Oh, man, I'm so sorry."

"Thank you."

She picked up her keycard and stepped over to the little alcove, where she found a toothbrush and pocket-sized tube of toothpaste for seven dollars, and a tube of aspirin for two. She paid and went out, climbing up the stairs to the second floor. Her room was on the corner.

Letting the borrowed knapsack drop to the floor with a thud, she looked around, inhaling the lingering scent of lemon-scented industrial cleanser. When she pulled aside the curtain, it revealed a view of Pine Road and the railroad crossing. She let it fall. The room brimmed with noise and the smell of copper. After a few more seconds, she recognized one of the noises as an air conditioning unit. She found the thermostat and the Off switch. The bed's lime green bedspread was a fashion crime, but she folded it back and forgot about it. In the base of the beige lamp bolted to the bedside table, she found a pair of USB ports and an electric jack. She plugged in her converter, added the charger cord and her phone. The lightning bolt symbol flashed up on its black screen.

The noise: cars, horns blaring, distant sirens, clunks and echoing voices from downstairs. It wasn't a noisy room, it was a noisy *world*, and she wasn't reacclimated yet. She sat on the edge of the bed, staring at the remote next to the lamp base.

She needed to call the Agustos. She should start searching for local stores for the tech stuff Mei wanted. She had to find out where she could get gas cans. And Tasers. And while she was here, what about her parents? Had she walked past their bones an hour ago, buried in the ash and wreckage? Could she find them and get them buried while she was here? She didn't have much cash with her, but she had a savings account at the local branch of the family bank if it hadn't burned. And there was a safe deposit box there too, and she was a co-signer on it, but she didn't know where the key was. Melted somewhere. How was she going to get around? Use the bus? There was ride-share, and she had the app on her phone, but her credit card had melted. She looked down at her hands, which shook slightly. She didn't think she could do this. Mei should have come. She was so smart, so take-charge. A little thing like a Taiwanese passport wouldn't have been a problem.

She propelled herself off the bed and into the bathroom. There was good water pressure, but the first swallow of water made her gag. It wasn't just the chlorine, which she had expected; it was the taste of various metals, nothing like the sweet spring water in her water bottle. Grimacing in advance, she swallowed two aspirin with a slug of the metallic water.

Her email was still loading, and her text bucket was full. When she called, Remedios Agusto's number dropped her into voicemail. She left a message, and one for Daniel too, telling them they and the lantern needed to go back with her. Then she started scrolling through texts.

The Piersons, who owned Pierson's Grocery, had left many, mostly variations of *R U OK?* She deleted all but the most recent. There were three from the county sheriff's office, and a handful from an insurance company, about the house. A few texts from the mortgage company, no surprise.

Various acquaintances, variations on the Pierson theme. There were about twenty texts from law firms. She deleted all those.

The bill for her cell phone account was available for review online. She'd missed the payment date. She'd better pay it while she was here; she was going to need the phone.

The phone buzzed in her hand, Remedios calling back. "Erin, are you all right?"

"I'm okay. Things are...it's hard here."

"What's going on?"

"We need you and the lantern. It's too complicated," she said. "I can't go into it right now, but we need you. Mei's there, and we're trying to shut them down and—"

"Shut who down?"

"The parasites. It wasn't like we thought. Vianovelle wasn't in charge, they are." She closed her eyes and made herself stop talking.

"Erin, how long have you been back?"

"Couple hours."

"Have you eaten?"

"Yeah. This morning. Before I left."

"Okay. I want you to get something to eat. I'll tell my work I've got a family emergency, and we'll get the earliest flight we can. But you, you need to eat, and then get some sleep."

"I'm fine, really. I don't think I can sleep."

"You're not fine. I can hear it in your voice."

"But there's so much to—" her voice veered away from her and she was sobbing, her chest shaking with each inhalation. She curved her free hand over her eyes, the sobs wracking her. "I don't know, I don't know what I..."

"Take it easy. We'll be there. You won't be by yourself. Erin? Erin, food."

"I'm s-s-sorry, I..."

"Hush. Food and a nap. Right now. We'll call you back with our plans. It's going to be okay."

She stammered out a goodbye and disconnected. Phone clutched in one hand, she cried until her skin was tingling. Back in the bathroom, she took shallow breaths through a wet chlorine-scented washcloth until self-control returned.

Across the street, the Taqueria Mi Nave anchored a strip mall. Inhaling the smell of pork and chiles, she felt a sense of sanctuary. She ordered and sat down at a pastel blue plastic table with a molded orange chair. The sports section of the local daily hung over the table's edge. She straightened it and read a headline about the 49ers, and somebody named Garoppolo.

The woman at the counter called her number and handed her the burrito and two bottles of water, and plasticware wrapped in a paper napkin.

Unfolding the loomin foil, she stopped to stroke its smooth surface. Was this something they could use? Would it hold a charm? The smell of the roasted pork and the beans took over, making her stomach rumble, and she stopped thinking. The bottled water tasted of plastic, but she could live with it.

With half the burrito eaten, she went back to the texts and deleted a few more. The sheriff's office asked her to reply because they were seeking her whereabouts. There was a number. She wasn't sure she wanted to do it yet. She didn't want to call the Piersons yet, either. She tried to think about what the best first thing to do was. Money? Check with the bank?

She rewrapped the burrito and took it back to her room, stowing it in the tiny fridge. A quick search showed her bank branch had survived unscathed. Now was the time to find out if her ride-share app still worked.

A gray Toyota showed up ten minutes after she called, and a young mom with curly blond hair drove her up the bank, sharing a list of friends who lost homes, businesses, cars, and pets because of the fires. "At least the air is finally clearing up," she said.

Erin had two thousand in her account, and she cashed out all but two hundred. On an impulse, she said, "Can you print out my most recent statement for me? It'll have my address."

The woman printed it and slipped it into an envelope for her. She was about to leave when she remembered the box. "Can I get into the safe deposit box? I lost my key in the fire."

"You need to be on the signature card."

"I am."

"I'll get the manager."

Erin spent five minutes in an interview with the manager. There was a whole process to go through when someone said they lost their key, but the bank expedited it for fire survivors. The manager walked over with her and used her own key to open the box. "Do you need the room?"

Erin had seen the box six or seven times with her mother, and opened her mouth to say "No," on autopilot. She stopped herself. "Yes, please," she said.

She had never seen "the room." It was office-sized, windowless, with a small table and two chairs. She flipped the metal latch and lifted the long lid of the narrow container.

Right on top, a sealed plastic sandwich bag filled with little copper disks. At first, she thought they were pennies. She picked up the bag. Charm disks, just like the ones the charmcasters used. Underneath, a desiccated sticky-note, with her mom's writing. "These came to us with the book. (Not the sandwich bag.)"

She closed her eyes. Mom's humor.

After a few seconds, she dropped them into her messenger bag.

A folded manila envelope with a copy of the family will and a prepaid funeral agreement at East Woods Memorial Park and Mortuary. Another envelope with a copy of the deed, the mortgage, some insurance stuff. Under those, bundles of cash.

She recognized her father's touch in the neat stacks of twenties, edges even, nicely banded with paper. Without thinking or stopping to count, she scooped them up and put them in her messenger bag. At the very bottom, a small velvet jewelry box. Her throat ached when she saw it. When they'd moved to be closer to the frontera after the Carews were killed, she'd come with Mom, who'd put the box in here. "Just till we take care of this guy," she'd said, smiling, and they went out to the car, her left hand ringless for the first time since Erin could remember.

One of them had come back here, added, or taken out something, before Oshane Langtree attacked them, because the ring box was at the bottom now.

The will and the burial plan, she thought. That would have been Dad again, Mr. Practical, putting the Important Papers in a place where they were safe, where Erin, if she lived and they didn't, could find them.

She emptied out the box. She didn't tell the teller it was empty. She didn't say she didn't know if she would ever be back.

The second ride-share driver was quiet, and halfway back to the motel —she stopped looking out the window, she couldn't stand the devastation —Remedios called her.

"Okay, we've got a flight out tomorrow, later than we'd like, but we'll rent a car and we'll be at your motel by four tomorrow, your time. Did you sleep?"

"No, but I ate, and I feel better."

"Okay. We've reserved a suite at the conference center downtown and you're coming there with us."

"It's really not—"

"Oh, Erin, don't argue," Remedios said.

"Okay. Thanks, then."

"How…" Remedios's voice grew soft. "How bad is it there? I mean, we've seen pictures."

"Really bad." There wasn't anything more to say about it. She cleared her throat. "I think I have to get my parents buried. Maybe tomorrow…"

"Why don't you wait until we get there? You said Mei gave you a shopping list, maybe pick off the easy stuff on it. And get some sleep!"

"Okay. I will."

The room, when she was back inside, felt stuffy. Once again, she went to the window. It still didn't open. The late afternoon sun turned the world copper, and the aspirin was already wearing off.

The phone needed four hours to fully charge. With it tethered to the wall, she searched for stores selling the electronic gear. A couple of the locally owned hardware stores even had what she wanted. She was forced to check into E-Stuff for the rest of it. She thought about counting the money her father had left in the box. She thought about going downstairs and buying a newspaper. She thought about watching TV.

She thought about Trevian, and Mei, and Lauris Diebell. How much damage had he done?

What was happening back home? Back *there*.

Remedios kept saying she should sleep.

She didn't think she could. The smell of copper distracted her. More— the scent of copper everywhere made her sinuses ache. Her copper-hunter skills had come to life in Trevian's world, and here they were a big drawback. Copper was everywhere here.

Noise, distant but constant, flowed into the room. It was time to take a shower.

26

Once Erin and her guards were out of sight, Trevian found he missed her very little. The first three hours, while he helped refresh charms and gather materials from the supply depot, he only thought of her every few minutes. Later, there was only a faint emptiness behind his breastbone, and he only turned to speak to her, ask a question or make an observation, a dozen times or so. The scent of her hair, the shape of her smile, only came back to him in those vacant moments when he was walking, standing, or waiting. Or eating. Or waiting to eat.

Fortunately, there was much to be done, and he could fill the emptiness with necessary tasks. After so many sennights when he was unneeded, it was pleasant to be helpful.

What if Erin decided to return to her home? Wouldn't anyone? He had fled his, but if things had changed there... Even now, for the first time he could imagine dinners, Midwinter and Long Year festivals, with his sister and his wife. Except, in those fancies, Erin was by his side.

Under Yorita Mei's direction, he and another laborer pulled out one of the machines she called a generator and hauled it into the middle of the main corridor. Mei hoped Erin would return with some sort of fuel. Trevian suggested double-distilled lick.

"Is nothing else is available, it's worth a try," Yorita Mei said.

After, she asked Trevian to help her in the supply depot, where they both began to dismantle the steel shelves. Mei stacked them in the middle of the floor, ordering them by length.

"What are these for?" he said.

"In case we need an antenna."

"What is a nantenna?"

"Radio waves move along line of sight," Mei said.

"Can you not see from here?"

"The mountains block the waves, like a dam blocks ripples in a pond."

Trevian nodded and set to work pulling apart another set of shelves. He was surprised Elmaestro Melendres had approved this, but maybe she wanted to keep Mei occupied.

"I need to get up to the top of the mountain," Mei said. "There had to be a nantenna array here before, but I can't find a sign of it."

Trevian thought there was no easy way to the top of the mountain, but David LaFish was his salvation. Hearing of Trevian's charge, the copper-hunter said, "I know a way. It is treacherous, and takes some skill, but it's passable."

"All the way to the top?"

David gave a nod. "We once thought there would be an opening into the caverns from up there. We must go around the hill, past the east opening and along the ledge, and then it's an easy climb."

"You've been there?"

"Of course! There is a huge sheet of steel right by the east opening. Miriam wanted to bring it out in one piece, but we never managed."

Trevian put David in charge of the expedition and included two Copper Coalition guards armed with crossbows. Draped with their moonstone chains, the guards armed with bows and clubs, they set off around the northern flank of the mountain.

The track they followed was hardly a "trail." Trevian kept looking down the steep cliff to the trickle of the stream far below. This creek, swollen with floodwaters, had carried Aideen and Ilsanja away from Vallis's mestengo lair. Trevian doubted he would survive a fall to the creek now.

As his foot skidded on gravel, he wondered how they would bring materials up this track. Beyond his right shoulder the sides of the mountain rose smooth, white, pale gray, streaked with strings of rust red. A few hardy shrubs grew out of the cracks, but most of the bluff was naked rock.

The decline flattened, and the track widened. Large, rounded boulders littered the skirt below them. To the east, the terrain turned green with trees and bushes. David turned, climbing up a set of rocks arranged like giant steps.

Their guards stopped them at once, calling David back. One guard ascended first, her bow at the ready, and stood watch at the top as David, Mei, and Trevian followed. The second guard brought up the rear. They stood on the broad ledge that held the eastern opening to the cavern complex.

David led them past the blocked opening, up another incline, although this one was wider. Looking northeast, Trevian could see sections of the trail to Lily Bend, and the notch between the mountains. He noted where the trail branched and led to the rock overhang Vallis and his mestengos had used. Another narrow, deep canyon separated those mountains from Orchard Hill, as if someone had pushed the land like a carpet, creating deep folds in the fabric.

The last leg of the climb was not as arduous as he'd feared. The sun was out, making the sweat on their faces sparkle as they stood on the broad mountaintop. At its southern edge, three or four tarps lay tacked to the stone. "That must be where they covered the holes in the room with the Pit," Mei said. "Remember? Ruth told us."

Trevian nodded. Beyond the tarps, the rock face sheared away and formed one wall of the deep, crooked ravine dead-ending in a rockfall. There had once been a southern entrance to Orchard Hill in there, but it was blocked, Stillwater said. He looked about. North, he could see the peaks of other mountains. The southern wall of mountains between White Bluffs and Merry Lake blocked any view of his hometown, leaving only green unbroken sky. Minding his footing, he walked to the west edge. Merry Lake glowed like a green jewel in a rust-brown setting, while small figures wandered about in the toy-sized buildings of the dead town. Farther west he could make out the west trail, curving up into the hills.

And all around this the sky stretched.

"Is this high enough?"

Mei approached him. "Probably. We'll add some height with the tower itself."

"You said you need energy to feed it," he said. "How do you plan to string copper so far?"

She shrugged. "There's the opening we passed on the east side. We could open it up."

The first guard heard them. "Unsafe, yorita. It leaves us vulnerable to an attack."

"We might have to risk it."

A swirl of blue at the corner of Trevian's vision made him look south. Now he saw nothing but air and the wall of rock. He touched the moon-stone chain looped across his chest.

Mei was debating with the guard, and Trevian stepped away to give them some privacy. A discoloration in the rock beneath his feet caught his eye. He knelt. "David? What do you think this is?"

David joined him, squatting balancing on the balls of his feet. "A purple stone of some kind?"

Trevian brushed away the rock dust. The colored spot spanned the width of his palm, stippled lavender to deep purple. He rapped it. It had the feel of glass.

David glanced around. "There's another." He stood and began search-ing, ranging in a circle. "There are five here."

"And more here," Trevian said.

"What are you doing?" Mei said.

"Tracking these odd purple patches in the rock."

She came over. As Trevian had, she knelt and brushed one of them clean. Then she bowed and put her eye down to one. "They're skylights. People drilled into the rock and capped each end with glass, to let in more light."

"This isn't a roof or a wall, it's a mountain," Trevian said.

She tapped on the spot. "Yes, it took some serious drilling, for sure."

Trevian stilled his protest. After all, Yor Montez's drills had probably gone as deep as these tools of the Ancient had.

He drew his knife and tried to pry one of the purple stones free, but could get no purchase with the tip of his blade.

David laughed. "You've forgotten your roots, Trevian. This is a prospector's job." He knelt before one of the patches and took a chisel and small hammer from his satchel. Placing the chisel carefully, he tapped three times on the butt. The purple stone fizzled to powder, falling like rain into the smooth-walled hole beneath it.

"There's another cap at the bottom," Mei said. "To disperse the light. Where is this? I mean, in the caves. What room are we over?"

Trevian shrugged. His mind didn't work that way, but David's did, he said, "The rubble room. We're right above it."

Of course they would be—the deadly room housing the frontera.

Mei sucked in her lower lip. She was remembering Lauris, he thought. Then she lifted her head. "Good. Once we have power, we can run the cords straight up through these holes."

"How do we break the bottom caps?" Trevian said. "Lob stones down on them? Drop plummets?"

She gave him a look.

"A plummet is a weight with a sharp point at the end," he said, "tied to a cord. It's used to determine if a wall is straight upright."

"Miriam has some of those," David said.

Mei smiled. "Great! We can use those. Maybe we can break the glass from the inside."

"I remind you the room's unstable, and we can't reach the ceiling."

The guardian was the most pleased he'd ever seen her. "We'll figure something out."

She whirled away from him, marking off paces out loud as she planned for her tower.

He met Harald at the bottom of the trail. The justice arm was frowning. "What were you doing?"

"Walking on the top of the mountain with Yorita Mei."

"Why?"

"She asked for my help. She means to place a tower there, for the radio waves."

"A *tower?*"

"Yes, a nantena."

"Come with me." Harald led him through the camp and waved down the first Copper Coalition guard he found. "Find Profesor Stillwater and Elmaestro Melendres and have them meet me in the town hall at once." He hesitated. "And Capitan Espinosa."

"Why?" Trevian said.

"She cannot build a tower," Harald said. "Did you not hear Tregannon explain what Alker Holay said? A tall metal pole is what the New Way wish to build."

"I heard nothing of it," Trevian said. "And if it were so, why wasn't Yorita Mei told?"

Harald frowned. "It seems we cannot imagine every single thing we must tell Yorita Mei *not* to do," he said. "Come. You will tell them what you know about her activities."

Trevian stood his ground. "Why? I see nothing wrong with Yorita Mei's work."

"Then you can explain it."

"Have Yorita Mei explain it. I'll attend, but she is the expert."

"She's reckless," Harald said. "She's building them a gift. Does that reassure you?"

"She's building *us* a tool to defeat them."

"We need to let Elmaestro Melendres know at once what the guardian is doing." Harald took several steps away from him.

"Do you think you failed, Harald, with Lauris? Is this why you are so concerned?"

Harald spoke over his shoulder. "I *did* fail with Yor Diebell. I won't fail again." He kept walking.

After a moment, Trevian followed.

M elendres swept back and forth, her fists clenched. "I'll have an armed guard on her day and night if I must."

"What crime is she committing?" Trevian said.

Profesor Stillwater said, "Building the very thing the New Way wants!"

"You judge the Señorita without a single question to her," Espinosa said.

Melendres glared. "I do not know why Justice Arm Stuart included you in this meeting," she said.

Harald stepped forward. "This is a team of several nations. All nations must be included."

"Madlyn isn't," Melendres snapped.

Harald flushed. "My error, Elmaestro. I didn't remember. I'll find their charmcaster—"

"No. This is fine; this is *more* than enough." She stared around the room. "Are we in agreement now? The yorita's actions are rash and dangerous?"

"I am not," said Espinosa.

"You, Capitan, may very well be in league with her."

"So, everyone who disagrees with you can be dismissed," Espinosa said.

"I am not convinced her acts are dangerous either," Stillwater said. Melendres's head snapped around, her eyes wide.

Stillwater seemed to consider her words. "I do not question her *motives.*"

"You have never, before now, spoken any word about a tower," Trevian said.

"Everyone knew," Melendres said.

Harald held up his hand. "I knew because Tregannon briefed me," he said. "But I was not present when Holay was interviewed. Neither was Capitan Espinosa. Was *he* informed?"

Now Melendres's face tuned red. "I do not know. I assumed Tregannon had explained."

"There was a fear they would reopen a frontera using a device. It was never specified," Espinosa said.

Melendres stopped her pacing, and stood, her arms folded. "Why did she embark on this sudden fancy? I thought she wished to experiment with her raydee machine."

"You should ask her that question, and not me," Trevian said, "but I will say what I think. Yorita Mei wishes to move quickly to stop the parasites. She cannot experiment with her radio because another machine needs fuel to power it. And the waves that travel through the air are blocked by mountains, so she wishes to build a platform to lift the device high enough to send them free over the mountaintops."

"Well," Ruth said, "That sounds...logical."

"No doubt it's the same reason the New Way wanted *their* tall pole," Melendres said. She shook her head.

Trevian said, "Yorita Mei is a guardian. Should we not be guided by her knowledge?"

"Why should we? These stories of the Four Families, they are fireside tales and the stuff of mystery plays. Why must we automatically trust out-of-worlders who know nothing of us?"

"Because they are our history," Ruth said. "We should at least listen to them."

"History!"

Ruth said, "Everything Yorita Dosmanos has said has been borne out by other sources. This very place, Elmaestro...they understand it better than we. We should at least have Yorita Mei explain the purpose of her tower. And we should tell her our concerns."

"She listens to nothing."

Ruth raised a finger. "That's not true. She acknowledged the machines might be dangerous."

"Not the one she wanted."

Trevian said, "She *wanted* to experiment with all of them. She conceded to you about the boxes in the laboratory room."

Melendres said, "Brel refused to destroy this place, and now we build the very structure the New Way wants. This is backwards. Councilmember Farway had it right."

Harald said, "Councilmember Farway was so negligent she sent a spy into our midst."

Espinosa shifted his sling. His voice was calmer, a little softer than usual. "Elmaestro, I fear to speak again, because I know anything I say you will distrust—"

"Would you be any different?"

He hesitated. "I would not. Our countries...distrust each other. We both must decide if we can trust these people, the ones you and Elmaestro Tregannon assembled, and the guardians who are so much a part of your history. I know you question my thoughts about Señorita Mei, but what I see in her is a woman dedicated to defeating the creatures who had her parents killed. She believes they threaten her world as well."

Melendres held up her hand. "Let me be clear to everyone. I may have spoken harsh words in anger, but I do not question the ycrita's motives. I only say she is reckless."

"Erin is also reckless," Ruth said. "She was impossible to hold back. Carving that charm onto herself with no discussion is only one example. It took her into the heart of the New Way, where we could have lost her forever, but got us vital information, and it helped Trevian close the frontera."

"Your point?"

"We can trust them. I think, if we are less angry and fearful, we can direct Yorita Mei."

Trevian doubted it, privately.

"So, we build a tower. Brel spoke of honey in the bottom of a jar to attract the New Way. Now we build them a nameday gift. Is this our plan?"

Harald said, "We strengthen our wards, and we prepare to hold our borders, and we let Mei build what tools she needs to defeat these creatures once and for all."

"If you will allow me," Espinosa said, "I have experience strengthening borders."

Melendres stared at him and gave a little huff. "In his message to Harald, Elmaestro Tregannon explained why he hadn't notified me you were part of the team, Capitan. He said he had *forgotten* our border disputes and didn't realize *we* thought they were so important."

Espinosa snorted too. For a moment the two of them were united in indignation. Trevian wondered what Erin would say when he told her. Then he remembered she was gone.

"However, one thing I do know. Perlarayna has strong borders. I accept your assistance, Capitan Espinosa."

He bowed, wincing.

"Very well. This is reckless turviness. Let us make it the best reckless turviness we can," Melendres said.

Profesor Stillwater came to him while he was helping a charmcaster sort metals. "I would like to extend the wards, especially toward the canal tunnel road."

"It is a public road," he said, "though little used."

"I know it's questionable, but I think we must."

He stood up. "I will help," he said.

"Good. I'll get a pair of guards and we'll go together."

"Are you worried about a specific attack, profesor?"

Half-turned away, she looked over her shoulder. "Worried is too strong a word. The people who have harried us have been ignorant people, deliberately misled by rumors, but several...engagements? Is that a military term? Have come from there."

"Perhaps those are meant to be distractions," he said.

"Perhaps. And those distractions will be met with robust wards."

He followed her back to the town hall, where she chose two guards, one of whom was also a copper-hunter. Even with the new company from Duloc, the guards were running themselves threadbare. Tregannon needed to send still more. Melendres had said more Crescent Council guards would be joining them soon.

As Stillwater led them toward the canal tunnel, Trevian thought of Mei's comment about the human-made tunnels. Had she really thought they didn't know? The evenness of its shape, the gray walls, the strange smooth substance, neither rock nor earth, lining the floor. She, like Espinosa, really did think they were primitive. Perhaps they were when he considered the things Erin and even Mei spoke of. Tubes of loomin flying people through the air, clear around the world—he had grown up with that fireside tale, but apparently it truly happened in their world. And—the strangest part—not powered by elementals.

Halfway between their camp and the tunnel, the profesor stopped. She shaded her eyes and looked at the steep cliff rising next to them. "What about those? Should we plant some wards up there?"

They had warded the long plateau that led into Orchard Hill, and Trevian thought this was an equally good precaution. "It's a steep climb," he said. He'd made worse. "As I recall, there are small caves and overhangs along this face. An enemy could gather and hide there, I think, but I do not know where they would have come from."

"Through the tunnel, in the small hours of the night, with no light and dark clothing, hiding themselves from our guards?" Stillwater said. She'd given this much thought.

One of the guards nodded.

Trevian held out his hand. "I'll plant them," he said, and Stillwater poured eight charmed disks into his palm.

The copper-hunter guard insisted on accompanying him. Encumbered with a club and a crossbow, he climbed more slowly than Trevian, but they made it up to a narrow ledge looking down over the lake. Trevian raised a hand, and Stillwater waved back. If he planted a ward here, if would extend the protection given by the charm the profesor was currently planting. The difficulty, he discovered, was not in the climb but digging in the rocky soil. The other guard helped him, chipping away rock with his knife, and soon they had the first one placed.

Trevian peered up, thinking. Another few, along the ridgeline, would slow any New Way hosts who tried to come over the western hills. The climb was a challenge, and he widened the gap between himself and the guard. Sunlight still struck the high points of the ridge, and it was warmer here. He found a spot to stand and wait for the guard to catch him.

A shout echoed off the mountains. The guard with Stillwater fell, an arrow springing out of his thigh. Stillwater caught the guard, pulled him back, and shouted, waking the warding charm. A group streamed out of the tunnel, three on caballos, the rest—seven, eight?— on foot. One mounted rider held a longbow.

Trevian dropped belly-down on the rocks. He peered the other way, to see the copper-hunter guard crouched back under a boulder, loading a bolt into his crossbow.

A second arrow stuck the ward and ricocheted, skidding into the mudflats.

The lead rider shouted something, words bouncing off the rocks, but Trevian caught the word *infestation*. He looked back down at the crouching guard, who was leveling his bow, and made a frantic hand-sign of negation. Even from here, he saw the guard's eye narrow, but the man nodded, holding off on his shot while keeping the crossbow ready.

As stealthily as he could, Trevian let himself slither down and to one side, hoping to come around behind the group. He didn't recognize a single person, but he would have wagered his entire claim they were from White Bluffs. Crouching behind a boulder, he pulled his mourning scarf up over his nose and tied it tightly. If there was a host among them, he didn't want to be recognized.

"Clear out! You're not wanted! You bring a plague!"

"You are attacking the Copper Coalition! And we bring no disease!" Stillwater shouted back. She had knelt by the injured guard, supporting his weight, but now he sat up on one elbow, and she rose to her feet. "You'll answer to your sheriff for this."

Trevian's skin began to itch, growing to a sting as he climbed. He waited, curled behind a rock, scanning the group. There was a host among them.

"The Copper Coalition's in league with them! Everyone knows it, they have been for years," the archer shouted.

"In league with what?" Stillwater put her hands on her hips.

The riders reined in, caballos milling and stamping at the edge of the ward.

"Well? With what?"

"The...the plague!" The lead rider shouted. "They've used prospectors to spread it!"

One of the men in the group shouted, "Charge the ward! It won't hold forever! Let's cleanse this place!"

"You are fools!" Stillwater said. She wasn't shouting, but her voice carried. Sadly, it was making little difference. Without looking, Trevian knew the guard on the cliff was marking the longbow holder, and if that man nocked another arrow, he would fire.

"This excavation is a venture between the Crescent Council and the

Coalition! You are attacking the Council. Are you aware of the penalties for that?"

"You're lying!" the bow holder shouted.

The stinging of Trevian's arm grew close to unbearable. While their attention was directed at Stillwater, he slipped down on a diagonal. The mark began to burn. Somewhere at the back of the cluster, the infected host waited.

Behind Stillwater, at least a dozen people came running, armed. He thought he saw Genaro.

The walkers crowded around, pushing against the ward. Good, they gave no thought to what might happen behind them. Trevian dropped onto the shore. There, a young woman stood, pointing, speaking softly, at the very back. She wore a simple blue skirt over trousers, jacket a little too big, her hair held back with a ribbon.

Trevian tucked all but one of the charms into his pocket and slipped his rebar club off his belt with his other hand. As he watched, she called, "Father?" Two riders reined their caballos around to face her.

Trevian crouched and sprinted, whirling his club. Gravel spurted out from under his feet. He raced up behind her as her father urged his caballo forward. Trevian shouted, "Aooooguh!" and swung the club in front of the caballo's face. The mount reared, pivoting into the second caballo, and the bow-holding rider cried out and fell. Trevian grabbed the girl by the arm, spun her around, and pulled his club against her throat. His arm felt like it was on fire. He spoke the work to wake the charm in his hand.

"Stay back!"

The young woman whimpered. "Stop him, please! He's infected! Don't worry about me!"

He sidled toward the edge of Stillwater's ward.

The head rider drew a knife. "Let go of my girl!" he shouted. "Mestengos! Monsters!"

"You must stop them all!" the woman shouted.

Trevian walked backward, dragging the woman, as her father charged his mount at his ward. The caballo struck it, and staggered, screaming. Pain blew through Trevian's bones. He kept backing away, toward Stillwater.

"She's infected," Stillwater said. "I feel it from here!"

The father was off his mount now, brandishing his knife, hacking at the ward. "Get your filthy hands off my girl!" Trevian felt each blow, but they were an annoyance only. The air around him compressed as the edges of his ward bumped up against Stillwater's.

Six guards stood alongside Stillwater now, crossbows loaded and pointing, while a healer knelt beside the downed guard. Trevian didn't turn his head, but he knew the guard on the cliff had reloaded too.

The attackers milled around, growing silent. Their bow fighter, rocking back and forth moaning, a crossbow bolt in his leg, and had silenced them. Only the father was still charging.

"Ready?" Stillwater said.

Trevian nodded. She spoke, putting the charm to sleep and he back-stepped, dragging the girl with him. As the attackers rushed, Stillwater reawakened the charm. Bodies thudded off the ward and Stillwater staggered. Genaro caught her arm.

"Profesor, are you well?"

"I've never felt that before," she said between gasps.

"Father! Don't let them take me! They'll infect me!" the host shouted.

Genaro came forward with a short riata in his hand. Trevian put his own ward to sleep, and Genaro caught the woman's hands, lashing them together. The attackers set up a clamor, throwing themselves at the ward.

The young woman began to thrash. The top of her head struck Trevian's chin, driving his teeth together before he could dodge.

"Profesor, you'd better be the one to do this," he said. To the attackers, an innocent young woman was being dragged off by men. Tearing at her clothing would spill lick on a blazing fire if he or Genaro did it. He nudged the host's knees out from under her and forced her down. She whipped her head around like a kiote breaking an ardiya's neck, her teeth clacking.

Stillwater drew her knife and approached. Standing beside the woman, she yanked the oversized jacket down over the woman's arms. "Be silent!" she shouted.

After a second, the crown quieted.

"Do you see her blouse? Do you see she is unharmed?"

"I see you have a knife!" her father shouted, and the crowd at the back began to shout and curse.

Stillwater put the tip of the knife against the fabric and ripped. Trevian, expecting trouble, tightened his hold as the woman began to thrash. The New Way didn't care if she were injured or died; they only wanted to remain undetected. Now it was a race; could Stillwater reveal the parasite before it flattened and turned gray?

With one hand Stillwater tore the cloth away. The father roared, charged the ward again, fell back and froze. "What have you done?"

"You all saw I did not touch her."

"What *is* that?"

"Dios!"

"By the Mother. Is it…a tumor?"

Stillwater slipped the flat of the blade underneath the parasite. It stopped its pulsing and dropped from the woman's skin, shriveling like a fall leaf, to land gray and flattened on the pebbles and sand. The young woman sighed and fell back. Genaro and Trevian caught her.

"*There* is your parasite! There is your infection!" Ruth said.

The man with the long bow sat up. "Milan? Did you know of this? Did you bring us up here *knowing*?"

The father whirled, his back to the ward. "I did not! How could I know?"

"You told us *they* carried it!" someone at the back shouted.

Milan said, "Drop this ward, let me attend my daughter."

"She's a spy!"

"She is no spy," Stillwater said. "The parasite controlled her behavior. *She* was not to blame."

"You whipped us up, Milan! You said we had to keep our town safe, when sickness was right among us!"

Another attacker ran forward, grabbing Milan by the collar. "How many of us did she infect? How many!"

Stillwater dropped the ward and Genaro seized Milan, forcing him down and binding his hands. Harald must have given him all the riatas. The guards advanced on the group, crossbows aimed, and the attackers gave ground slowly.

Stillwater said, "We carry a charm to warn us if there is an infected one in a group. The rest of you are not, but you have injured an agent of the Copper Coalition and attacked the Crescent Council."

"We were lied to!"

"Misled! You can't blame us!"

Stillwater jerked her head at Milan. "We're taking your daughter for medical care along with our guard you had shot. You will accompany us." She raked the group with her glance and raised her voice. "You and she will give us the name of each person here, everyone who attacked a peaceful expedition of the Crescent Council and attempted murderous harm, not to mention bringing an infected person into our midst."

The group murmured, shifting from one foot to another.

"This is not an ordinary disease," Stillwater said, letting her voice grow a bit softer. "These parasites are driven by a hive mind from beyond a frontera. They wish to subjugate us. When you follow their wishes, as you just did, you are aiding them."

"We didn't *know!*"

"Did you ask the same kind of questions you would ask any merchant, if you were buying a cart or a new harness for your caballo?"

They were silent and Stillwater gave them a sharp nod. "Of course not."

"We trusted Milan!"

"You *must* ask questions. Speak to your sheriff. She is aware of the infestation and will help you protect yourselves."

"You said there is a charm! Why don't we have it?"

She raised her voice again. "You must ask your town council. You came here intending to harm us, you shot one of our guards. I have no more time for you." She turned her back and woke the charm, leaving them shifting and muttering.

As Trevian caught up with her, he said, "Is that wise?"

"I gave them things to think about." She slanted a glance at him. "Trevian?" She touched her chin.

He touched his own, fingers on skin. The scarf had torn loose and lay against his neck. He closed his eyes.

"The New Way knows I am here," he said.

"And they know you can close a frontera."

"If there was any doubt before," he said. "Now there is none. They will come."

27

Erin woke up a little after six in the morning. After she popped two more aspirin to beat back the copper headache, she took another shower. The motel's shower dispensed a gaggingly sweet bodywash and shampoo from a box on the shower wall. She went back to the taqueria and ordered coffee and a breakfast burrito. The coffee was overcooked, with a metallic taste. She remembered sisuree—pepper and pear.

Back in her room, she pulled out the bundles of cash and counted them up. With the money from her own account, she had a little over six thousand in cash. Maybe she'd buy Mei a generator. Reading down Mei's list, she decided she could pick off quite a few things before the Agustos arrived.

She pulled up one of the sheriff's texts and called. The outgoing message referred her to another number. She listened to its message, identifying it as a non-profit whose offices opened at eight. Rather than wait, she called for a ride and went to the neighborhood hardware store where she was able to get most of Mei's gauges. While she browsed the aisles, she saw a box reading "battery charger," and flagged down a woman in an orange smock to tell her what it worked on. After a pretty long conversation, Erin added a cordless drill, drill bit set, cordless screwdriver, spare battery, and battery charger to her cart. On her way up to the counter, passing the two shelves of office supplies, she grabbed a lined yellow pad and a pack of pens.

The clerk looked at her. "Got a DIY project, hon?"

"A big one."

By then it was after eight, and she called the non-profit. They had a contract from the county to help locate people identified as missing after the wildfire. The specialist asked for her name and date of birth. She gave it. There was a pause. "Erin, is there anyone with you right now?" the woman said.

"If you're going to tell me my parents and my grandmother died in the fire, I already know."

The woman moved on, asking her if there was anything she needed and offering a referral for services. She was clearly working off a script, and Erin's loosely concocted story about where she had been did not get much scrutiny. After five minutes, she thanked the woman and disconnected.

She paid her cell phone bill at the service center. The man who helped her had to activate the safe from his device and take her cash away behind a door that locked behind him. While she waited for him to come back, another box, like the battery charger, caught her eye.

"Power bank? What is this?"

"Super long-life battery," he said. "You know, if you had to evacuate, like the fires last month? Or if you lost power. Mega-useful. They'll run a laptop or a tablet for six hours, and a phone for over eight, as long as you're not watching a movie or something. And they recharge in about four hours."

"You can run other devices on them?"

"Sure. They get great reviews, want to see?" he reached for his phone, but she shook her head. She bought six. He was a lot happier opening the safe in the locked room this time.

The next logical thing was to call the memorial park, and she pulled out her phone, then tucked it back into her bag. It was probably still too early. She didn't want to call them from the backseat of a car with a stranger hearing everything. When she thought of calling the Piersons, her heart fluttered and she had a hard time getting her breath, so she settled for texting them.

The motel room seemed like a cell now. The smell of fabric softener filled the place, battling with the copper smell and making her more nauseated than she'd been before. This wasn't good. She sat down at the tiny table by the window and wrote out a letter for Mei, telling her what she'd bought. At the bottom, she put the local time and said she would be back at the frontera at 5 pm her time, the next day. Her hands shaking slightly, she wrote a short note to Trevian telling him she missed him.

She called for another ride and went back to East Woods Road. Perkins Security shouldn't be able to roust her, not with the bank statement, complete with address, on her. Sure enough, the white car followed her ride hail. She pulled out her documents, and they waved her through.

She had the driver let her out in front of her lot. When the car was out of sight, she walked over to the culvert.

Sitting cross-legged under the culvert bridge, she opened her book. She'd never watched a frontera open before. The shadowy space filled with a pulse of lavender light, then white, like bright sunlight. She spoke the words to activate the puerta stone, rolled the letters into a tube, and held them over the stone. They vanished.

She closed the frontera and walked back to East Woods Road. In front of the burned-out strip mall, she called for another car, and waited, staring at the western horizon, blue hills capped by a blue sky.

S he remembered coming back to the room, but she didn't remember falling asleep. When she woke up, dry-mouthed and disoriented, she saw she had a voicemail from the Piersons. They were relieved to hear from her, glad she was alive, sorry about her parents, and they had her final check for her. Did she want it mailed?

Mailed to where? She checked texts and emails. There was nothing from the Agustos, but the phone buzzed while she was holding it. "Hi, hon, we're about twenty minutes out," Remedios said.

"I'll get packed," she said.

The last time she'd seen the Agustos they'd been pale and sick from being held in a stupor by the New Way parasites, their energy fueling Oshane's copper magic. Now they looked like the couple she'd seen on videoconferences in the old days. Remedios's tanned skin was smooth, with a little puckering under her chin, and Daniel's greenish eye were clear and bright. He looked at the boxes by the door and said, "What's all this?"

"Mei's shopping list."

He scooped up the closest two. "Is she building something?"

"I'll explain."

She got a refund for the third night and climbed into the backseat of the rented Avalon. Her sinuses itched again. They would never stop. Now she could sense copper, she would feel like this all the time.

The convention center sat in the southwest corner of town, about half a mile from the railroad tracks, overlooking Prince Green Creek. In one more year, the county's commuter train would stop right next to it. She'd never been to the center before.

Their suite was on the third floor. Erin got into the elevator and almost passed out from the burnt hair and licorice smell. She stepped out. "I'll take the stairs," she said as the door closed.

The hotel used a vineyard and grapevine theme, barely audible instrumental music piped in from somewhere. The stairs were lined with large graphics of moments from the town's history rendered in tasteful sepia. From in here, you could almost pretend nothing had changed in Fountain Grove. The jade green carpet figured with brown and green swirls, the maroon walls...it was like playing a video game or watching a movie. Everything was slick, shiny, clean.

"I didn't think you were claustrophobic," Remedios said, settling her on the loveseat with a bottle of designer water.

"I'm not. It's...copper. Metals. I sense them now, and it's unpleasant sometimes."

"When did this happen?"

Erin shrugged. "Sometime while I was over there." She knew exactly when. Walking with Trevian up the empty streets of Merrylake Landing toward the old sheriff's house.

"Is it like an allergy?" Remedios sat beside her. Across the good-sized sitting room, Daniel finished fiddling with the coffee maker, which gurgled.

"Kind of." The smell of fresh coffee wafted around them. Erin relaxed against the back of the seat.

She swallowed some water and began, starting with the threat first. Once again, it was a relief to discuss the New Way as a networked consciousness without having to cast around for wild analogies. Daniel was particularly interested. "If it's AI, someone programmed it," he said.

"It's not AI now. It's descended from AI, and it's somehow connected with elemental energy. I don't want us to get trapped into thinking we can just, like, reprogram it or something. It's a life-form."

"Any you're sure Langtree isn't controlling it? He was manipulating those, those things."

"He isn't controlling it. They worked with him, reluctantly, because he's one of the rare few who can't be controlled. In fact, we think they've kicked him to the curb."

"Coffee? Take anything in it?"

"Black's fine, thanks."

He carried over the cups and sat down across from her. "You and Mei think the lantern and the compass will close the frontera, so what will a radio do?"

"Block their signal and destroy their local network. The frontera has to be closed first. If they manage to open it, they'll bring an invasion force through. They've got energy weapons, they'd be unstoppable."

She started explaining the process. This part didn't go as smoothly, because she ran right into problems of governments and ruling parties, military or no military, and who was in charge. She kept stumbling and having to back up. It wasn't that their questions weren't good. She just didn't know the answers.

Remedios narrowed her eyes when Erin showed her the mark. "That's mutilation, Erin," she said.

"It's not, though. Look, the book shows us—" She pulled out the book and flipped to the page with the drawing. "It isn't any worse than a tattoo."

"That doesn't make your case," Remedios said. "Are you going to want to carve that mark on us before we go back there?"

Erin nodded. "And it's an early warning system. You can sense them."

Daniel said, "Does it keep you from being taken over?"

"Not exactly." She explained. Halfway through, Remedios shook her head and walked over to the window.

"So, if it doesn't work, why do it?"

"It *does* work. It's an espionage weapon. And it works great. I only know what they are because I was merged with them. Otherwise, we'd still be underestimating them, thinking they were being controlled by the locals, like Langtree, and they'd have conquered his world. Once they did, they'd have access to all the linked worlds."

"Why do you say that?"

"All the frontera open there. It's like a hub."

Remedios fiddled with the coffeemaker. When she came back, she looked skeptical. "You said you already tried to close this second frontera."

"We had six people. It wasn't enough."

"Including you? You're magical now. More than you were already, I mean."

"Yes, including me. It didn't work. But Mei's compass started reacting. And there was a major earthquake."

Daniel said, "Are you sure you've got the cause-and-effect right? Maybe the quake opened the frontera."

Had it? She swirled her coffee cup. Was she remembering wrong? Sitting in the glossy luxurious suite, she was suddenly not sure. No—there'd been the yelling outside in the corridor before the ceiling collapsed, before Lauris... "I've got it right," she said. She stared at each of them. "I've been over there for weeks now. Every single day, this is what I've been fighting, or studying. You're acting like I'm traumatized or drama-queening it."

"No," Daniel said.

Remedios spoke over him. "Of course we don't think that. But you're exhausted, and this is hard to wrap our minds around. We only ever really saw Langtree, and he was in control of those elemental creatures."

"It's hard to let go an initial assumption," Daniel said.

"Is that directed at me?"

He smiled. "No. It's about us." He glanced at his phone. "Okay, I know it's not dinner time here, but I'm starved. Do you want to order room service, or should we go down to the restaurant?"

Their body-clocks were on Florida time. "Let's check out the restaurant," she said. "And..." She leaned forward, set her cup on the glass coffee table, well away from the edge. The clink as the ceramic struck glass shivered through her fingers. "My parents. I have a prepaid funeral plan and I, I should have called today, I..."

"We'll help you," Remedios said. "First thing tomorrow."

"Shouldn't we be shopping first thing tomorrow?"

"I think the list will go pretty quickly," Remedios said.

Erin sat back. A weight fell off her chest, and she sucked in a deep breath, maybe the first one since she'd landed back here.

The Brasserie was done up in shades of brown and gray, with gleaming metal accents, a carving station, and an open kitchen, where a black marble bar seemed to run on for a mile. The smell of roast beef and frying fat filled her nostrils, conjuring up a juicy burger, a carpet of cheddar cheese melting over the pebbled surface of the meat, the pillow of the bun compressing, juices running down the corner of her mouth.

They got a booth. There was a Wagyu beef burger on the menu, and Erin ordered it with a green salad. The Agustos got drinks with their orders.

Remedios sipped her margarita and said, "It sounds like you've been learning something about their society, their culture, and their history. We weren't there...well, conscious, anyway, long enough to understand, but they seemed technically primitive."

"Mid-nineteenth century?" Erin said. "They have machines, they have clocks and timepieces, but they don't use clockwork for other machines. They rely heavily on the elementals." She speared a half cherry-tomato. It was ripe, sweet, and tangy. She missed tomatoes. "They're like, raging capitalists, as near as I can tell, and they haven't a war in a couple hundred years."

Daniel said, "That seems contradictory."

"I know. I think maybe there just weren't enough people. Mei says..." She relayed what Mei had told them of Perlarayna, pausing when their entrees were set in front of them.

Remedios nibbled a slice of the baby squash accompanying with her chicken breast. "Do you think it was our world? An identical planet, I mean?"

"I do, but the pre-collapse culture was different. There were differences in religion and government. In some ways, they're sexist, but they're not puritanical. It's...weird."

They were mostly silent as they ate. She didn't know them well; they were another guardian family, but all the videoconferences had been artifact-related, primarily. Erin's grandmother and Remedios had been friends, bonding over television shows. "Are you still watching *The Crown*? Is it still on?" she said.

"You haven't been gone that long. Yes, I am. I think of Dolores every time I sit down to watch."

She was only able to finish half her burger. They skipped dessert and got to-go boxes. Back in the suite, Remedios read over the list. "Tasers?"

"Yeah. They should disrupt the node's communication, and you can fire them from a short distance away. You don't have to get within knife or club range." She looked at their faces. "The people we'll be fighting, they're controlled. No one wants to *kill* them."

Remedios shrugged. "Okay." She grabbed her tablet and started searching.

They watched the local news—the fire was still a big deal—and then a costume drama on PBS. Remedios said, "Erin?" and woke her up an hour later.

She trudged into her bathroom, brushed her teeth, and got ready for bed. If she dreamed, she didn't remember.

She ate the rest of her burger for breakfast. After she showered, she pulled the necessary papers out of her bag before she could come up with another reason to stall. "I'm going to call the mortuary."

After a moment on hold, she connected with a woman with a professionally soothing voice who have them an appointment for nine. Erin took an aspirin for her copper headache and put on her shoes.

Remedios handed back the list. "I added a few things."

First aid supplies—yeah, good. Socks? Underwear? They had underwear in Trevian's world, but another pair of shoes, some hiking boots, weren't a bad idea.

They drove north, the horizon still smudged with a brownish tint. "Is the sky ever going to be clear again?"

Daniel said, "It will."

She could see more scars of the fire. She thought it had burned from the north, but at some point, it swung around and came at the town from the east. A hill on the eastern outskirts spread a flank of black instead of the golden tan common this time of year. The city was more broken than she first thought.

As they pulled into the Memorial Park's lot, her heart began to race. Across the threshold, her feet sank into the thick carpet. The woman at the desk welcomed them, directed them to a siting area and offered them coffee or tea. A dwarf Japanese maple filled the space beyond the single window with edged crimson.

Robert Knowles approached, shook hands with everyone and led them back to his quiet, word-paneled office. Some certificates, framed in dark cherry wood, hung on the walls, and four-color brochures filled the side table. He expressed sorrow at her loss and said he was glad she had a support system.

She handed him the papers. He smoothed them out and opened a pale blue folder sitting on the blotter. "I guess you were out of town for a while," he said.

She launched into her rehearsed story. "I left the night before the fires. Visiting friends in Idaho and…they're really off the grid."

His eyes skimmed the paperwork.

She said, "I don't have death certificates, but I'm sure I can get them. And they, the, the remains, I don't know how to—"

"Erin," he held up his hand, speaking softly. "We will do all of that." He walked her through the process. The mortuary would order the death certificates and have the bodies released to them.

"Do you prefer a full burial?" he said. "Cremation is an option, but many people have opted—"

"Cremation is fine."

Remedios whispered, "Really?"

"It's all right, they're already…" Her voice wobbled out of control again. "… it's purer."

She requested inexpensive urns, to be buried next to her brother and her grandfather.

He made some notes. "A service? Would you like it here?"

"No service. There's no one—" she planned to say, "there's no one to attend," but the words stopped her. There was no one.

He explained. Once the remains were transferred, cremation and burial would happen quickly if there was no memorial service. Then he went through the paperwork with her. She signed her name three times and initialed things twice. "Prepaid" didn't really mean there was nothing left to pay for. There were fees and other costs. At the end, she carefully counted out twenties onto his desk. He left to get change. When he returned, he handed her a brochure for a survivors' support group. "I'll call you later on this afternoon, Erin."

"Thank you."

"Would you like to spend a few minutes in our meditation garden before you go?"

"No. Thank you. I'm fine."

Outside, the sky directly overhead was clear blue, and two more ginkgo trees dropped yellow fan-shaped leaves. The rented Avalon gleamed silver and a light breeze moved the air around her.

"You okay?" Daniel said again, as he opened the door for her.

"Yeah. I was stupid, I should have said I was deployed."

"No, it opens up too many questions," he said. "You made a good choice. You don't owe anyone an explanation."

She slid in.

Remedios leaned in between the seats. "How are you feeling?"

"Like I'm a bad daughter."

"Erin, never think that! They don't."

"I don't know. I'm burning their bones and leaving a day later like—"
Burning their bones, a phrase from Trevian's world.

Daniel reversed out the space and swung the car out onto the road.
"None of them, of *us*, ever thought we'd really have to go into another
world, let alone fight off an invasion there."

"Erin, your dad, your parents and your grandmother are proud of you
right now," Remedios said.

"Yeah, I'm just a hero."

Remedios slumped back into her seat with a sigh. "Your mother was
really angry when Chip enlisted," she said. "It wasn't only because she
feared for his safety. She thought they were cheating you. Your father's
approach was, well, Chip'll finish his tour, come home and it will be Erin's
turn to go to college, have a life. But that wasn't what happened. You had
to sacrifice everything."

"Chip sacrificed everything, too."

"He did. It doesn't lessen what you did."

"What we're trying to say is we think you're heroic," Daniel said,
glancing in the rearview. "So, how about taking the victory lap?"

Despite herself she laughed. "Okay. Victory lap. I'll try it."

Whether it was sporting goods, automotive or electronics, not a
single sales representative in a single store reacted oddly to their
shopping demands or the cash payments. One of Mei's electronic gadgets
required a visit to a specialty store, but even the Tasers weren't a challenge. There was a background check requirement which meant they
couldn't pick them up until the next day, but buying fifteen wasn't a problem, and they didn't need to trot out their cover story about providing
security for a public event.

It wasn't like they were buying the components of a bomb or anything,
right?

The pile of stuff filled the trunk of the rental car. Hauling it back
through the frontera might become more of a problem than she'd first
thought.

"Will they let us take gas cans into a burned area?" she said, envisioning the white security car prowling the neighborhood.

"We'll need to think about that," Daniel said.

Remedios squeezed the bag of gauges into a corner of the trunk. "What's left to burn?"

"There's plenty," Daniel said, "at the edge of the zone. You've seen the rumors already on OurTown."

Erin said, "You joined OurTown for here?" OurTown was an online community divided up by addresses.

"Right after we got back," Daniel said, making sure Remedios was clear before he closed the trunk. "It was a way to keep track of things."

For lunch, Remedios directed them to a downtown pizza place she'd read about. Erin's headache raged up like a migraine, and she could smell nothing but copper.

While they were eating, the mortuary called. Her family would be buried the next day. Cremation would take place at eleven, if she wanted to attend. She told him politely she didn't plan to.

She thought she should feel more than she did.

"We can go," Remedios said. "We can pick up the Tasers after."

Erin shrugged and took a bite of her slice of thin-crust pizza Margherita. "I don't need to," she said. She wasn't sure it was true, but she really didn't *want* to.

The Agustos exchanged a glance and didn't reply.

28

They carried the injured guard up to the camp. Trevian guided the host woman while Genero prodded her now-silent father along.

The woman was dazed, shaking her head and muttering. She wasn't in a deep stupor like many in Madalita had been, which meant, or seemed to mean, she hadn't been infected long, just long enough to persuade a group of gullible fools to attack them. What had the New Way found out while she was merged with them?

"I couldn't stop," she muttered. "I knew what I was doing, but I couldn't stop it."

"We know."

"How did this happen to you, Celisa?" her father said. "I saw no change in you, none!"

Stillwater snapped. "Later! She will answer questions when we all can hear. You, yor, would better spend your thoughts on how you will explain your attack on us to the Crescent Council Justice Arm."

She was still angry.

Harald met them with one of the healers and a tarp for the wounded guard, who refused it and insisted on hobbling to the medical cabin. They took Celisa and her father into the town hall building. "Tell me what happened."

Stillwater ran through it in short sentences, her lips clipping the ends of her words as you might slam the door on a cat trying to come inside. Twice, Celisa's father interrupted and twice Stillwater's glare silenced him.

"So they know Trevian is here. They'll be on their way, no doubt in force. You—" Harald looked at the young woman.

"Celisa Fenster, Justice Arm."

"How did you get infected?"

"My husband. He rode to Three Springs to bring back a load of wool. When he came back, he said he had something I needed to see. This was a sennight ago, a little longer."

Her father said, "A sennight!"

"Are you weavers?" Harald asked, softening his tone slightly.

She jerked her head in a nod.

"What were you and your husband doing during this time?"

"I...I was talking to my father and his friends. I told them Joseph heard tales of the parasites, coming down from Merrylake Landing. I..." she glanced at her father. "I pretended I was fearful and asked if they had seen or heard anything. I, in the market, I'd flinch and gasp when I saw a prospector pass me. When Father would ask what was wrong, I'd say it was no matter."

"I thought you were frightened!"

"It is what we, *they* wished you to think."

Harald said, "And Joseph? What did he do? Did he also spread rumors?"

"No, he...he has a friend with a tavern on the southern green, where Jefe Silvestro of the Langtree Company often rides with his friends. Many days, in the afternoon, they stop for ale or a shot of lick before returning home. Joseph offered to help with washing up, and he asked lots of admiring questions about the jefe, about the progress of the company and what steps they were taking to protect the cages. Jefe Silvestro spoke openly of it."

Stillwater murmured, "This is very bad."

"I must let Aideen know at once."

She held up her hand. "Let's get as much information as we can first."

"Do you know their plans?" Harald said.

She stared past him, blinking. "I know some. It's like a dream, so real when it happens, but fading already. They need the cages, and they have among them a host with a weapon that shoots lightning. And there's a frontera nearby, one they need to open."

271

"When? When will they attack the cages?"

She rolled her shoulders in a helpless shrug. "It was not given to us to know."

Harald's eyes narrowed. "Can the New Way choose what you know and don't know of it?"

"I...I think so. It didn't seem like that. It seemed like I was part of a great family, all warmth and joy...but shouldn't I know when the attack is planned, if I were truly one with them?"

"A good point," Harald said. He shifted around to stare at Celine's father. "Your name?"

"Milan Markow."

"We know you are not infected," Harald said, "but I'm inclined to keep you here under guard, since you may be working for the parasites for coin or some other advantage."

Markow sputtered. "What? I knew nothing! My daughter and son-in-law had tales, they sounded true, I only wanted to protect—"

Harald said casually, "When did you first meet Lauris Diebell?"

"Who? I know of no one by that name."

Harald stared at him without speaking. He shrugged. "Very well. We will hold you both here until the sheriff or her deputies come to claim you." He switched his attention back to Celisa. A chill skittered down Trevian's spine at the complete coldness with which Harald dismissed Markow.

"Yora Fenster, is there anything else the New Way revealed to you?"

"There is someone they call the unreliable source. They are wary of him, and they believe he is operating against them, in this area. He is somehow connected with an air elemental."

"And why was this important, do you think?"

Celine wet her lips. "They do not like air elementals. Earth elementals are a worry because they can consume a host. But air elementals are another matter, and they wish to keep their distance. They would destroy them all if they knew how."

"Why?" Harald's tone was gentle.

"I don't know."

Harald and Stillwater shared a glance. "Very well." Harald got to his feet. "We will see you and your father are kept comfortable and closely watched until the sheriff's people arrive."

As they all rose, Markow muttered, "We were duped. I don't see why you must—"

Stillwater whirled and nearly ran to him, thrusting her face into his. "Shall I tell you *why*? You rode down on us and attacked with no warning. That is not the act of a protector, or a righteous person. It's the behavior of a mestengo."

"We believed you were a threat to us," he mumbled, looking at his boots.

"*You* were the threat." She marched past them all. "Guards!"

H arald summoned Capitan Espinosa, Mei, and Elmaestro Melendres and gave them the warning. At Melendres's direction, he and Trevian quickly wrote reports to the White Bluffs sheriff and Aideen, while Melendres composed an urgent note to Tregannon. She summoned two riders and sent them off, one north to Duloc, the other to White Bluffs.

"We don't have enough guards," she said, watching the haunches of the caballo as the one ride headed north. "We are vulnerable. At least we have the wards."

"Aideen said she had warded the cages, so that is some comfort."

"Sixteen trained guards will not be enough to protect the town." The elmaestro kept her gaze trained on the trail, the rider now vanished from view around a curve. "This weapon like lightning, do you know it?"

"Yes. They struck me with it. It burned like fire, and it jolted in a way I've never felt before."

"Can it kill?"

"I think it can."

"But only one, this woman said."

"One she knows of. She pointed out to us she did not know everything the New Way knows."

"I thought they shared knowledge instantly." She stared at him now.

"There is some...aspect? That seems to guide what the hosts know."

"A ruler of some sort, a jefe?"

"I do not think our images and words match them," he said. "Erin has thoughts on this, but I don't think she'll say the New Way has a jefe."

"Perhaps a sieve?"

"Yes, maybe more like that." He cleared his throat. "This vulnerability to air elementals interests me, Elmaestro, especially if the Pit is home to some. Could we not aim them in some way at the nodes?"

"All we know about air elementals is that they can kill," she said. "Let's not drink poison to forestall the enemy stabbing us."

"The one my uncle uses is controlled, like the flames that killed Erin's parents. We do not know them in their native state. They may not be poison."

"And we have no time to learn. Trevian, this whole expedition is about people, the Ancients, us, wielding power with catastrophic results, whether it's imprisoning elementals or trying to open frontera between worlds and fusing those worlds together. I will not be the one who creates the next catastrophe."

"I understand," he said. He did, he simply thought she was wrong.

He found Harald and Stillwater sitting together in the dining hall. Harald held both her hands. They looked up when he entered. He was ready to veer away, but both of them smiled.

"Are you still angry?" he said as he sat down next to Stillwater.

"I am, sadly. I pride myself on remaining calm, using self-control, but those *people*. And I know it's not their fault," she said, as if to head off his comment.

"They had reason to fear, and reason to question us, not to fire on us without a word," he said.

Stillwater sighed heavily. "When Tregannon sent me here as Elmaestro Melendres's second, I was confident. This is my strength; history, scholarship, organizing things."

"And you are doing it well," Harald said.

"No. I'm in the mountains without a map."

"We are all in those mountains," Trevian said, "and there is no map."

"You guide us, Ruth," Harald said. "And you nudge Melendres forward when she would balk and shy away."

"Which is not often," Stillwater said. "She's no coward."

"No, but she is lost in the mountains, too, and she doesn't have the experience we do."

"She's getting it daily."

Harald said, "I believe Markow had no contact with Lauris. I hope Councilmember Farway will take the right steps."

"Perhaps Elmaestro Tregannon will nudge *her*," Trevian said.

"Drag her by the reins, you mean," Stillwater said.

A t dinner, Mei brought him a strip of yellow paper. 'Erin sent you a note," she said.

"You had a message from her?"

"Yeah, good news." Mei scanned the group.

Trevian pointed to where Harald and Melendres were sitting. "May I give you a reply to this?" he said.

"Yes. Sure. She's opening her frontera tomorrow, about this time, and we'll exchange notes then."

"The frontera has to be open?"

"Seems like." She started straight for Melendres's table.

He unfolded the thin paper, slightly slick compared to what he was used to. Pale yellow, with light blue fibers running through it. As he followed her words, he decided they weren't fibers, but rather lines painted into the paper for guidance.

Composing his response in his mind, he left the table, planning to go to his cabin to write his answer. He looked over the lake as he walked. Twilight was falling. The shadow of Orchard Hill cast across the lake like a blanket. Flocks of sprites darted over the surface of the lake, splitting and merging like a whirling, turvy scarf. He wondered if he could describe it in his note to Erin. As he watched, the shimmering flock parted again, dividing almost in half. One half curved like a knife blade and shot toward him. The air above them flashed blue, and the sprites vanished.

He stepped back, shocked. He spun around and shouted, "Hey!" He cupped his hands around his mouth and shouted again, for Harold, for Melendres.

Espinosa, Harald, and Melendres crowded through the door and rushed toward him. "What has happened?" Harald shouted.

Trevian turned, waving an arm at the lake surface. When he turned back, only a fringe of sprites remained, clustered in the reeds along the shore.

"What is this?" Melendres slowed. "I see only sprites."

"An air elemental," he said. "It was feeding on them."

Espinosa's mouth curled. "You mean the sprites flew away?"

Melendres said, "We've seen the elementals feed on sprites in Pais Lewelyn. Do you think it was a wild one, or the one your uncle has tethered?"

"I don't know."

"Could you see it?" Espinosa demanded.

"No. I could see the sprites racing to avoid it, and I saw a flash of blue above them."

"Much like what we saw in the cavern, when the rubble room collapsed," Melendres said. Spinning on her heel, she scanned the lake. "Well, it's gone now."

"What does it mean for us?" Trevian said. "Do you think it came from the Pit?"

"There is no evidence the air elementals come from the Pit," Melendres said.

Trevian held his ground. "Except the copper-hunters hear the sound of air elementals from it."

Melendres shrugged. "We'll have no answers tonight." To Harald she said, "Are the wards at fullest strength?"

Harald stepped closer to Trevian. "We will check," he said.

I wish I could be with you. I wish I could share your burdens, he wrote. *This evening I watched the sprites swirl over the waters of the lake like a scarf.* He decided not to tell her about the attack. She would only worry, and there was nothing she could do.

He folded the paper and put it in his pocket to give to Mei. Any air elemental could have been drawn to the lake, because of the sprites, or even because of the activity in the caverns. It didn't have to be Oshane's. It wouldn't be his first assumption, if a worker hadn't been killed from a fall, and another disappeared.

The revelation of his mother's murder was at the front of his mind. Perhaps it was only a dark hope that his uncle was close enough to lay hands on, render justice to, or his fear that Oshane would still find a way to harm Erin. He gazed at the knapsack at his feet, the golden collar with the blue stones nestled into the bottom, safe from Oshane or the New Way for now.

Outside, Mei sat with several others around a glowing whiterock fire. He gave her his folded letter and sat beside her. Mei slipped the paper into her pocket. "I want to visit the tunnel project tomorrow. Will you go with me?"

"Along with a guard, of course."

276

"I feel like I shouldn't pull a guard away from the camp or the cave complex."

"You are vital to our defense, Yorita Mei, and you will have a guard."

She rolled her eyes. "All right, fine."

"And the Capitan?"

"I'll explain to him," she said.

They left early in the morning, Mei, Trevian, and a guard with a crossbow, all garlanded with moonstone chains. His sister wasn't present, but Yor Lopez rushed to greet them, grinning widely as he shook Mei's hand. Stepping over a stack of quartz sheets, he escorted her to a U-shaped work area, where a curl of papers nested, and weighted down the edges of the top one with rocks. Trevian trailed behind.

"We're drawing off more radiance each day," he said.

Leaning against the table, Trevian studied the square conduits of quartz, the sides fastened together with charmed copper, exactly like his father's cages, except long and narrow, with no copper mesh and no prisoners. "Why didn't my father try this first?"

Yor Lopez paused with his finger on a pentagon drawn on the sheet. "He did, but the copper kept melting."

"Do they disturb you, the flames? When you're working?"

Lopez snorted a laugh. "Daily! We wear leather aprons and hoods as a protection. At least one a day rises out the rifts to visit us."

"They attack?" Mei said.

"Oh, no. They're curious."

Mei looked at Trevian. "I'm confused. Do they think or not?"

"We don't know the answer to that," he said.

"I don't believe they think, yorita," Lopez said, "but they do watch." Lopez moved his head. "Is this the best place for us to begin entwining the feeder cords?"

"Show me in real life," Mei said. Lopez looked puzzled but led her around the glowing rifts to the conglomeration of machinery and materials. Memory tugged at Trevian. He knew those spools of copper, the charmed leather tubes, the machines, from the cages.

Two other sheets of paper formed a pad beneath Lopez's schematic of the tunnel project. Idly, Trevian nudged one of the stones, and the top sheet curled up, revealing the one beneath.

It brought back memories too, hours trapped in his father's study, forced to review the schematic of the cord strung and buried throughout the town, harangued to memorize line numbers and junction numbers, frostbitten by his father's disapproval when he failed.

Yor Lopez had marked two key lines and a central junction with ink. "Yor Lopez? A moment?"

"Certainly." Lopez wended his way between trailing cords of copper, smiling. He saw the curled top page. His smile didn't falter but his shoulders tensed.

Trevian said, "What are these marks?"

"Ah, well, we will have to run cords to your cave complex," he said.

"These don't show that."

Lopez smoothed out the top sheet and set the rock back in place. "You'd have to discuss it with your sister—or your wife."

"It looks like you're redirecting lines."

Lopez's gaze slid from one side to the other, like a frying egg in hot oil. "A project only, jefe."

Trevian wanted to press, but he had made a promise to Ilsanja. He would be free, and the running of the company would rest with her and Aideen. He would make sure Aideen was aware of the changes to the schematic, certainly. "I know Yorita Mei is helping you. I'll let you get back to it."

"Thank you, jefe."

"I prefer 'yor,' or even Trevian, Yor Lopez."

"Thank you." Lopez hurried away as if he could outpace more questions. He caught his foot on one loop of leather and plunged forward, catching himself in the next stride.

As a boy, Trevian hated the cages and resented every minute he spent there. Watching Mei and Lopez, he grew interested in spite of himself. The engineer outfitted the three of them in the long aprons, gloves, and hoods, and Trevian watched silently as Mei and Lopez pawed through the material, with Mei scratching out calculations on bits of paper, with Lopez either nodding agreement or snatching the paper and making changes. Trevian played a hand of cards with the guard, but when a worker on a rest break joined them, he felt himself drawn back to the equipment, where workers were twining several inactive cords of copper into a thick strand.

Just beyond this mound of machinery, he thought, his mother had been buried for sixteen years.

The air above a long rift shimmered, turning violet and yellow. "Mei," Trevian called, "Turn slowly and look."

She did, caught her breath and backed into a spool of copper string as the flame faded and reappeared, close to the strand of cords. The workers eyed it but didn't stop their work. It pulsed above their heads.

"What's it doing?"

Trevian said, "Watching."

She reached for it, and he said, "Stop," but she already had, her open palm facing it.

"It's hot," she said.

Lopez said, "Hot, yes," without laughing.

"Where'd it go?" She stared around as the flame vanished.

Lopez draped the thick copper rope over one of the spools. "Back to the rift, probably," he said, "Or out somewhere."

"Trippy," said Mei.

She worked with Lopez for three hours. He served them strong tea and flatbread. Mei swallowed and said, "You need a way to gather the cords when they run from the conduit before they're entwined. They're a hazard—you nearly fell over them yourself."

"The space at the cages is wider," he said.

Mei nodded, with the vague expression Trevian recognized. She was thinking.

They mounted up. The sky was high overhead. Mei tipped back her head and closed her eyes. "Plenty of time left to work on the tower," she said. "It's really exciting to see what Aideen and Lopez are doing. It's like traveling back in time, in a way, to the days of Westing House."

"What was Westing House?"

"Not a what, a who. He discovered alternating current. Your sister's a visionary. Do you have that word?"

"If you mean brilliant, I've always thought so."

The trail curved left onto the broad flat stretch at the base of Orchard Hill, past the narrow ravine. The walls of the ravine shared the reddish rock of the cliff behind him, formed the curve of the valley holding White Bluffs on one face and the white stone of the mountain housing Orchard Hill on the other. Erin's story, of one world sprouting out of another, foreign mountains ripping up through the skin of the earth, made more sense when he looked at that narrow opening or thought of the deep folds in the mountains on the east side of Orchard Hill.

The guard's head jerked and his caballo danced in place as a stone bounced down the ravine's side. Trevian moved his mount between the canyon and Mei. "What?"

The guard, crossbow up and ready, didn't answer immediately. "Just a loose rock," he said. "Only one. I feared a rockslide."

"They're common enough. Mei?"

She stared back at the ledge trail they'd just left. The tunnel was not visible from here. "That's a long way to string wire."

"They'll walk up to where they can see this, the plateau," Trevian said. "Then a longbow arrow with a string tied to it will be shot, and copper cord tied to the string, and we will pull it across."

She looked into the gap, calculating. "That would work," she said.

The guards at the edge of the compound ward put it to sleep so they could enter. It awakened again behind them, filling Trevian with the faint sense of well-being copper gave him. Mei pushed her mount to a trot, eager to get to work on one of her machines. Trevian hoped he would remember, in his next message to Erin, to ask her what "trippy" meant.

s soon as Erin opened the frontera, the book buzzed like a cell phone on a table. She opened it and took cut Mei's reply. Folded inside was a short note from Trevian.

"Mei's happy and she wants four more power packs," she said.

"We can pick those up tomorrow before we leave." Remedios made a note in her phone.

Erin wrote her responses on Mei's note and sent it back. Sitting cross-legged in the culvert with the book on her lap, Daniel and Remedios watching her, she couldn't think of anything to say to Trevian, and settled for writing, *I miss you and I'll be back soon.* She sent it off and closed the frontera.

The sun had set, and the sky turned a deep lavender. Headlights glowed like a string of pearls, heading north, as they drove toward the hotel. Those were the commuters returning from their work in the bay area. Halfway back, Remedios said, "Have you thought about what you're going to do?"

"I'm leaving most of it up to Mei."

"I mean after."

"After…"

"After you defeat the parasites." Daniel changed lanes to pass a sluggish pickup truck.

"Oh. Well, there's still another possible frontera, at Aperture One. We should make sure it's really closed."

Remedios's voice was gentle. "What are your plans? Long range."

In the dark car, no words came to her. Long range? "Well. I can't afford to live here."

"You can stay with us for a while."

"But the frontera."

Daniel said, "You were never the guardian of the frontera. You're the guardian of the *book*."

"That's true… "

"If these artifacts have served their purpose," Remedios said, "maybe we and our descendants don't have to dedicate our lives to them anymore. Maybe the artifacts belong over there now."

"I never thought about it."

Daniel said, "You need to check with the insurance company. You have some money coming for the house. It might buy you some time to decide."

Go to college, get a degree in geology. Could she live with the stink of burned hair and licorice in her nose every single minute? Could she move somewhere off the grid? Idaho? Alaska? And do what?

"Just give it some thought," Remedios said.

Three hours past dark, Juanita Gunnarsdottir came to Trevian where he sat by the fire, sipping lick. "Will you help me persuade the guardian she needs to rest, not draw strange shapes and scribble plans until sunrise?"

He nestled his cup into the fine gravel. "I can try."

Mei muttered to herself as her pencil flashed across paper. She didn't even acknowledge Trevian's entrance.

"Yorita Gunnarsdottir thinks you need to rest."

"What? I'm fine. Some more tea and I'll be good for a couple more hours."

"Everyone else worries when you don't sleep," Trevian said.

"Oh, please, that's so transparent." Mei sighed like an actor in a stage play and set down her pencil. "How about if I spend some time looking over that second metal book? Would that be acceptable?"

"Is it a rest?" Yorita Gunnarsdottir said.

"It would be acceptable," Trevian said. "And if you wished, you could share with us what's in it. It is more of a mystery to me than Erin's book was."

"Hokay." Mei picked up the lamp.

Sprite lamps still shone brightly in the library room. Mei flipped metal pages. "I did find this," she said, "It's about the four families."

"Their origins?" Gunnarsdottir settled herself on a chair near the door.

"Yes. I mean, still no time frame. But they had found a couple more frontera, and they went through at least one because it's where the collar came from."

"Is this after the cataclismo?"

"Oh, yes." Mei sat down on the table, her legs swinging.

Trevian said, "Erin thinks the collar is not from this world, and neither are the puerta stones."

"She's right about the stones at least," Mei said. She cleared her throat.

The town has fallen to the twin armies of Genrell Kellogg and Butcher Montrose. We have given what help we can to the refugees, and now embark on our final plan. These pages are the last piece of it. A messenger will carry this book into the mountains where it will be kept safely for those who come after us.

Days ago, when we saw how things would go, we sent off four families of travelers, to various frontera across the land.

Our scientists worked diligently and risked much to craft tools to control the elementals. By far the most powerful of these is the collar of puerta stones, which allows the wearer to direct the actions of the flames. If we had more stones and more time, we could use them to turn the tide of this battle. And for that reason alone, the collar must never fall into the hands of the warlords.

The other objects fail to control elemental creatures but are still powerful. The lantern, crudely fashioned, melds and distills the charmforce of copper-hunters and charmcasters. The compass of puerta stones works with the lantern, expanding the range of its influence. We also believe, although it is not proven, that the lantern and the compass affect air elementals in some way. All this information and more has been placed in a book like this one. That book holds necessary charms and warnings, and will help those who wield our tools, when they return to this world, to do it well. Pages have been stolen, but more than enough vita information is still preserved.

We have, as best we can, mapped all the frontera we have found, and located four that open to the world that seems the safest, most like our own, not the blighted ones.

We note for history the heroic women and men who entered those frontera, to keep these tools out of the hands of the warlords:

Margaret and Conrad Carew, whose town was burned by the warlords, their daughter Annika, son Jason. They hold the puerta stone collar.

Wing Genki, first to go through a frontera and return, first to bring us the puerta stones, who lost his wife, his mother, his father, and his grandmother in the Montay Ray massacre. He holds the compass of puerta stones.

Madeline Talavera, granddaughter of Beatrice, holds the lantern.

Evalina Dosmanos, widowed at the battle of Ponderay, her son Hector, daughter Marta.

She holds the first book of metal leaves.

Our scientists risked much to create these potent tools, and they must not fall into the hands of the warlords. Our travelers will hold them safe. In ten years, we will send messengers to them, and in another ten, until such time as they can return these objects safely to our world.

The rest of us will protect this stronghold as long as we can. We know we cannot hold it, but our lives buy precious hours for our travelers. Dios los proteya.

"The last part is cut or scratched into the page, not stamped," she said. "Like they ran out of time. Or maybe it wasn't part of the official script, just the thought of the writer."

"Dios protect them," Gunnarsdottir said. "That is what the last sentence means."

"Yes."

"They intended to return," Trevian said.

Mei carefully closed the book. "Right. Once things got better. My ancestor...he lost his whole family."

"Did you speak of messengers, in your world?"

"I never heard of any. Something broke down, obviously."

Perhaps something as simple as this book being lost. Trevian said, "So the compass and the lantern do work together."

"I don't know if that's going to help or not," Mei said.

"I think it will."

Mei nodded. "I think the cataclismo explains your magic. The charms."

Gunnarsdottir said, "In what way?"

"I think the influx of energy from the other world triggered some kind of conversion. Either that, or that energy itself contained paranormal properties." Her gaze seemed to lose focus. "Erin said something about that."

Trevian said, "What are you saying?"

"It brought the...energy that awakened the elemental creatures."

Trevian glanced at Gunnarsdottir and shrugged almost in unison with her. It made as much sense as any story. He wondered what Erin would make of it.

Mei's face stretched in a yawn she barely covered with her hand.

"Perhaps you should sleep," Gunnarsdottir said innocently.

"Hokay, hokay. You've convinced me."

I t wasn't even nine yet, but the Agustos hadn't questioned it when she'd excused herself. She lay on the comfortable bed in the air-conditioned darkness.

She had no family left here, and no purpose. It wasn't like she had a purpose in the other world either, once they shut down the New Way. She couldn't really say she and Trevian didn't *have* a future. It was more like, what would a future with him look like? Did they even have dentists, vaccines, or birth control? If she stayed, would it be in a society where a third of the women died in childbirth? And what could she do? Interpreting texts for Ruth Stillwater at the Copper Coalition could only go so far.

Once the frontera were closed, her book would have served its purpose. And so would have she.

She didn't belong here, but it was hard to say she belonged there, either.

T he first thing Mei wanted to do in the morning was go to the supply depot. She didn't say why. Trevian went with her and insisted she use the harness. "I just need to get a couple of things," she said.

It was more than a couple and once she'd made a pile in the center of the room, they found a worker to help haul everything up to the gallery. Several more pieces of metal seemed destined to be part of the tower. He helped her carry some items, including a coil of something half rope and half fabric. In the wide east-west corridor, Mei laid out the metal pieces and knelt, unscrewing nuts, removing bolts, carefully setting them aside.

"And this?" Trevian rolled his shoulder, which held the strange coil.

"Oh, yeah. Could someone take it to Mr—to Yor Lopez? You know how he was staggering over those feeder cables? He can use that to lash them together. It's less of a tripping hazard."

Trevian examined the strand. The line was flat, as wide as his thumb, a pale gray, with a smooth texture. The woven strands showed up clearly. "Is this some variety of tree silk?"

"It's called nigh-lawn."

"I'll take it to them," he said.

She sat back on her heels, looking slightly shamed. "Trevian, you're not my errand boy."

He understood after a moment. "Is it a useful task?"

"I think so. It might prevent an injury."

"I like to be useful," he said. "And I have little else to do here."

"They include you in all the planning sessions."

He shrugged. Including him was a courtesy only; Mei did not see it. "You have guards and helpers, you have Yorita Gunnarsdottir and Profesor Stillwater to assist."

"And Miriam LaFish. She's great."

"And her. I'll go at once," he said.

He considered asking a guard, but they were stretched thin enough. In a quarter of an hour he was mounted and riding across the plateau, the coil of nigh-lawn strapped to the back of his saddle, his moonstone and plata chain chiming softly. The usual sounds from the camp bounced off the rock face around him, and as he passed the narrow ravine, they faded from his hearing.

There was less activity at the tunnel today. A worker stopped him at the entrance to the tunnel but nodded and stepped aside when he recognized Trevian's face. Lopez and another person hunched over a spool of copper beyond the rifts, and as Trevian approached that person straightened up and turned. His sister blinked. Her smile filled her face. "Trevian, you shocked me!"

He hurried to her and embraced her. "It's a surprise to me, too. Mei sent me here to deliver this coil of nigh-lawn line to Yor Lopez."

She fingered the nigh-lawn. "What does it do?"

"It will hold the cables together."

"I tripped on one yesterday, and the yorita was worried," Lopez said.

"Well, why not? This is such a narrow space. It will make it easier for the workers. Can you stay, Trevian? Will you come to the house?"

"No, not today. I plan to help Mei with her charmed tower for her machine."

"A tower now?"

He told her what he knew of the tower, guiding her away from Yor Lopez. When he believed they were beyond the engineer's hearing he said quietly, "Do you know Yor Lopez has made notes on the general schematic of the lines and the junctions?"

"How do *you* know that?"

"I saw them, yesterday."

Aideen nodded slowly. "I am aware. He reviewed them at my direction."

"I only wanted to be sure."

"The improvements Yorita Mei offered have already increased the amount of energy we harvest. We hope to string cord to Orchard Hill by tomorrow and begin furnishing you energy by no later than the next day. But I worry about this report the sheriff made to us, about the Fenster family and the Markows being infected."

"Only the Fensters, I think."

"The sheriff said the husband got information from Ilsanja's father."

"He had his friend who owns the tavern ask about whether you were being more watchful at the cages. It was a way to find out what changes you've made."

Aideen closed her eyes. "That man."

"He thought he was reassuring an anxious townsperson."

She rubbed her forehead with her hand. "You're right Anyone would have done that. *I* would have done that. And the man asking was not infected." She sighed. "So all our work..."

"Still provides protection."

"I hope it's enough."

He didn't want to add to her burdens, but she needed to know, so he told her the New Way definitely knew where he was.

"We are as prepared as we can be," she said. She hugged him again, suddenly. "And you? Are you protected?"

"Safe. Armed, or behind wards, and with a charm that holds off air elementals," he said.

"Then stay safe and come visit us soon. Bring Erin and Yorita Mei if they wish. Ilsanja enjoys talking to them."

"I will," he said.

He let his caballo rest for a bit longer before he took his leave. Clouds filled the sky now, and he wondered if they would get rain. The breeze was cold enough to make him shiver. His caballo swished his tail and worked the bit as he trotted up the ledge trail. Staring up at the top of the mountain housing Orchard Hill, Trevian imagined the apparatus Mei was building perched there. From here he could see nothing, but he guessed David and Miriam LaFish were showing other workers how to hammer into the rock the looped stakes meant to tether the tower. Strange that the metal book Mei read from last night did not say the compass opened a frontera, unless those Ancient writers hadn't known it. They spoke only of it strengthening the force of the lantern. The frequency, that strange word Erin and Mei used, and appeared in Erin's book. The speed of the little waves of charm—or no, how many waves of charm appeared in a minute, and not just charm. The little waves carried voices and pictures. It was all vague. Copper-hunting was more logical.

Light drizzle filled the air, sheening up on his mount's coat. He couldn't see beyond the mountains to tell whether there was a table of cloud and real rain coming, or if this was just a cap called up by the moisture of the lake below. He turned the caballo onto the plateau.

Aideen was already planning to switch parts of White Bluffs over to energy from the tunnel. Did the partners know? He guessed she would say, if asked, she was simply trying to be prepared. Still, she must be awfully confident of the success of the project. In that way, she was like their father. While in social situations his sister seemed almost timid, there was at her core a deep confidence, and clearly confidence drove her now.

His caballo's neck curved, eared pricked. They approached the mouth of the ravine and Trevian heard a muffled shriek, echoing off the rocks. He drew his mount to a halt. For a second, the only sound was the softest patter of drizzle on rocks and brush—then, a warbling scream of pain, bouncing and lowing.

"Hello!" he shouted. Half the word played back to him.

He nudged the caballo closer. He could not ride the animal into the ravine; it was too narrow, the way rock-strewn and uneven. "Is someone hurt?" he shouted.

The sound again, not words, trailing upward.

One of the guards? Trapped beneath rocks? The stone bouncing down the rock face yesterday, perhaps it had been the tail of a rockslide deeper into the cut. No one had mentioned a missing guard. Perhaps it was a member of the New Way? More likely someone from White Bluffs. He looked around. He had his knife and his club; moonstones glimmered across his chest, and he had copper disks he could charm if he needed to. Even mestengos deserved help if they were injured. Still, the camp, and guards, were close. He could bring back help.

A warbling shriek bounced off the rocks.

Dropping the reins, he dismounted, resettled his knapsack, and approached the mouth of the ravine.

"Can you answer me?"

High-pitched, gobbling, the sound baffled him. It came from deeper in the ravine, but beyond that he couldn't tell. Gripping his club, he started in.

The mouth of the ravine was clogged with stubborn, resinous brush, and the trail narrowed quickly, blocked by boulders of red stone and gray. The only way in was up, and soon he had climbed up above the twisting floor of the canyon. He looked up. The walls above him curved in, red shading to rainclouds. Nearby a caballo snorted, and he started. It was his own mount, well beyond the mouth of the ravine, the sound carried to him by the tricks of the rocks.

"I'm coming to you!" he shouted, wrapped in echoes. Silence greeted him.

The outer rocks were slick with drizzle but farther up, sheltered by the curve of the walls, the way was dry. He still needed to use hands as well as feet in several places. How far in had he gone? The canyon was so narrow it seemed like he could touch the plata-colored rock on the other side. Unlike the top of the dome, which was mostly smooth, this face of the mountain was checked and cracked, marked by a few broken ledges, narrow hammocks of rock.

The shrieking started up again, cut off abruptly.

He crept along, not wanting to fall himself and add a second casualty to the day. There was no easy way to go forward now, except up. The ground beneath his feet was closer to soil than gravel.

His old prospector training flowed back into him, and he picked up speed, climbing more easily. Something else flowed into him as well, so slowly he didn't recognize it at first: a yearning. It was the sense he had when he was close to a frontera. He'd felt it, in its purest form, when he searched for the Madalita frontera. There was a frontera in this canyon, or nearby.

Of all the things they had planned for, he never thought of that.

It wasn't *so* close, and he pulled his attention back to the injured person in the rocks.

"Hello?" He stood, waiting.

After a moment or two, he moved on, climbing up an incline to a broad spot beyond the overhang of the ravine walls. Straightening up, he scanned the earth before him, sweeping his gaze across the humped and rubbled floor of the ravine, the tops of the walls, then back and forth across the north ravine face before him.

Nothing.

Screams started, high-pitched, like a kiote in a trap, and he wondered for an instant if he had come all the way in for a wounded kiote. The screams trailed off into a sobbing sound that could only be human. A shudder shook his whole body and Trevian's stomach dropped. He brought up the club, stepping back, putting his back against the rock.

Words, now, lower in pitch and clear as quartz. "Remove the moonstones."

"Where are you? Show yourself." There was no need. He knew who he was confronting.

Movement at the tail of his eye. Across the ravine a figure moved out into view on one of the hammocks of rock, higher up the rock face than where Trevian stood. He pulled something else into view at his feet, a person, kneeling. Soft keening washed over Trevian, doubled, and trebled by the walls.

"Let them go, uncle," he said. He couldn't see Oshane's prisoner clearly. Their hands seemed pulled behind them, and a twisted cloth gagged them. Oshane held them up straight with one hand twined in their hair. In his other hand, he held a knife.

"The charm," he said. He wore an ash gray scarf, tied at the back, dropping in a triangle until the head of his prisoner hid it from view.

"You're wearing a mourning scarf," Trevian said. "You dare."

Oshane's musical tenor filled the ravine. "For my brother."

"You killed him!"

"I still have the right to mourn him. No one can deny me that." Oshane lowered the hand with the knife. "And for the last time, nephew—" His captive arched their back, twisting their head. The keening became a muffled shriek as Oshane pushed the knife into their back.

"All right! Enough!" Trevian seized the plata and moonstone chain, yanking it free. He held it out.

"Drop it over the side."

He did so, flitting his gaze back and forth across the sky. The air elemental was not in view, yet. He dropped his gaze to the ground. The ravine was deep but narrow, and if he could find a rock...

"Take the charm disks you carry and drop them as well."

It took him a moment, but he did. His heart shook his chest. He could not let Oshane get the collar, but he could not watch his uncle harm an innocent either. Who was the captive? He said, "The New Way approach. Shouldn't you flee? You are no friend of theirs, these days."

"When I control the power they need for their frontera, they will heed me again," Oshane said.

"They've abandoned you."

Oshane moved his head as if to shrug. "I was too strong-willed for their control."

"It's a defect of the brain," Trevian said.

"Another lie from your out-of-world woman. We would have ruled two worlds, Trevian, if you hadn't betrayed me, but everyone does."

"Like my father, who you killed? Or my mother? Or the New Way themselves? You are the betrayer."

"What makes you think of Serafina?"

"We just burned her bones," Trevian said.

Oshane's posture softened slightly. "She was the first one I had the elemental kill," he said. "I wasn't sure it would—or could. But it did, it took the breath right out of her."

Black spots filled Trevian's vision. "You cannot win here, uncle. Take your elemental and go south, where they don't know you. Make your fortune there."

"Dump out your knapsack," Oshane said.

Trevian's heartbeat raced. He laughed. "Oh, do you think I have the collar? You've wasted time and effort, uncle."

"I think not."

"It was entrusted to Erin."

"I know the Four Families. One guardian would never hold two objects. It's against their beliefs. And you, Erin's tethered dog, are the only one she would trust."

Trevian shrugged. "If you think so. You failed to get the compass, you failed to get the collar, and the cages are beyond your grasp—"

"Yes." Oshane's knife arm twisted and his captive shrieked again, curling over, until he hauled them back upright. "The *cages* are."

"Release your captive," Trevian said. "I'll give you what you want." The sky had lightened somewhat, and he saw Oshane held a woman. She hadn't once looked at him, instead stared straight ahead as if she would not, by any conscious gesture, ask him for help.

Oshane moved, and the hand that held the knife appeared, now holding the flautine. He put it to his lips.

Trevian sprang, up and across, hoping to seize the rock ledge with his free hand. His fingers found rock and clung. Singing filled his ears. The elemental pulled him up, dangling.

"Drop your knapsack."

His legs kicking in spite of himself, Trevian twisted around, sliding the straps down his arms. The knapsack, and the collar thudded onto the ground. "There!" he said. "Let your captive go."

Oshane made a circular gesture with the flautine, still playing it. The ground receded, Trevian paddling wildly as if he were in water instead of air, as the elemental lifted him up, up, past his uncle and the captive woman. His gaze found hers, dulled with pain and resignation. Up, higher, and suddenly his ear canals fluttered, and the world spun, and everything was upside down. His club swung down, bumping him in the temple. Blood rushed into his head. The mist-slicked dome of Orchard Hill curved around below him. He gasped, but there was no air.

"I'll release her now," Oshane said.

Trevian shouted *No!* but he had no breath to scream. Oshane dropped the flautine and drew his knife again. With one stroke he cut the woman's throat. Below Trevian, blood gushed in a jet. Oshane stepped back and kicked the woman over the edge. Her body fell like a bundle of rags, bounced off a ledge and thudded onto an outcropping. Trevian's lungs fought for air as his vision narrowed to a tube, the rest of the field growing dark.

In his mind, he twisted and contorted, but now he could see nothing. Sound fled. Now, nothing held him, and the jagged rocks rushed toward him. Sensation left him. He plummeted.

30

W hat do you mean, he's lost?" She swayed where she stood. "Ilsanja! Harald, what's happened? Was there an accident?"

Ilsanja hurried up the hall. "Are you well? Harald? What has happened? No, wait, let's go into the kitchen where you can dry off."

"We think your uncle has taken Trevian," Harald said, his boots squelching on the tile. Dolores hurried to find towels, and Susannah immediately heated water for sisuree. "No, thank you," he said, as the cook offered a plate of cakes.

"Dolores, join us," Aideen said. "I saw Trevian only yesterday morning. Tell us what happened."

Harald murmured thanks to Susannah and curled his hands around the warm cup. "I will tell you what we know. He never returned from the tunnel. We found his mount standing ground-reined at the mouth of the ravine at the edge of the plateau."

"He didn't take a guard? Why didn't he take a guard?"

"We searched into the ravine and found his knapsack and the moon-stone charm. And...Aideen, we found the body of a woman. We are bringing her back to the sheriff. She has been...hurt, and her throat was cut."

"Was she one of the workers, or the Copper Coalition charmcasters?"

"None of us recognize her."

Aideen's lips felt numb. "Yora Ousten," she whispered.

"We can't assume," Ilsanja said. Her voice was silken, but she clutched Aideen's fingers.

"No. And we'll soon know. But where's Trevian? Why would Oshane take him?"

"I fear he hopes to extort Erin or Mei by holding Trevian captive."

"Or force Trevian to find an open a frontera for him, since he no longer can," Aideen said. She stood up. "I need to go to Merrylake Landing. We need to help with the search."

Harald said, "Will you come to the sheriff's office first, and tell me if you know the woman? I will accompany back you to the camp."

"I... Yes. I will," Aideen said. Her mind was a whirling blank, no thoughts she could find or follow.

Ilsanja rose. "I will go with you to the sheriff. If this woman is Melya Ousten, I will go the cages and let them know."

"Yes." Aideen took Ilsanja's hands. "We'll do what's needed."

"Sprite cart or caballos?" said Dolores. "Justice Arm, we've already stabled your mount."

Aideen said, "Sprite cart."

Dolores nodded and left the room with a snap of her skirt.

When they arrived, Sheriff Tanden looked as grave as Aideen had ever seen her. "Her throat was cut," she said, "but worse still was done. Her fingers have been broken, and she is cut, over and over, deep gashes, on her chest and back, including a wound where the knife went in and twisted. If she had been rescued, I fear there would not have been enough blood left in her body to sustain her."

She led them into the cold room, where a shrouded form lay on a bench. The sheriff drew back the cloth.

At first, there was nothing familiar about the face Aideen stared into. The skin looked waxy, the eyes dull, and a wet gap ran between the woman's chin and her chest. It was a face of absence, as bland as a statue, because the life that sparked through it was gone. It was like a dead copper cord. Aideen stared at the straight nose and the distance between the eyes, imagining life running beneath the cool skin, and she could see Melya Ousten now; a gifted charmcaster, and expert at the cages and the mesh, quick to laugh, hot-tempered, and yet calm and happy around the flames. Tears heated her eyes. "It's Melya," she said.

The sheriff pulled the cloth back up, tucking it in around the dead woman's head. "We will notify her husband. I will let him see her face, but he does not need to know the rest of it."

Aideen said. "Someone broke her fingers to get her to tell them about the cages and the charms. Was it Garth?"

"We've seen or heard nothing of Garth since he vanished."

Harald said, "Nor of Langtree, but there is no doubt to me who has done this, and who has abducted Trevian."

Or worse. Aideen didn't say it aloud. Surely if her brother were dead, there would have been a body, like this one. She said, "Joseph Fenster. Does he know of this?"

The Sheriff looked thoughtful. "He said nothing of it. His charge, he said, was to find information from Jefe Silvestro."

"He was part of the New Way. If they had a hand in this, he might know of it, or his wife might," Harald said.

"Do you wish to question him, Justice Arm?"

Harald paused to think. "Aideen, you need me to escort you to the camp—"

"I don't need an escort."

"I think you do. If this is Langtree, he has tried to kill you before. If it is the New Way, we must assume your family and company are targets." He shifted his attention to the sheriff. "Can we get Fenster here quickly?"

She gave a nod and beckoned over one of her deputies.

———

"Harald is right. You need protection," Ilsanja said, as she fastened her coat.

"What of you? You're going to the cages."

"The cages are protected, and I'll bring a guard from the offices with me."

Aideen put her arms around her friend, holding her close. "I fear the worst," she whispered.

Ilsanja wrapped her arms around Aideen's waist. "If he were dead, they would have found him, just like they found Yora Ousten. He lives, and we will find him."

"Please, please, be safe," Aideen said.

Ilsanja held her at arm's length and smiled the familiar half-smile. "If you will as well," she said.

They parted, Ilsanja in a caballo-cart to notify the manager at the cages, Aideen with Harald, back up mountain to the camp. Joseph Fenster had known nothing of a woman abducted from the cages, or of Trevian's disappearance.

The rain dwindled and by the time they reached the camp, the sky over Merrylake Landing shining green. Genaro and another guard took Aideen into the ravine, but there was nothing more to find. Yora Ousten's body had been discovered on the north side, and Trevian's effects on the south, across from one another.

At Aideen's request, Genaro guided her up to where Yora Ousten had been found.

She leaned down as Genaro carefully tipped a rock to show sticky blood underneath.

"Her throat was cut, why isn't there more blood?"

He said, "It rained last night. I wish the Justice Arm were here. He might glean more from the scene."

There was no blood trail, or any other marks. An air elemental could kill without leaving a mark, but wouldn't Oshane leave Trevian's body, to taunt them?

"What of Erin?" she said as they returned to their mounts.

"Yorita Erin went into her world and is due back here tomorrow. Profesor Stillwater rode north to meet her at her frontera and tell her the news."

"Tell me honestly, do you think he is dead?"

Genaro stared at his caballo's mane, patting the animal's shoulder. "I think we would have found a body," he said.

"Have they looked in the lake?"

He nodded once. "We have two guards searching. The lake is shallow close to shore, and there are no broken reeds or other indications of something falling, but they are wading and poling."

If Oshane had dropped her brother's body into the center of the lake... but it would float, unless he weighted it. If so, they would never find him, his bones would never be burned... "Is this meant to distract us? To pull us away from an urgent task?"

"It seems likely," Genaro said.

She didn't speak the trail her thoughts followed; if it were only a distraction, then her brother was most likely dead. She stiffened her shoulders and tilted her head back, as if she faced Jefe Silvestro across a table. "Then today we will begin stringing copper to Orchard Hill, and we will feed Yorita Mei's machine." She slipped her foot into the stirrup. "I'm going there now."

"We'll accompany you," Genaro said, and the guard beside him nodded. The other headed his mount back to the camp, to assemble another party of searchers.

Yor Lopez himself met them at the mouth of the tunnel. Genaro dismounted and froze, staring. Aideen wondered what he made of it. Tips of square quartz conduits poked up in various places along the lines of the rifts, like fishing poles from a basket. Charmcasters moved back and forth, stepping over serpents of leather, holding glass globes trailing copper wires, checking the evenness of the flow. Despite everything she felt a glow of pride.

Yor Lopez fell silent at her news. "Yorita Aideen, I have no words," he said finally. "Melya was one of our most talented workers. Good journey to her. And Yor Langtree…"

"I do not assume my brother is dead, Yor Lopez, and I am confident we will find him. Was Yora Ousten a dioso? If she was, Ilsanja will want to light a candle, and have prayers said for her."

"I think she was."

"Very well. In the meantime, I want us to move up the timetable. Can we string copper to Orchard Hill today?"

He chewed on his lower lip, watching the workers. "I believe we can get one uncharged line delivered to Orchard Hill before sunset," he said.

"Why doesn't the copper melt?" Genaro asked.

"Ah!" Lopez explained about the enhanced charm on the quartz, and the steel tips of the gathering cords, which acted, he said, like a wick in oil.

"But doesn't steel melt? And aren't flame colonies hotter than most fire?"

"Years ago, Yor Montez brought in a charm to reinforce the drill bits we used to drill into the colony over at the cages. It kept the bits from softening. It does the same with the first hands-width or so of steel cord."

Genaro nodded. "It's a wonder," he said. "Do you need a longbow archer?"

Lopez looked over his cadre of workers before nodding.

Genaro said, "I will return with one. Yorita Aideen, will you join me?"

For Aideen, it was a point of pride to watch the first line strung, to show whoever had done this they would not be stopped. She rode back with Genaro, who found a guard from Pais Lewelyn, Artemesia Cantu, a master with the longbow.

The riding was making Aideen sore, but she kept her back straight. At the edge of the plateau, with the ledge trail in sight, they stopped to set up a rough target put together from Orchard Hill scraps. Genaro remained with the two workers, and the guard, Artemesia, and Aideen rode on.

Yor Lopez waited for them beyond the tunnel, and from where he stood Genaro and the target were in clear view. Cantu dismounted, strung her bow, and checked the direction of the wind. "These first shots will help me gauge the weight and the wind," she said. Her first arrow went straight into the target. The second shot, with a line attached, fell just short of the edge and Aideen's heart dropped. Yorita Cantu did not seem worried. She moved a few feet closer, tied a line to the third arrow, drew back the bowstring, and released. The arrow plunged into the center of the target and Yor Lopez gave a cheer.

Across the chasm, the workers pulled the line, and then the copper cord, and then the thicker copper cord. One of them began the walk back to the opening of the cave complex, while Yor Lopez supervised the unspooling of the wires, so they didn't crimp or break. Aideen felt a pressure leave her chest. This, at least, was going forward. "I must return to town," she said.

Yor Lopez nodded. "You'll take the guard with you," he said.

The guard spoke up. "Yes, she will."

The trail home was now as familiar as the road to the offices. She passed the house, the guard at her flank, and continued into town. In the company offices, Ilsanja broke off a conversation with Paloma Quinn and Petrie when she saw Aideen.

"People are shaken," she said. "Madalena believes they can run things with a limited crew, so we let several people go, to grieve. Her husband looks shocked and numb."

"You notified him?" Aideen squeezed her friend's hand. "You didn't need to do that."

"I did. And I asked my father to visit the family and pray with them. I hope you don't think I overstepped."

Aideen thought back to how concerned Jefe Silvestro had been when they found the body of Sykes. "I think it is a good thing," she said. "At Orchard Hill, they continue to search for Trevian, and we have stepped up our timetable. We're stringing cord now. I'll return to the tunnel tomorrow, to see how we've progressed."

Ilsanja closed her eyes. "I wish this would end," she whispered.

31

From her room, where every outlet had a power strip and every device they bought was charging, Erin watched Taser training videos on her phone. It looked pretty easy. Remedios moved around the room, packing up the fully charged items.

At eleven, instead of watching the coffins holding her family trundle into the flames, Erin had picked up the Tasers and the final few things on Mei's list. They'd decided to leave mid-afternoon. A car stopping at the edge of the neighborhood in daylight would arouse less suspicion, Daniel thought, than at twilight or dark. Erin contacted the insurance adjuster and gave them the Agusto home address in Winter Garden as a contact.

"I'm worried about the rental car," Remedios said. "It'll probably be impounded."

"We'll sort it out when we get back," Daniel said. Erin admired his casual confidence.

She closed her eyes and thought about Trevian for a minute. It made her feel better. No matter how dire things were over there, she could count on him, her foundation, her gleam of light even when she was completely bummed out or afraid.

At three o'clock, they loaded everything into the trunk of the rental and drove north. Erin waited for the emotions; sadness, regret, but she felt only eagerness, a desire to be back. As they turned right onto East

Woods Road, she said, "Let's go in the back way. Maybe we can avoid the security people completely. Turn left on Jonagold Road."

Daniel did. The people on the east side of Jonagold Road had intact houses, but nearly a third of the ones across the street were damaged, and they drove past two burned-out lots. At Gala Street, she had him turn left again. "This will take us right up to it."

Daniel pulled over and parked where the dirt shoulder widened slightly. A dog barked somewhere, and the hiss of cars was audible, but otherwise things were quiet.

They covered the four gas cans with lightweight plastic tarps and lugged them down first. Everything else was in boxes or bags, and they each took an armload. Remedios went back and carefully locked the car.

When they were ready, Erin opened the frontera. Daniel and Remedios picked up the gas cans and carried them through. Erin held her breath. What if there was a problem? A minute later they appeared, outlined in white, and stooped to pick up some of the boxes. Erin grabbed the last two and stepped through behind them.

In Trevian's world, the frontera opened in a narrow passage in a hill, really a conglomeration of collapsed buildings, dim and cluttered now with the boxes and cans. She blinked and flicked on her flashlight. "Everyone okay?"

"We're fine," Daniel said. "Okay, do we need to start schlepping this stuff out?"

They started again with the gas cans. Halfway down the uneven passage, Erin heard voices. She raised hers. "Hello?"

"Erin?" Lantern light filled the passage, and behind it, shadows outlined Ruth Stillwater. "Are you well? Are you all well and safe?"

"We need help carrying things," Erin called back.

Ruth spoke over her shoulder, and three men crowded around her. They wore the green and blue of the Crescent Council. They took the cans and boxes. Daniel and Erin held onto the bags, and they followed Ruth out into the green sunlight. Erin made quick introductions and looked around. "Trevian didn't come?"

"No." Ruth turned away, speaking to one of the new guards. At the foot of the hill, a group of armed people, some in Copper Coalition red, some more in blue and green, and a crowd Erin recognized as prospectors, waited.

"He must be busy," Erin said, feeling deflated.

Ruth stepped to one side and put her hand on Erin's arm. "I wished to wait to tell you this," she said, and cold swept over Erin. "Trevian is missing."

"Missing? Is he in the cave complex somewhere? You should check the Pit."

"He did not disappear from within the complex. We can trail him as far as the ravine between the plateau and the cliffside. We fear his uncle had a hand in this."

"He had the protection charm."

"We found it in the ravine. And there is more. There was a dead woman, who worked in his sister's company. We believe the two things are related."

"Are you looking for him?"

"Of course, and we'll keep looking, but returning you safely to the camp was my priority. We hold onto hope that he lives."

It was the kind of thing you said when you thought someone was dead. Erin clenched her fists. "I'll help search as soon as we get back."

"We need you working with Yorita Mei."

"No, you *don't*. I know how Trevian thinks, and I know how Oshane thinks. I have a better chance of finding him. You don't need me running a screwdriver."

Ruth's face made it clear she had no idea what she meant. "Erin…"

Over Ruth's shoulder, Remedios's gaze was concerned and sympathetic, and sympathy was the last thing Erin wanted right now. "Let's get going, then," she said. "We need to get to the camp. Oh, and tell your army not to freak out if they see fire elementals. They come when I'm upset."

"Freak out?" Ruth murmured, but she gave directions to the guards, and they trouped down the hill. Under the supervision of one of the squad leaders, the guards split up the four gas cans between two mulas and loaded the rest of the equipment into saddle bags. It didn't take as long as Erin felt it did, as she paced back and forth.

Oshane had to be holding Trevian as a bargaining chip. Her stomach clenched, and a chill ran up her spine. "Ruth, did you find Trevian's knapsack?"

"We did. His belongings were scattered about and we couldn't tell if anything was missing."

Oh, shit. "Oshane has the collar," she said.

"He what?"

"He has the collar. He can take control of fire elementals."

Ruth spun. "Can he control yours?"

"They're not mine, and I don't know. I don't *think* so."

"I thought you had sent it to your world," Ruth said. "I thought it was safe."

"It *was* safe."

"If we had known—"

Erin walked away from her. Her whole body shook. Everyone felt fine second-guessing every decision she made. And Ruth was right, the collar obviously *hadn't* been safe with Trevian. Trevian hadn't been safe. She'd endangered him.

A Crescent Council guard handed her the reins to a caballo, and she swung into the saddle. Remedios guided her caballo over. "Take a breath," the older woman said. "You're doing the best you can. We're *all* doing the best we can, and we'll take care of this."

"Oshane getting the collar is the worst thing that could happen."

Remedios raised her eyebrows. "Really? I thought the *worst* thing was the New Way opening a frontera and mind-controlling this world and then ours."

"Well, yeah. Of course."

"We'll find Trevian, and we'll recover the collar."

Erin said, "I hope so."

She tried not to think about it as they set off. Few prospectors had mounts, so they would come behind. It was a makeshift army, but it was what they had.

The last time she had been on a ride at this pace, she'd been coming back from Madalita. Trevian was at her side, and she thought they were on the verge of winning, of defeating the New Way. This time, coldness filled her belly and when she let herself think beyond the steady lope of her mount, her eyes stung, and her throat swelled up. Where was he? Was he alive?

The sun dropped behind the mountains, and they were forced to slow their pace, but they pushed on. Ahead of her, a couple of mounts whinnied and balked. Beyond the lead riders, two flames danced. The company slowed.

Ruth joined her. "Are those yours?"

She didn't bother to say, *they aren't mine*. She could feel them. They weren't under a compulsion. She pushed her caballo though the ranks, dismounted, and walked up to where the funnels of blue flame twirled. *I'm sad, but I'm all right*, she thought. She wasn't sure they understood "sad."

A sense washed over her, bereavement. They read the disappearance of Trevian as a loss of…family? Well, pretty accurate. Her web of belonging was torn. Vaguely, she knew "web of belonging" weren't her words.

She closed her eyes and sent them an image of Oshane. *Not safe*, she thought. She pictured the collar.

Both elementals flared up, hot enough to force her back a step. They recognized the collar. And they were angry.

Safe, be safe, she thought at them. *Far from me.*

Web of belonging wrapped around her like a blanket.

Stay safe. She turned her back and approached the humans and their mounts. From the expressions of relief on the faces of the guards closest to her, she would have known the flames were gone, even if she hadn't felt the tiny absence inside her.

She didn't speak until she was back in the saddle. "We can go on," she said. "They aren't controlled."

The squad leader said, "Will we meet others that are?"

"It's possible," she said.

They rode for another hour, and Ruth trotted her caballo up alongside again. "The other guardians told me not to speak to you," she said, "But you are a grown woman."

Erin didn't answer.

Ruth said, "I understand why you made the choice you did at the time, but I wish you had trusted us more."

"I gave the collar to the person I trusted the most."

"If you had told us, we could have protected Trevian better."

"Or Tregannon would have tried to get it away from him and put it somewhere for 'safekeeping.' Like he was so eager to get his hands on the book."

"Well, if he had…the collar would be safe."

"Would it? Or would Tregannon be out making deals with political leaders to get more power and more coin into the Copper Coalition? Really, Ruth. Wouldn't he be tempted if he thought he could control elementals?"

The hoofbeats of Ruth mount were the only response for a few heartbeats. "In normal times, I wouldn't say you were wrong," she said finally, "but I thought you trusted *me*."

That stung. Erin said. "I trust you. I trust Harald. But Trevian had the collar, and I knew where it was and I...there were other things going on. I didn't think about it."

"I understand. Anyway, the collar is less important than this equipment you bring back for yorita Mei." She looked around, clearly ready to change the subject. "While Trevian's prospector friends will be helpful, and I am glad of their loyalty, I worry about bringing such a group close to White Bluffs, with the rumors the New Way have so carefully planted."

Ahead, lights flicked on as the various riders awoke their quartzlight charms. It was a dangerous trail to ride in the dark, but they had no choice.

F rom the top of the trail, the camp looked like an illuminated snow globe. Ruth rode to the front of the line and spoke with the guards who put the wards to sleep. Erin suddenly wondered if they had enough food and supplies for all the reinforcements Ruth brought.

Mei ran up and threw her arms around her. "I'm so sorry! We'll find him. We'll find him, I'm sure of it."

Erin hugged her back, letting herself sink into comfort for at least a second. "I know we will," she said.

Mei hugged Remedios and Daniel. She pulled open the bags like a kid on Christmas morning and no one stopped her. Harald appeared, hugged Erin too, and gave the Agustos a short bow. Erin introduced him. Ruth led them off to meet Melendres and Espinosa, while Mei sorted the equipment into piles.

"Gasoline, thank God! And these—" she waved one of the power bank boxes. "I can't wait to power up the radio and start playing with frequencies."

"While you're doing that, can you bring me up to speed on other things?"

"What? Sure. Okay..." Mei looked up from the stacks, smiling. "We can energize the tower with flame-power! Oh, ugh, it rhymes. Anyway, we're drawing power from the tunnel! We strung the line earlier today and it works! Well, I mean, we have lights at least. We'll need more juice, but—"

"That's really not good," Erin said.

"What are you talking about? It's great!"

"Oshane has the collar. He can control fire elementals."

"What? How could he get the collar?" Mei's hands dropped into her lap. "You gave it to Trevian?"

"Don't start," Erin said.

Mei shrugged. "It's what I would have done. Anyway. We'll need to let Aideen and Mr—Yor Lopez know right away. They'll need those force fields or something."

"Wards."

"Yeah, those." She bounded to her feet. "I need to talk to Capitan Espinosa, maybe we should put more guards down there too."

It was hours past dark, but the camp was bustling. Ruth introduced about half the copper-hunters and charmcasters to the Agustos. People were working in shifts. They were going around the clock now.

Erin met with Harald and Capitan Espinosa to demonstrate a Taser and help decide who should be trained on them. Espinosa's arm was still in a sling.

"Mei and I each get one, and Aideen Langtree gets one," she said. She expected Espinosa to pull a power-play, but the capitan nodded.

"Sound strategy," he said. Harald made a list of candidates. They agreed Erin would show them how the weapons worked in the morning. She found Mei who was scratching formulae on a piece of paper. "Figure four hours per gallon in the generators, best-case scenario," she said. "We'll make it work."

"If they work, we'll need one to recharge the Tasers."

Mei shook her head. "You'll need power strips for that."

"Remedios bought five."

"The woman's brilliant," Mei said. She dropped the pencil. "I know I said I'm sorry, and we'll find him, but...do you need to talk about it?"

"I need to know what happened."

"They started searching about dusk and found his horse. He'd been gone for hours by then. And then they found that poor woman, and his knapsack, with the contents dumped out."

None of this was good, but Erin said, "If Oshane attacked him, he probably kept him alive. He wants the compass now, so he can bargain with the New Way. He may be using Trevian as a hostage."

"Well, we can't..."

"No. We can't."

Mei was quiet for a moment. "How was it...? Back home?"

Erin tried to think. "A lot of the town burned. I didn't know that. And nothing seemed right anymore."

"It's an adjustment. Like getting home from a long trip. Once you get home for good, it'll come back to you."

The changes went deeper than that, but Mei didn't feel the same way and she wasn't up for that discussion. "I'm giving you a Taser."

"Kay." Mei turned back to her numbers, and Ruth came to ask Erin to debrief Harald and Elmaestro Melendres.

Erin hadn't thought she'd be tired, but her vision blurred, and it was getting hard to find words. The fourth time she yawned in the middle of trying to answer one of Melendres's questions, Ruth stood up. "You are exhausted," she said.

"I'm not."

The profesor didn't listen. "We expect a lot from you tomorrow, Erin. Rest now."

Erin let herself be persuaded and went back to the house she shared— had shared—with Trevian. Ruth had built up a whiterock fire in the hearth and the bedroom was warm. She pumped some water into the sink, brushed her teeth, and washed her face. The two sleeping bags— they didn't call them that here, they called them bedrolls—lay on the mattress where she and Trevian had left them. He had smoothed them out the way he always did. Tears filled her throat.

She climbed into the roll closest to the wall and lay down. Trevian's scent surrounded her. She rolled over and pressed her face against his bedroll, to inhale him, and to muffle the sobs.

At about ten o'clock the next morning, everyone in camp started or jerked up straight, heads turning in unison, even Erin's, toward the mouth of the cave complex. Most of them had never heard such a sound before. Erin halted her Taser demonstration, listening to the echoing roar of a generator. Just like at home during a power outage. She pictured Mei whooping in triumph.

Harald and Espinosa had chosen archers to wield the Tasers. She didn't doubt they had good aims, but a fake pistol didn't point like an arrow. With the roar of the generator, relief filled her. They could practice without worrying about depleting the charge.

Less than an hour later, two workers lugged the generator down the trail into camp, Mei following with a gas can. They carried the equipment into the town hall. Erin gave her group a break and walked over. Remedios joined her.

"Where's Daniel?"

"In the latrine."

"Is he all right?"

"I think he's having a reaction to some of the dried fruit. We have water and trail mix bars. He'll be okay."

The generator sat directly underneath a window along one side of the town hall. Inside, Mei directed three people Erin didn't know. Two strung ropes across an unused room, while the third draped tarps over the ropes. Mei walked a narrow table into the space.

"What are you doing?" Erin lifted the other side of the table.

"I want to start testing frequencies with this radio, and I don't want the node to get a visual feed," Mei said. "Now I've finally got reliable power. It took me an hour to get it started."

"Do you think the radio will work?"

"It's the next thing to test."

"Do you have earplugs?"

"What for?"

Erin looked around. "The generator."

"Earplugs!" Remedios said. "I didn't even think of those."

"Check with Ruth Stillwater or Harald's valet, Genaro."

"Harald's got a valet?"

"Genaro's more like a personal assistant. Anyway, they'll come up with something."

"On my way."

The tarps cut the light from the far window, leaving the shrouded space pleasantly dim. Mei put the radio on the table sideways and rummaged through the various connecting cords they'd brought back until she would one that fit into a socket. Erin slipped the plugged end into the white power strip on the floor, which ran to the extension cord snaking out the window, where it plugged into the generator.

Remedios returned with strips of soft cloth. She showed the workers how to roll them and stuff them in the ears. Not one of them demurred. They'd probably been in the cave complex when Mei started up the machine the first time.

Erin and Mei followed suit. Mei went outside, and the rackety roar started up again. It wasn't as bad with the cloth wads. Back inside, Mei knelt, plugged in one of the gauges and began turning the dial on the radio. Erin leaned as close as she could. "Should I be able to hear anything? I mean, nobody's broadcasting, right?" Her voice sounded funny through the plugs.

"Except us." Mei made notes. "Okay. I'm going to ask Profesor Still-water to bring in one of the nodes."

"Do you need my help?"

"What? I don't think so."

"Well, don't forget, you have Taser practice too."

"Really?"

"Have you ever used one before?"

"Of course not."

"So, then, yes, really."

Mei waved a hand without looking up. "Kay."

Genero insisted on accompanying her, with a guard, to the tunnel, so she could show Aideen how to use a Taser. Two horses stood, ground-reined, at the rock-choked mouth of the ravine. Genaro pointed with his chin. "Jefa Langtree hired two trackers to continue the search for Trevian," he said.

Jefa Langtree—Ilsanja. "Good," she said, staring over the edge of the plateau where a copper line swayed like a spider web, glinting in the late morning sun. "And that's the power line?"

"Yes."

It couldn't have been more obvious if they'd painted an arrow on the ground. Oshane would know exactly what was transpiring. Erin hoped Aideen would listen to reason about putting up some serious wards. Until you'd seen the flames attack, you couldn't really imagine how bad it would be.

Like Mei, Aideen hugged her, and like all the others, she said, "We will find him." Erin just nodded.

When she explained about the collar and Oshane, Aideen's eyes narrowed. "What does he need to do to imprison an elemental? Must he draw it out first?"

"I don't know how that works," she said. "He lured the two he had away from the colony in some way before he trapped them, that's all I know."

She nodded. "Possibly, what we do is more interesting to them than what Oshane can offer. But we'll take steps. He will not get control of this, I swear it."

"Well, this other thing is for you. It's a weapon." Erin unwrapped it and held it out, explaining it was non-lethal. Aideen didn't want to touch it, and it took her foreman or engineer, Lopez, to persuade her. Erin led her over away from the workers, showed her how to check the charge, and had her shoot it at the wall.

"It's like the jolt you get from flame-charged cord," Aideen said as the cartridge struck and sizzled.

"Right. It incapacitates the person you hit. I'm hoping it disrupts the parasite too, but we don't know."

Aideen carefully engaged the safety and restored the cartridge. "How many of these do you have?"

"Fifteen. It would have been hard to get more, and I didn't know if we could power them up."

"No. This is good. Thank you for thinking of me, Erin." She looked around, then slipped it into her waistband. "I hope I won't need it."

Erin nodded. She was afraid they would.

32

He touches the book and pain whines in his fingertips, flies up his arm. Force throws him back, his feet skidding on the floor of the cavern, until he crashes into the wall behind him.

Eyes, greenish-gold, dull, staring past him into the rain. Wet warmth.

He approaches the book. Its copper cover is dulled, brown in spots. A streak of light from somewhere plays along the bottom edges of the loomin pages. Grit shifts under his feet. He reaches for the book. At the joints of his fingers, the skin is creased. Shallow ridges run the length of his short nails, the curve of fingertip visible beyond their edges. His thumb points away from the other fingers, curving back toward them at the top joint.

The air, cooler than the air outside, smells of rock.

The rings binding the book have a faint sheen, catching the same errant streak of light. Air rushes through his nose, down his throat, as his lungs inflate. Warmed, it flows out.

Wetness. Water from the sky drenches him. Beneath him, something wet and soft cushions him.

Motion. Dizziness. Gray clouds. Darkness. The smell of rock.

His fingertips grip the smooth wrapping of his club, his spine, neck, and shoulders adjusting to the shift of weight, stress in his wrist and elbow as he holds out the club, prods the book, and the force slides him away from it, his boots shushing on the cave floor.

Darkness.

This. Before.

A voice. A woman's voice. *"How have you denied us home, traveler?"*

Pain in joints and bone. Why? A ward. Others hurl themselves against it, and he feels each blow in his bones.

Before. This all happened before.

Was this death? The reliving of one memory, forever?

If he could choose, it would be a memory of finding copper, or of Erin, across the campfire, eyes veiled in shadow, smiling at him—not the closure of the Madalita frontera.

Erin. Dark smudges under her eyes, throwing herself into his arms. The scent of her skin. Her laugh. Her curls against his cheek, his chest. Erin, eyes cast down as she reads the pages of the book. Erin, kneeling, the collar flashing as it rotates through the air, and she catches it. Erin, freeing the two flames.

And now a rush so fast he can't comprehend them all. Erin, Harald Stuart, Ruth Stillwater, sunlight across the face of the Merry Lake, his claim, the warmth of copper all around him, belonging, Aideen laughing, the yearning of a frontera, Ilsanja, her gaze weighing him, his father frowning, the chafe of his thighs against saddle leather white lick clean and harsh down his throat the burst of the first ripe berries sunset over the mountains rimming them with gold the flashing pink stone of his mother's necklace the pressure of guitarra strings against the pads of his fingers his mother's fingers guiding them her voice her smile her eyes lit by the gold of a sprite lamp a boat of copper in a flat lake at night.

He lay in the bottom of a flat-bottomed boat of copper, drifting on the mirror smoothness of Merry Lake. Not memory, dream. He gazed up at the bluff beyond the plateau, green-white in the dark, lit by the full moon. He'd dreamed this, more than once.

His stomach cramped. He rolled over and got to his hands and knees before he spewed. Fortunately, there was little in his stomach. Pain stabbed his side with each heave, and every joint ached, down to his fingertips.

Dark where he was.

He crawled backward to avoid the pool of vomit, its acrid smell filling his nostrils.

Where was he?

Dead people didn't spew, he was quite sure.

Why *wasn't* he dead? The elemental had sucked the breath from him. It meant to kill him.

His face itched. He rubbed it, and something flaked off against his knuckles. He smelled it: blood. His mourning scarf was stiff and sticky, reeking of blood too. He straightened to a kneel and examined himself with his hands but found no wounds.

Not his blood.

Eyes, dull, greenish-gold, inches from his, staring sightlessly up, blood still oozing from the slash at her throat, leaking onto him, wicked into the fabric of his mourning scarf.

So much like the one Oshane wore.

He'd landed on the woman Oshane had killed. Oshane hurt her, over and over, then cut her throat and kicked her over the edge like a sack of refuse.

Why wasn't Trevian still there? And why wasn't he dead?

Oshane wanted him dead. Of that there was no doubt. Dead, his body found with the woman's, a final taunt or threat.

The elemental had killed before. Could it make a mistake?

And where was he?

He stood carefully and didn't fall over. Success.

It was dark, yes, but a lighter gray shown ahead of him. Not bright enough for him to see his boots, but enough so he could see the walls, less than an arm's reach away on either side, pinning him in. He reached up, touched rock scant inches above his head.

Motion, dizziness, the rush of air. Something carried him here. Oshane's imprisoned elemental? Why?

Had Oshane had him carried away so he would die never found, his bones never burned?

Oshane would not leave Trevian unattended in the hope he would die. He was not a fool. His confidence in his tethered elemental, though, was absolute. If he'd ordered it to kill, he might not check. He would assume it carried out its task.

He touched his belt. He still had his purse and his club, but his knife was gone, probably fallen free while the elemental dangled him upside down.

One hand on the wall, he shuffled toward the circle of gray in front of him.

"Wards will be a problem, yorita," Lopez said after Erin had left. Aideen nodded. As they'd discovered at the cages, wards slowed the flow of energy drastically. "We will have to create a corridor again," she said, which made the ward less protective. "And perhaps more guards. I wonder if they need our energy at all, since Yorita Mei has fired up one of the Ancient machines."

Lopez sighed, his face as wistful as a boy's. "If only I could see that," he said. "But you ask a good question."

"I'll send them a message," Aideen said, "since I didn't think to ask Erin."

She wrote a quick note and gave it to one of the Copper Coalition riders to take back. Things were in hand here, and there was no word from the Coalition about her brother, so she mounted up and rode home, the yellow weapon Erin had gifted her bumping against her hip.

"What is *that*?" Ilsanja said when she got home, so Aideen described it and let her friend hold it. For those few moments she didn't think of her brother. She said, "Any word from your trackers?"

"Nothing. I think they will hear at the camp before I do. But we will not stop looking."

Aideen said, "I know."

They sat down to dinner, a simple meal, speaking little. The triumph of the tunnel project dwindled in comparison to Trevian's disappearance. Was the Langtree line cursed? Aideen took a sip of wine. It was, she thought, and the name of the curse was Oshane.

As Dolores brought out a bowl of fruit, the lights went out. This happened from time to time, but even as Aideen waited for them to flicker and glow again, she folded her napkin and pushed back her chair.

"Perhaps we had better..." Ilsanja said.

"Yes."

Dolores spoke from the doorway. "I'll have Nila get the lamps out and send for your caballos."

Outside, the sprite lamps lighting the street shone like yellow stars. Every house on the street was dark, and as they mounted up Aideen heard windows opening, questions called. No one was panicking, since this *did* happen from time to time. Aideen rode into the center of the street and called out that she would send word back when she knew what had happened.

The sky to the east bloomed with spangles of golden light as if a giant sprite lamp hung in the sky.

"The beacon," Ilsanja said.

They pushed their mounts as fast as was safe through the dark town. Here and there, a blackrock lamp already glowed in a window. The company offices glowed greenish with the light of the lamps. They tethered their mounts and Aideen opened the door, to find Paloma Quinn already in the lobby. "I came straight here," the accountant said as she set lamps in the windows. "Edmund is with me. Because of the beacon, we've sent a squad of Copper Coalition guards up to the cages, but I have heard nothing so far."

Outside a caballo whinnied. A moment later Armando Montez came through the door. "If they sent a rider to us, they'll be at the back," he said.

The beacon meant an attack.

Aideen hurried through the building with Armando and Ilsanja behind her. Hoofbeats sounded as she flung open the door, and a lathered caballo appeared. The rider threw himself off. "Yorita, Jefa, they've attacked us," he said. "Yor Potter sent me."

Armando took the mount's reins and began to walk the animal back and forth. Aideen put all her attention on the rider. "Breathe and calm yourself. Is Yor Potter well? Is the ward holding?"

"There was a man with a weapon that spat lightning. I do not think the ward will hold."

"He did right," Aideen said. "Come inside and tell the Jefa everything you can remember." The weapon that spat lightning came from the New Way. "Ilsanja, please send an armed messenger to the tunnel."

"At once," Ilsanja said.

Armando tethered the caballo and pumped some water for it. "I think we can do little here until we have more information. We should be ready for casualties."

She wondered if the energy from the cages was already in the control of the New Way, and exactly what it meant.

She and Paloma Quinn reviewed the plan they had made days earlier, with a thought to starting it tomorrow; delivering lamps and sacks of blackrock to all the people who purchased power from them. The door flew open. "What's happened?" Silvestro demanded. "The town's dark!"

"The cages were attacked, Father."

"This is Langtree's doing!"

The messenger, who was sipping water, shook his head. "A crowd of people came over the mountains from the east."

"An army?" Silvestro frowned.

"Not…not an army, Jefe. A crowd. I don't know a better way to say it. We were startled, not alarmed at first. They looked like townspeople who had gotten lost in the mountains. Many were limping. Yor Potter thought they might be refugees from a wildfire or an earth shudder, until we felt those marks on our arms burning. Yor Potter sent me away immediately. As I rode out, I saw the lightning weapon."

Aideen cleared her throat. "Paloma, can we send a messenger to Yor Olafson and the other doctors nearby? I fear we may have wounded."

Paloma nodded. "I'll wake all the messengers and have them at the ready."

"Is this a group from Sheeplands who has gone turvy?" Silvestro demanded, sinking down into one of the seats.

"We think these are people controlled by the parasites," Ilsanja said.

"This is all madness and fury," Silvestro said. "We need to get those cages up and running again, not sit around here. Surely we can herd away a group of exhausted turvy-ones from the plant."

"Let us wait until we have some facts," Ilsanja said.

Within fifteen minutes, Yor Olafson and two other town doctors had congregated in the lobby, and in another ten, there was a commotion at the back, and Aideen ran out to help the first of the wounded. Thus, she learned the ward had collapsed, and her workers had evacuated the entire plant, which was now in the hands of the New Way. Threedeer Potter was not with this group, but he had appointed a speaker, who said they had passed the guards on the road.

They had six wounded, two severely. One lolled, barely conscious, as her fellows carried her inside. She'd been struck hard in the head, twice. Others had cuts from knives, and broken bones. Olafson took charge, laying the wounded down in various parts of the lobby.

Aideen found one of the charmcasters standing near the door. "Did you have time to remove the charms?" she said.

The woman nodded. "As soon as our arms began to sting, Yor Potter called me over and I removed them. They have the plant, but it's useless copper and quartz to them now, the flames all released to their rifts."

"Where is Threedeer?"

"He would not leave until everyone one was out. There is another van of riders coming, yorita, and more wounded."

315

"I've heard it described as a crowd. How many attackers were there?"

The charmcaster made a helpless gesture with her hands. "Twenty, twenty-five? They didn't even fight as well as prospectors. They seemed like exhausted townsfolk, but they stabbed and struck and didn't seem to care if they were injured."

Ice coiled in Aideen's belly. Twenty-five fighters who didn't care if they were injured. Would they attack the town next? Were the remaining guards enough? She found Paloma and asked her to send a second message to the guards. "Perhaps they should guard the east edge of town," she said, "but what if this is a distraction and another group means to attack the town from the Sheeplands Roads? I don't know what to do."

Paloma rested her hand on Aideen's arm. "And you don't have to," she said. "We will send the message. The squad leader will know what steps to take. And by midnight we should have word from the camp."

Edmund welcomed in a handful of other office workers. Aideen sent them into the supply area, where the smallest cache of blackrock was stored. She gave them the lists of customers and asked them to separate sacks and lanterns by street, so they could be delivered quickly in daylight.

Ilsanja moved among the wounded, fetching what supplies she could find. Her father knelt awkwardly beside a worker with a splinted arm and spoke with him.

A second group of walkers and riders arrived. The most able-bodied of them took charge of the caballos. The rest were helped inside. Three-deer Potter came in last, cradling his left arm. The cage work was a business for burns, and Aideen had seen several, but this one made her catch her breath. It was bloody, patches of skin blackened, with a clear liquid seeping from them. Threedeer's eyes were glassy, and he swayed where he stood. "Everyone's out, yorita. Everyone's safe. I got them out."

"You did. Come sit down." She waved at Yor Olafson and guided Potter to one of the chairs.

"Everyone's out," he said to Yor Olafson as he approached.

"You did very well, yor," the doctor said. He held Potter's chin and tipped his head up. "Yor Potter, did you hit your head?"

"I don't remember. Maybe not. My arm got burned, but I got everyone out safe."

"A flame?" Aideen said.

The night manager shook his head. "A man."

"Follow my finger with your gaze," Olafson said.

"He had a wand of lightning. He brought down the ward. They weren't even mestengos, yorita."

"Can he have water?"

Without looking at Aideen, Olafson nodded. "Ilsanja has a powder, have her put two large pinches into the cup and stir it briskly. The pain is dazing him."

Aideen found her friend and brought back the potion, which Olafson cajoled Threedeer into drinking. A healer who dealt mostly with herbs had seen the commotion from her house, and joined the group, but the company's office lobby was not an infirmary, and Aideen gathered the partners together in a corner. "Can we bring the wounded to our houses? Surely conditions are better."

Silvestro said, "No need to scatter them among several dwellings. We will bring them all to my house. There is enough room."

His house *was* large. Aideen was silent, searching for words, but Ilsanja reached out and squeezed her father's hand. "That is a good solution."

"We should send a messenger to the house and harness up some carts."

"I'll see to it," Aideen said. As she wound her way across the lobby, Silvestro called for everyone's attention behind her.

Throughout the night, Aideen, along with others, caught brief naps in one of the chairs. The doctors agreed moving the wounded into one house was a good idea, and soon a caravan of carts went up the hill to the Silvestro house. Sometime later, Crescent Council guards arrived, stationing themselves along Sheeplands Road, while a double handful of Copper Coalition guards rode up to the cages. For hours, it seemed, they heard nothing. The sky outside grew lighter. Townspeople had appeared throughout the night, many to offer help, but some just lined up along the shore of the canal, whispering and watching. As dawn came, more people appeared. Aideen sent a message to the *White Bluffs Report*, in the hopes the daily newssheet would provide enough information to satisfy people.

As the day reached full light, a foursome of guards, two in blue and green, two in Copper Coalition red, rode up and dismounted. The speaker for them required a doctor at the cages. "We have no injuries ourselves," she said, "but we've captured three of the marauders, and they are weak and dazed."

"And the rest?"

"A group has backed into the cave, and they are still fighting, but the three we hold say more than half the group left, among them two out-of-worlders."

Paloma sent a message off for a doctor and offered the guards sisuree and fruit. Aideen let her knees unlock and slumped onto the carpet. A moment later Ilsanja joined her.

"Was this all just a...a game? A hoax?" Aideen said, trying to make sense of the senseless attack.

"A game with too many people left hurt, and our town without power. Once we have control again, how long will it take to re-establish the flow?"

Aideen closed her eyes and calculated. The charms were not dangerous, but they were complicated, and each cage and each copper mesh had to be re-charmed. A day, at least. Then flames had to be lured or coaxed back into the cages, another day or more. Unless they rebuilt the cages now, going to the siphon-like system they were trying at the tunnel. Only, reshaping the cages could take several days. She pressed her hands over her eyes.

"Three days," she said. She could not use this crisis to push forward her innovation. At least, not yet.

"But you have the rest of your plan," Ilsanja said.

"Only for a few buildings in the center of town. The sheriff's office, the *Report* building, and the town hall."

She rested her head on Ilsanja's shoulder and closed her eyes. Only an instant later, it seemed, Paloma Quinn said, "Yorita? There is a large group outside, demanding answers. Jefe Silvestro has gone to his house. Can you and Jefa Langtree address them with Yor Montez?"

Her skin seemed to shrink, but someone had to, and she was a partner, after all. The three of them met briefly to work out what they wanted to say, then peered outside.

The crowd had grown, spilling down both ends of the street, and another crowd jostled across the canal. Her heart dropped. They would not even be heard by these people. Paloma Quinn came out behind them and handed Ilsanja a copper cone about the length of a kitchen knife. "It's charmed," Paloma said. "It amplifies sound."

Aideen wondered where the accountant had found one.

Ilsanja straightened, lifted her head, and led the way out the door. As soon as they saw her people began shouting questions, and Aideen could only make out snatches of words. From where she stood on the top stair, she saw the sheriff, astride a caballo, at the edge of the crowd, next to a wagon harnessed up to a pair of mulas. When she looked, she found the faces of the few deputies she recognized.

"...a war?"

"Were these mestengos?"

"...lights be on? And..."

"Are we attacked?"

Ilsanja held the cone close to her mouth. "Let us speak, and then we will answer your questions."

A wave of quiet, starting near the front, rolled through the throng.

Ilsanja spoke clearly and briskly. The cage had been attacked by an unknown group, apparently suffering from the parasite sickness. Most of them had already fled. The Crescent Council and the Copper Coalition guards were retaking the plant, and more guards were coming to protect the town.

Someone shouted, "Is it prospectors? It's prospectors!"

"It is not," Ilsanja said.

Groups of people took up the refrain, but another question got shouted out of the crowd. "When will we have light again?"

Aideen held out her hand. Positioning the cone as Ilsanja had, she said, "We must first regain control and determine the amount of damage. If there is no damage, we will have lights again in three or four days."

"Days!" The word flashed through the crowd. Aideen heard, "...pay you!" distinctly from several groups.

She held up her hand. "You *do* pay the Langtree Company to provide you with light, and we will to the best we can. Already, our workers are distributing blackrock supplies to each household, from our stockpiled stores, and lanterns—"

A man near the front yelled. "What? You knew this might happen, and you did nothing?"

Anger flooded her. She breathed deep and tried to stay calm. "We *feared* this might happen, and we *planned* for it."

Just then, Paloma Quinn came out, followed by five workers. Four carried boxes filled with sacks of blackrock, while the fifth box overflowed with lanterns. Paloma stepped to one side. In a procession, they paraded past her down the steps, skirted the crowd and mounted the wagon next to the sheriff's mount. The people quieted, watching as the wagon turned, rolling into the nearest neighborhood.

Ilsanja murmured, "I did not know Yora Quinn had worked in the theater."

It was the only explanation Aideen could think of for such perfect timing. She grabbed the opportunity. "We will resolve this as soon as we can. This was an attack by an outside force. As well as re-establishing the lights, we must care for our wounded and make sure the plant is safe."

"Where is Jefe Silvestro?"

Aideen searched the crowd for the voice. It was one she knew. The editor of the *White Bluffs Report*, Yor Genrey, pushed his way up to the front.

Yor Montez took the cone. "The jefe is at his house, seeing to our wounded who are getting care."

"Does Jefe Silvestro have lights and warmth in *his* house?"

Yor Montez was calm and genial as ever. "He has blackrock lanterns and whiterock burning in the hearths, I'm sure, so the doctors and healers can give the best care to your neighbors and family members."

The editor was not finished yet. "If you planned for this, how were the cages so easily overrun?"

"Had you come by and offered to help, and seen our wounded, you would not think it easy. Our plant was attacked by an armed mob of more than twenty people. Our plan, Yor Genrey, developed by the partners, is to assure every customer has lanterns and enough blackrock to last a sennight."

"Surely this eats into your profits," Genrey said. A few in the crowd laughed.

Aideen held out her hand and Armando handed her the cone. "It does," she said. "We are concerned with profits, but we are more concerned for the safety of the town. We are your neighbors, too."

People grumbled, but the edge of the anger had vanished.

Aideen took advantage of the moment. "You all heard Yor Genrey's questions just now. The *Report* is the most consistent, and best, source of information for all of you. I will come here at ten in the morning each day and meet with Yor Genrey and any of you who have questions, until things are back to normal."

A rush of sound came from the crowd, and it took her a second to identify it as positive.

Armando called out, "All three of us will." Ilsanja nodded.

She handed the cone back to Ilsanja, who took a few questions, but people were walking away, some following the second wagon loaded with lamps and bags of blackrock.

Aideen used the cone one last time. "Yor Genrey, will you join us for a moment inside?"

His eyes widened, but he nodded and loped up the steps.

"I'm waiting for the sheriff and at least one of the town council to join us," Aideen said.

He looked wary. Yor Genrey was something of a mystery in town, an outsider who came from down mountain. Aideen thought he was from Pais Lewelyn originally.

The sheriff strode in. "I saw no sign of the council anywhere in the crowd," she said.

"We'll start with you two then," Aideen said. As they'd agreed, Ilsanja and Armando let her take the lead. "This is what we mentioned to you earlier. Do you wish to have some light from our experimental location, at least a few hours a day?"

"Your power does more than shine light on my work," Genrey said. "It powers my press. Why would you want to keep the *Report* in business?"

"For the reasons I just gave to the crowd."

Genrey gave Armando a raised-eyebrow look. "Even though *you* tried to shame me, Yor Montez, for not rushing to your aid?"

Armando said, "You are not a good neighbor, but Yorita Langtree sees some value to you."

The sheriff said, "We'll be happy to have lights, but if you have this source why not direct the energy to the town?"

"Because it is unstable. You will know that and adjust. We plan to include the town hall, if the council is interested."

Yor Genrey nodded as if he'd had a calculation come out the way he expected. "We are your test, then."

"Yes."

"Well, I'm willing to try it." He jammed his hat on his head and grinned at Armando. "To help out a neighbor."

Aideen told them when they could expect details. When the lobby was finally nearly empty, Ilsanja hugged her. "I thought Yor Genrey would turn the crowd against us, but you two managed him."

"It was Armando who calmed them."

"It was all of us," Armando said.

Aideen beckoned Paloma over and handed her the cone. "How did you come to have this? And how did you know to bring out a handful of workers at that exact moment?"

The accountant blushed. "My mother was part of a group of traveling players," she said. "And...I put this the supply room because I thought if we ever did have a serious problem, it was the easiest way to be heard."

"You are a wise woman, Yora Quinn," Armando said.

"You see?" Ilsanja smirked as the accountant went back to her tasks. "I thought it would be theater."

The roof of the tunnel got lower, forcing him to stoop. He could see his boots now. A high-pitched whine filled his ears, making his neck vibrate. The sound descended to a lower register, like singing, like the rush of water, like the sound an air elemental made. He ducked, staring around, but he was still alone in the tight passage. Ahead of him brightness grew.

The rock beneath his feet shivered and a cracking sound ran the length of the passage. He crouched, his arms curved over his head, waiting for the fall of rock, but only a faint curtain of dust drifted into the space. He edged forward, stopped again, sure this time he heard voices. They fell silent and he shouted, his words ringing off the walls around him. No one answered.

It was a fancy, his turvy senses mocking him.

He lost his balance. The floor was even beneath his feet, but he wavered, falling against the wall. Even braced, dizziness rolled over him in waves. He felt as if he were lying in the bottom of a boat, the lakes waves gently rocking him. Above him, the western face of Orchard Hill shone whitish-green in the night.

This was a dream; he remembered it, from the night Erin had leaped through her frontera, and come to his world. Even then, it felt like a dream he'd had before. He'd never seen a boat of copper, but somehow the streaks of greenish moonlight down the pale rock face, the undulation of the water, and a sense of...belonging, he knew it. As if he'd felt a long time before and forgotten it.

Why was the memory of a dream assailing him now, just when he needed to move?

The images faded and he stood again, as upright as he could. The oval of gray light before him grew broader with each step.

Hours passed while Trevian had not touched Aideen's thoughts once, and now she felt guilty. It mattered little; thinking of him, not thinking of him, nothing had changed.

At noon, a van of guards rode into town, corralling a line of tottering prisoners. At the back, four guards carried two bodies on planks. The squad leader beckoned Aideen and Ilsanja over.

"These are the ones we found at the cages," she said. "At least ten more fled during the night, they said. They are free of the parasites." She waved her arm at a sealed basket one of the Crescent Council guards held. "Those two are badly burned, I fear they won't live."

Aideen marched past the attackers, a sorry lot, downcast, wounded, to where Yora Lucien, the doctor for the Silvestros, stood by the planks. The doctor said, "I would guess you know these injuries, yorita."

"We haven't had one in years." The skin of the man closest to her was so blackened it was impossible to distinguish the scraps of charred cloth from skin. Standing next to the doctor, Ilsanja turned away and put her sleeve over her nose and mouth. "They tried to lure, or chivvy, a flame into a cage, knowing nothing, and this is the result."

A spurt of hot satisfaction filled her, as she thought of Threedeer, his eyes glazed, blood weeping from the blackened cracks in his skin. *I got them out.* These men deserved their deaths. Instantly cold shame filled her. This was not a belief for someone who sought to follow the Mother. She glanced up and found Ilsanja's gaze on her.

Ilsanja said, "They attacked us, wounded our people, and cast our town into darkness. They did this to themselves."

The sheriff did not have enough cells, so she took use of a warehouse. Lucien attended to the wounded, who were mostly burned although many had bruises and cuts. Aideen and Ilsanja stayed while the sheriff questioned a dazed woman who made the most sense of all of them. Everyone in the group came from Doris Flats, a small town in Sheeplands, nine leagues down mountain. Aideen knew the name well. The current stretch of copper wire, part of the Sheeplands expansion, ended there.

There was not a single tracker, prospector, or guard among them. The woman they questioned owned a guesthouse; her husband, one of the dying ones, worked in the town banco. Two were sheep ranchers, one a potter, two weavers, and a merchant. The woman's fingernails were split and caked with dried blood. Aideen didn't know what to make of it.

The woman's speech halted and broke, and she stared past them, as if searching the air for words. Grief, perhaps, or the state of confusion Trevian and Erin had spoken of.

"There were four, wool merchants from Madlyn. They welcomed me first…"

"Welcomed?" The sheriff frowned.

Aideen murmured. "The word they use when they attach a parasite."

The sheriff shuddered. "Ugh! Go on."

"And I gave one to my husband, so he was welcomed too. He took four nodes to welcome others. We, they, needed to control the cages at White Bluffs, so we could send a signal once the frontera was opened. They, we, distant in Madlyn who had—"

"What are those nonsense words?" the sheriff said.

Aideen raised a hand. "She is speaking in the forms of the New Way. There is home, here, and distant. I don't fully understand it, but I think she means another host."

"Continue," the sheriff said.

"…an informant at the Crescent Copper Coalition, and we were directed by that one."

"A Madlyn council member?" the sheriff said.

The woman blinked and shook her head. "No. A dioso padrey."

"What did they want?" the sheriff said.

"We… They…"

Ilsanja said, "Speak as if you were still part of it."

The woman's eyes closed. "Near, we will find and open the frontera. Here, we need the energy of the cages to send a signal. We will build an apparatus to send the signal distant. It makes the chaotics calmer, easier to welcome into the New Way."

"What are chaotics?" The sheriff had her hands on her hips.

Ilsanja said, "We are."

"So, they mean to render us docile with this signal? And then you and yours would implant those nodes?" Aideen said.

The woman nodded, her eyes still closed. "Our plan was to build our pylon at the cages. We still needed copper, so we dug up what was buried—"

"You did what?" Aideen said.

"We dug up what was buried…"

"The copper cords we *just* finished stringing, nine leagues of it?" Aideen took the woman's hand. "You all, you dug it up by hand?"

"Yes. We did. It was needed."

"Where is my copper?"

"It is with us, one from Home."

"The out-of-worlder," Aideen said, unclenching her teeth.

The sheriff shot her a glance. "But now half of you are gone, including the out-of-worlder, so what is the plan now?"

The woman shivered suddenly and opened her eyes. "I don't know, exactly. When you are with them, it feels like you are at home with your family, nothing to question, nothing to fear. He...had others carrying the coils of copper. We knew from distant in Madlyn that the Copper Coalition went to a place called Merry Lake, but we didn't know the purpose. As we traveled, we learned that the copper-hunter who attacked us in Via Nueva had come to the lake, so we knew it was the right place."

"Where is Via Nueva?" the sheriff said.

Aideen explained. Beyond the captive woman, the warehouse door opened, and a man came in. She didn't know him, but his black attire and the white bib he wore attached to his collar identified him as a dioso padre. Ilsanja hurried across to him.

"What did you mean to do, at the cages?" Aideen said.

The woman looked around. She seemed a bit more lucid. "Redirect the power," she said. "Everyone knows how the Langtree cages work. You lure a flame into the cage, and its heat fills the wires. Then you attach the wires to what you want powered."

"You thought it was that simple?" Aideen shook her head.

"When we got there, the cages were empty. You'd destroyed everything. Nothing worked. We were... They were, well, they don't *get* angry but—"

"They were angry," Aideen said.

"And so, many of us left but some, us, were told to stay behind and get the cages functioning."

"Where did they go?" the sheriff said.

"North," the woman said.

"How? There's no road, nothing but mountains."

"There are hunting trails," Aideen said. "Primitive, but passable."

"We can climb," the woman said. She frowned, staring back into her own memory, Aideen thought, of the rough journey she'd been unready for.

Yora Lucien approached with the padrey and touched the sheriff's arm. "This woman's husband is close to death. If she is going to speak to him…"

"You may take her," the sheriff said.

The padrey put his hand on the woman's shoulder. "Come, my child, say your farewells."

She looked around, and began to sob, a deep wrenching sound. She rose and followed the padrey and the doctor. Ilsanja looked away.

Aideen moved to her side. "Who sent for a padrey?"

"I did." Ilsanja's tone did not invite further questions.

Aideen said, "I'll meet Yor Lopez at the cages and see how badly things are damaged. But Harald and the Copper Coalition need this information since that is where the New Way is going."

"I'll see to it," Ilsanja said.

The sheriff joined Aideen at the door. "Your line of copper did not run along Sheeplands Road," she said, "but through the back country. They've been on their way sennights, marching off with little food and no water, digging up lines by hand and fighting, injuring themselves."

"The New Way has no regard for them," Aideen said. "We are less than caballos to them. A person tends to a caballo."

The sheriff wrapped her arms around herself. "Can a node be taken from a dead person and attached to another?"

"I assume it can. I don't know."

"Dark times," the sheriff said.

33

E rin didn't know when Mei turned off the generator, but the camp was quiet when Remedios called them together for practice. Mei, looking half-awake, cupped the compass in her hands.

"I want us to rehearse these notes," Remedios said, "away from the chamber so we don't cause a collapse, but I want to see how—if—these artifacts function together."

"Where are the caps?" Erin said. She looked around. With Trevian and Lauris gone, they would have been two down. If her status as a guardian gave Remedios the needed energy, as it seemed to with Mei, they were still one short from the image in the book and she didn't know if it would work.

"The caps fed our energy to Oshane's collector, the big column of copper wire he had. It was for his use. The lantern doesn't need it. I think the nodes were simply experimenting with a parallel technology."

Looking around the circle, Erin thought Remedios lost most of them at "parallel technology," but now wasn't the time to translate.

"Can we please get started?" Mei said.

"Yes."

Erin held out the book. She sang the five notes, shifted up and sang them again. Remedios and Mei came in on the second repetition. The puerta stones on the compass flickered. The others joined in. Erin's hands tingled and a gentle pressure built around her. The notes seemed to come from all around her. It wasn't like being absorbed by the New Way, but similar, a pulsing net of awareness and energy. The stones on the compass flashed in a rippling rhythm, faster and faster, Erin's breath synchronized with those around her, webbing them into one orb of power.

Remedios slowed the cadence of the chant, softened it, and stopped it. The air felt a little colder. Everyone looked around.

Miriam LaFish said, "I felt that. Did everyone? It seemed like everyone did."

Nods all around the circle.

"Do we just continue until the frontera closes?" Remedios said.

They needed Trevian more than ever. Erin said, "That's what Trevian did. I'm still worried that the compass seemed to open this one, though."

"But the book shows us doing this."

Erin knew she couldn't start doubting the book, the *books*, now. "Is anyone else hungry?" Suddenly she was starving.

"I am, but I want to get back to work," Mei said.

Remedios stepped across the circle. "After you eat," she said firmly.

The dining hall was nearly empty but plenty of food remained. Mei scarfed down some sausage and excused herself. A few minutes later the rattle of the generator filled the camp.

"I'm going to find out if there's any word about Trevian," Erin said.

"I've asked Ruth Stillwater to take us up to the complex." Remedios sipped sisuree, made a face, and sipped some more. "I want to see this chapel room, or as much of it as I can."

Erin found Genaro and Harald talking to a pair of trackers she didn't recognize. It turned out Ilsanja had hired them. They had climbed up the rockface and gone into a couple of openings but found no trace of Trevian.

"If Oshane is holding him, I suspect we'll hear from him soon," Harald said.

The two trackers were going back out. "I'm going too," Erin said.

Harald shook his head. "It's not safe, and you're needed here."

"I'm really not. Remedios, Mei, and Ruth all have what they need from the book. I'm not mission critical."

"You are a copper-hunter," he said.

She sucked in a breath to argue.

Harald folded his arms. "Erin, we can't lose you too."

"You won't."

With Genaro, she walked the ravine for over an hour. He pointed out where the moonstone chain had been found, and Trevian's knapsack. Erin went over the same ground, hoping for something, anything. They found nothing.

It was hard to climb up to where the dead woman had been found, but she managed it. She found no clues. Scrambling back down, she glanced over at a slash in the rocks. Bracing herself with her feet and one hand she pointed. "Genaro, what's that?"

"Another hole," he said. "One of the trackers climbed inside. It's narrow, seems to curve upward. There was no blood, no trace of Trevian. Why?"

"I don't know." There was no reason to linger here. The fact they hadn't found a body might be good, it might mean Oshane was keeping him alive. Or it might mean Langtree fed his body to an earth elemental. She flinched away from the thought. "I'm sorry I wasted your time. Let's get back."

"It isn't a waste," Genaro said.

She couldn't figure out what was different in the camp until Ruth hurried up to her. "Please, Erin, will you help Yorita Mei? I fear she'll injure herself." The camp was quiet again. The generator wasn't running.

Daniel and Remedios stood by as Mei, who had opened up the compartment of the generator, poked at it. She was swearing. For someone who reacted to foul language, her own range was pretty impressive.

"What's going on?"

"The generator stopped," Remedios said.

Mei's head snapped up. "I was narrowing it down! I had a window! And then this—" she stood up. "This piece of *shit!*" She kicked it before Erin could stop her and then folded over, swearing even more, clutching at her foot.

Erin reached out and steadied her. "Breathe," she said. "We'll get one of the other ones."

"This was—ow, ow—this was the only one that would start! And now it's dead."

Daniel said, "It started running rough and then it coughed and died. We added fuel, everything."

It wasn't a good time to remind everyone the generator was three hundred years old. "Okay. We switch to those power banks."

Mei dropped to her knees and put her head on the machine. "I thought this would *work*."

"It did. You're five hours ahead of the game. You saved nearly one complete power bank."

"Every time I think we're moving forward…"

"Yeah, welcome to my world." Erin patted her shoulder. She felt awkward doing it. "Stand up. We'll break out those power pack things and you'll go kick some parasite ass." She sounded like a character in a movie, but Mei sat up and sighed heavily.

"Okay."

Daniel brought in one of the power packs and a selection of adapters. Inside her alcove, Mei soon had power to both the radio and the gauge. A shrouded cage sat next to the machine.

Mei turned the dial. Her eyes never left the gauge. Remedios and Daniel backed out of the space. Erin pulled the blankets together and folded back the lampcloth on the cage. The node rose and fell in its usual sleepy rhythm.

"Do you need anything?"

"Mmm. No, thanks."

Erin looked over Mei's shoulder. The buttons on the machine face had various labels, like Lock, and Squelch, which made no sense to her. She leaned closer. "What does that mean?" She pointed at a three-letter set she'd seen somewhere before.

"Kilo-hertz. It's the frequency. You'll see kHz and mHz."

"Okay…" Erin tried to remember. Somewhere in one of the many stores she'd been in? No, it was here. She tried to mentally zoom back on the memory, to see the place, but no luck. "I'm going to go get some sisuree," she said.

"Okay…could you bring me a tea after all?"

———

The passage ended in a haze of gray light. He stepped out onto a narrow ledge of rock and stared down into a wide well of silvery gray. Far below him, sparks danced on a translucent membrane of some kind, and through it he could see…he wasn't sure what he was seeing. Clouds? That made no sense. Large patches of green, dark green, blue. Holding onto the side wall, he looked upward into darkness, and knew then where he was. This was the Pit.

He stepped back and sat down suddenly, leaning against the wall.

With luck, he could climb up to the rim.

But below…it fell for so far and *not* into darkness.

He heard music.

His fingers tingled. Five notes, a key shift, five more. He closed his eyes.

Remedios Augusto stood before him, holding the lantern, which glowed blue in his imagination. Sound buoyed him up, and Erin…Erin was here.

"Erin."

The sound stopped, and his ear popped, ringing faintly. A fancy only, he was alone in the passage.

He wasn't sure he could climb, but he had to try.

He wasn't alone in the passage now. He couldn't say how he knew, but there was a…being with him. No change to the light or the pressure of the air. His ears… Yes, air pressure. He breathed shallowly, in case it was the air elemental, planning to throttle him.

He lay in a boat of copper, rocking like a child's cradle, staring up at the whitish-green bluff.

The whitish-green bluff. The outer wall of Orchard Hill, where the Pit was.

He formed words in his thoughts. *Is this you?*

The dream image solidified; he could taste the air, watch the ripple of light on the rock face.

What are you?

An image of the Pit, beyond the sparking membrane. Suddenly the stretches of blue and patches of green grew, not closer, but clearer in his mind: rivers and lakes. Trees. Meadows. Above it, whirling, dancing entities. A rush of freedom overtook him, and he laughed.

Are you…the one my uncle has tethered?

A different memory now; him, leaning against the barrier at the Pit, thinking of his mother. This was the elemental's way of telling him it wasn't the one his uncle controlled. Or at least, he assumed that.

Why are you helping me?

Notes, music scraping his throat, his scratchy voice echoing from the walls. Five notes, a key shift, five notes, the smell of rockdust in his nose as the frontera rippled, ready to close. Because he'd closed the frontera to the homeworld of the New Way.

Copper boat, the mountain.

A code for yes, he decided.

How are you doing this? Can you do this with every human?

At first the image seemed like the dream-image, but things were different. The coarse sand crunched under his feet, and he looked up at his father, who directed them to a roundish boat, painted white, with a curved neck and a beaked face for the prow. The prow's head had glass eyes glowed because of a charm. Trevian could barely keep from jumping up and down. It was the first time Father had brought him to the Merrylake Landing Fair. This was one of the famous swanboats, and Father had rented it for just the two of them.

Across the lake, the town of Merrylake Landing glowed like charmed glass itself. Bits of music bounced over the water, swirling and parting like the carpet of glimmering sprites. Trevian jumped down into the boat and ran to the side, peering out at the smooth water reflecting the glowing creatures. His father said something, and he answered. The arched side of the boat, carved to represent a swan's fin or wing, was firm and cool against his hand. Whitish-green, the mountain to the east shone like a full moon. A line of shadow two thirds of the way up, a plateau, that led across to the eastern pass to the North Road. Father said there were caves there. Someday Trevian would explore those caves and—

No need for nonsense, his father said.

Trevian stared at the cliffside. Something there, something above the line of shadow, touched him, filled him with yearning. He would go there. He would.

"I was nine," he said, aloud. Affirmation from the elemental, which had taken a familiar form now, a ball of pale blue light hovering in the passage.

"Back then? You knew of me back then?"

Copper boat, the mountain.

"Do you know the New Way?"

His lungs filled with heat. He gasped. Red flame burned around him, searing him, and all around him they were dying, his family, his community, suffocating in the...

He retched, flailing with one hand. "Stop!"

But it didn't stop. So quickly he was dizzied, he dropped through the membrane and hurtled down into the land below. His stomach roiled again. He whirled over the tops of a forest, clearings with small settlements of human dwellings flashing by below him, until he hung above a vast stretch of charred earth and a dome. Within the dome, a complex grew, built in no form he recognized, layered and squared, somehow fluid, like an ants' nest and yet structured like the sides of a crystal. He pressed himself against the wall of the passage as hard as he could, needing earth to steady him. After a moment, or several, he didn't know, he said, "They came to your world? They tried to destroy you."

Affirmation.

"What do you need from me?"

So strong it filled his vision; a golden broach of a four-horned ram, its red eyes glinting, melting into golden slag.

Watching the cups carefully, she picked her way back to the cabin and left Mei her tea. Outside, she heard Ruth's voice and followed it until she found the profesor talking to charmcasters.

Ruth's voice. It connected to the memory somehow. She waited until the charmcasters left. Ruth smiled at her. "Is there something you need?"

"I'm trying to remember where I've seen something, and it's related to you. Do the letter kHz mean anything?"

Ruth blinked and frowned. "No...not immediately. Why?"

"It's a radio term. It stands for kilohertz...something to do with the frequency we're looking for."

"Something from your world?"

Erin shook her head.

"Something you saw in the radio room?"

"I don't know. Maybe."

"Sorry I'm not more help."

Erin shrugged. She didn't know why she was getting obsessed over it, if she was even remembering it right. She decided to look for David and Miriam. She hadn't talked to them much. She didn't know them well, but she at least knew them.

Two buildings away from Mei's cabin, the vagrant image bloomed in her head. Not the radio room. The laboratory. She wheeled. "Ruth!" She ran back after the profesor, liquid sloshing over her hands.

"What? What is wrong?"

"The binder. The one with the image from my book, the dissected node, do you have it?"

"Yes, we brought it down to study. Although I don't know why, it makes no sense to us."

"The library room?" Erin was already backstepping away, preparing to run.

"Yes, but—"

"Thanks!" Erin sprinted for the house.

Mei was still staring at the gauge when Erin ran inside, panting, and plunked down the binder.

"Look!"

"What? Slow down, Erin."

"Is this, is this useful?"

At the bottom of the page, in a box, the column of numbers sat, taunting, kHz after each pair.

"Oh, God," Mei said. "Yes! Probably!" She fiddled with the gauges. "Look! Tell me what it's doing!"

The node shivered, contracted into a ball like a piece of silly putty, flattened again. "It's expanding and contracting, very fast, and it doesn't seem happy."

"Oh, it is unhappy?" Mei practically purred the words.

"It's turning gray at the edges," Erin said, as the parasite flattened. The thing blew outward, and Erin squeaked, throwing up a hand to shield her face. Bits of greenish-pink jelly dripped down the side of the box. "It exploded," she said, "So, yay. And eeuuw."

"It's down near the amateur-radio bands. I thought it would be closer to cell phone range or even military."

"We had it the whole time. And we know it works!"

Mei corrected her. "We know it worked on *one*."

"Mei, that was pretty dramatic. When the New Way shut them down, they flatten out and turn gray. This one blew up."

Mei twisted her torso and did an arm stretch. "Yes. It's good news, but now I'm worried about the power. I was counting on the generator."

"We've got flame energy."

"If I can convert it."

"If we run flame energy up your tower, but use the power pack things to run the radio, would that work?"

After a long pause, Mei said, "It might."

"Mei. You're making progress."

Mei sighed and looked at Erin. She looked lost. "I hope so."

34

E xcept for the guards on watch, the approach to the cages looked no different. Inside, the damage was obvious. Leather insulated lines were unhooked, gauges disconnected, apparatus strewn about. Each quartz cage in the row was empty, and the one closest to the rifts had a shattered wall, shards of sharp-edged quartz littering the ground. "What happened here?"

Lopez said, "I'd guess this was where the two got fatally burned. They lured in a flame. Without the charm to reinforce the walls, they wouldn't hold one for long. It no longer wanted to stay, it burned through the quartz and returned to the colony. Perhaps they thought to herd it back in some way. Because they were fools."

"A banco worker and a shepherd."

Lopez nodded.

Aideen looked at the other three walls, which seemed intact, as did the copper binding. Perhaps these could be repurposed... She resolutely turned away from the thought of refitting this damaged cage as a set of siphon conduits. "Can we set the intact pieces aside for now?"

Lopez smiled, then sobered. "Of course, yorita." Perhaps the thought had visited him too.

She walked the rest of the plant. They were without equipment and short of workers with so many from one shift injured. "How much time to repair, do you think?"

"They rummaged around and cluttered the place, but the actual damage looks limited." Lopez put his hand on a second cage which sported a jagged crack like a lightning bolt in one wall. "This is worthless, even charmed."

"I think this damage came from the energy weapon," she said.

"With a partial crew, a full day for repairs. And we are now running energy from the tunnel site, and I don't want to pull workers away."

"I understand. Two days, then?"

He sighed. "Yes. I'm sorry, yorita. I know it's not what you want to hear."

"Why are you sorry? We were attacked by a mob who broke through a ward and destroyed our installation."

He met her gaze. "There is good news, it's summer, not winter. Demand will not be as high."

"True." She waited for a few seconds. "About these two damaged cages...we will take them out of the line, of course. Is the rest of the cage useful?"

His little smile came back. "We'll test, but I'm sure of it."

"So, if we *wanted* to experiment, would it be possible?"

"We would limit power distribution, with two cages off the line. If we tried the siphon method...I do not think it would delay operations. If that's what you want to do?"

She looked around to be sure no one else was within hearing range. "Tell me honestly, Yor Lopez, am I taking advantage of the attack?" *Am I doing the wrong thing*, she wanted to say.

"No." He looked puzzled. "Why would you think that?"

"Very well. Let's convert these two cages into siphons. But first get the cages ready, so we can bring in some flames."

"I'll start at once."

"Is there someone you trust the work to? I want you at the tunnel if you can be spared."

"Yora Alturas can handle things here. I'll send for her."

Aideen rode back down the hill. She stopped at the offices. Most of the office workers, and many cage workers, were assisting with the delivery of lamps and blackrock. Energy was trickling to the *White Bluffs Report* office, but she wasn't sure it was enough to power the press. There were guards in the street, but most were posted at the main roads into town.

She feared an attack on the town less than an incursion against the tunnel project.

Ilsanja looked up when Aideen came into the office and pushed aside a stack of paper. "The town council arrived, made me repeat all the answers I had already given to the crowd, and said they would be content to have some lights from the experimental site."

"Content, would they?"

Ilsanja smiled. "Yes, they are a magnanimous group." The smile vanished. "Have you slept?"

"As much as you. I thought to go up to Merrylake Landing and to learn if there is any news."

Ilsanja looked at her and said nothing.

"I know it's foolish," Aideen said. "I know we will hear as soon as there's news. But...my family fades away around me like smoke in a wind. And I...I can do nothing."

Ilsanja came to her side. "We'll find him. And you still have family. I'm family, and Erin will be."

"You'd accept Erin as family?"

"I think I would have to, since Trevian has."

Aideen tried to untangle Ilsanja's logic and gave it up. Her words gave comfort, and comfort was enough right now. She steadied herself, sat down in the chair Ilsanja had just vacated, and filled in her friend on the status of the cages.

Once she was done, Ilsanja half-bullied her into going down to the messengers' room. She found an empty cot. Sleep claimed her almost immediately. When Ilsanja woke her later, she was startled to find two hours had passed. "Will you sleep?"

"We have news. I'll lie down for a bit after," Ilsanja said.

Armando Montez sat in the conference room, and so did Jefe Silvestro. Ilsanja's father looked every day of his age. She doubted he had slept either. A Crescent Council guard joined them, and Yora Lucien. Edmund sat near the door until Aideen directed him to sit at the table where it would be easier to take notes.

What most of the prisoners needed, the doctor reported, was water, food, and rest. "The sheriff is writing a complaint to the Doris Flats sheriff, although frankly I hardly know why," she said. "These people are no more guilty than a clutch of dolls in the hands of children."

"Our people are doing better," Silvestro said. "Yor Potter is more lucid, although still in great pain. His burns are clean, and there is no infection. We are confident they will all recover."

"That's very good news." Aideen, who had kept pencil and paper for her own notes, jotted it down.

The guard said, "Two Justice Arms have been sent up from Sheeplands because they are the closest. They are bringing a posse and will begin to search the mountains for the rest of this mob."

"It's hard going," Armando said.

"Several topnotch trackers and climbers are among them."

Aideen briefly updated them on the cages and the expected progress. Mindful of Silvestro, she touched only lightly on the experimental lines. It wasn't light enough. His head came up.

"You're already running energy from up there?"

"Some."

He glared at her. Aideen left her hands relaxed on the table and stared back, monitoring her breathing.

"It is working?" he snapped.

"Only a trickle, but yes."

"As long as it's working, and you don't make a wild offer to the entire town," he said. He twisted in his seat, as if in discomfort. "Last night it came to me. This is part of a well-planned, serious attack that has been in play for several months." He looked around the room, chewing on his lower lip. "Plainly, Yor Oakley and Oshane Langtree were part of it all along."

Ilsanja's eyelids fluttered as she suddenly grew interested in a flaw on the table's surface. Aideen stopped herself from snickering. It was the closest Silvestro had ever come to admitting he'd been duped, and probably the closest he would *ever* come.

Armando said, "I believe now they were the first wave. And the deaths of our two workers must be the result of Oshane. I know some believe he no longer helps the parasites, but I question that."

"Even if he is not working with them now, his aim is the same as theirs," Aideen said. "But our people are healing, and no one else was killed."

"And the equipment is salvageable," Armando said.

They thanked the two guests. Alone, they reviewed the plans. The blackrock distribution was going well enough. There had been no violence and no attacks on the town. That was the best they could hope for.

It was her turn to bully Ilsanja into resting. Back in her office, she read a message from Yor Lopez. They had made faster progress than he had estimated, and all but two of the cages were ready and connected. Two fabrickers were re-shaping the damaged cages into conduit, and the cords were all sorted and correctly attached. If they continued at this rate, they might be ready to re-charm the equipment by the next day.

———

E rin decided to let herself be happy for the rest of the day about Mei's breakthrough. There was plenty else to be worried about. She managed to keep her resolution until late afternoon, when Ruth sent for her to attend a short meeting with Melendres, Harald, and Capitan Espinosa.

There were two bad things. The first was an attack on White Bluffs, shutting down the cages. A group of twenty or more had attacked it, but the really bad part came next. One man had a tube that shot bolts of light, and it had taken down the ward around the cages.

"The New Way homeworld guy," Erin said. "Probably the same one who attacked Trevian. Did they get him?"

"They did not." Ruth glanced at some notes she'd written. "As you know, a volunteer army of prospectors came with us, and they've camped along the trail. There is a place where the trail branches, passes a ring of standing stones, and ends in an overhang."

That was where the mestengos held Aideen and Ilsanja prisoner.

"They reported they saw moving lights in the cliffs to the south of that place early this morning."

"Like fire elementals?" said Melendres.

Harald shook his head. "The movement was not fluid, and the light was the color of blackrock."

"Lanterns? A group moving up from the southeast?"

"So we think. That is rough, rough going, and they will need to climb to reach the east side of the plateau."

"If it's even passable. No one has scaled it before," Ruth said.

Melendres turned over one palm in a questioning gesture. "What did the messenger from White Bluffs say about the mob of fighters? Are they guards or soldiers?"

"They were townspeople, armed with knives and clubs, ready to die, but not trained. And they'd been driven."

Melendres stared down at her hands as if they held an answer. "So, while the climb up the cliffs cannot be done safely, it can still be done if the climber doesn't care about living?"

Espinosa stirred and flinched. "Someone must make it to the top, to attack, or there's no purpose."

"They have a weapon that destroys ward and burns people. It seems only one or two of them must make it up the cliff, as long as it is the right one or two."

"They aren't superhuman," Erin said. She rephrased. "Not gods. And we have some weapons they're not expecting, too."

Espinosa said, "We must not assume the cliff is a defense. These people will go to extremes we do not imagine."

"We must ward the top of the mountain," Melendres said.

"That might be a problem."

She stared at Erin. "Why?"

"Um, the generator Mei got working broke. We'll need power from the Langtree installation at the tunnels, and apparently warding charms block it in some way."

Melendres sighed. "Of course, because nothing should be given easily to us."

Ruth said, "Once the wire is inside the wards, Yorita Mei plans to string it through the ceiling of the rubble room. We can safely ward the mountaintop."

Erin wondered how they were going to do that.

Harald said, "We will have to leave a gap in the wards below, at the western mouth of the complex. And we will have to concentrate our fighters there. We will split our force."

"Not ideal, but necessary."

Melendres sighed. "And now comes the moment when I, who did not want this metal tower at all, must ask us to please help Yorita Mei complete it as quickly as she can, so we have some defense against these parasites."

"She's found the frequency," Erin said.

"I suppose that is good news," Melendres said. She folded her hands. Her face was calm. "Capitan Espinosa, I must call on you for a favor."

Espinosa straightened up. "Elmaestro?" He stumbled over the pronunciation.

"We need someone familiar with battle plans. Will you lead our guards? Harald will assist you."

Erin couldn't imagine how much that had cost Melendres to ask.

Espinosa stood up and bowed. It clearly hurt his arm and ribs, but he did it anyway. "It would be my honor," he said.

———

L ugging pieces of Mei's tower up the trail to the mountaintop kept her mind off Trevian for two hours, and once the pieces were in place, she helped assemble it. Mei was thrilled with the battery-operated screwdrivers, and so were many of their local helpers. Miriam LaFish looked smitten, and Erin wagered that if they got on the other side of this, Miriam would take one apart to figure out how it worked.

Tipping the thing upright was not easy, but they managed. They lashed it to the bolts already hammered into the rock, with their metal loops on top.

That done, she hiked back down the cliff and rode with Genaro to the tunnel project. Lopez, who was part manager and part engineer, looked like he'd just come in. He met them next to the cutting table and updated them on what happened in town. "The jefa and the yorita are unharmed, and we will resume operations soon, but we have many wounded."

"And you're staying up here?" Erin said, surveying the tunnel. It looked operational, the bulbs glowing and the vaned windmill gauges rotating, workers moving from station to station as if they'd worked there for months.

"I have good people in place, and they need me here, especially since we are directing some energy into the town." Lopez clasped his hands.

"How's that working out?"

"It's a trickle, but steady. With Yorita Aideen's approval, we may activate another conduit and provide some power to houses in the neighborhood close to the newssheet office."

"Through the wards?" Genaro asked.

Lopez made a face. "We can't send enough power through the wards, so we aren't awakening them."

Erin said, "Even though you've already been attacked? And you know Oshane has an artifact that lets him control fire elementals?"

"Yorita, do you want power to your complex, or do you want us warded?"

"I want both."

He shook his head.

341

"Can you at least ward part of the openings?" She remembered what Harald had said at the meeting. "Then put your guards at the gap?"

His shoulders shifted backward, and his gaze grew level. Before he could answer, Erin said, "Hey, I *know* I've got no right to tell you your job."

"The yorita is correct."

"I just don't want you to die."

He half-turned away. "I'll discuss partial wards with Yorita Aideen."

"That's all I can ask for," she said, "Even though you're mad at me—"

"I am not angry, yorita."

Yeah, right. She pushed on. "Can you show us how it works, now it's running? I don't understand how you connect up a line without getting shocked."

He bowed. "Come this way and I'll show both of you."

Each quartz tube ended with a band of copper, a toothed wheel of PVC attached to each side, and a loomin tag on top. The lines of copper ran through a copper cap. The wheels mounted into a set of tracks into each shaft. A set of clamps held each conduit, a tall lever made of PVC upright at its side. Erin guessed PVC wasn't conductive either.

Lopez pointed to the tag. "Each tag has a number corresponding to our copper lines. This one will connect with the line to the *Report* building." He gestured to the sheathed copper line snaking out of it. "This conduit, as you see, has not been lowered into a rift yet. First, we connect it to the board."

The three stands Erin had noted before stood near the tunnel wall. A river of sheathed cords snaked out behind them, running in both directions. Some of the cords were bundled together with flat nylon rope.

On the stand closest to where they stood, the globes glowed above each socket, and the copper vanes of the carousel crept through a rotation. It was slow, but it was spinning.

"Once we've connected the cord to the right socket, we close the clamps and turn the wheel, which lowers the tube into the rift," he said. "The clamps keep it from falling all the way in, where it would be lost."

"Wow," she said, nodding.

Genaro said, "This is a wonder, Yor Lopez."

He shrugged. "I'd seen the tracks in a blackrock mine, years ago. They use them for the carts, and they weren't hard to adapt. This substance," he tapped the lever, "deadens the energy like the charmed leather does, so no one is jolted or burned."

"It's amazing," Erin said. She touched the lever too. "A lot of this stuff is hollow."

"Yes, I've seen it."

"In my world, they run wires through it. Underground."

His body language changed. "Truly?"

"Yes."

"Huh. ...thank you, . That makes me think..." He faced her fully. "Yorita, I *do* see the risks, working here without wards. I saw the wounds to my people. My night manager is badly burned. But this energy is important. I have to weigh risks and make the best decision I can."

She bent her head. "I understand."

"We want the same thing," he said.

Finally, she hit on something that might not offend him. "Is there anything you need from us?"

"A fabricker would be helpful."

"I'll check with Elmaestro Melendres as soon as we get back," she said.

"I'd be grateful."

As they rode up the trail, she said to Genaro, "I handled that badly."

"He is exhausted and worried."

"And I insulted him."

"You held up a mirror to his fears," he said. "You weren't wrong. And you gave him a boon. He will search out more of that peeveesee to sheath his copper lines."

"And an additional fabricker will help."

Back at the camp, she talked to Melendres. "I will see who can go," she said. "Yorita Erin, Yora LaFish plans to draw copper cord up to the mountaintop today, using the holes Trevian found. Would you assist?"

"What? What holes?"

"Oh, you weren't here. There are holes for light in the rubble room, and Yorita Mei and Trevian decided the energy-bearing lines could extend up to the tower from there. At first, Yora LaFish was going to clamber up a rickety ladder that looked like death on legs, but it's not possible in that room, so someone will drop a line from above. If you would assist..."

"Sure." It beat pacing the floor of their room waiting for news on Trevian.

Genaro said he and Harald would escort the fabricker to the tunnels, and Erin joined the next group starting up the trail to the Orchard Hill complex.

A line of unsheathed copper wire already ran along the east-west corridor, and they followed it. The floor here was rock or concrete, and the wires would remain exposed no matter what. Erin hoped they were planning to bury it where it approached the mouth of the cave. Otherwise, anyone attacking them could simply sever the line and kill their power—or the camp's own fighters would get badly shocked. It seemed simple to string wire, but there were so many details to be considered.

She'd barely ever thought about the energy grid at home except to complain about it.

Miriam LaFish joined them at the doorway to the rubble room. She touched Erin's hand. "Is there any news?"

"Nothing new."

"I know they will find him."

Erin nodded, swallowing hard, and didn't speak.

The room was dim and seemed worse than when she'd seen it before, even though she couldn't identify where anything had changed after the cave-in. She stepped inside. Reflecting in the beam of a quartzlight, two white ropes dangled down from the ceiling, dancing like snakes. Miriam pointed at the coil of copper wire near the door. "Can you help me?"

"Of course." Erin stooped down to pick up the wire. The coil she held was really two coils, two lines of power. Mei had wanted energy to each leg of the tower. It looked like she'd get half that. Erin hoped it was enough.

She traced her way to the two separate ends and spent a few minutes separating the circles of wire. Being careful not to kink it, she played out one line, climbing over the piles of rock, and handing the end to Miriam who had already clambered up on the top of a pile of rocks and held one of the ropes in her hand.

Miriam pulled a flat circle of metal out of the pouch on her belt. About the size of a quarter, it looked like a washer. She looped the copper wire through it and twisted it back on itself, then ran the end of the thin rope through it as well, tying a couple of intricate knots. At her tug on the dangling line, the copper began to climb up through the air. Whoever was drawing it up from above needed two tries to get the washing aligned with the skylight hole, but after that the copper rose smoothly and Erin had to scramble down to keep the wire uncoiling smoothly.

One down. Half done.

They repeated the process. Now that Erin knew what do to, the second line went up even faster. She imagined that above, Mei was directing people to attach the copper to the tower.

Once they were done, workers would wave a flag from the ledge below, and the tunnel crew would answer. They would attach the lines to a conduit, and everyone would know whether this was even going to work.

35

Trevian felt as if he'd just awakened after a long night of drinking bad ale. The air elemental could only communicate with images, and those, it seemed, must come from Trevian's mind or memories. It was no easy process, and he wasn't sure he understood things completely.

This elemental wanted to untether its trapped fellow. On this, they agreed. While the notes of the flautine seemed to aid in the transmission of Oshane's orders to the creature, the broach tethered it. Destroy the broach and it was freed.

The air elementals had known of this world for a long time. Using his memories of Orchard Hill, it stitched together a story for him, about the Pit, a frontera, and about occasional visits from curious air elementals. Many stayed. Some were killed by fire elementals, and a few were imprisoned by charms.

Trevian had no way of distinguishing elementals, although they did among themselves. With the aid of this one, the tethered elemental had managed to veer away from Oshane's command to kill Trevian. The effort had weakened both creatures although this one was recovered.

More than this elemental hated Oshane, it hated the New Way. The burned ring around the strange structure in the air elemental world had been a fire storm that had killed hundreds of them. It had been long ago, Trevian thought, but not in the elemental's reckoning.

He understood more. Humans lived on the air elementals' world but not in such high numbers as here or other worlds. Eight billion, Erin had told him once, inhabited hers, and she hadn't been joking. It was not as easy for the New Way to infest an area there, although they continued to try. If he understood the imagery right—the elemental had rummaged through his thoughts and drawn out machines, clocks, charms, and a sprite cart as examples—inside their strange structure, the New Way were trying to fabricate a new kind of host. And they were intent on destroying the elementals for a reason he didn't fully understand but had to do with a sound, one the New Way did not like.

"We must stop them here," he said. "And soon. I must help my people too."

Various images. Agreement.

"I need to get back to my people."

The elemental did not respond.

M ei waved the gauge over her head and shouted "Woo-hooo!" and the group clustered around the tower gave a cheer that carried down to the watchers far below them on the ledge. The tower had energy. They were going to leave it charged. Even with the semaphore process, it took too long to signal the tunnel workers back and forth. Miriam awakened the warding charm after the last of them climbed off the mountaintop.

Something was going right, Erin thought as she tramped along the trail. She stared over the edge of the eastern cliff. Could someone really scale it? It seemed nearly impossible, which meant she couldn't disregard it. She couldn't take anything for granted.

Remedios Augusto took charge in an unexpected way after dinner, marching up to Mei and Erin, pointing and them an announcing, "You two are going to get some rest right now."

"We're fi—"

"Don't argue with me."

Behind her, Ruth didn't even try to hide her smirk. Melendres, more solemn, nodded.

"Okay, fine," Erin said. Mei shrugged, and they went off to their cabins. Erin knew Remedios was right. They planned to close the frontera first thing in the morning, and she and Mei were both wiped out—Mei more than her, even though muscles she hadn't known she had were sore from all the lifting and carrying.

She hated the bed and the silent room, though, hated trying to sleep without Trevian there.

Eventually, though, she did, and sleep was deep, dreamless, until she plunged up from sleep, heart racing, every nerve humming.

The camp rang with clamor. She crawled out of the bedroll and ran to the door. Outside, lanterns swung everywhere, and it was a scene of directed chaos. She stepped outside. "What's happening?"

Someone stopped. She didn't recognize the voice. "Stay inside for now, yorita. You're too valuable to risk."

"To risk? What do you mean? What's happening?"

"An attack."

"What?" She froze. Mei, where was Mei? And where were the Augustos? She whirled, took three steps to the bed, snatched up her shoes and her bag.

They needed to close the frontera now.

The tunnel was providing enough energy to the *Noticias* to power its press, which was a triumph. At Lopez's suggestion, Aideen had the lines to nearby buildings opened. The light provided was dim but steady.

Ilsanja suggested they meet with Yor Genrey now instead of waiting until the next morning. Armando agreed, since they had good news. The three of them went to the newssheet's office, where Genrey served them tea and asked many questions. His edge did not seem quite so sharp today, though.

"By tomorrow, we may have full power back," Ilsanja said as they returned to the office.

"We may. I don't wish to assume it."

They met with Paloma Quinn to see how the emergency expenses were affecting the budget. The funds they had set aside would clearly cover the necessary repair. The wages for the workers would be covered, but Yora Quinn warned they would need to dip into company reserves for the payments to the doctors and apothecaries.

"It can't be helped," Ilsanja said. "We'll bring it before the partners, but there should be no argument."

No, Aideen thought, the argument would come when she talked about making a transition to siphons up at the cages. She said, "There are leagues of copper line to be replaced, remember, on the way to Sheeplands."

Ilsanja sighed sharply and shook her head. "I'd forgotten."

"I hadn't," Paloma said, "but I think you will need a payment plan. Unless the copper is recovered?"

"They have thrown it so far down a canyon we can't reach it, I'm sure," Aideen muttered, her anger against the New Way flaring up again.

After the meeting with the accountant, Aideen reviewed paperwork. She was halfway through the quarter's payroll—nothing unusual until the past few sennights, when all this began—when Ilsanja came and lounged against the door jamb, grinning.

Aideen closed her file. "What?"

"Suppose they *didn't* throw it so far down a canyon we couldn't reach it?" she said.

"What? Our copper?"

Ilsanja's grin widened. "Probably not all of it, but searchers found several coils at the bottom of a cliff. They sent down a climber on a rope and hauled it up. It's on its way back to us by caballo cart now."

"Wonderful news!" Aideen frowned. "It's wealth. Why would they discard it?"

"Why would they invade the cages and then flee? Nothing they've done makes good sense."

"Good sense to us. There must be a reason and it won't be to our good." Aideen fiddled with her pen. "I'm delighted we can salvage some of our copper," she said.

"You're hiding that delight well."

"I *am* delighted. But I'm worried they will seize control of Yorita Mei's machines."

Ilsanja nodded without speaking.

Reluctantly, Aideen said, "I think it is beyond our reach to help."

"We do not have an army, and we need our guards here," Ilsanja said. "I think they are well prepared at Orchard Hill."

Aideen hoped so.

Barely an hour later Ilsanja returned, this time marching into the office, settling herself on a chair, a paper in her hand. "Report from my trackers," she said. "No word on Trevian, but one of them is sure she saw a trio of air elementals above the ravine."

"So many, in one place?"

"Could Oshane have control of all of them?"

Aideen swallowed, suddenly cold at the thought. "What if, somehow, they are in league with the New Way? After all, Oshane partnered with them." Another thought struck her. "What were they doing, did she say?"

"She saw three whirling circles of bluish light, far above them. She felt as if the creatures were watching them, but they did not approach as fire elementals sometimes will, and then, she writes, they dissolved into the sky."

"Where did they go?"

Ilsanja shook back her hair. "A mystery."

"A worrisome one."

When Aideen went downstairs to get a report from Paloma, she noticed the accountant looked exhausted. Paloma had been with them since last night, and Aideen did not think she had taken advantage of the messengers' cots. She ordered the woman to go home and took over the list herself. More than eighty percent of the allotments of blackrock had been delivered. As it grew closer to dusk, she sent for Ilsanja. "I'm going to ride into the neighborhoods and see people have what they need," she said. "Can you continue with the distributions? Simply check that they make it onto the cart."

"I'm the majority partner. Should I come with you?"

"If you wish, but we must get this last bit out to the people on the outskirts of town."

Ilsanja smiled. "Can you dodge questions nimbly enough?"

"I will pretend I'm you," Aideen said. Ilsanja laughed and took the list from her hands.

Aideen encountered plenty of angry townspeople, and more who were fearful, but most offered her hospitality. Houses glowed bluish with the light from the lanterns. Closer to the Noticias building, several people pressed her about the light from its windows, and she explained the experimental source of power. She got snorts of disbelief, but not as many as she'd expected. She told everyone that Yor Montez and Jefa Langtree were at the offices working, and Jefe Silvestro still helped tend the wounded. She wanted the town to know the partners were working to fix the situation. Most people didn't seem to care.

It was past full dark when she returned to the office. Ilsanja met her in the lobby. "All the blackrock has gone out," she said. "Shall we start preparing the second bags?"

"No. Let our people go home and rest."

"There is a message from Yor Genrey. The lights have dimmed and glowed several times. He does not recall that happening before."

Aideen suppressed her sigh. "I'll go speak with him."

"I've sent for a caballo, and I'll go with you."

"As the majority partner?"

Ilsanja nodded and swept past her.

In the block that held the newssheet's building, Aideen saw the irregularity herself. The windows would fade in brightness, then surge back. It was a slow interval, but definite.

"We got tomorrow's sheet printed," Genrey said, as they stood in his lobby. "It is no great tragedy, although it's hard on the eyes, but since this is an experiment, I thought you should know."

"We thank you," Ilsanja said. She glanced at Aideen. "The power is not flowing regularly?"

"It seems not. If it were a problem with one of our junctions, the power would simply fail. This would seem to originate at the source. I will ride up there tonight."

"Tonight? Can't it wait until morning?"

She didn't want to speak of the Orchard Hill project in front of the editor of the newssheet, but if there was a problem with power fluctuation into town, the same problem might be occurring at Orchard Hill, and Aideen didn't know what it would mean for Mei's weapon. "I think tonight is best," she said.

"I'll join you," Ilsanja said.

Yor Genrey had been staring at Aideen's hip. "A question, Yorita Langtree. What is that object on your belt? I noticed it earlier."

Aideen glanced down, confused, and nearly laughed. "It's a..." She didn't want to tell the news editor she carried an Ancient weapon. Well, it wasn't Ancient, it was from Erin's world, but still. "A piece of Ancient," she said. "A recent gift."

Genrey sucked in his lips, nodding. "It's very...yellow."

Ilsanja favored him with a brilliant smile. "It is! I hope Yorita Aideen will let me borrow it one day. It matches a dress I have. Good night, Yor Genrey."

Genrey nodded, and they took their leave

As they unhitched their caballos, Aideen said, "Are you sure you wish to ride up there? I will be safe enough on my own."

"I *am* the majority partner. And I've had little chance to spend time with you, alone. A ride under the stars, the two of us, will be pleasant."

"I think so too."

They set off through town. Under the gentler glow of blackrock lanterns, the town had a peaceful quality Aideen had not seen before. The stars stood out, twinkling green, more plentiful than usual. Their mounts were familiar with the trail now, and beyond the houses, Aideen reached out her hand, and Ilsanja took it.

What if every night in a life could be like this, riding in the dark of a warm summer night with the one you loved? Life did not work that way, but for the rest of the ride, Aideen pretended it could be so.

The tunnel was quiet, light filtering out. She hadn't approached the project at night, and she didn't think Lopez would be here. They tethered their mounts. As they approached the entrance the filtered light flickered. The color was strange, more orange than the glowing bulbs usually gave. She quickened her pace.

Her toes struck the ward a second before her nose did, and she managed to bring a hand up in time. This entrance was warded. Was this what was causing the fluctuation? "Hello!" she shouted. A guard appeared at the entrance, crossbow ready, then lowered it and gave her a nod. There was a gap in the ward where the guard stood.

"Yorita Aideen?" Lopez hurried toward her. "I wasn't expecting you. I sent a rider half an hour back, to your house. We have a pulse in the flow, and we're trying to regulate it."

Aideen looked around. Six workers comprised the night shift, several studying the boards, others calling back and forth as they disconnected and reconnected the copper lines. "It's why we came."

He beckoned them over. "It seems to be the rift closest to the north opening. Perhaps the elemental colony is agitated in some way."

Ilsanja walked away from them, staring out the north opening across the lake. "What's happening over there?" she said.

"Is there something? This rift is the wavering one. Perhaps they sense a disturbance..." Lopez strode over and peered over Ilsanja's shoulder. "What *is* happening?"

"Lots of lights."

"Can we keep energy flowing to their machine?" Aideen said.

Lopez pivoted toward the stands. "I believe so." He stepped over a line of cords, heading for the stands. Aideen followed him.

The board that monitored the lines going to the tower looked good, the carousels rotating steadily, lights glowing. Muscles in Aideen's neck and shoulders relaxed suddenly. At least power was flowing where it was most needed. All was well here. She and Ilsanja could return home.

"Aideen!"

She spun, to see Ilsanja scrambling back, one arm up to shield her face. The air filled with a driving wind, blasting grit at her face and hands. Like Ilsanja, she threw up her arm.

"Get to cover!" Lopez yelled. He seized her arm, dragging her back toward the cutting table, past the stack of quartz sheets. She stumbled over the cords, caught herself.

The night shift workers yelled. The yells became panicked screams. "Yorita! Yor Lopez!"

Lopez yelled back, "Get to cover, everyone!" He pushed her down behind the table, where Ilsanja already crouched. "Dios!" Lopez whispered. Aideen followed his gaze.

Like an arrow of steam from a boiling kettle, flames rippled up out of the northernmost rift. Some swirled up to the top of the tunnel, forming a ceiling of flame. A moment later, three darted like crossbow bolts at the fleeing night shift workers.

The workers ran, pushing through the gap in the ward, the elementals harrying them. Lopez plunged his arms into the shadowed space under the table and pulled out...leather. The aprons and hoods. He thrust one at Aideen and one toward Ilsanja, pulling the third hood over his face with the speed of habit. Aideen turned the hood, trying to find the opening.

"What is happening?" she said, peering from under the table.

From the glowing ceiling, two tips of fire arced down, aiming at them. There was no place to hide.

36

Her bag tight against her side, Erin sprinted for Mei's cabin. Mei met her outside, and the Augustos were with her. So was Ruth.

"There's been an attack on the trail from Lily Bend," she said. "The prospectors held them off, but they are throwing themselves against the ward, and it will give way. And a smaller group has attacked from the west pass. Our guards are holding them, but..."

"We need to close the frontera," Erin said.

"That's what we thought," said Daniel. "Miriam and David LaFish are on their way."

"Elmaestro Melendres is bringing the other charmcasters and copper-hunters."

Mei said, "The tower?"

"No sign of an attack on the east side yet," Ruth said.

David and Miriam appeared out of the shadows, two other copper-hunters with them.

"How well armed are the attackers?" Erin said.

Ruth hesitated. "I'm not sure. Bows, knives, and clubs, I think. Some copper-hunters in the group. About thirty of them. Dorotea and her group whittled them down, but it's a good-sized bunch attacking the wards."

Mei swung around. "I need the transmitter," she said.

"Now?"

"Assume we won't be able to get back to the camp."

Daniel said, "I'll get it. Do you have the gauges you need?"

"In here," Mei said, tapping the Death Note pack slung over her arm.

Daniel emerged carrying the transmitter, and they made their way toward the trail up to the cave, Erin right behind Ruth. The rush of activity around them wasn't chaotic. Everyone knew what they were doing and where they were headed...even them. At least Erin hoped so.

Up on the ledge, Daniel stopped. "I'm taking the transmitter up to the top of the mountain."

"Is it safe?" Remedios couldn't keep a warble of fear out of her voice.

"It's worth the risk. It'll be ready when Mei's ready."

"...okay."

Melendres and a cluster of others waited them at the cave entrance. The guards shone quartzlight beams on each face but let them through. As they entered the complex, Erin did a quick head count. They had ten people who were either charmcasters or copper-hunters, and two guardians, who seemed to be able to feed the charm just as well as a magical person. They had the lantern and the compass—

"You did bring the compass, right?" she whispered.

"Of *course* I brought the compass! Did you bring the book?"

"I did."

Ruth's long strides looked relaxed, but Erin was out of breath when they reached the rubble room. In darkness, their lamps and quartzlights sent of shafts of brightness making the shadows longer and darker, the room looked more dangerous than ever. Erin, moving gingerly, led the way, and they formed a rough circle around the place Trevian had pointed out.

Erin felt the slightest tinge of...something, from the peak of rubble. The frontera slept, but it wasn't closed and locked on this side. Well, they were going to take care of that.

She wondered how they would know when it closed, or if they would know. Would they just stand here forever, chanting? Trevian said he could feel it, but Trevian wasn't here.

She consciously drew a long deep breath from her diaphragm.

Remedios unpacked the lantern and held it. "Is everyone ready?" Far from echoing, her voice sounded flat and tiny.

A chorus of assents ran around the circle.

"Mei? The compass?"

"Are you sure? You weren't here, but last time it caused an earthquake. And someone..."

Remedios said, "Then why is it in that image in the book?"

Mei's voice wavered now. "I've got it, but can we try it without the compass first?"

Remedios looked at each of them. "Okay." She shut her eyes, breathing as deeply as Erin had a moment ago. Within a few seconds they were all matching her breathing, almost without realizing they were doing it.

Remedios started the chant, the five notes. She repeated the refrain without changing key until everyone had joined in. The sound grew. Now there were echoes...not echoes, really. It sounded like there were others, around them, taking up the chant. The lantern seemed to glow in the murk.

She shifted keys.

Erin's energy melded with those around her as she sang. She closed her eyes. Against her eyelids, lines of energy twirled, interweaving, forming a cylindrical basket around the frontera, rising higher and higher. They were succeeding.

Trevian woke. He sat up from where he'd slumped over against the rock. How much time had passed? The passage was darker. He crawled to the opening and peered down into the pit, which still radiated light. Above him, the shaft faded into darkness.

He didn't sense the elemental anywhere about him.

He crawled farther out onto the shallow ledge and ran his hand along the side of the Pit's wall. It wasn't perfectly smooth. Perhaps it could be climbed. It didn't matter whether it *could* be—he was going to have to climb it. His gut crawled. He had climbed before, but never without a rope. And if he fell, he would fall into another world, dozens of leagues below him. And his friends, his world...who knew what would happen?

At the top of the Pit, Erin waited.

He would be well, as long as he didn't look down.

The cone of energy grew, but the sense of the frontera, like a flickering campfire, did not fade.

Remedios broke off the chant.

The chanters blinked and looked around, like people who realized their last beer was wearing off. Erin assumed she looked the same.

Remedios said, "Mei?"

Mei's voice trembled. "I don't want anyone else to get hurt."

"It's worth the risk, Mei," Erin said.

"Easy for you to say."

"It's not."

Miriam said, "Not easy to say, but true. We must close this door and lock it. It's worth our lives to do it." She looked around. A few looked reluctant—hell, Erin wasn't thrilled at the idea of dying—but everyone nodded.

Mei stared at the rocks under her feet. She was going to refuse, Erin just knew it, but Mei sighed and opened her pack. She lifted out her artifact, cradled it.

They began again.

He thought he'd climbed for hours, but the top was no nearer. He risked a look down. Well, the opening *was* far below him. Not far enough though. Plainly, time was a substance that stretched like warm tree sap when you were in pain.

Finger and toeholds were getting harder to find.

What if he could not go forward? He doubted he had the strength or dexterity to climb back down. Would he just cling to the rock like a fly on the side of a cup until exhaustion claimed him and he fell? Most likely.

Why had the elemental abandoned him? Why did it refuse to help him? He had missed an opportunity to bargain. He wished his sister had been here, and Ilsanja. Yes, Ilsanja would have driven a shrewd bargain with the creature. He laughed and made himself stop, afraid of jarring himself loose.

He shifted his right foot up until he found a roughness in the rock, jammed his boot toe into it. Stretching, trying to ignore a stitch in his side, he put his weight on the foot and straightened his knees. His questing fingers found a crack and a bump, and he clung to them.

Looking up again, he discerned faint cracks running horizontally along the wall of the pit. If those cracks were wide enough, and he could reach them...

He reached up.

The web of belonging enfolded her as the glowing lines twined and rose, whirling up to a point near the ceiling. Erin expanded beyond her body, selfhood merging with those around her and another, nearby. Trevian? She thudded back into herself, and the notes wavered. Cursing silently, she refocused. Five notes, five notes and shift. Five notes, five notes and shift. Tendrils of connection snaked out around her. It was like the New Way, only healing instead of toxic.

Against her eyelids, she could see the steady flashes of the puerta stones in the compass, and now she could see the shape of the frontera, violet and silver light. They all could. Fear gripped her body, but she didn't let it distract her.

The frontera was *not* opening. The light grew away from violet and lavender, fading into white and a color beyond white she couldn't name. The air pressure in the room changed, and rocks shifted around them. Beyond the walls of the room, others were present, many others. She didn't allow herself the distraction. Those others weren't human.

The frontera shrank in on itself, a pinpoint of burning light, and vanished. Air blew past her from the back, eddying around the space the frontera had claimed.

Remedios gave a huge sigh and stumbled. Erin caught her. The others looked around, wide-eyed.

"Did it work?" Mei whispered.

"It worked." Erin scanned the rubble room. The sense of the, the others had vanished. "I thought Trevian..."

"I thought so too."

"And others," Miriam said. The copper-hunters from the Copper Coalition nodded.

"We felt them. They weren't...enemies. But they just..."

They'd been waiting, Erin thought.

Mei ran her hand through her short hair. "Okay. Now, we broadcast. Who's coming with me?"

Remedios said, "Can we have a moment to celebrate?"

"Sure," Mei said. She waited for less than a count of three before asking, "Is that long enough?"

The cracks were big enough to slip his fingers into. He tried to hang there, but his side and his fingers shrieked in pain, and he scrabbled until his left foot found a bump that would hold him. The pain ebbed and a dangerous feeling of well-being flowed through him. He rested his cheek against the rock. Voices welled up around him, holding him up, Erin. Erin was there. A basket of glowing lines surrounded him. This must be a vision brought on because he was close to death, but in his mind, he saw the room the Ancient had called the chapel, a circle of people chanting the notes he'd chanted at Madalita, and in his mind he joined them.

And others joined him.

From the trail, in the darkness, Erin had no idea how the battle was going, if it was even still going on, until David LaFish gasped and collapsed. Miriam shouted and knelt at side.

Melendres had met them on the ledge, to say Espinosa sent a group of guards to the east side. He thought the attack from the western pass was a feint, meant to draw them away from the true target.

"Guards! Crossbows!" Ruth shouted. The lead guard fired a bolt into the dark.

"Quartzlights off! Get up behind the boulder!" Melendres said, and they rushed to huddle behind the big chunk of rock that stood up beside the trail. Erin stooped to take David's arm and he shouted, cutting the sound off and grunting.

"Oh, God, I'm sorry," Erin said. A crossbow bolt still quivered in the dirt beyond him, and in the dark the stream of blood down his arm gleamed in the pallid moonlight. "Can you stand?"

Mei shouted. "Erin, get to cover!"

David staggered to feet. "It didn't touch a large vein or tear the muscle...much." He panted, and Erin thought Miriam was holding him up. "I'll be fine."

They crouched behind the rock.

Melendres murmured, "They've made it through the ward."

Now Erin heard shouting, but it seemed to come from every direction around them.

Ruth whispered, "Mei and Erin, we go. Be dead silent and stay close to the ground. No lights."

"We'll distract them," Melendres said. She moved, but it was too dark for Erin to see what she did. Handed something to Ruth, she guessed, because Ruth whispered, "Thank you."

Ruth crept away from the boulder, and Erin and Mei followed. Erin felt like her senses stretched out past her body, her ears nearly tingled. A bolt hummed, from the trail out into the canyon, and Erin swore she heard a grunt from below them.

Bunched together, they moved slowly at first. "I've awakened the ward Noemi gave me," Ruth said. She rose to a crouch and picked up speed. They followed, stumbling up the trail, working to stay within the circle of the ward.

Across the canyon, light exploded like fireworks. Arrows whistled through the air. Erin ducked instinctively. Glancing back, she saw none of them were striking close to the boulder. Whoever the attacking archers were, they weren't experienced.

Melendres's guards fired back, and from the screams, their bolts found targets. Erin's toe caught a rock, and she flailed forward, barely catching herself. No more looking back.

Spots flickered in front of her eyes, and her lungs where pumping like a bellows when they reached the flat area in front of the eastern opening to Orchard Hill. Ruth called a password to the guards, who were on high alert. They stopped to get their breath. The number of guards here was higher, even though the entrance was almost completely blocked. They had Tasers. The lead guard nodded to Ruth and said, "Profesor, we heard the fighting around the edge of the mountain, but it's been quiet here. We've seen and heard nothing."

"Good news. More guards will be joining you. Is the entrance warded?"

Again, a nod.

Ruth put her hands on her knees and breathed deep a few more times. "Are we ready?"

"Ready," Mei said.

He was alone again, like waking from a deep sleep and a pleasant dream.

Hanging for an instant by his hands, he drew up his left leg until he could fit the toe of his boot into the crack. It was almost like standing. He found the next crack, not as deep, but enough for a fingerhold. He pulled himself up.

Aideen pulled the heavy apron over her head as the fire elementals dove at them. The air around grew hot as an oven. Ilsanja made a sound like a whimper, and Aideen groped until she found her friend's hand and clutched it.

"Yor Lopez, what did we do to the elementals?" She couldn't see him under the tent of her apron.

His voice was muffled. "Nothing. I've never seen flames act this way."

Perhaps the siphons upset them more than the cages did, but why would they wait to attack? Were they drawing too much radiance…?

The heat vanished. Heart pounding, Aideen peeked out from under the apron. The dome of flame still flared above them, but no individual elementals attacked. She scanned the whole room before her, and her heart dropped into her stomach.

He stood just inside the tunnel from the ledge trail. They had left a corridor unwarded, so the radiance could flow. One side of his face was scarred with burns. A gaudy mess of gold and blue twinkled at his throat, and he wore a gray mourning scarf. Terrified as she was, Aideen felt a tongue of anger lick up at that mockery.

Oshane waited until he knew she had seen him. Like a man strolling along the canal on a festival day, he sauntered for the lit-up board at the north end of the tunnel.

With the half-moon above them, the climb up to the top of the mountain was easier to see at least. Erin had thought she was in better shape than this, but she was panting—again—when she reached the top.

Ruth spoke the word to put the ward to sleep, and they stepped over it. She reawakened it behind them.

Mei bolted across to the tower. "Don't touch the legs or the wires, they're hot," she shouted over her shoulder.

"Then how are you going to—"

Mei knelt and unzipped one of the compartments. She pulled out a pair of the long leather gloves. "Lopez gave me these. Erin, light?"

Erin dug out her flashlight and aimed it at the base of the tower where Mei was working.

Mei touched one of her handheld gauges to a dangling wire. "We've got juice," she said.

Ruth said, "Juice?"

"Power."

While Erin trained the light on her, Mei took a few minutes to connect the transmitter to the wire. Erin couldn't figure out a way to plug the power cell into the frequency meter without putting down the flashlight, so she just held it while Mei connected all the equipment.

"Get ready," Mei whispered.

"Trouble!" Ruth shouted.

"Keep working." Erin ran to Ruth's side. Lights sparkled below them, coming up the eastern cliff.

Ruth cupped her hands around her mouth. "Guards! Invaders on the eastern cliff!"

As Erin stared down, four people crawled up over the eastern ledge. As the guards charged them, one pointed a bone-colored wand, and the space below crackled with lavender lights. Screams followed.

"Oh, no." Erin said.

The person with the wand headed for the trail at a run, another close at his heels, two more, armed only with rocks, shielding them. Two of the Copper Coalition guards were down, and the others charged but had to deal with still more climbing over the cliff. And the lead attacker fired the energy weapon again.

"Is that the…?"

Erin gulped and nodded. "Yes." She spoke over her shoulder. "Mei! *Crank* it!"

A bove Oshane's head, the flames parted like water before an anguila. The cluster of blue and gold, it was the collar. The flames weren't agitated by the siphons; they were controlled. Was he controlling all of them?

"The collar," she said. Lopez gasped, and she knew he understood.

A soft sound filled the tunnel, faint, repeating. Was Oshane *humming*?

He studied the board and the lines of copper back to the siphons. From where she crouched, she could read his smile as if it were aimed at her. Before she could speak, could shout "No!" or even move, he stepped up to one of the siphons, wrapped both hands about the clamp's lever, and pushed. The clamps released, and the siphon slid down, leaving a dangling line. As it vanished, a globe went dark on the board.

O nly two made it up the trail, but it was enough. Erin knew they were the two from the New Way homeworld.

"You're too late," she shouted though the ward. "We've closed your frontera."

The woman said, "We'll make another."

"Mei?"

"It's working!" Mei said. "I'm broadcasting!"

Ruth said, "Look below, strangers. Your plan fails."

Erin risked a glance. On the flat below them, the attackers had fallen. Some were kneeling, holding their heads, while others held up both arms, hands empty. The signal was working.

More guards spilled onto the ledge, Espinosa's reinforcements.

"It's in unimportant," the man said. He and the woman seemed untouched. Erin grabbed Ruth's arm and pulled her back.

He aimed the weapon, standing at a forty-five-degree angle to it, and fired on the ward. The barrier rippled. Ruth curled in on herself, groaning.

It wouldn't hold long.

37

Images flooded Trevian's mind: his mother, Aideen, and Oshane. Oshane! Mocking him, across the ravine, holding that poor imprisoned woman in front of him like a shield. Red eyes winking in the face of Cheviot, the four-horned ram.

Blue and gold filled his vision, so bright he couldn't see around it, and then it was dark, and he was back in the field of Ancient, staring at the body of Cosigan, his chest burnt open. He watched as, from the scraps of Ancient littering the ground, the imprisoned flames drew to themselves carapaces of metal, teeth of gleaming flame. Aideen, and lines of copper cord, Mei speaking, Trevian himself, playing a hand of cards with a bored guard…

He started, lost his footing, and nearly fell, hanging by fingertips until his foot found purchase. "Oshane's attacking the tunnels!"

Copper boat, the mountain.

"What am I to do, hanging here?"

Air billowed around him, blue and singing. The sound grew louder and steadied, and he rose, rose, cracks in the walls streaking past him, through a line of darkness, his gaze blurring as he swept up into the room of the Pit.

O shane opened the clamps of the next siphon. When it was slow to move, he nudged it with his foot. The quartz conduit glided down and vanished.

Aideen reached for her knife, bumping her hand against something on her belt. Nudging the hilt loose in the sheath, she drew her feet up under her.

"Aideen, no," Ilsanja said.

She couldn't listen. She had to stop him. She sprang out from the under the table, catching herself on one hand, and launched herself as Oshane. She plunged into heat, but the apron deflected the worst of it.

Fire wrapped around her, but she reached him. Pulling her arm free of the leather, she cut upward with an underhand motion. He saw her move and dodged aside, so she only cut a few links of gold from the collar at his neck. Someone was screaming in rage—it was her—and she lunged forward again. Oshane dodged and pulled his own knife. It was too late. Triumph rushed through her as the tip of her blade lodged between his neck and the weight of the collar. She pulled, scraping the soft gold against the edge of the knife's blade.

Her arm burned, and the pain flooded her. Gritting her teeth, she kept carving.

A wall of fire struck her. She hurtled backward until her head slammed into the cold metal of the cutting table.

Someone shrieked like a kiote. Someone was in searing pain. She wondered if both were her.

T he New Way host pointed the energy weapon and fired again. The ripple sent Ruth staggering back, falling to one knee.

"Ruth?"

"I'm well." From her voice, that wasn't true.

"Mei?"

"On it!"

Erin sidestepped to stand between Ruth and the New Way. It wouldn't do a bit of good, but it felt right anyway. "Your foot soldiers are failing," she said. "You won't win."

The woman spoke again. "You, you are a recidivist chaotic. We will prevail here, and we will create another conduit. This is a structure we can use."

"Wow, points for using 'recidivist' in a sentence," Erin said, just to say something. "There's lots of uninhabited land on this world, why don't you all just go somewhere and live out a human lifespan?"

"This world and the other elementals worlds must be protected from the worst impulses of the chaotics."

"Yeah, always with the 'protecting.'"

Suddenly Mei screamed curses into the night. "I've lost power!"

He whooshed past guards before he could think, and the stars opened up above him. To the north, the Copper Coalition guards and prospectors beat back a group of attackers, but the air elemental flew in the other direction, away from the cave mouth, across the glittering lake, and he could see nothing. He looked up and saw flashes of light from the mountaintop. "Erin! Let me help them!" But the elemental would not stop, would not turn.

Ilsanja was shrieking. She bolted across the tunnel, the apron snapping around her, her arm raised. Flames swept down in a wall, and she burrowed into the apron and charged through them.

Yor Lopez darted out and followed her. He held a blade in his hand, one Aideen didn't recognize, longer than a knife.

Her arm flared pain with each heartbeat, and something hard dug savagely into her hip with each inhalation. Into her hip...Erin's weapon.

She rolled, driving her teeth through her lower lip to keep from screaming.

Oshane had his hands around Ilsanja's neck. Aideen remembered the grip of his hands, her vision fading, her lungs screaming for air.

The wall of flame rippled between them and where Aideen crouched.

She stood and ran toward the mouth of the tunnel. The flames swarmed Lopez, leaving the air between Aideen and Oshane clear. She ran as close to the rift as she could, raised the weapon, and remember to slide the little button forward to take it off "safety." She pointed it and pulled the trigger.

The square at the muzzle end shot free, trailing wires, as a regular snapping filled the space. Oshane staggered, his body jerking. So did Ilsanja. Oshane went to his knees.

Lopez grasped Ilsanja around the waist, grunting a curse as he did so, and tugged her free. He dropped her on the floor, turned and hacked down with the long blade—it was a quartz saw—at Oshane's neck.

Oshane screamed. A second blow, and the collar fell free.

Lopez scooped it up, panting. His eyes gleamed through the shroud of the hood. With an underhand toss, he hurled the collar into the rift. It landed on one of the conduits and, gleaming, slithered down its length. A tongue of flame sprang up.

Aideen dropped the yellow weapon and rushed to Ilsanja.

Oshane lay groaning, one hand pressed against his neck. Blood pulsed out, and shudders shook his body. Before she could blink, every flame vanished back into the rifts.

She knelt by Ilsanja's side. "Ilsanja!" She looked up at Lopez. "Yor Lopez, are you well?"

"That out-of-world weapon has a nasty bite," he said.

Ilsanja shuddered and lay still. "It does," she said, barely audible.

"My love, I am so sorry."

Grit swirled around them, and Aideen's ears rang. Lopez covered his, ducking down next to the boards. The air turned blue, and Oshane floated up into the air.

"No!" Aideen stood, intending to grab him, but the pain from her arm froze her.

Oshane's eyes were white all the way around. "Stop!" he shouted, as he swept out over the lake.

Aideen threw down her knife. "He escapes *again*!"

"Don't wager all your coin...on that," Ilsanja said. She opened her left hand. Blood streaked the mound below her thumb, welling from the point of a pin driven into her flesh. At the end of the pin, swinging like a door in a high wind, the face of Cheviot the Ram stared up at them, red eyes blinking.

"Oh!" Pressing her fingers on either side of the pin, Aideen removed it. She bent and kissed the bloody spot gently. "Yor Lopez, do you have a bandage?"

"Power first, yorita," he said.

Ilsanja nodded.

Aideen tore a scrap from her mourning smock, wincing with each movement, and handed it to Ilsanja. She stood, wobbling only a little. Copying Lopez's gesture, she threw the pin into the rift. Staggering slightly, she followed Lopez to the boards.

The next pulse of the weapon and the ward shivered into nonexistence, knocking Ruth to her knees again.

"Mei!" Erin screamed. "Your Taser!"

She turned her head and reached out, as the blocky weapon hurtled towards her. The man raised his weapon. She slipped off the safety and pointed it, praying the videos got it right.

The wires stuck, and he juddered like a shaken doll and fell. The woman gasped. He still clutched the energy weapon, and the woman reached it before Erin could.

"Erin, do something! I need juice!" Mei shouted.

The elemental dumped Trevian at the mouth of the tunnel. He skidded, his hands scraped, but he barely cared. He ran inside.

Ilsanja stood, gripping the edge of a U-shaped metal table, while beyond the rifts, Aideen hurried toward the stands, clutching a cord in her gloved hands.

"Trevian," Ilsanja said, her voice reedy and thin. "Help them!" She waved a hand.

He took four long strides. Aideen whirled, her hand on her knife, and relaxed when she saw him. "Trevian, thank the Mother you live!" One sleeve was gone, the edges blackened, and blisters rose on her skin. Her hair made a frizzed half-crown.

"By the Mother, Aideen, what happened?"

"Help. Here." She rummaged around and tossed a pair of gloves to him. "Oshane destroyed two siphons. We must get the power back to Orchard Hill in case they need it—"

"They need it now. The attack has come. Yor Lopez, where do you need me?"

"Here, take this," Lopez handed him a cord, pointed at the board, bounded over several lines, and knelt at its base, threading cords awkwardly with the thick gloves.

"Oshane is where?"

"Gone. A story for later."

Trevian carried over two lines and watched as his injured sister connected them. Now, every globe on the farthest board glowed.

"There." She sat down and fell over sideways. Ilsanja pushed him away and knelt by her side.

The woman raised the weapon. Erin couldn't think of anything else to do except rush her, but something shot past her, barreling into the woman. Ruth.

The weapon discharged, a lash of light whipping across the night sky. Erin pulled her knife and ran forward.

The woman rolled, pinning Ruth beneath her. She knotted her fingers into Ruth's hair, lifted her head and slammed it down on the rocks.

"Get off of her!" Erin kicked the woman in the ribs as hard as she could. She slashed down, cutting through fabric and skin on the woman's back.

"It's working!" Mei shouted.

Work faster! Erin thought, as someone grabbed her from behind and threw her sideways. She hit hard and rolled. The man had staggered to his feet. He wasn't a hundred percent, but he was up, and he was heading straight for Mei.

"Mei! Incoming!" Erin scrambled for her knife and went after him.

A streak of light flashed across the sky. Ilsanja looked up. "What is the name of Dios was that?"

Lopez knelt at Aideen's side, a pile of soft cloths and a pot of salve next to him.

"I'm all right," Aideen said.

"I must get back to the camp," Trevian said. "Erin is up there, and that was the bolt of one of the New Way's weapons."

Aideen took a deep breath. "We have caballos. Take one."

"Are you sure—"

Ilsanja said, "Go. You've helped, the power flows again, and I can tend things here." She stared at him, and her expression softened. "I can tend things here, husband," she said. "Your sister will be well."

"Thank you," he said and strode for the hitching post.

E rin closed the distance when the man pulled another weapon out of the back of his belt. Oh, shit. Of course.

"Mei! Gun!"

Mei threw herself flat and the first shot vanished into the night. As she fishtailed around the leg of the tower—there was no way it provided cover—he aimed lower, and Erin cannonballed into him as hard as she could.

T he caballo shied violently, hooves sliding on the rock, its head tossing, as air elemental surrounded them. Trevian thought to drop the reins as he was sucked out of the saddle. "Wait! What?" Why now? Why not when he had needed them?

The ground fell away beneath him, and he ascended the cliff. As the mountaintop came into view, he shook his head and blinked. He was surrounded by air elementals, more than he had ever seen at one time. They flowed down onto the domed top of Orchard Hill. His feet touched stone, and he ran toward where Erin struggled, a man on top of her, choking her.

He drew his club and struck, again, and kept striking until he heard Erin crying out his name. The man lay still, the back on his head dark with blood. Erin, sobbing, threw her arms around him. "Are you alive?"

"I'm alive." She was warm, and he pulled her even closer. "Are you well?"

She pushed back. "Yeah, but we lost power, and these guys, well, they're tough, and...we've got to get this broadcast thing going."

She dragged him over to where Mei crouched, peering at the face of some apparatus, frowning. "It's going out, but there's not enough range."

"It looked like it was working," Erin said.

Trevian looked around, finding Stillwater kneeling over a prone person, binding their hands. Figures appeared at the edge of the trial. He gripped his club, but then he recognized them.

Melendres ran to them. "Yorita Mei, the parasites are dying," she said "But only the ones here. We have to get them all."

Erin said, "We *have* to. That woman said they can create another frontera."

Remedios Augusto limped over. "What about augmenting it with power from us? From the lantern?"

"Isn't that what Oshane did?"

"Yeah."

"That's bad," said Erin.

"But it couldn't hurt," Mei said.

"There's a difference when we choose to do it," Remedios said. "Trevian. Good to see you alive."

"And you," he said.

Melendres glared at him. "Did you call the air elementals? I wish you had told us you could do that much earlier."

"What? I called nothing."

"They came to our aid, on the east flank. The nodes…dislike them, I guess."

David LaFish had been injured, he saw, and Miriam was supporting him. The others seemed unhurt. Stillwater *was* hurt, he thought, but said nothing as she joined the group.

"Okay, let's try this," Remedios said.

"Do we have to connect the lantern to the tower?"

"Let's see."

"Are we doing the same notes?"

"Yes. Let's imagine we're sending energy into the transmitter—the box there, it's broadcasting the frequency."

"This sounds pretty vague," Erin said, but then she shrugged. "But I'm game."

Remedios led them, suggesting they close their eyes and envision the nodes dying. She started the chant. Trevian absorbed the welcoming energy, the sense of belonging. Each person was distinctive, and the lines of power crossed and wove in a cone surrounding the tower.

Singing.

It wasn't a song he knew. It was a harmony not coming from human throats. He opened his eyes. Everyone else had too, staring wide-eyed at the rushing ring of air elements who whirled around them, filling the air with their sound.

"This is…working," Mei said.

Remedios Augusto gasped, and Erin said, "Wow," and others called out to deities, as they felt—he felt—hundreds of minds, suddenly free, aware of themselves as selves, not as part of the New Way. And dimly, underneath the awakening of the imprisoned people, ran a thread of growing silence. At first, he could not place it, and then he knew. The unattached nodes, dying in their hiding places.

3 8

Lots of stuff happened afterwards, and Erin even remembered some of it.

She limped down the trail with everyone else, bleeding from a cut on her neck she didn't remember getting. She stayed close to Ruth's side as they carried her down in a tarp. Ruth said she was fine, but Erin knew a concussion when she saw one. She held Ruth's hand in her right, and clutched Trevian's with the other.

Harald pushed his way through the crowd. "Ruth!"

"She's all right," Erin said, and he nodded without looking at her. She stepped away as he took both of Ruth's hands in his own.

"Harald, I will be well," Ruth said.

"And I'll be here."

The camp was filled with people who were confused, mortified, injured, and finally free of the parasite. As soon as they tended their own wounded, Melendres sent climbers down the eastern cliff face. Two dozen of the New Way hosts had fallen when Mei's broadcast severed their connection to the nodes. Four were dead and ten had serious injuries.

Trevian was fretting over Aideen, who'd gotten burned in some way Erin didn't completely get yet. "Where's Oshane?" she said.

Instead of answering, he fetched her a cup of sisuree. When he set it down, she put her hand over his. "Where's Oshane? Did he get away again? Is that why you're so twitchy?"

"He did not escape." His gaze flicked away from hers. "I'll lead them to his body tomorrow."

"What aren't you telling me?" she said.

He leaned forward and put his forehead against hers. "Please don't make me speak of it," he said.

———

His heart lifted when he saw Aideen in the camp, being tended by a Copper Coalition healer. "It's only a burn," she said. Her hair on the right side of her head was a short frizz, the rest burned away.

"I can't believe you flung yourself through a wall of fire to reach him," he said.

"Ilsanja did too." She pointed.

Ilsanja, who sat by the cot's side, raised her eyebrows. "We're both fools."

"Heroes," he said. "The fodder of fireside tales and stage plays, possibly for generations."

"You see? I told you there would be a play about us." Ilsanja turned her skeptical glance on him. "And where did you skitter off to for so long? We thought you dead."

"I thought I was as well." He told them what Oshane had done and explained, as best he could, about the air elementals.

"So, you and Erin both have some kind of charm over elementals," Ilsanja said. "It seems you'll be the ones to be the subject of legend and song, not us."

"It's not a charm. We—well, I—have no power over them. They selected me. And they were not as helpful as they could have been."

Aideen shifted uncomfortably. "They put their needs first, do you mean?"

He laughed. "Yes."

She smiled but did not join his laugh. "As we do," she said, nodding.

"We had mutual needs in the end, and they aided us."

He took his leave. He glanced back to see Ilsanja lean forward, her lips meeting Aideen's, and it made him yearn for Erin.

———

He led a group with a tarp into the same ravine where Oshane had attacked him. His uncle's body lay draped over a point of rock, lifeless. He did not explain how he knew where it was. He did not explain what the elementals had shown him in memories—they had tossed Oshane back and forth through the night air like a pair of kiote cubs toying with a raton, how they drew the breath from his lungs again and again, before they rose to a suitable height and dropped him onto the rocks.

The group carried him back.

"We'll burn his bones in three days," Aideen said.

Erin gripped Trevian's hand. "I'd like to attend," she said.

"Are you sure? There is no need for you to subject yourself to that."

She looked at the body in the tarp. "I want to be sure he's dead."

***

Erin sat down to enjoy her first real meal since the battle, with Mei, Remedios, Daniel, and Trevian, when Melendres found them. "You five, I have something I want you to see."

"Right now?"

"Better before you eat, I think."

Erin sighed and pushed away her plate. They followed the Elmaestro down to the cabin they were using to store bodies and do death examinations. Both of the New Way homeworlders had died when the nodes did, and Erin thought this had something to do with that. She was right. Both bodies lay on their stomachs, and someone had peeled away their back skin and muscles. Erin's stomach flopped and Mei shut her eyes for a moment.

"We could not see where a node had attached to them," the doctor said, pointing. "But this…"

Cross-wrapped across the spine, with tendrils running up into the neck and out into the muscles, ran pale green lines and dots of copper and gold.

"Ugh," Remedios said.

"Did this take the place of the nodes?"

"Maybe this was what happened when you wore a node long enough, like, since you were ten," Erin said.

Mei shivered and turned away. "I *don't* want to think about this. Can we go?"

Melendres nodded. "This is what you saved our children from. I thought you should know."

"I see." Erin did see. This was Melendres's weird way of saying thank you.

The doctor said softly, "Yor Langtree? Yorita Dosmanos? Can you stay a moment?"

"Sure."

The others left. The doctor tipped her head toward a wrapped body in the corner. "There's no need to show you this, but I examined your uncle's body."

"He had a lot of broken bones," Trevian said.

"Yes, as expected, a half-healed wound in his shoulder. His kidneys though, they were covered with tumors."

Trevian blinked. He reached for Erin's hand without seeming to realize it. "Tumors?"

"Yes. Charmcasters often succumb to the tumor disease."

"They do?" Erin said.

Trevian nodded. "Shandren died of it, Ilsanja's mother."

"Oshane wasn't a charmcaster."

"No, but he fed on copper-hunter power for a time and used their power as if he were a charmcaster. I don't know exactly how long."

"That might explain it."

"Well." Trevian shrugged. "Thank you. I'll inform my sister, I guess."

They walked outside. Erin said, "Do you think he knew he was dying, or thought he was?"

Trevian shrugged. "I cannot tell."

"I can't figure out why he decided to help them, at the end. He had to know they'd get rid of him as soon as they could. The only thing that stopped them originally was his trapped air elemental."

Trevian shook his head. "He never intended to help them. He meant to show them he had control of the power they needed. Up 'til the end, he was speaking as if he would outwit them."

"If he knew he was dying," she said, "this might have been a desperation move."

Trevian walked for several feet without answering. "I don't think it would have mattered to him. My father and my uncle both were bitter, angry men. They lived their bitterness in different ways."

"I'm going home," Mei said. "As soon as we mop up here, whatever that means, and debrief people at the Copper Coalition or whatever it is they do—"

"I think they call it debrief."

"Anyway, Espinosa and Juanita are heading home to Perlarayna and I'm going with them, and then home."

Erin wasn't sure what to say. "I'll miss you."

"I'm not needed here," Mei said. She'd been quiet and standoffish since Melendres had shown them the bodies. Erin waited, sure there would be more, and finally Mei said, "I killed those people."

"Radio waves, not you."

"Radio waves I generated."

"We didn't know that could happen. We didn't know they were different. That guy was coming at you with a gun."

"They're dead as a direct result of what I did. That's who I am now."

Erin moved closer. "This may have been the shortest war in history, Mei, but it was a war. And people die in wars. You saved thousands from enslavement and death. Doesn't it balance out?"

Mei gave a sob. "It probably should, but it doesn't."

Erin put her hand on Mei's shoulder but couldn't think of anything else to say.

Finally, Mei said "Do you want to come back with me?'

"No, thank you," Erin said politely.

"Are you going to go home?"

"Not right away."

Guards were still in place at the perimeters of the camp, but the wards were down during the day. With Trevian, Erin rode out to a safe distance beyond the boundaries. From here, she could see the tip of Mei's tower, which still stood. Ruth planned to send for scholars from Pais Lewelyn and Madlyn to experiment with radio waves. Station KMEI, coming to you live from Orchard Hill.

Her last conversation with Ruth hadn't been comfortable. Ruth had picked up the New Way homeworlder's gun. She intended to take it to the Copper Coalition. When Erin asked for it, the profesor refused.

"We've found these before in veins of Ancient," she said, "but we didn't know how they functioned."

"It's a lethal weapon," Erin said.

Ruth raised her eyebrows. "It hurls scraps of hard metal into flesh faster than a crossbow can. Of course, it's lethal."

"You're sure you want to go down this road, Ruth?"

"We're scholars," Ruth said. Though she was weak from her head injury, she was still stubborn.

"Weapons never stay in the hands of scholars."

Ruth crossed her arms. "Erin, you are brave, you have helped us in many ways. I'd say you and Trevian saved us. But you do not guide our future."

So much for that. It wasn't like *Erin* had brought a gun, after all. She looked around. Trevian watched her. She smiled, comforted by his presence.

She dismounted and walked away from the caballos so they wouldn't spook. Clearing her mind, she reached out. The flames appeared a few feet away. Curiosity.

She closed her eyes again and imagined the rifts in the tunnel. Then she imagined a question. Would they be happy there?

Willingness. She couldn't describe it any better than that. She remounted, and they rode up to the project. This was the trail that led past the canal tunnel. It was a slightly longer ride than the ledge trail. Aideen and Lopez waited for them, but Lopez had sent the workers on a break, so that no one would disturb the flames.

Aideen had a bandage on her right arm. Her eyes widened when she saw the flames, who appeared as soon as Erin walked inside, but she stayed where she was. "Do they wish to join the colony?"

"I don't know, and I don't know if this colony will accept them, but it seems like it's the closest to a real home they're going to have."

"Shouldn't they stay with you?"

Erin didn't answer because, *"They should do what's best for them"* sounded snarky.

The flames rotated, changing shades from pale yellow to blue and lavender. They vanished, and Erin felt a moment of loss.

Joy. The web of belonging.

"They're in," she said.

"Did they even say farewell?" Aideen said.

Erin stared at the rift. "Yes. They did."

J uanita Gunnarsdottir was not returning to Perlarayna after all. She had sent a request through the compass and been granted leave to study at the Crescent Copper Coalition. It was an experiment, Ruth said. She and Juanita were jubilant.

The Agustos were also ready to go back through Erin's frontera, recover their rental car, and face the consequences. The last night they were all together, the camp held a banquet. Instead of the town hall building, they ate outside, under the stars, next to the lake.

At the end, Remedios cleared her throat and stood up.

"I have something to say," she said, as the camp quieted. "Well, something to do, actually. I've been talking to Mei, and it turns out the artifacts were always supposed to be returned to your world. I am giving the lantern to the Crescent Copper Coalition, in care of Profesor Ruth Stillwater."

Ruth, fully recovered, hugged her, and took the lantern, holding it close to her. She sat back down next to Harald.

Trevian shifted closer to Erin and whispered, "The guardians always meant to return." Erin had missed Mei's discovery in the second book.

Mei stood up. "And I think Elmaestro Melendres should have the compass." She and Erin had discussed this. Mei asked Espinosa first, but he made it clear Perlarayna didn't need or want any charmed Ancient artifacts. The Elmaestro had been delighted to take it.

Melendres rose, bowed, and said, "We are honored, Yorita Mei."

Erin snuggled closer against Trevian.

"Well?" he murmured, brushing his lips against her hair. "Will you go with the Agustos? Will you go home?"

She looked at the bluish whiterock fire, the rough-clad people sipping really bad booze or a stimulant drink that would never be coffee. In some places, they had electric lights. They'd never in her lifetime have television or microsurgery.

She would always be strange here, but there were still things to do.

She twisted around and put her open hand on his chest.

"I am home," she said.

39

"Yorita?"

Aideen, halfway up the stairs, turned. A woman from the cages stood a few steps below her, come to pick up her pay envelope or some other business. Aideen recognized her but didn't know her name. She was about the age Aideen's mother would have been.

"May I...?" The worker held out a prayer bead.

Aideen cupped her hand under it. "Thank you. I never refuse a prayer."

"For all you did for us."

Aideen felt her face flush.

The woman stared at Aideen's right arm. Most people glanced and looked away. There was nothing to be done about the scars. She hadn't lost any feeling, or any use of her fingers, and she could be content with that. And her hair was starting to grow back on the right side, although she still looked like a child's doll left in the rain for a sennight.

The woman said, "You have a badge."

"A badge, is it?"

She rolled back her own sleeve, showing a line of shiny skin like a brand. "Burns are what you get in the business. You're one of us now." Her face changed. "I mean no disrespect."

Aideen felt her face flush with warmth again. Her eyes prickled. "There is no higher compliment you could give me, Yora."

The woman gave a jerky bow, grinning. "Thank you, yorita."

Aideen hurried up the stairs. Armando Montez was already present, sitting calmly, staring out the window. He smiled when Aideen came in. "Good morning."

"Good morning. Ilsanja will join us soon. The last of the wounded went home yesterday."

He nodded. "And she visited to see all was well," he said. "You did your share of visits, as I recall."

"As did you."

He gazed out the window. Yor Montez was comfortable with silence, a skill, or a state, Aideen hoped one day to achieve.

The door opened. Ilsanja's narrow skirt, in dark blue, was made of the finest of fabrics, but it mimicked something Yora Quinn would wear. Her friend was experimenting with a more severe look for the office. Aideen wore a slim dress of misty green, the color Ilsanja had chosen for her. They were both making changes.

"Good morning! And what are we discussing today?" Ilsanja said.

"Your favorite thing," Aideen said. "Shares in the company," as if she and Ilsanja had not explored the topic for an hour the night before.

"Let me guess, Armando, she wishes to give you all her shares?"

He laughed. "No. Aideen did offer me a greater share in the partnership, since it's my drill bit charm that helps siphon up the power."

"But Yor Montez has a different offer for us."

Ilsanja set her elbows on the table, folded her hands, and rested her chin on them. She didn't even try to look surprised. "Let me see if I can guess. You wish to sell us your shares."

Armando's smile widened. "In one guess, Jefa."

"Exactly what you predicted," Aideen said.

Armando leaned forward. "When my son was engineering in Pais Lewelyn, he found a huge rift field. It's a few leagues from the city of Sandoval. He, Lucia, Valentin, and I plan to move there, and re-create the Langtree Company. I need coin for my share of the initial expenses."

"I am worried, Yor Montez, we will lose access to your steel charm when we need it more than ever."

He shook his head. "I will license you to use it. The Langtree Company will pay me an annual fee. We will revisit the contract every eight years."

Ilsanja tipped her head. "You'll need a copper charm. Or do you have one?"

"I hoped to trade some of my shares to Yorita Aideen for that, since it is a family charm."

Ilsanja smiled. "Trevian owns the charm, as he owns everything not specifically named in Don Oswald's will. I am Trevian's agent."

Montez nodded.

"I like this idea of a license," Ilsanja said. "I think I will give you a license to use it, for two percent of your company's profits."

Armando raised his eyebrows. "What if there are no profits?"

"Oh, there won't be, for the first year at least," Aideen said. "We all know that."

Armando said, "Yes, I remember those lean days."

"But eventually there will be. And for you," Ilsanja said, "you will have an established company with direct interest in your success."

He raised his eyebrows. "Or a competitor with its fingers on my coin."

"We do not gaze to the south," Aideen said. "My interest points north."

"With the Copper Coalition's help?" he said.

She smiled.

"My shares, then?" They settled on a price. He and Aideen shook hands. She was buying them from her blackrock profits, which left her with few cash reserves, but the Sheeplands project was going forward once again, and she was less worried now than she had been in months.

"Thank you both," he said. "And Aideen? May I speak personally?"

"Of course."

"Your father let his anger claim him. When I watch you, I see brilliance and inventiveness at least the equal of his. It has been an honor to watch you come into this company. And the two of you together..." He shook his head. "It has been a wonder."

For the second time in an hour, Aideen blinked away tears.

Ilsanja said, "No doubt my father wonders much as well, Armando."

He laughed. "Don't you worry about your father. You've given him back social standing, and he'll be no obstacle." He rose. "Good day, Jefa, Yorita."

"You won't escape so quickly," Ilsanja said. "I need dates from you, Yor Montez, since I intend to throw a party in your family's honor, one that will put this town's grandest nameday celebrations in the shade."

"I don't know whether to smile or shudder," he said. "We'll speak soon."

When he left, Ilsanja said, "As expected. And now, you're the majority partner, with thirty-nine shares. You can outvote my father."

Aideen laughed. "My love, I can outvote you!"

"I hoped you hadn't noticed."

"We're not done yet," Aideen warned. The next part of the conversation would prove the more difficult.

Ilsanja sat back, waiting.

"Yor Lopez."

"Bringing him to the partnership table in place of Yor Montez." Ilsanja raised one eyebrow.

"How did you know?"

"Do you think I don't know you yet?" She sighed. "Yor Lopez saved my life, but that's not reason enough to do it."

Tension gathered in the pit of Aideen's stomach. "What *is* reason enough?"

"Does he bring enough of value to the company to become a partner? To speak in the decisions that guide the company, to share in the gains and losses directly?"

"And does he?"

"*You* think he does."

"Ilsanja."

She shrugged again. "He brought an experimental idea to working life in a matter of sennights. He persuaded my father to do the right thing. He gets the best work out of people. He'll never be a jefe, you know."

"Well, I'm no jefa, except in family name," Aideen said. "Can he work and be a partner?"

Ilsanja shrugged. "I suppose, if he wishes."

"I plan to give him ten shares."

"Leaving you with fewer than me," she said. "Do you *fear* leadership, Aideen?"

"I don't fear it. I just don't link it to how much of the Company I own."

Ilsanja scooted forward. "Let us try this. You give him five shares. That leaves you with thirty-four, and *I* give him five, which leaves me with twenty-six."

"Fewer than your father?"

"We still have the majority share."

Aideen sat silent, watching her partner's face. "Are you sure you wish to do this? I understand you too. You see shares of the Company as control."

"And we will still have it," she said. "If you're willing to share."

Aideen reached across the table. "With you, my love? Always."

Ilsanja folded her fingers through Aideen's. "And we will work wonders."

END

ACKNOWLEDGMENTS

Once again, thanks to the great folks at Falstaff Books; John Hartness, Melissa McArthur, Erin Penn and Tuppence Van de Vaarst in particular.

Another year of infection and staying close to home rolled by while I worked on *Golden Rifts*, reminding me again of the vital importance of medical workers at all levels. Thank you for everything you do. Thanks to US Postal Service workers, for being champions, even when you were overwhelmed with work and there weren't anywhere near enough of you.

Thanks to the folks of FOGCon, our local SFF convention; to Marta Randall and the Saturday Writers Workshop for critique, insight and support; and to Brandy Mow. Thanks to my wonderful neighbor Carol. You are the best fan ever.

Thanks to teachers everywhere.

And thanks to readers, especially you!

ABOUT THE AUTHOR

In addition to THE COPPER ROAD series from Falstaff, Marion Deeds is the author of *Comeuppance Served Cold* from Tordotcom Books. Her short fiction has appeared *in Podcastle, Daily Science Fiction* and several anthologies. Deeds is a columnist and reviewer for Fantasyliterature.com. She lives in Northern California with her husband, volunteers in a second-hand bookstore, and feeds the local crows. She enjoys watching the backyard squirrels do yoga.

ALSO BY MARION DEEDS

From Falstaff Books

Aluminum Leaves

Copper Road

From Tor.com

Comeuppance Served Cold

Anthologized Work appears in:

Strange California, (Falstaff Books)

The Wand that Rocks the Cradle (LaGrange Books)

Beyond the Stars; Unimagined Realms (Astral Books.)

www.ingramcontent.com/pod-product-compliance
Lightning Source LLC
Chambersburg PA
CBHW020527110726
47899CB00004B/1283